False Light

Seth Alexander

Cover art and design by Rob Cannon
To see more of Rob's fantastic work, please visit:
RCannon.Design

Chapter 1

William

Tick-tock. Tick-tock. The clock in my kitchen keeps ticking. Time is spinning like a top, and it drives me crazy to sit and watch. Clocks remind me how fast everything moves. I've never been a fan of moving too fast. Deadlines were a problem with my landscaping business, but I lived up to my promises. I took my time and made sure everything was right. Meticulous, one man called me. I laughed because I didn't know what it meant. Now I do. He was right. I'm meticulous.

Sixty-eight years in this world, and I'm still learning. I may not be the smartest around, but I've seen enough hours spin by to deserve every bit of smarts I can call my own. Hell, I've forgotten more than most people remember.

That clock keeps on ticking at me, so I slap together a pimento cheese sandwich and head on out to my garage. It's pleasant this time of year with the garage door open. Today is a little warmer than it's been. Nowhere near as hot as summer. Summer can be hell.

I've grown up in the Florida heat. After a while, it becomes a part of you. I can't even remember the number of times I worked on a lawn with the sun beating down, drenched in sweat and happy as could be.

It must take growing up in the heat to love it because most people here can't survive without their air conditioning. I planted some palms for a British guy on the other side of the Intracoastal years ago, and he called air conditioning the 'air con.' Said he couldn't live without it. But winter in Florida is when the natural 'air con' kicks in. Lucky for me, I live at the beach. The beach is always more pleasant than inland. We get breezes people across the ditch would die to call their own.

It's nearing time for me to check the mail. Eleven to eleven-thirty is the sweet spot for not looking too eager. Sometimes it's there. Sometimes it's not. Today, it's not. Nothing too unusual about that. But the SUV parked outside my neighbor's house is unusual. There's a man inside, waiting. Flynn runs a business out of his house, and he's not fond of being disturbed before noon. A client polite enough to wait might be a first.

My gray braid bounces back and forth across my shoulders as I walk back into my garage to focus on the business of a retired man. The rusty Ford pickup with my old company's logo on the side stays in the driveway, leaving plenty of space for a reclining chair in the center of the garage. Hand tools and yard equipment, both old and modern, cover the walls. Organized by type and then by age, the collection forms a web across almost every inch of wall space. Fourteen shovels, all but one still caked with dirt, form a centerpiece.

The shovels hang from a wooden frame I built myself and bolted to the wall. Each shovel has its own designated space and represents a member of my family and the time we spent together. Every speck of dirt reminds me of moments I never want to forget. Some people collect snow globes and shot glasses to say where they've been. For me, a shovel feels right.

"Who's that in front of my house?" asks a squeaky voice, sweet like an adorable mouse. The childish innocence of it is beautiful.

"I don't know, Lily."

"Do you think Flynn is okay?"

"Flynn's always okay."

Lily pouts and then looks concerned. "Do you think he misses me?"

"Everybody misses you, Lily. Everybody but me."

"I'm glad you're here, William. I don't want to be alone."

"You'll never be alone again. Now you're with family."

My mother, Beatrice, and father, Martin, are at the top of the wall. The shovels continue down like a family tree. My sister Susan and her boys, Ethan and John, are on the left. My other sister Emily and her children, Walter and Rita, are in the center. My brother, James, is on the right with his namesake, James Jr., and his daughters, Emma and Isabelle. Lily is unique, occupying a place of her own to the right. The final shovel is the only clean one of the bunch. It's up there as a symbolic gesture for my future.

The years of long hours spent building my business kept me from having a family of my own. My neighbors became my family. That suited

2

me just fine. Unlike kin, if I didn't like someone, I could forget about them altogether. Then the property value for anything near the beach shot up like a rocket. All the neighbors I knew and loved disappeared. All I have now is Flynn and Lily. They are my adopted children.

"I don't like everyone here, William."

"Why's that?"

Lily urges me to lean forward. She covers her mouth to make sure only I can hear what she says. "Ethan's mean. He pulled my hair."

I stand up straight and march over to Ethan.

"Dammit, Ethan. I told you to be nice to Lily."

Ethan doesn't say a word. He shrugs his shoulders and pretends he can't hear me.

"When Susan gets home, I'll tell her what you did. We'll see what your mother thinks about your behavior."

Lily sticks her tongue out at Ethan and disappears. In the fading glow of her light, her shovel still stands out. I used that shovel to create the memorial garden for Lily after she vanished. Watching their family dissolve nearly killed me.

I taught Flynn how to surf when he was little. He loved it. He loved it so much he left his sister alone years later. No one blames me for her disappearance. But they'd be justified if they did. The day Flynn's father, Herman, left was the day Flynn destroyed all his boards. I haven't seen him touch the ocean since. Now and then, I catch Flynn standing on his patio, staring out at the water.

The sight of Lily's shovel makes me nostalgic. That's a word I like. Nostalgia is about all I have left these days.

My sentimental side takes over. Updating Lily's memorial garden crosses my mind. I crack open a PBR and pick up a pen off my kitchen table. The table doubled as my office for years. One of the best parts of retiring was cleaning off the junk. All that's left are office supplies and a stack of paper with my company's letterhead. I grab two sheets and head out to the garage.

The recliner in my garage is where I'm most creative. Ideas become doodles. Doodles become plans. Plans become sidetracked when the thought of that man parked outside of Flynn's starts bothering me. I take a gander and see that he's still sitting there waiting. It's been close to an hour, which means it's about time for an exchange of words.

Chapter 2

Stephen

Creativity is not my strong suit. The last time I flexed my creative muscle, I wrote my wife a poem. Most people write poems about love. Mine was a reminder of how to file mail in my color-coded filing system.

Blue is for bills, I recited to Helen six days after returning from our honeymoon, *the most important of all,*
Filed by season: winter, spring, summer, and fall.
Maroon is for magazines, both his and hers.
This spot is for mine, and this spot is for yours.
All the personal mail, like a birthday card,
Will go in the section as green as our yard.
Junk mail won't stop no matter how hard you try,
Put it in the section as black as night sky.

Helen tells the story of my mail poem every time family or friends comment on my need for order. They laugh the same way Helen laughed that day: loud and clear. The story ends with the second time I tried to recite the poem to Helen after she misfiled some junk mail. She laid down the law. My options were to stop reciting organizational poetry or find a divorce lawyer.

My typical Monday routine begins with an alarm at six in the morning. After waking up, I drink eight ounces of water from a full sixteen-ounce glass. My morning jog starts no later than ten minutes after six. An hour later, I return home and sit down at the table where Helen has everything set for breakfast. I finish the remaining eight ounces from my glass of water with breakfast and then shave, bathe, and dress so I can be on my way to work by eight o'clock sharp.

This Monday broke from my routine at eight o'clock. Instead of going to the office, I tended to other errands. Now, at eleven fifty-nine, I'm sitting in a Ford Explorer outside of a two-story home on a beachfront lot in Atlantic Beach. Years of regimented lunch breaks beginning at noon have conditioned my stomach to expect food within the next eight minutes. The rumbling sounds of a hungry stomach fill the car while I survey the house. A four-foot wrought iron fence circles the lot on the front and sides, with openings for the driveway and a walkway to the front door. Manicured gardens surround the two-story red brick home with an older model Toyota Camry sitting in front of a detached two-car garage. The sight of this house keeps me looking back and forth at the business card in my hand. It surprises me every time the address corresponds to the fading bronze numbers on the side of the mailbox.

A man's head rises from underneath the driver's side window. He presses his forehead and nose to the glass, placing his hands around his face like blinders.

The man stays put as I lower the car window. His face leaves a streak of oil where it touches the glass.

An ocean breeze fills the car with the scent of salt and the faint sound of a child's laughter. That laughter brings a tranquil smile to my face.

"Hello," I say.

"Hey," says the man, who backs up but keeps his hands on the door. His tanned face wrinkles like a prune when he smiles. The gray hair tied back into a single braid bothers me. "Name's William."

William's appearance is at odds with the polished look I've worn for over a decade. The only time I might have accepted a man like William was during a trip I took at age eighteen. My friends and I drove across the country, smoking pot and drinking whatever we could afford. Seventeen years later, my jaw tightens and the hair on my head cut to military specifications stands on end when I extend my hand.

"Good afternoon, William. My name's Harold."

This business needs to be under another name. Using an old buddy's name provides me anonymity. Harold used to slack when we scrubbed pots together on KP. He owes me one.

William looks down at my hand.

"You been parked here a while, Harold. Long enough for me to take notice."

"I'm looking for Flynn Dupree. I have his business card here."

William takes the business card from my hand and holds it up and away from the car, examining it more than necessary. The tattoos above

William's knuckles catch my attention. 'L-O-V-E' is tattooed on his right hand and 'M-O-R-E' on his left.

"He still might be sleeping," William says before returning the business card.

"Really?"

"It says it right on the card." William points at my hand. "It's at the bottom."

No contact before noon.

"That's why I was waiting. It's after noon now."

I exit the SUV with two briefcases.

"William," I say, walking toward the fence surrounding the property, "it's been nice meeting you, but I need to go speak with Mr. Dupree."

"Make sure you call him Flynn. He prefers that."

"Thank you, William."

A path of paver stones begins at the opening in the fence, makes a detour under a vine-covered trellis, and ends up at a wooden front door with a glass pane at eye height. The melodic doorbell chimes and dies away with zero response or movement. A second attempt produces the same results as the first. Nothing changes with attempts three, four, and five. Discouraged, I step back onto the front lawn, weighing the options of checking the windows or walking around to the back of the house in case Flynn is on the beach. Before I can decide what to do, a disheveled man in red plaid pajama bottoms and a light blue t-shirt opens the door.

The choice in clothing, the ragged beard, and the scent of beer and marijuana emanating from this man are in contrast to this stately home while precisely what I expected based on the business card. Nothing would make me feel better than telling this immature man in his mid to late twenties that it's not too late in life to get a job and stop leeching off of society. But I need his help.

"Yeash," he says, rubbing his eyes before putting on a pair of square-framed glasses. The sunshine coming in through the open door lights up his golden eyes. Amber eyes are rare. The only other pair I've seen were darker in appearance. This man's eyes shine like golden filaments when the light hits them just right.

"Are you Flynn?"

"Shore nuff," Flynn says, rubbing his face. He tries to run his fingers through his hair but abandons the attempt when his fingers end up caught.

6

Long hair on men bothers me. Flynn's locks are long enough to irk me, but not long enough for me to show my disapproval. It isn't as bad as a ponytail. However, it falls over his ears and is well on its way to ponytail territory.

"I have a business card I received from an associate who would prefer to remain nameless."

"Right," Flynn says. "And how can I help you?"

"I'd like to hire you."

Flynn motions for me to enter. "Come in."

Next to the door is a mirror with black tape running across it horizontally at eye level. In the center of the tape, two eyes stand out in golden ink. The tiled entryway leads to the back of the house where French doors open out onto a patio overlooking the beach. A stack of numbered boxes forms a barrier to my right, blocking my view into another room. On my left, a wide arch frames a kitchen.

Flynn ushers me toward the kitchen table. A glass water pipe and a white bakery box occupy a prominent position at the center of the tabletop. The pipe is a hippie wet dream of swirling green, white, red, and yellow glass. The colorful swirls are almost hypnotic. Flynn does not notice me staring at it.

"Want a drink?"

"No."

"That's fine, but you need to eat cake." Flynn points to the bakery box in the middle of the kitchen table.

"Thank you. I'm not hungry." My stomach growls after the words leave my mouth.

"C'mon. That cake's gonna go untouched if you aren't hungry. It's from my friend's bakery on Seminole and Atlantic. She's been there a while now and keeps on putting these cakes and things in my hands. I can only take so many sweets 'cause, you see, I'm more of a salty guy—"

"Fine," I say. "I'll have a piece. I'd like a glass of water to go with it, please."

"Gotcha." Flynn walks back to the sink and pours me a glass of water. He pulls a plate from the dishwasher and a fork and knife from a nearby drawer.

Flynn opens up the box and pulls out an ornate white cake decorated with red and black frosting. 'I'm sorry I ran over your baby' is written across the top.

Instead of giving in to curiosity and asking about the baby, I accept the piece of cake and smile after placing a forkful in my mouth.

"Delicioso, huh?" Flynn asks.

I nod. I'm not sure what to say about the pipe next to my plate. My eyes keep focusing on it. It looks more and more like a multi-colored hippie dragon.

"Oh," Flynn says, finally noticing me staring. Flynn picks up the pipe and moves it to a spot on the kitchen counter. "Sometimes, I forget to put Alien up when I have surprise guests."

"Sorry for not calling ahead."

"No biggie. Aside from the cake, how can I help you, Mr.—?"

"You can call me Harold."

"Harold, how can I help you?"

"Well, I'm working for a client who requires the utmost confidentiality. And from what I've heard, and from what your business card says, you maintain secrecy quite effectively."

"Mind if I peruse it?"

"Peruse it?"

"The business card."

"Um, sure." I hand Flynn the business card.

The business card says 'Confidentiality guaranteed' right under Flynn's name, address, and the phrase 'Florida's cheapest consultant,' but above 'No contact before noon.'

"In ink on paper." Flynn walks over to a drawer in the kitchen. He pulls out several business cards and hands me two. "Here's my current card. One for you and one for your client."

The old and new business cards are the same in all respects except the new one replaces 'Confidentiality guaranteed' with 'Confidentiality possible.'

In this world, there are people to buy and people to force. Flynn's business card confirms he sells himself to the highest bidder. The only unknown is the price. Starting too low runs the risk of being dismissed outright. Starting with something reasonable creates a gray area for

8

negotiation that can result in a lot of personal questions. Those questions fall by the wayside when a substantial amount of money is on the table.

"Would five thousand dollars ensure confidentiality?"

Flynn's eyes widen. The reaction indicates the offer is substantial enough.

"How much work are we talking about?"

"Today only. Everything is set. We need you to place it into motion."

"Sounds like it could be complicated."

"Not your role. Your role is simple. I cannot go any further until you agree to participate."

"Do I get the five thousand now?"

"No. What I will do is provide you with two thousand now and the remaining three once you've completed your task."

"You've got the biggest Kinderhook I can offer."

"Kinderhook?"

"Big O—K—" Flynn emphasizes the letters more than seems necessary. "Martin Van Buren. Old Kinderhook. Popularized OK with his election. It's older, though. A bastardization of the phrase, 'All correct.' Or so I've read."

Both of my briefcases are important. One has a manila folder full of papers and pictures. The other has sensitive equipment inside. Flynn takes the folder from me and spreads its contents onto the table.

"This woman here is your task for the day."

I hold up a picture of a blonde woman in a waitress uniform.

"Who is she?"

"A call girl who also works at a diner on Third Avenue in Jax Beach. Your job is to convince her to meet you at a motel later today where she will entertain another man. You have an allowance of three thousand dollars at your disposal."

"Is this money I receive ahead of time?"

"No, I will bring that money when I bring you the remainder of your money. You will both be paid afterward."

"And if she won't partake?"

"Most of her life is laid out in this paperwork. All of her embarrassing little secrets are yours to dispense as you see fit."

"Can I keep the difference if I talk her down?"

"No."

9

Flynn exhales deeply.

I hold up a key and a picture of a motel.

"That's on Atlantic?"

"Correct. You will have this woman meet you there at six o'clock." The urge to say eighteen hundred instead of six almost gets the better of me. A simple slip like that reveals more than I want. "This is the most important part of what needs to happen." I hold up a remote small enough to fit in the palm of my hand. "She needs to go inside and wait until a man comes to the room. He will arrive at six-thirty."

"I don't see a picture of this man." Flynn holds his hand above the folder's contents. "What does he look like?"

"That is of no concern to you. He will go to this specific room." The key I hold up is for the motel room door. A small fob with the corresponding motel room number is attached to the bottom. After holding the key up for Flynn to see, I place it back on the kitchen table. "All you need to know is that he will be there."

"Gotcha."

"This man needs to be on the bed when she presses this button." The red button stands out against the gray plastic of the small remote. The remote is light. After placing it onto the table, I can barely tell my hand no longer carries its weight. "When she presses the button, a camera will start recording. All we need is enough footage to prove who the man is and establish that they are together in a tryst. He cannot know we are recording him. The bathroom has a perfect view of the bed. To prevent him from being suspicious, I'd suggest she press the remote while in the bathroom."

"Why did you choose this woman?"

"She is the client's type and was recommended by someone I trust."

"Let's make sure our ants are marching in the same direction. I convince this woman she needs to do this for us. Once she shows up, I provide her with this remotamajig and ask her to push the button. The mystery man shows up at six-thirty. She pushes the button from the bathroom, which starts a camera recording the two of them together. Everything marching one-by-one?"

"Yes."

"Hurrah—"

"And the final piece is here in this other briefcase. This contains the recording device. The camera hidden in the room is too small to have enough storage, so inside this briefcase is a recording device and enough batteries to keep it active for some time. You need to be parked in the parking lot of the motel for this device to receive the feed."

"Can I open it?"

"No. The only way to ensure the authenticity of this video is for the briefcase to remain locked. I do not want to provide anyone the opportunity to claim that the video is fake."

"That's it?"

"That is all you need to do."

"That's it, dotted and crossed, for five grand?"

"Yes. And here is the two thousand I promised."

I hand Flynn a nondescript envelope from my briefcase. Without hesitation, Flynn opens the envelope and counts the twenty hundred-dollar bills twice.

"Anything else?" Flynn asks.

"No." I close my briefcase, pull a pen from my pocket, and write the number of my recently purchased cell phone on one of Flynn's new business cards. "If anything goes wrong, call me immediately at this number."

"Shore nuff," Flynn replies.

Chapter 3

Flynn

It takes me a while to realize the state of my breath. It always does when I wake up. The stench of stale beer hits only after meeting with Harold. Non-pickled gray cells tighten my jaw, forcing me to keep my damn mouth closed and leaving me to wonder if Harold could smell the beer. From prior experience, I know the embarrassment that comes when my clients see the aftermath. Most leave. But those judgmental eyes stick around. I added 'No contact before noon' on my business cards to prevent people from seeing me in any state other than alert. Although, generally, even if I wake up late, I don't show up at the door smelling like beer. Or forget to put up Alien.

It doesn't matter in the end. Harold hired me. All that matters are the twenty kite-flyers in my pocket and the thirty more to come. For what? Hiring a hooker for someone who doesn't know they're on *Candid Camera*? If Harold sensed the aftermath, then he understands that drinking problems don't fall too far from the tree of loose morals.

Not to say I have a drinking problem, but I did sleep on the floor last night next to my Super Nintendo and a pyramid of empty Pabst cans. Retro night went off the rails at some point. It's hard to say when in hindsight.

Playing video games required sobriety back in the day. As a child, I took them too seriously. It bordered on being an after-school job. I remember sitting on that rumbling school bus, anticipation growing with each stop on the route home. After the bus hissed to a standstill at the end of my street, I would run home as fast as my legs could move and bolt through the front door. My backpack full of textbooks and notebooks would fall off somewhere on the way to a reach-out-and-touch spot in front of the TV where I'd play *Dragon Warrior* on my Nintendo, hunting silver slimes with the tenacity of a hound dog. At this point in my life, the appeal is waning. These days, when I sit down, I need a beer to stay focused. One leads to another and then another. Before I know it, the night disappears, and I'm facing the aftermath.

The rickety Pabst can pyramid I built last night is in danger of collapsing. The specter of my father, a man who raised me to keep things respectably clean, propels me across the living room carpet. This house had been my father's pride and joy, right on the beach with a beautiful view. My mother picked it out while she was preggers with me. When my parents divorced, my mother received the house with my father paying the property taxes in perpetuity. My mother re-gifted the house to me as a college graduation present. All I need to cover are the utilities and whatever other expenses stick.

With my father's dislike of dirt and stains still on my mind, I focus on ferrying the Pabst cans to the recycling bin outside of the kitchen. My first attempt at ferrying fails due to a can-hauling calculation snafu overestimating my hand size.

A wise man once told me from failure a phoenix flies. He was probably speaking about something a bit larger in scale. However, another wise man once told me dimes make dollars so that that scale can kick rocks.

My next attempt touches genius by factoring my shirt into the can-hauling calculation. The results shit Mensa bricks as I stretch my shirt out by the bottom hem, place the cans onto the extended fabric, and then pull the hem up to my chin to hold them all in place. Some cans still contain a combination of backwash and dregs. This becomes obvious as a warm sensation crawls down my chest. The leaking liquid speeds up my conscientious ferrying to a scramble. A blue recycling bin sits outside of the kitchen door on a concrete walkway to the detached garage. I open the door and lunge at the bin, releasing the cans to fall with a clatter onto dozens of others. My squishy tee removed, it falls with a slosh onto the laundry room floor.

My focus turns to exorcising the beer demons that passed out in my mouth last night after tangoing with my taste buds. Ten seconds of gargling mouthwash to the tune of "Largo al factotum" precedes brushing my teeth and tongue in small circles for what feels like an eternity. It takes another session of mouthwash and brushing to reach a contented clean.

Black tape partially obscures my reflection in the mirror. The tape covers my eyes, but I can still see the foam from brushing my teeth stuck to my beard. The whitish hue on the dark brown hair at the edges of my mouth clowns up my face with a faux smile. Despite being shower bound in seconds, I use a towel to get rid of that smile.

Some people live for long showers. Surely, those people stand around like in the movies, rubbing soap into a ridiculous lather while singing or dramatically massaging their neck with steam curling around them. That kind of wasted time doesn't appeal to me. A quick shower is a good shower. This day is no exception.

Once out, I towel off and rub some baby powder underneath my pits. Deodorant is irksome. The artificial slick can become a sticky mess. For my comfort, and to appease the nation's nose, my mother recommended baby powder. More recently, my mother bought me a collection of colognes. I've never been a cologne guy. The word 'cologne' conjures images of magazine ads where a confused and angry shirtless man stands alone in a canoe on the open ocean. I never wanted to be that guy, but the pride my mother took in the gift convinced me to spritz myself with some stinkwater. After only two months, cologne became a part of my routine.

With my mother on my mind, I use the Aventus she gave me for my birthday. It takes only two sprays for me to smell all kinds of French classy.

My bedroom is a mess. That mess ascends into a mound of clothing on top of my dresser. All I can do is rummage for something to wear. The collection combines clean clothes from the dryer and clothes not dirty enough to throw on the ground. Best in show of the clothes pile is a pair of cargo shorts and a shirt from the middle of the top.

When I opened the front door for Harold, I noticed it had warmed to the high seventies, which, while not entirely out of the ordinary for November in Florida, is pleasant enough not to dress in layers. This weather means I'm able to wear the short-sleeved eighties blazer I picked up on a scavenging trip to Goodwill. It still has the plastic wrapping from the dry cleaner when it comes out of the closet. The white blazer slips on like silk-lined butter. I stop at the front door on the way out and grab my keys and Cubs cap, Mordecai the Fourth.

A fitted cap deserves a fitting name. A fitted Cubs cap deserves a fitting Cubs name. Mordecai 'Three Finger' Brown was a Cubs pitcher during the dead-ball era. Our shared love of throwing curves makes the name apropos. Mordecai the Fourth and I have been together for the past three years. It was a challenge to love another cap after the washing machine massacre that took the life of Mordecai the Third. Somehow, I have persevered.

The black tape on the mirror hanging near the front door has two eyes drawn in gold ink. The gold eyes line up with my own. My friend Misty drew them on to spice up the plain black tape. The reflection is like looking at a secret identity, a hatless bandit version of myself. The real me always wears Mordecai. He's essential. I learned years ago that the shade from Mordecai dulls my eyes enough to appear darker. It helps keep the gawkers' chins in check. The new hair I've produced in recent months makes Mordecai a tighter fit. Pulling most of my hair back helps him snuggle on.

The salt-tinged November air is a glory to behold. The last time I watched the news was two days ago. They failed to mention that it would warm up this much. High-seventies in November is something to mention, even if it only stays for a day.

I'm in my car before I realize I've forgotten the information and briefcase Harold provided me. The trip back inside takes me to the kitchen where a brown leather portfolio and Harold's briefcase sit side-by-side on the table. The portfolio was a gift from my father after I graduated from college. He thought it would be the perfect thing to carry around résumés for job interviews. It's hard to say whether he'd laugh or be angry at finding out I'm using it to carry around the life story of a prostitute told through pictures and documentation.

The briefcase and portfolio end up on the passenger seat of my '92 Toyota Camry. My Camry purrs like a drowning cat when I start it up and pull out of the driveway. The back streets of Atlantic Beach vary from pristine to crumbling and wide to narrow. They are a product of growth. As houses sprouted up, so did roads. Speed limit signs line the streets, but whoever is in front of you dictates your speed. On most of the back roads on a temperate day, bikes and their slow-moving operators control the flow. Whether it's a person roaming back and forth in the lane to keep their balance while holding a surfboard or an entire family meandering down the road like a family of ducks on bikes, someone will raise your blood pressure. Instead of wasting time, I make a beeline from my house

15

to Seminole Road, which is a main road near the beach where the elderly and the impatient collide, making it unappealing to anyone on a bike who values their life.

Two small shopping centers flank the sides of Seminole Road where it meets Atlantic Boulevard. On my right, a bakery sign stands out as soon as I clear a small group of trees next to a duplex. A smile gets creepy on my face at seeing the open parking spot in front of The Cake Mistress Bakery awning. That spot is my Camry's second home.

Both the awning and the storefront are alive with color compared to the rest of the businesses. The pastels that make The Cake Mistress Bakery sign and surrounding frontage jump make my insides smile. That happiness comes less from the colors and more from a sense of accomplishment. The space used to be a drab laundromat around the corner from my favorite bookstore since childhood, Tappin Book Mine. I worked with the bakery's owner, Misty Harris, over several days to turn it into a more lively space. The entire design came from Misty's artistically inclined significant other, Elizabeth.

A black '55 Chevy hearse sits in the spot next to mine. Misty's father, Leslie, gave her the hearse as a gift when the bakery first opened. Leslie converted the hearse into a delivery vehicle at his custom auto shop in Mayport, west of Atlantic Beach. He kept the fin taillights, chrome detailing, headlights that look like tired eyes, and bright whitewalls, but altered the delivery bed to secure cakes instead of coffins. Programmable LED billboards integrated into the sides of the hearse flash the bakery's daily deals in bright red to all passing traffic.

Clumps of bells jingle when I open the door. The pastel colors continue into the bakery until Misty shows up to greet me.

Misty's appearance bothers many people. If they don't like her black clothing, black boots, black eyeliner, and black nail polish, then they find fault with her piercings. With four earrings in each ear, three in each eyebrow, one in her nose, and two in her lower lip, they have their pick. Most people see Misty and assume she has tattoos as well, but she never liked them. Misty once told me that tattoos are for those looking to hold on to memories, whereas piercings are for those who want to create memories and experience sensations in unique ways. After asking her for further explanation, she told me that the skin around the piercing is like a raw nerve that fades into a pleasant tingle. Loving a pleasant tingle as much as the next guy has never tempted me to test the veracity of her claims.

The black clothes and piercings migrated from the Hot Topic to Misty at age fifteen after her mother's death. Misty was never ominous and moody, or pretending to be casting spells and conferring with the dead; the black was a sign of reverence. There was an extended period of mourning and quiet when she, as the eldest child, took over for her mother around the house. It took time, much like the raw nerves of her piercings, but her sunny disposition returned while the black accoutrements remain.

"Where in the hell did you find that jacket?" she asks, laughing out loud. "Did you rob Don Johnson?"

Misty rolls up the sleeves of her black chef's jacket.

"Actually, it was Philip Michael Thomas. If you're going to make fun of my threads, at least tidy up your facts."

I suck in my cheeks to give myself a gaunt look before spinning like a model in front of the cash register. It's only after that I realize the gaunt look never materialized because of the amount of facial hair I'm sporting.

"It looks better on you than it did on him."

"Thank you, dear," I say, walking behind the front counter to give Misty a quick hug. Misty, blessed with the height of her Filipino mother, comes up to my chest. Instead of shoving her face right into me, Misty leans backward when she hugs me to avoid smearing her black makeup on my white jacket. Looking down, I can't help but notice the spiked dog collar hanging around her neck. After a quick look at the collar, I take a seat on one of the empty worktables.

"I had a client come by today. He knocked out some of that cake you gave me."

"You gave him some baby cake?"

"Yeah, he seemed to enjoy it."

"Did you explain that the cake was an apology for running over your bike?"

"Didn't think it was relevant."

"He's going to think we're odd here."

"Says the woman adorned with a dog collar."

"Oh, yeah. It's new. Tin and I bought matching ones to show our commitment to each other."

Tin is Misty's girlfriend's nickname. Elizabeth went by the name Liz when she met Misty. The first time Misty's father met Elizabeth, he brought up Tin Lizzy being the nickname of the Ford Model T. Elizabeth thought the name sounded fun and, over time, became known as Tin.

"Most people buy rings for commitment."

"It's different and fun."

"It's different."

"What's that supposed to mean?"

"Nothing. Just repeating. I love Tin. I prefer you being you is all."

"I'm still me."

"I know."

"Did you just come in to let me know someone liked my cake?"

"Kinda. I also wanted to check in and see how everything's going."

"You mean business?"

"Mostly, but I could go for some intimates as well."

"Business is fine. We've been slower than I'd like."

I've lived my entire life at the beach. Small businesses appear and disappear in the blink of an eye. It boils my blood when insincere locals complain about how important it is to keep franchises and big-name stores from invading the Beaches. Once they've complained their way onto a high horse, they gallop across the ditch to one of the many discount chains while ignoring small businesses at the beach that need their money to survive. It's impressive how activism and support dissolve at the first advertisement of a two-for-one sale.

"If you need any money to help stay afloat, let me know. I fell into work."

"I don't want any more of your money."

"I know. But I'd rather you don't trip on that fine line between want and need."

"Thank you, but no."

"That's fine. Figured I'd let you know it was available for parading before I drink it all away."

"If you have another Islay Single Maltapalooza event, let me know so I can participate this time."

"That's my girl," I say with a smile. "Well," I look down at my watch. The time remains constant beneath the shattered crystal. "It's time for me to go take care of business."

18

As I walk past, Misty holds up her hand for a high five. When our hands connect, Misty holds on and turns me around.

"One more thing you might find interesting," Misty says, reaching up and taking Mordecai off my head.

"Be careful. Mordecai isn't used to being handled by the fairer sex."

"I think I know how to handle a gent."

"I beg to differ."

The innuendo merits me a punch in the shoulder and an "Asshole!" declaration from Misty.

"Also, he hasn't been cleaned in a while, so you're probably violating health codes by touching him."

I run my fingers through my hair. It has a habit of drying in tousled clumps if not given a little attention.

"Anyway," Misty says, making a snapping sound with her tongue before continuing. It's a personal belief that the brief snapping tongue sound is becoming the official sound made by women aged fourteen to thirty-five to indicate a subject change. "I just hired a Cubs fan to work here."

"That's nice. Misery loves company."

"And she's cute."

"Now, I'm actually interested."

"I knew you would be. And she's bound to have low expectations since she's been a Cubs fan her whole life."

"That's true. Her tolerance for failure has to be exponentially greater than a normal woman."

"See, she's perfect for you. She starts tomorrow. Make sure you stop by."

"I'll mark it on my calendar," I say, taking Mordecai from Misty. I smooth my hair back and reattach him to the skull he calls home.

While the ringing bells announce my exit, I can't help but wonder if the Cubbie girl likes fantasy baseball.

Chapter 4

Flynn

"Hi," I say to a young lady behind a hostess stand. Her blonde hair falls in loose curls and frames her face. "I'm supposed to meet Edith Danes here. She said to let the hostess know."

Edith Danes called me yesterday evening after someone broke into her apartment. We agreed to meet in Ponte Vedra during her lunch break. The job for Harold is a priority, but a promise is a promise. The leather portfolio in my hand is a reminder of the work ahead.

"Yes, Edith told us she'd be expecting someone. Follow me."

A faint aura of apple and peach surrounds the hostess. It lingers in her wake as I follow her through the restaurant to a table in the back. A raven-haired woman wearing wire-rimmed glasses stops eating her salad and looks up at me. Her eyes widen as though she's shocked at my appearance. I can't tell what she expected. Whether I'd be older, fatter, darker, lighter, well-groomed, Sam Spade-like, or something else. All I know is that I'm not what she envisioned from our brief phone conversation.

"Mr. Dupree?"

"Ms. Danes."

"Please have a seat." Edith nods toward a chair across the table. "You sounded bigger on the phone."

I sit down and place my portfolio in front of me. I'm unsure how to feel about Edith's comment. It makes me curious about why she wanted to speak in person rather than over the phone. Edith said she believes an abusive ex-boyfriend broke into her home. The size comment makes me wonder if she's looking to get back at him physically.

A waiter comes to the table and fills up my water glass before trying to hand me a menu.

"Water is fine. Thanks," I say, pushing the menu away.

"Nothing to eat?"

"No."

"How's the salad, Miss Danes?" The waiter adds an emphasizing wink to his question.

"Great, Brian." Edith smiles as she watches the waiter walk away from the table.

"Should I call you Edith or Miss Danes?"

"Edith is fine."

"Sure thing, Edith. You told me over the phone you're having trouble with an ex."

"Yes. Jason, my ex, broke into my apartment yesterday."

"Do you live in Ponte Vedra?"

"Yes."

"Hasn't there been a string of burglaries in the area? The Haiku Bandit, right?"

"Nothing was taken. And no haikus. He left a box of chocolates and a dozen roses in my kitchen and a pair of black panties with a matching camisole on my bed."

"How do you know it was your ex?"

"Because it has to be him."

"Was the underwear your size?"

"I didn't think to look. The police took it."

It's a shame she doesn't know. If the underwear were in Edith's exact size, it'd be an indication that this intruder has an intimate familiarity with her.

"Any secret admirers or someone at work you catch looking your direction every now and then?"

"No. This is the kind of thing Jason would do to get under my skin. He started hitting me. I ended our relationship. He started showing up at my door, screaming his head off. I called the police."

"Did they arrest him?"

"Yes, but they couldn't do very much."

"Why's that?"

"I didn't call them when he hit me. By the time I did, he had a story prepared about me having burned an entire closet of his clothing. He told them that was the reason he was so angry and that he'd leave me alone.

Since he had nothing on his record prior, they dismissed it as a petty squabble."

"Now that his behavior is on record, why don't you call the police again?"

"I've tried. Jason learned from what happened last time. I recorded some of the messages he left and brought them to the police." Edith pulls a digital audio recording device out of her purse and sets it on the table. "The police looked into it and said the calls are coming from payphones. On top of that, he's masking the sound of his voice."

Payphones? I can't remember the last time I came across a working one.

"Go ahead and press play."

The recording starts with a lot of background noise. Ambient sounds continue while an automatic voice says that there is one saved message. It sounds like Edith held her cell phone up to the recorder to make a copy of the voicemail.

"You are mine." The distorted voice sounds like a person talking through a sock with an unnatural throaty and deep croak. Edith knows whoever left the message. Otherwise, there would be no reason for this person to try so hard to sound different. "If you can't get that through your skull, then I will crush it."

The message ends. Edith's eyes tear up.

"How many more are like that?"

"There are ten on the recorder, but there've been more."

Edith dabs her eyes with the napkin in her lap.

"Were the police able to figure out how he got into your apartment?"

"No. He had to come in through the door."

"Does he have a key?"

"He had one, but the maintenance man has since changed my locks."

"When they change locks in an apartment, they usually use similar locks with similar keys. He could have turned your old key into a bump key and got in."

"What's a bump key?"

"It's like a master key. You can make them by filing down an existing key. They're easy to make. He could have found a video online for specifics."

"You're saying he can walk in whenever he wants?"

22

"If somebody wants to get to you, they can. You can buy a lock pick set online and become proficient in a month. You can climb in an unlocked window or kick in the front door. If somebody wants something enough, they'll get it."

"That's reassuring."

"That's reality."

"Which is what I want from you."

"What? To kick in his door?"

"I want you to provide him a dose of reality. I want you to show up to his apartment and make him feel afraid in the same way he's made me."

"You want me to go to your ex's place and attack him?"

"Yes. Jason likes to hit women, but he's afraid of most men. He's the pretty boy type who's terrified of getting hit. You're not as big as I'd like you to be, but he doesn't have any training. You'll be able to hurt him pretty easily."

"This will not solve your problem."

"My problem is that no one else cares about what he's doing to me. My problem is that the police can't lift a finger until he attacks me. My problem is that when he finally does attack me, I think he's going to kill me."

Edith is right. The police can only act when something reportable happens. She's reported the threatening messages, and they've looked into it. That's as far as they can go. The police can't turn Jason's life upside-down because Edith believes he's leaving her threatening voicemails. But I disagree with her about the beating.

If a jilted lover is angry and looking for revenge, then a beating will only fan the flames. It sends a message in the worst kind of way. Anything she does to challenge his authority will escalate his behavior. The only way a beating might work is if it sparks a new obsession. Hurt and humiliated, Jason will need an outlet. The first step for most people after a mugging or an assault is to take self-defense classes. Edith's ex would probably take boxing or MMA lessons, which can be a perfect outlet for someone who enjoys hitting other people. If he follows this route, he will gravitate to this new circle that embraces his violent tendencies. The camaraderie may be enough to help him forget all about Edith. Or none of this will happen. He could blame Edith for the attack and beat her to death in a fit of rage.

23

"Are you all right?"

"What?" I ask, confused.

"You zoned out for half a minute and were muttering the word 'peach' over and over again."

"I'm fine," I reply. "If I do this for you, then you need to be more careful."

"Why?"

"Because there's a chance this will cause his behavior to escalate."

"If you give him a good beating, then he'll know I have protection."

"People that do this," I say, tapping the audio recorder, "people that leave messages like this are stalkers. Stalkers know and follow routines. They wait for the perfect time to strike. He'll know you don't have full-time protection and that you're often alone."

"I'm not alone that often."

"Often enough."

"How would you know?"

"The hostess didn't bat an eye when I said your name. So either you made a great impression when you told her I'd be joining you or you're a regular. Also, she called you Edith when I referred to you by your full name. The hostess looks like she's about nineteen. Most nineteen-year-olds would instinctively say Ms. or Mrs. Danes when referring to a woman in her thirties. That tells me she's more familiar with you than she would be with a typical regular. I'd say you see her so often that you've told her to call you Edith rather than Ms. Danes. Best guess? You've come here at least two times a week for months."

"The salad's worth it. They make their own raspberry vinaigrette. But that doesn't mean I come here alone."

"The waiter called you Miss Danes despite a noticeable piece of costume jewelry on your ring finger. It's big and flashy and gets the point across: *I'm off the market*. I know you're wearing the ring because you don't want to end up caught in another bad relationship and need some time to yourself, but he doesn't know that. Or at least he shouldn't. Despite the ring, he still called you Miss Danes, not Mrs. as the ring should indicate, but Miss. He winked at you when he left the table. Innocent enough, but he's not a child. He's in his thirties and should know better than to flirt with a married patron. I think he knows you're single because you come here alone. He calls you Miss Danes because he

24

wants you to correct him and say 'Mrs. Danes.' You have never corrected him, so now he's trying to flirt with you. You brightened up the moment he came to the table and then checked out his ass as he walked away. I'm not judging. It's quite lovely. If my preferences leaned that way, I might come here for some vinaigrette and a good ogle. The kicker is that he notices you noticing him."

"What point are you trying to make?"

"The best way to hurt your ex is to hurt his ego. Take off your ring and find someone new. That waiter is interested in you. You are interested in him. Forget about your ex, and date this guy. He looks nice. I'm sure you'd be great together. And if your ex is stalking you and sees you out on a date, then there's just as good a chance of him hittin' the hills because of this new man than if I beat him for you. At least this way, you can be happy and move on. Because, honestly, you're hurting yourself a whole lot more than your ex is hurting you right now."

"I told you what I want," Edith says in a cold voice. "Are you willing to do it, or do I need to find someone else?"

"I feel for you. I've never been in a situation like yours. It's hard for me to understand how you feel—"

"Damaged. Weak. Scared."

This is devolving into one of the most depressing lunches I've had in the past year. Edith's eyes are puffing up. The modest makeup she carefully applied in the morning will run if I don't give her a quick answer. Her erratic breathing is a sign that she's about to break. The flawed and fragile woman she's been holding in is about to come pouring out. This could be dangerous. Cracks in our facade let out the light and invite the darkness. There's no telling what she might do if I turn her down. The best of us can become the worst in an instant. With her back against the wall, there's a chance she might strike out against her ex in unforeseeable ways.

"I will help, but you need to change things. I'm fine with you not listening to me about dating the waiter. I respect your decision. However, you need to change your routines. Something as simple as showing up here a couple times a week makes it easier for someone to follow you."

"Jason knows enough about me to find me wherever I go. He knows where I live and work. He could follow me from either."

"But the routine is the problem. Your routines make it easier for anybody to find you."

"I'm an error control specialist. If I didn't have routines, I'd have been fired long ago."

"That's work. You can change things outside."

"My entire life is routine. I eat at the same time every day. I wake up and go to bed at the same time every day. I only shop on specific days so I can pick up and drop off dry cleaning on other specific days. I'm at work a lot, and that only leaves me so many hours in the day to do things. I need to order them so they can end up done."

"That's fine. Start with minor changes. Try to stay in areas with lots of people. Leave work with a group. If he's afraid of confrontation with men like you say he is, then he'll only attack you when you're alone."

"I have a little trap set up for him at the door if he tries to get inside again."

"Is it lethal?"

"Why?"

"You realize when you answer 'Why?' to a question like that it means 'Yes,' right?"

"It's not lethal. He'll just be very surprised."

"If it's lethal, you can go to jail for a long time."

"He's the one breaking into my house."

"As an American, it's your God-given right to want to see him dead on your doorstep. It's not your right to pull the trigger, only hope that it's pulled. You setting up a trap isn't considered hope; it's considered action. And we're a country of hope, not action. You can hope and pray for all sorts of awful things to happen, but acting on those urges will get you a concrete cell with a piss-poor view for the rest of your life."

"Are you done?"

"It's premeditated. And you live in an apartment. Think of what would happen if the maintenance man shows up."

"I told you it's not lethal."

"Fine. Before we put this to paper, I need to provide you one more reality check and remind you that there's a decent chance this will not work."

"For me, it's worth the risk."

"I'll need his address and three hundred dollars."

"Three hundred?"

"I'm taking a lot of risk in doing this."

"Oh, I know. When you told me to bring cash, I brought five." My eyebrows raise when she pulls out a wad of Old Hickories and starts counting. "Too late, you said three."

"Do you have a mailbox or mail pickup at your office?" I ask, taking the stack of Old Hickories from Edith.

"Yes," she says.

I pull an envelope out of my portfolio and push it across the table.

"We'll be square if you mail this when you get back to work."

Edith picks up the envelope and glances at it before smiling.

"Who's Sergeant Sexy?"

"An old friend. It's an inside joke."

"I'll drop it in with the outgoing."

"Thanks. What time does Jason get off work?"

Edith slips the envelope into her purse and hands me a piece of paper with an address on it. It's an apartment complex in Ponte Vedra. A drinking buddy of mine lived there for a while. Our late-night hijinks left me familiar with the layout of the area.

"He works from home and should be there now. He usually goes out at night to troll around the Beaches and drink."

"Do not tell anyone you paid me for this. Even after time passes, don't."

"My lips are sealed," Edith puts her fingers to her lips and pretends to turn a key.

The waiter returns to the table with a carafe of water. "Would you like me to top you off?" he asks.

"Yes, please," I say, handing him my glass. "I've got a quick question if you don't mind?"

"Shoot," he says, filling my glass with water and returning it to the table.

"My cousin Edith is looking for a new gym." I smile at Edith across the table. She puts her hands in her lap. A look of terror creeps across her face. "It looks like you frequent the gym."

"Four, five times a week," he says with a smile so hard I can tell he flosses.

"She left her last gym because she didn't know anyone there."

"You should join up," the waiter says to Edith. "I'd love to show you around."

"You hear that, Edith? He'd love it," I say, standing up from the table. "I've got to go. You two should exchange information and set up a date and time to meet up. Edith, tell Aunty I said, 'Hi.'"

Chapter 5

Amy

It takes Marty half a cigarette to find me smoking behind the diner. The other waitresses can burn through an entire cigarette, while my personal best tops out at three-quarters. The others huff and puff as quickly as they can, but not me. Slow, measured drags work like breathing exercises, and the calming influence of nicotine relaxes me enough to go back to work with a smile on my face.

"What'n the hell are you doin' out here?" Marty's rotund belly bounces when he pushes the door hard enough to hit the concrete block wall. A hellish lunch service left his white shirt and blue tie stained by grease. "You need to be inside waitin' on yer damn tables."

Marty pulls a long drink through a straw from a sixty-four-ounce plastic cup. This specific cup is in Marty's right hand so often that everyone working in the diner calls it Rosie. The once red plastic is now a faded and spotty orange, while only a white outline remains from the gas station logo that covered the front.

"Calm down, Marty. Dammit! I just needed a minute to relax."

The southern twang in my voice never works on Marty. The accent started as a childhood phase. Everybody told me how adorable it sounded. I kept using it until I stopped having to try.

"Relax on your own time." Marty points his fat index finger at the phone in my hand. "And you better turn that thing off. I see you textin' on the clock again, and it's goin' in the sink."

The cursor on the unfinished text message blinks at me. Marty's eyes are bulging out of his head, and the sight encourages me to lock my phone. It bothers me that I'm not able to finish texting my sometimes here and sometimes not boyfriend who is currently in Scotland. I'm supposed to pick him up at the airport on Saturday. Those plans are up in the air until he responds to my text messages.

"See," I say, throwing my cigarette to the ground and rubbing it into the asphalt with the toe of my white non-slip sneaker, "all done."

"Better damn well be," Marty shoots back, holding the door open while looking me up and down as I walk back inside.

Marty's eyes are always watching me. There are times his stare could burn a hole in the knee-length black skirts we have to wear as a uniform. The bottom hem of the skirt and the sleeves of our white blouses and socks all have the same white frill, evoking some perverted little girl fantasy.

Marty closes the back door and follows me through the kitchen. We part ways when I walk past the display case full of pies and back onto the black and white checkered tile floor. An older waitress walks up to me with a sour look. The sight of her in the frilly clothing, trying to work the schoolgirl fantasy, makes me snicker every time I see her.

"What's wrong, Carla?" I ask, keeping any semblance of a smirk off my face.

"Some man in my section is askin' for you directly. I'm gonna give you the table, but I'm expectin' one of yours shortly. Don't wanna see none of you cuttin' into my tips today, sweetie."

I smile politely.

Men tend to ask for seats in my section. I'm a breath of fresh air compared to Carla, and easier on the eyes. Being blonde and petite helps me sell a lot of pie. My appearance isn't the only reason men want me as their server. The reality is that I treat my customers better. A smile and a little flirting go a long way in repeat business. On a typical day, three or four people ask for me and only me.

Recently, some of my coworkers, Carla included, decided to get back at me by unloading customers they think will be poor tippers.

"Did he really ask for me?"

There are zero familiar faces in Carla's section.

"Table eight, sweetie," Carla says with a wink.

The man is a stranger. My best guess is late-twenties, but the month-plus of growth on his face makes it hard to pinpoint an age. The dark and wiry beard shows no attempt to trim it. A beard like that means he's self-employed or out of work. No type of management would tolerate something that untamed. His clothes are worse than his beard. They look fresh from a church's charity bin. His short-sleeved jacket and beaten-up hat stand out much more than the olive cargo shorts and thong sandals.

Two thoughts pop into my head simultaneously: The man is homeless, and Carla's a bitch.

Approaching the table, I try my hardest to imitate a genuine smile. The man takes off his glasses and starts cleaning the lenses with the shirt he's wearing underneath the jacket. The orange They Might Be Giants t-shirt with a snowman warming his hands over a fire made of money is one my first high school boyfriend wore all the time. It makes me like this guy even less.

"What a sharp jacket," I say, trying my best to make initial small talk and show interest in the customer.

"Yes, ma'am. I bought it at the Goodwill for four cherry choppers. Thought I might take it out on tour now that it's comfortable out."

I have no idea what a cherry chopper is. My first instinct is that he's crazy. Then I see the leather case sitting closed on the table. The case is expensive, too expensive for someone shopping at Goodwill. My second instinct is that he's crazy and full of shit.

"My name's Flynn," the man says, leaning back in the booth and tipping his hat.

"They call me Amy." The gesture he made seemed odd, so I respond with a feigned cowboy accent and the tipping of a pretend hat. I flash my best smile, the one that makes customers come back to me time and again.

"I know," Flynn says. "I asked that lovely lady if I could have you as my waitress and sit here where it's nice and quiet."

"I'm sorry, but you don't look familiar—it was Flynn, right?"

"Yes, and we've never met." Flynn extends his hand, which I shake daintily.

Sitting down in a booth next to an unaccompanied man makes him feel like he's got himself a lady to eat with, and a man with a lady always tips better. This is why I take a seat right next to Flynn, even though I wouldn't sit in the same row as him in a movie theater.

"So, Flynn, how did you know to ask for me?" I lean against the table and toward Flynn.

Flynn still appears homeless, but sitting close to him reveals well-maintained teeth and pleasant cologne. My eyes wander to Flynn's left

31

wrist, where a gold-colored watch with a broken face stands out under the diner's bright fluorescent lights.

"Expose that to the light of day for me," Flynn says, tapping the leather case.

"Huh?"

"Open it."

The fake smile I'm wearing fades to shock when I open Flynn's case. A photo of me walking to my car sits on top of a stack of pictures and papers. I'm wearing my work uniform, but the background is not the diner parking lot. The car parked next to mine is my neighbor's. Someone took this picture in front of my apartment in Atlantic Beach. It's jarring because I look oblivious to anyone photographing me.

"Why do you have this?"

"Miss Wright, please keep your voice down. I'd hate for anyone in this restaurant to overhear us."

I recoil at the sound of my last name. Flynn moves my picture off the top of the papers and reveals a family photo of me with my mother and father. It's a smaller version of a photo my parents keep over the fireplace in their home. Flynn flips the photograph; on the back are my parents' names and their home, work, and cell phone numbers.

"How do you have all of this?"

I can feel my face turning red. Tears fill up the corners of my eyes.

"Miss Wright, please keep calm. I need you to do a favor for me."

"I don't even know you, and you come in here with these pictures asking for favors."

"No, I'm being polite. You need to do what I want, or I will call your parents and let them know how you support yourself."

"What do you mean?"

"I'll tell them you're a hooker."

It takes a second for his words to hit home. When they do, I place my hand over my heart like I'm struggling to keep it in my chest. My mouth stays open as I stand up from the table to look around and see if anyone else is reacting. The surrounding tables are empty. Flynn spoke quietly enough that no one is paying any attention to us. I try my best to ensure my facial expressions appear both angry and clueless about Flynn's accusation.

"How dare you!"

"Fine. Let's just say you provide the girlfriend experience to men with enough money to buy your time. Is that better?"

"What are you, insane?"

"Well, I ain't been right since I grew above my elbows."

"What does that even mean?"

"Sorry, not sure what I said," Flynn shrugs. "I associate things awkwardly, and sometimes I say things without realizing it. My father calls them Flynnoquialisms. Great word. Etymologically suspect."

"Seriously. You need to leave before I call the cops."

"The job pays two thousand for only an hour of your time."

That misty feeling on and around my eyes dries up. The tears slow to a halt. A stern look draws my eyebrows together, something my mother told me not to do because it causes wrinkles.

"You said two thousand dollars for an hour, right? That wasn't another Flynnoquialism you don't remember?"

"Two thousand dollars for one hour of your time."

"What are they looking to do?" I ask, sitting back down at the table.

"You don't technically have to do anything."

"Are you a cop?"

"No."

"Now it's entrapment. You know that, right?"

"Yes. I'm offering you a deal. Two thousand for an hour of your time."

"Where and when?"

"There's a small motel on Atlantic Boulevard not too far from Third Street. Do you know where that is?"

I've never been to the place, but I've seen it while driving on Atlantic hundreds of times. The motel looks sort of dingy and questionable, so I always stay away from it.

"The one next to the church?"

"Yes. I'll be in the motel parking lot at six o'clock tonight. Be punctual."

"Don't worry. I'll be there."

"I have the number for your cell phone. If you're late, I'll be calling."

I walk away from the table and quickly turn back.

"Did you want anything to eat?"

"No. Thank you. I live off of a liquid diet."

33

I walk away from the table again, heading back to my other customers. The next time I turn around, Flynn is gone.

Chapter 6

Flynn

Jason Daniels lives in a bottom floor apartment in Ponte Vedra. I've never understood the appeal of living on the bottom floor. It's necessary with a house. Outside of a Howard Hughes scenario, I can't think of a situation where someone would only live on the upper floor of their home. These apartments are different. They are only two stories, and the second floor has to cost about the same as the first. There may be a slight increase for vaulted ceilings or other amenities that are not possible on the first floor, but the benefits are worth the cost. The ability to open up the windows and let the sun and breeze come in on a beautiful day, without having to worry about the gawky neighbor's prying eyes, is worth a minimal rate hike. That annoying sound of sprinklers hitting the walls in the early morning is somebody else's problem. Even the random lawnmower buzzing across the grass sounds distant and pleasant when it has a one-floor buffer.

Apartment complexes like this provide other amenities to keep the bottom dwellers from complaining about their upstairs neighbor's inconsiderate stomping all hours of the day and night. They'll toss in track lighting or a free painted accent wall, fans in every room, maybe a substantial pantry or direct access to a garage. Some provide privacy hedges, which are the amenity equivalent of socks on Christmas. Privacy hedges are pointless. It's nice not to worry about seeing neighbors in awkward positions, but that's why blinds exist. The only real benefit of a privacy hedge goes to the criminal element. Those green blockades make it easier for someone to sneak up to an apartment and stay hidden.

Jason's apartment has a thick privacy hedge in a concrete planter near his front door. Sitting in my car, I can barely see the apartment number on the yellow plaster next to the door frame. This privacy will make it easier for me to get in and out unseen.

I remove Mordecai and my eighties blazer and set them in the passenger seat. Before getting out of the car, I pop the trunk. The packed trunk has a collection of hats and shirts, some notepads, three pairs of shoes, some pens and markers, a crowbar, a light-up pizza delivery sign for my roof, and several identical packages covered in brown paper. I put on a brown hat and a brown button-up short-sleeved shirt. I use a black marker to write Jason's address on one of the paper-wrapped packages. There's a phone book underneath the brown paper, which gives it the perfect package size and shape.

Ringing the doorbell while committing a crime is a terrible idea. It's always better to knock. It's easy to slip up in the heat of the moment and leave a fingerprint.

My disguise isn't much of a disguise. It only works from the waist up, which is all that's necessary. If Jason looks through the peephole and sees a person wearing brown and holding a package, he will open the door. Odds are he won't immediately look down and realize my lower half doesn't match the upper. That delay gives me enough time to do my job.

The faint light coming through the peephole disappears. The deadbolt pops before the handle turns. My mind is prone to wander off on fanciful tangents. It's something I don't realize happens until it's too late. At certain moments, I need to focus on reality. My therapist tells me a commonsense way to keep focused is to take deep breaths and count to ten. She's wrong. The heavy breathing makes me worse. Huffing away right now would look suspicious. And counting to ten? That's the kind of mindless recitation that breaks my concentration. Making mental lists is a helpful middle ground that hones my focus far more than counting. I don't list groceries or anything that would require an excess of creative thinking. All I list are facts.

George Washington.

"Jason Daniels?" I ask when he opens the door. The man is tall. A step up into the apartment adds to his height and forces me to look up at him.

John Adams.

"A package?"

"You're Jason?"

Thomas Jefferson.

"Yup. Do I need to sign?"

Edith was right, Jason is a pretty boy ... *James Madison*. The part in Jason's auburn hair looks like Moses' best work. A luxuriant wave of hair rises from one side of his head and rolls to the other, blending in like it's crashing on the shore. He looks like an all-American football star who's aged gracefully into his thirties. The time he invests in his hair alone makes it hard to believe he spends his nights trolling beach bars ... *James Monroe*. That said, he could be one of those creepers trying to recapture their glory days by flirting with barely legal women, or Edith could have been exaggerating his behavior. What stands out most about Jason is that he works from his home and still dresses and fixes his hair like he's at an office. *John Quincy Adams*. Wearing a tie while sitting in your apartment feels like something from 1950s TV.

The easiest way to incapacitate a man is to kick him in the balls. The current height difference requires an alternative approach. A quick punch is rarely enough to bring a man to his knees. Follow through and grip strength help pick up the slack. These special circumstances remind me how grip strength is truly an underappreciated asset.

Jason's knees buckle. I release my grip. Both of Jason's hands are engaged in cradling himself, which makes him an easy target. "Andrew Jackson!" I reach back with the phone book and come across his face with a blow from which he bounces right back. It's almost like a Bobo doll regaining its equilibrium and waiting for the next punch. "Martin Van Buren!" I swing the phone book once more. This time he hits the carpet with a muffled thud.

William Henry Harrison.

Jason is still breathing, which is a relief. But he's not moving. Half of his face is red and beginning to swell. I grab Jason's tie, yanking his head off the floor. *John Tyler*. Edith wanted a beating, and I'm certain she wants more than some slaps with a phone book and a pair of sore balls, so I punch him hard enough to ensure he'll have a black eye.

"James K. Polk!"

Moments like these make me hate what I do, but it's better I'm here with Jason than some knuckle-dragger who will beat a man until he's nothing but pulp. "Zachary Taylor..." These wounds are superficial. They'll heal up and leave no lasting damage. In the meantime, Jason will see his pretty face in the mirror and stop and think. "Millard Fillmore..." Maybe he'll think about the times he hit Edith and realize that the feeling

37

of being damaged, weak, and scared is now something they share in common.

"Franklin Pierce…"

It's all wishful thinking.

Life trains us to see only so much. Damaged, weak, and scared is an apt description of anyone willing to look into a mirror. Emptiness and hollow words define reflections; fanciful images etched in glass for the world to see. There is no good in our eyes. There is no evil in our hearts. There is only emotion, bridging the gaps like scars on our skin.

James Buchanan…

Chapter 7

Amy

My headlights pass over Flynn standing next to a Toyota Camry. In an instant, he fades to a silhouette in my rear-view mirror. The parking spot I choose is on the opposite side of the lot from Flynn. Keeping my distance makes me feel better. I'm still afraid that something might go wrong. The distance gives me time to turn around and head back to my car. The dome light reveals marks on the palms of my hands matching the textured cover on my steering wheel. Any other time, I would smoke a cigarette to calm down, but one of my rules is to smoke only after business is complete. Instead, I take a deep breath before opening the car door.

An ocean breeze rolls through the air, moving the branches of the tall oak trees like puppets. The creaking sound some of the older branches make adds another level of eerie to the night. I approach Flynn cautiously. He's no longer wearing the short-sleeved jacket, but the cargo pants, They Might Be Giants t-shirt, and old hat remain. The parking lot lights hit Flynn in such a way that the brim of his hat hides his face in shadow.

"I'm here," I say, adjusting a black canvas tote on my shoulder. The bag is something I usually bring to yoga. Today, I'm using it to carry the necessities.

"Such perfect timing," Flynn says, tapping the broken face of his wristwatch. "Six on the nose."

The fingers on my hand roll out one-by-one into an open palm. "Where's the money?"

"Is that how you handle a transaction?"

Flynn's comment bothers me. I try not to show it by taking my open hand and using it to readjust the bag on my shoulder.

"You promised me two thousand for an hour of my time."

"And you will receive two thousand once the hour is over."

"How do I know you'll pay me?"

"You'll just have to rely on me being an honorable man."

"You're blackmailing me."

"I would call it forcing you into a business opportunity."

"And why me?"

"Because you are perfect for the part."

"How so?"

"Well, there's a man who will show up here in about half an hour. He prefers women like you, blonde and—" Flynn whistles and makes a curvy outline of me with his fingers. "All you need to do is get him onto the bed and push a button. Spend a minute or two on the bed with him. Titillate and whatnot. It'll be over before you know it."

"What button do I push?"

"This one." Flynn gives me a plastic remote with a red button in the middle. It's similar in size and shape to the keyless entry for my car. "Just don't touch it until he's on the bed. And you need to use it from the bathroom to keep him from seeing it."

"Why not? What does it do?"

"It starts a camera."

"No way. There's no way I'm doing anything on film."

"You don't have to do anything. Just make it look like something is happening. A couple minutes of video, and we're good to go."

"Then why do I need a button? Can't we just start recording now and not have a button? Don't cameras record for hours?"

"Some do, but this one doesn't. The button needs to be pressed only when he's on the bed. Is that clear?"

"Yes."

"Good," Flynn says, pulling a key from another cargo pocket. "This is for your room. Go get ready."

Reluctantly, I take the key and shuffle toward the room. The remote disappears into a small pocket on the inside of my tote. A bright light shines near the door, illuminating the surrounding area. I've seen this motel from a distance, but never up close. It has an undeniable charm. The squat building makes me imagine what the Beaches were like during the old days. I've lived here for most of my twenty-six years, and it's hard to believe Florida used to be full of motels like this one. Sadly, these places will all disappear in the next decade, replaced by something bigger and flashier.

The door's hinge squeaks as it opens. A musty smell rolls out of the room. Moments like these make me realize that as much as I love the old beach aesthetic, sometimes the old beach odors might merit a wrecking ball.

The room is dark inside. Before closing the door, I hit the light switch. Two lamps reveal a simple room with off-white textured walls. An abundance of wicker stands out. A wicker headboard and two wicker nightstands covered in peeling white paint look plain next to the floral bedspread. The fading floral mess of oranges, blues, and greens begs me to remove it from the bed. I pull the bedspread off and fold it neatly, setting it on the floor in the small closet.

Not knowing which is cleaner, the stained carpet or the hideous bedspread, I place my tote bag on top of the bedspread. The bag is full of goodies from ambiance enhancers to cleaning supplies. Two sheer pieces of midnight blue fabric draped over the lamps on the nightstands reduces the light in the room enough to make the peeling wicker stand out less. A can of air sanitizer, sprayed in a continuous stream, helps clear out the musty odor. The tub doesn't feel gritty or slimy, which makes it clean enough for my comfort.

It takes a minute of running water across my wrist before it reaches the perfect temperature. To complete the experience, I walk back to my bag and pull out a bottle of rose-scented bath oil. The bottle recommends a cap per gallon of water, but I pour the oil into the water until the entire bathroom smells perfumed.

While the water runs, I take off my clothes and fold them, placing each piece of clothing into my bag. After adorning myself in a black silk nightgown that reveals enough to keep anyone interested, someone knocks. I cough gently before opening the door.

My hand rests high on the door's frame as I open it wide and set my twang to seductive. "Hello."

"You must be Amy," he says. "I'm Paul."

Paul is in his mid-fifties. The bright bulb outside lights up his smile, revealing yellowing teeth partially hidden behind a large mustache. Streaks of gray run backward from his temples through his black hair.

Suspenders hold up his gray slacks and press his white dress shirt close to his body.

Paul reminds me of my father. To prevent the inevitable awkwardness, I think of celebrities that bear a resemblance to Paul. Picturing a combination of Tom Selleck and Jay Leno forces the thoughts of my father to fly away into the night air.

"Please come in," I say, continuing to push the seductive angle.

"Thank you. I'm delighted you could meet me on such short notice."

"It's my pleasure. Please, have a seat on the bed."

"No, thanks. I'd prefer standing for a moment. I've been sitting all day. My legs could use the practice."

"Feel free to get more comfortable." I add a dash of Southern darling to my voice, hoping it will make Paul relax.

"Thank you," he says while taking off his shoes. "That's very kind of you."

I walk into the bathroom and turn off the water. The heat fogged up the mirror. Ever since I was old enough to reach, I've been drawing hearts in the corners of mirrors when they fog up. The sweet little girl I used to see when the fog cleared is smiling back at me from the other side.

"I was just going to take a quick bath to warm up. You're free to join me if you'd like."

Paul laughs with nervous confusion.

"No, thank you. I'm more than happy to wait until you finish your bath."

I'm discreet in picking up the remote from the closet. It hides among the handful of small bottles I carry to the tub.

Most men appreciate a brief show before the main event. Paul watches me untie my robe and averts his eyes before it hits the tile floor.

"Don't worry. I'm not shy."

"Maybe I should come back when you've finished."

"No. Please stay. It'll just be a minute till I'm ready."

"I'll wait," Paul says. There aren't any chairs in the room. Paul sits down on the bed and faces the wall. He pulls a pen and a small notebook from his pocket.

The rose scent floats all around me as I sink into the water. The open bathroom door provides an unobstructed view of the bed. Paul leans backward and acts as if he feels something strange beneath him. The mattress gives way in the center of the bed. Paul's balance shifts and he rolls toward the sagging center.

The remote's weight increases. The little hearts in the foggy mirror fade away. If I could see my face, I wouldn't be able to flip this switch. I close my eyes, take a deep breath, and open my eyes in time to see my thumb push down. A loud explosion erupts, sending black smoke curling around the frame of the bathroom door.

Chapter 8

Flynn

Smoking cigarettes is a nasty habit that grants me respite in times of stress. I smoked my first cigarette at a party Trudy Tellegio's older brother threw while their parents were out of town for the weekend. She invited me out of the blue. Needing to impress, and only thirteen-years-old, a cigarette guaranteed Trudy would see my cooler adult side. Not even being old enough to rent a movie on my own, I had to purchase two Lucky Strikes from a man outside of a Lil' Champ who smelled like he used beer as an aftershave. It all paid off when Trudy lit up at the sight of me strolling into the party like a tobacco-laden demigod among boys with a cigarette behind each ear and swagger unmatched since the days of James Dean. Hours of practicing the most impressive way to light a match paid off when a clump of three matches, bent and curled to scrape across the back of an attached matchbook, ignited in a bright blaze. I casually put the cigarette from over my right ear into my mouth and offered Trudy the other. She declined. Movies filled my head with the kind of nonsense that had me believing cigarette smoke would turn my tongue silver, which would allow me to beguile Trudy with an endearing smoothness. The results did not match expectations. The coughing? Kind of expected. The vomiting? Not so much.

That first taste of trauma is saccharine sweet in hindsight. Life heaped on the traumas and stuffed coal in my stocking every chance it got since, but, at that time, vomiting in front of a crowd of people felt like the end of the world. My embarrassment hit new heights when the Monday morning school bus ride turned into an ensemble singalong of a ditty titled "Flynnie's Gonna Yak."

Flynn, Flynn, Flynnie's gonna yak.
Gonna give poor Trudy a heart attack.

44

Here, here, here comes another round.
He won't be done till he's covered the ground.

Cigarettes bring back memories of that day. The good, the bad, and the mess I left in Trudy's back yard put me at ease and distract me from whatever bit of reality weighs me down. The knowledge that insurmountable problems will pass in time is comforting. Sadly, my brain associates that feeling with cigarettes. Happily, childhood traumas with accompanying schoolyard songs are a lot more entertaining later in life.

Every minute spent in the motel parking lot waiting for Amy is another minute of sitting on pins and needles. Half of that feeling comes from a damaged spring in the driver's seat; the other half comes from an inescapable feeling of dread at both knowing what I'm doing and not knowing why I'm doing it. Even cigarettes aren't helping. Typical problems require a single cigarette to help me move on to something else. Four American Spirits smoked in half an hour don't do the trick. Trudy's back yard fades away as soon as it comes to life.

Any paying job brought to my attention ends up being a job I need. The market for an unlicensed 'consultant' isn't booming. Turning away money, especially as much as Harold promised for the successful completion of only part of a day's work, never crossed my mind. But something doesn't feel right. Harold set everything in motion. Every bit and bauble is accounted for, yet he went out of his way to pay me five thousand dollars to contact Amy and be there when the plan comes to fruition. It doesn't make sense that someone would pay that much when they've already done all the work.

I've worked jobs similar to this one. Dalliances destroy marriages, but they also pay the bills. For me, an incriminating picture can be worth far more than a thousand words. These jobs begin with a blank canvas; I'm the one who paints the picture. Harold's job starts with me painted in a corner. He has lured Amy, the mystery man, and me to this location. This spouse or business partner or competitor trying to gain an edge, whoever hired Harold, intends to bring this man into a trap and have evidence against him.

There's a decent chance I might be overthinking. Harold appeared fastidious. When I first laid eyes on him, I could tell he takes pride in his appearance. The cropped hair and pressed clothing speak volumes about his personality. Harold trims his fingernails close and round, except for his thumbnails, which, although still rounded, are longer than the rest. A man so particular with his appearance will apply that to all aspects of his life. He could have pored over this plan for hours and prepared it over months, crafting this as a living Rube Goldberg machine and hiring me to push the first domino.

My father taught me a simple lesson when I was interested in following in his footsteps as a lawyer. I asked him how he could represent people that were lying to him. It took him a minute to respond. He stared at the wall before focusing back on me. "Money," he said. I waited for more. He laughed. "Empathy is what I should have said. Let's go with empathy."

Money is not the worst reason to do things, especially your job. My father's empathy for sketchy clients forced me to search for the 'Why' behind the money. Eventually, I concluded that we all connect in some way. My father's clients might have been terrible people, but maybe they had families, maybe they had a favorite hobby, maybe they had a beloved mother or grandmother. There are millions of ways we can connect. Once we find those connections, we can begin to understand them and their situation. Once you connect to people, you can see their peculiarities emerge. Those peculiarities can tell you a lot.

Harold's need for order exists in every perfectly ironed square inch of his clothing. But the flaw in seeing Harold as a man of order begins when I enter the picture. I can't understand why he would trust me with a plan nurtured like a child when it's a near-guarantee he wouldn't trust me with his daughter on a date.

For Harold, this could be the child he never wanted. Neat and tidy Harold certainly has a neat and tidy life. I, by all accounts, appear the opposite. A man like Harold isn't the kind of person one expects to spend an afternoon hiring a prostitute. Whereas, a face like mine is perfect for blackmail and solicitation. Five thousand dollars is cheap to keep a life neat and tidy. Harold's investment has made sure that, if it all goes wrong, I'll be the one stuck in a car with a mysterious briefcase waiting for a hooker to show up.

Harold's briefcase has done its best to earn the title of 'mysterious.' If it were alive, it would give me the old side-eye while sporting a lock-to-lock grin. But it's not alive. It's just a briefcase of secrets on the passenger seat of my car. Average in size. Covered in faux leather. Plain and simple. I'll admit that I tried to open the locks. Who wouldn't? My attempts at finagling did not include a screwdriver. There's no doubt in my mind Harold would notice suspicious scratches. Instead of forcing the locks, I tried to figure out the numerical code. The odds were against me divining the combination in time. The briefcase has two locks, each with three spinning numerals ranging from zero to nine. One million distinct combinations exist. Before trying anything, I thought of Harold. The organized man constructed in my mind lacks imagination. Subpar imagination winnows potential combinations down to simple sets of numbers or a personalization like a birthday or an anniversary. Knowing nothing about Harold left me with simple sets of numbers. All zeros, all ones, all twos. I went all the way through straight nines, and nothing happened. Ascending numbers. Descending numbers. Nothing happened. For about ten minutes, I pretended it was a safe and placed my ear against the sides of the briefcase, spinning the numbers and listening for the sounds of a clicking lock. No clicking occurred, but I swear I heard the faint whisper of a fan humming inside, the sound barely discernible over the marching beat of blood pumping through my body.

Amy arrives right on time. I explain the last-minute details and watch her as she enters the motel room. The motel is an unimpressive squat cinderblock building, a relic of Floridian architecture. According to Goethe, "Architecture is frozen music." If that's true, this motel is a symphony of frosty brown notes.

A man sitting alone in the parking lot of such an establishment could draw the wrong kind of attention. My cigarettes and I try to appear inconspicuous at a distance. The 'random beach rat standing next to the road waiting for a friend or family member' look is easy to pull off because I've been in that position more than once. The occasional driver passing by ignores me. A new Cadillac sedan pulls up. The driver looks back and forth. I check my pocket for my cell phone to pretend that I'm talking to someone. It's not there. In my haste to play it cool at a distance, I must have left it in my car's cup holder. Cadillac Jack doesn't waste his time on me. He parks and knocks on Amy's motel room door. The man's face is familiar. I can't quite place him, but the 'stache is a standout.

The cigarettes do their job, allowing me to reminisce about better times. Trudy's back yard fades away when an explosion in the motel

47

room shatters the window and blows the glass out into the parking lot. The shards of glass skitter to a stop in slow motion. Billows of smoke roll out through the windowless frame. My brain catches up to my feet as they plod toward the motel room door. As my pace quickens to a sprint, another explosion goes off. The pressure from the blast hits me from the side. Instead of running forward, I end up spinning to the ground.

Chapter 9

Stephen

Amy welcomes Paul Mahoney into the motel room. A pair of binoculars provides me a perfect view from my position at the end of the street. He enters as planned. Everything is on track. If Amy does as requested and puts Paul on the bed, then the bomb will do the rest.

The bombs' constituent parts are available in stores. Every detail matches online plans found on multiple websites. The triggering mechanisms are the only intricate components, but anyone with two spare hours and a fifth-grade education could turn the diagrams and instructions into functioning triggers. A disposable cell phone acts as a trigger for the pipe bomb in Flynn's car. When I call from a second disposable cell, the bomb will go off. Both phones were cash purchases from a store without cameras. The clerk was a skater punk whose only description of me will be 'tool.' As for the bomb in the hotel room, the trigger only works with weight on the bed. The emphasized importance of using the remote in the bathroom should force Amy to stay away from the bed. If she knows it's a trigger, any kind of trigger, then she knows to press the button where Paul cannot see her. Or at least I hope that happens. She is the one person I need to survive.

The intent is to make it look like Flynn committed the crime. If Amy tells the police that Flynn hired her to be there and meet with a man, then they will assume that Flynn orchestrated the entire bombing. The police investigating the explosion in his car will dismiss it as an accident or incompetence.

My job is specific: Kill Paul Mahoney at any cost. But something that specific is difficult. I rented the room in use, and the two surrounding it, with a credit card stolen from the center console of a truck I broke into earlier in the day. The last thing I want is for either of these explosions to

49

trace back to me. Unnecessary casualties are second to last on that list. Renting the surrounding rooms minimizes the chance of injuring others.

Placing the bomb in the bed required me to destroy the box spring. An increase in weight on the surface pushes the box spring down until it collapses and activates the bomb. Pressure is integral to the firing mechanism. Like a bullet in a chamber, it takes proper alignment for it to function. This safety measure keeps the button in Amy's hand useless until it is necessary.

The plan will fall apart if Paul realizes something is wrong. The mattress is light enough to keep the bed from collapsing on its own but thin enough to create an indent in the center above the bomb. Amy convincing Paul to take a seat should be sufficient. I removed the one chair from the room to leave the bed as the only option other than the floor. Sitting down should be enough. Any amount of additional weight can cause the box spring to collapse. That sudden inward motion should drop Paul back into the kill zone. Designed to blast sharp pieces of metal toward the ceiling, the bomb's cannon-like construction will kill anyone on the bed and leave those at least five feet away disoriented but unharmed.

The bomb in Flynn's car will go off when I push the call button on my cell. All I need to do is wait for the explosion in the motel room. Flynn has complicated my plan by not being in his car. The pipe bomb lacks the power and the shrapnel to kill a person outside of the vehicle. The concussive blast and the metal in the pipe provide enough impact and shrapnel to kill someone nearby, but the odds of it hurting someone outside are slim. My only chance at this working is if Flynn returns to his car before the first bomb goes off. Once the explosion inside the motel occurs, Flynn will be reluctant to be anywhere near the briefcase I gave him.

It feels like an hour while I watch through the binoculars. Only minutes pass. Flynn does not move from his position near the road. An ember at the end of his cigarette lights up and fades away, lights up and fades away. The bomb goes off in the room with more power than expected. The window blows out into the parking lot, and the door nearly unhinges.

Flynn stands still and watches. The cigarette falls from his hand and sends tiny embers shooting across the ground. Flynn runs toward the motel room. The most direct path to the door brings him within five feet of his car. I'm almost positive there will be enough of a blast to injure or kill him at that range. I push the call button.

The first ring ends with the pipe bomb going off in Flynn's car. It knocks Flynn to the ground, where he stays, immobile. The stillness is encouraging. If injured, he would try to move. This time and effort might pay off.

The sight of Flynn's lifeless body fills me with guilt. It could have been anyone on the ground, but he left his business card on my car while I shopped for groceries. I held on to that business card because Lou could always use a guy like Flynn. Rediscovering the card was the best kind of luck. Thanks to Flynn's sacrifice, my life can continue.

Before I can pack up and leave, Flynn's body moves. The burning car casts odd shadows, but I am certain he moved. His left arm and then his right. His right leg and then his left. Flynn is alive and moving. The plan is falling apart. People like Flynn always ruin everything. My plan was solid. It cannot end this way.

Damage control is the only viable option. If I can take Flynn out, the police still might blame him for the bombing. Adrenaline takes over. I start the engine and slam the gas. The tires squeal as the SUV takes off down the street.

Chapter 10

Flynn

Hydrogen.

The rough asphalt of the parking lot digs into my back. My car doesn't look right. It's all fuzzy. The windows are missing. Flames rise to what's left of the ceiling. How could I have been so careless? A burning cigarette must have fallen out of my hand when I went to put it in the ashtray. It rolled onto the seat. The seat covers burn easily. They've caught fire twice before. I was there to put the fires out those times. Where was I today? Away from the car. Smoking. Watching a man enter a motel room. That's when the fire must've started. I remember running. To put out the fire? No. To the door. The fire burned the papers that man gave me. Harold. He hired me. Harold gave me…

The dots of memory connect. The result is a briefcase.

Helium.

Everything makes sense now. Harold's briefcase carried a bomb. Something blew up in the motel room. When I ran to help, the bomb in the briefcase went off. I still need to help—need to try and help. But I can't. The timing of the explosion was too perfect.

Lithium.

If the explosion in the room triggered the bomb in my car, then the timing is all wrong. Instead of me being near the car, I would have been smoking across the parking lot. It took me at least five seconds to make it back to my car. And even then, the explosion went off when I was nearby. Not before I got there or after I left, but when someone who knew what they were doing would have set it off. The only conclusion is that Harold, or someone working with Harold, is watching me.

Beryllium.

Mordecai worries me. He stayed on when I hit the ground. The positive: The thin fabric might have softened the blow when my head hit the asphalt. The negative: If I move my head, it'll be like waving a flag to let people know I'm still alive. I'll be begging whoever triggered the bomb to finish the job.

Boron.

My glasses are on the ground nearby. The lenses focus the orange glow of the fire into misshapen circles on the ground. For me to reach the glasses, I'll need to move. Before I do that, I'll need a plan for what happens after.

Carbon.

My ears are ringing and my head hurts, but the rest of my body feels relatively unharmed. I tense the muscles in my arms and feel a twinge near my right shoulder. *Nitrogen.* My legs tense up and feel fine. *Oxygen.* The simple thong sandals I was wearing are no longer on my feet. The explosion went off behind me at an angle. It was like being blindsided by a wave. My body twisted. My feet collided. The back of my head hit the ground before I could use my arms to break the fall.

Fluorine.

Atlantic Boulevard is only two hundred feet away. If I can make it, I should be safe. Or at least safer. Any option other than continuing to lie prone in a debris field would be safer. Once near the road, there will be more witnesses. More witnesses mean that neat and tidy Harold will keep his distance.

Neon.

Grab my glasses and run. That's it. If I can find my sandals quickly, then I'll put them back on. Otherwise, I'll have to let the ground scratch my feet to hell. The lack of pain in my legs is a sign that running shouldn't be a problem.

Sodium. Magnesium. Aluminum.

I take a deep breath and scramble for my glasses. My eyes focus. My sandals are only a couple of feet away. A dizzying feeling hits me when I stand up straight. Despite uncertain balance, my feet end up nestled on the old leather soles of my sandals. I run toward Atlantic Boulevard.

Silicon. Phosphorus. Sulfur.

The sound of squealing tires behind me draws my attention. An SUV is barreling down the street in my direction. It looks similar to the one parked outside of my house when Harold visited me earlier in the day.

Chlorine. Argon. Potassium.

The escape route across the bits of glass and Toyota Camry littering the parking lot is as close as I'll ever be to John McClain running over broken glass to escape being shot up by the baddies in *Die Hard*. The thought of Alan Rickman's terrible German pretending to be an American accent and penchant for automatic rifles holds the dizziness at bay.

Calcium. Scandium. Titanium.

The only objects in the parking lot between Atlantic Boulevard and me that might stop the SUV are two cars parked side-by-side. The cars are approximately forty feet away. It will take me about four seconds to reach them at my current speed. The SUV's headlights are off, but I can tell the driver is aiming for a target on my back when it turns into the parking lot, bottoming out on the sudden incline from the road.

Vanadium. Chromium. Manganese.

When I reach the cars, I jump on the hood of the one parked closest to me and then on the one parked next to it. The SUV collides with the first car, forcing it into the second. The impact knocks me back onto the windshield. A deployed airbag hides the driver of the SUV. Instead of confronting my assailant, I slide off the car and let two birds fly their direction before heading west down the sidewalk.

"Iron! Cobalt! Nickel!"

The traffic on Atlantic Boulevard doesn't appear concerned by the fires. There are no looky-loos or stop-and-stares, only regular traffic. The explosions, although impactful up close, were contained. Someone driving by at that very moment might have heard something and dismissed it without concern.

It's clear after a minute of running that no one is following me. My run slows to a trot and then to a walking pace as I turn down a small alley between two office buildings. The alley takes me to Sturdivant Avenue, which I follow until I reach Seminole Boulevard.

The lights in Misty's bakery are still on. Despite the closed blinds, someone is inside. Misty always turns out the lights when she leaves. So either she is inside, or some stranger has broken into the bakery. Considering the day so far, a stranger running up the electric bill is not out of the question.

Harold could have covered this angle. The bakery is only a ten-minute walk from the motel. If he thought of everything, he might have someone waiting inside for me. Or Misty could be inside. It's not uncommon for her to close late. The hearse is the only car parked in front of the bakery, which is typical for this hour and not a surprise, in general, since Misty parks behind the bakery.

Debating out in the open wastes time I don't have; time Harold could use to track me down. It's better to be off the street. The metal frame of the bakery's door shakes as I pound my open palm harder than intended on the glass. Nearly displacing the glass in a fit of adrenaline overload slows me down.

The horizontal blind slats flip open. Misty is on the other side, brandishing a rolling pin at the idiot attacking her storefront. When she realizes I'm the idiot, she sets down the rolling pin and opens the door.

"Thank God you're still here."

"What the hell is wrong with you?" Misty hits people. It's part of her charm. She taps as she talks excitedly and punches when she's angry or upset. Misty punches me hard in my right arm.

"Dammit!" I shout. There is a bloodstain on my right sleeve. Either something hit me during the explosion, or I cut my arm tumbling to the ground.

"Oh my God, you're bleeding. I'm sorry. I didn't know."

"Just a leak," I say, locking the door and closing the blinds.

"Let me get you some towels or something." Misty runs behind the counter.

I peek out through the blinds before following Misty behind the counter. Misty comes toward me with a towel and a bottle of tequila. She pours tequila on the towel and starts rubbing my arm to clean off the blood.

"Is that Patrón?" I ask.

"I've been experimenting with a tequila sunrise cupcake and a tequila-lime tart."

"No rubbing alcohol?" I ask. Misty raises an eyebrow. "For the cut, not the cupcakes."

"No, but this should work fine."

Misty pours tequila over the cut. When she finishes, she takes a clean towel and ties it around my arm.

"Can I get a shot of that?"

Misty takes a metal quarter-cup measuring cup from a table dusted in flour and blows the remnants from it, sending a small cloud into the air.

She fills the measuring cup three-quarters full of tequila and hands it to me.

Downing half of the shot creates a burning sensation that cascades toward my stomach.

Someone bangs on the front door. Misty walks over and peeks through the blinds before I can stop her.

A male voice on the other side asks, "You open?"

I yank Misty back by her collar. She shakes me off while shouting, "What the fuck, Flynn?"

Opening the blinds reveals a man standing at a distance. It's too dark outside to see the man's face, but his body type does not match Harold's.

"We're closed," I say, closing the blinds and returning to the area behind the counter with my measuring cup of tequila.

"What the hell was that?"

"I thought someone might have followed me here."

"Why would anyone want to follow you?"

I finish my shot and return the measuring cup to Misty.

"Someone tried to kill me... twice."

Misty pours me another shot.

"This is about the money you mentioned earlier, isn't it?"

The entire drink goes down the hatch this time. "Yeah," I say with a cough. "A guy hired me to help him film what I thought would be a philandering husband. It turns out he really wanted to blow him up."

"Where did this happen?"

"Right down the street."

"I thought I heard a car backfire earlier."

Misty takes the measuring cup from my hand, fills it, and then takes a drink herself. The rings on Misty's lips make a clinking sound when the cup touches them. Misty fills it once more and hands it back to me.

"There was a man inside and a woman I was told to hire."

I take the shot and practically choke.

"Do you know what happened to them?"

"No. The explosion looked powerful. The one in my car had good pop, and the interior caught fire quickly. I'm not sure what was in the room. It was powerful enough to blast out the window, but not the door. There was plenty of smoke, though."

"Could they have survived?"

"If they weren't right next to it, maybe."

I hand Misty the measuring cup and shake my head before she can pour another shot. Misty places the measuring cup and the bottle of tequila on the wooden tabletop. I sit on the floor and drop Mordecai on the ground next to me. The feeling of defeat drains me. I escaped, but now what? I'm responsible for the deaths of two people. My life will become a living hell highlighted by prison.

Misty kneels next to me.

Not able to bear the sight of anything, I take off my glasses and place them on Mordecai. I rest my forehead on my knees and close my eyes.

"Flynn!" Misty shouts, violently shaking me.

"What?"

"You've been saying 'Our cells divide until we fall apart' over and over again for like two minutes straight. You wouldn't snap out of it."

"I'm fine," I say without conviction.

"We both know it's been a long time since you were fine, Flynn."

"I'm such an idiot," I whisper. "Five grand for a couple hours of work. I knew something wasn't right."

"Flynn," Misty says with her hand on my shoulder, "we need to call the police."

"No," I say before putting my glasses back on. "Not yet."

"Why not?"

"The man who did this was in my house. Remember the person I told you about? The guy who liked your cake? That's the guy. He knew every little thing about the woman he had me hire. He had all these pictures like he'd been watching her for a while—a real creeper, this one. And I bet he watched me, too. He probably knows where you live and where my mother lives. And I'm the only one that can identify him."

"Then we should leave."

I stand up, pull my hair back, and smile while placing Mordecai back on my head. The defeat is wearing off as the tequila buzzes my brain.

"I have a better idea."

"Does it involve calling the police?"

"Kinda, but you get some free advertising out of it."

"I'm listening."

"How long does it take to make a specialty cake?"

"It depends."

Chapter 11

Flynn

I've never liked to stand and smile in front of a camera. My mother tried countless times to make me. Her reward for the effort? Entire rolls of blurred film. My sister, Lily, loved to have her picture taken. Pictures of Lily cover the walls in my mother's condo. I make an appearance here or there, but the real star is Lily. Her bright smile shines down on my mother at all times. Taking a page from my sister's book, I smile wide.

Misty and I stand in front of The Cake Mistress Bakery, watching as a throng of people throw questions in our direction. We remain calm and keep on smiling.

"The announcement will begin at eight o'clock sharp," I say, my hands in the air to quiet the crowd.

We parked Misty's hearse askew to provide a backdrop for the cameras. The LED sign on the hearse lights up in red, displaying the bakery's name, hours, and phone number.

At eight o'clock, a hush falls over the crowd. They form a tiny Dead Sea of floating heads bobbing up and down behind a wall of cameras.

"My name is Flynn. I am a local private consultant here in Atlantic Beach. I've called you all here to provide information on the bombing that occurred down the road earlier this evening."

"For the record, what is your surname?" shouts a voice from the crowd.

"Mix-a-lot," I say plainly.

Misty disappears back into the bakery and returns holding a white sheet cake with a face drawn on the top.

"I met face-to-face with the person responsible for the bombing this evening. He called himself Harold and did not provide me with a last name. Out of fear for my life and the lives of my friends and family, I've asked the owner of The Cake Mistress Bakery to create a detailed sketch of the perpetrator."

Misty smiles as she holds the cake at an angle. The slight downward tilt of Harold's head works together with his beady black eyes to create an ominous look aimed at those viewing the cake. Countless flashbulbs go off, all lighting up the face on the cake. The quick flashing lights are an epileptic's nightmare that causes Misty's piercings to twinkle.

An existing sheet cake made the base of the drawing. Misty covered the surface in white buttercream and then added faux burn marks on the edges to make it look like an Old West wanted poster. My description of Harold became a pen and paper sketch Misty used as a guide. In a matter of minutes, Misty recreated that sketch on the cake with black frosting.

"I asked if she could make a 3-D version of the head. You know, the kind you see on those TV shows covered in fondant and painted. Apparently, that takes a lot of time we didn't have. However, Misty can make those if you contact her ahead of time at the phone number on the sign behind us. For now, you'll have to settle with this fairly accurate version. The eyes are a little off, and the hair is like something a caricature artist might do, but—"

"Shut up," Misty hisses. She levels the cake out and holds it in her left hand while hitting me twice with her right.

"Please ignore her angry words and small violent fists. It's the Filipino fire. She can't help herself."

"Mr. Flynn," shouts a male voice in the crowd. Floating spots from the flashing lights leave me uncertain as to which bobbing head is speaking. "In what way were you involved with this explosion? How did you come to see this man's face, let alone know his name?"

"I'm only here to release a prepared statement and this delicious sugary image of the perpetrator. I will not be answering questions. It is important to note that all children accompanied by adults who stop by The Cake Mistress Bakery will receive a complimentary sugar cookie. Thank you."

Various voices from the crowd shout 'Flynn' and 'Mr. Mix-a-lot' over and again.

Misty and I ignore the voices and walk back into the bakery, locking the door behind us.

"I think that went well," I say. "Can I get a piece of Harold's head?"

Chapter 12

Flynn

Reporters continue to knock on the bakery's door. Misty and I continue to ignore them. The occasional muffled question filters through the cracks around the door. Close to an hour after the press conference, the door banging hits new heights. Ignoring the knocking does not make it go away. A muffled, angry voice shouts, "Police, open up now!"

Misty obliges and directs the two men, one in uniform and the other in street clothes, toward me before disappearing into her small office. When they walk back, I'm sitting on a prep table next to what's left of Harold's face cake, drinking shots of Patrón from a measuring cup. I got greedy and ate both of Harold's cheeks before moving on to Misty's new tequila sunrise cupcakes.

"Flynn Dupree," a clean-shaven man in his sixties says with a fatherly air.

"Shit," I reply, finishing a shot of tequila. The bright yellows of his Hawaiian shirt signal it's time to pump the brakes. Business is about to commence. "Curtis Mother Fuckin' Vance."

Beachfolk, as a rule, dislike people from across the ditch. They epitomize bad neighbors by crossing the Intracoastal into our back yard, making a lot of noise early in the morning until late at night, and dumping their garbage everywhere. Despite the inherent stigma, Curtis Vance is one exception to the rule. The Beaches treat Vance to a hero's welcome when he graces us with his presence. During his former life as a lieutenant with the Jacksonville Sheriff's Office, Vance solved the biggest child abduction the Jacksonville Beaches has ever known, Lily Dupree—my dear sister.

"What are you doing here?" I ask Vance.

"I phoned your father after I saw you on the news. He asked me to help."

"Phoned my father?" I pour another shot in the measuring cup. "I guess I'm lucky you're not on a book tour."

After gaining notoriety from my sister's abduction, Vance retired and began writing. With my father's permission, his first novel was a fictionalization of my sister's kidnapping and murder. Vance made it possible for the entire world to read about how my sister died alone and in pain.

"My last one ended in September. Listen, I'm friends with the head of the local FBI branch, the mayor, and the sheriff. I made some calls. They thought that since we know one another, I should assist."

"Sounds like an interesting foursome for golf," I say before taking a sip of tequila. "Or hot tubbing."

"I knew you'd appreciate the help. I'm working as a temporary liaison. This is Officer Leonard Rittwell," Vance says, pointing to the officer at his side. "He's representing the Atlantic Beach Police Department. We will ensure you make it to the right people."

"What are you talking about?"

"I'm just here to assist."

"Yeah, you said that the first time. What, exactly, are you here to assist with?"

"We want you to be comfortable."

"Mr. Dupree." Officer Rittwell crosses his arms while smiling artificially.

Officer Rittwell arrested me two years ago for DUI. Not for driving my car while intoxicated. Not for driving a truck or a bus or a tractor through a field while pounding handles of vodka. He arrested me for riding my bicycle back from a bar. That bike ride cost me my driver's license. It took months of waiting and thousands of dollars in fees and court costs to have my driver's license reinstated. Being able to drive again felt great, but nothing holds a candle to spite. Spite kept me following Officer Rittwell day and night. Spite forced me to snoop into every little detail of his life while taking hundreds of pictures of him going about his daily routines. There were times when I not only delved into stalker territory but lived there for days on end. Why? Because spite makes people do crazy things.

Countless trips to Stalkerville with detours to Crazytown paid off when, one day, Rittwell spent an afternoon at the beach. The pictures

61

from that day are the highlight of my descent into spite. They perfectly capture the continuous bird's nest of hair covering the entirety of Rittwell's body and the purple bathing suit that fits him like a second skin. Every Monday, I mail a picture from the beach series to the Atlantic Beach Police Department, care of Sergeant Sexy. When the photo sequence runs out, which I've calculated to be in approximately three more years, the department will have a stack of photos they can turn into a flipbook of Officer Rittwell's day at the beach.

"That's my name," I say, my mouth full of cupcake.

"Stop being so smug. Do you realize what you've done with your little sideshow?" Officer Rittwell asks.

"No, Rittles, I don't."

"If that man really is the bomber, then he'll go into hiding."

"That was my intent. I'm the only person who knows he's involved, and I should have died. I need his face to be out in the open to take away his incentive to hurt me, my family, or my friends. Anyhoo, I think I can find him if need be."

I pour more tequila into the measuring cup while trying not to look at Officer Rittwell.

"We don't need any more of your kind of help, Dupree. You're a liar."

"I prefer 'fabulist.' It sounds classier," I say, bringing the measuring cup to my lips with my pinkie extended.

"I see you two know each other better than I had anticipated," Vance says, moving between Officer Rittwell and me.

"It's cute that Rittles is your pageboy for the occasion. You should make him wear a different hat."

"Keep in mind that I'm merely working as a liaison for the time being. And Officer Rittwell volunteered to assist me."

Vance's continual reminder that he's acting as a liaison piques my interest and provides me a better idea of what's happening. No one wants a big scene. The police sent Vance and Rittwell, two people I know, to take me into custody. Top brass, unable to shoot all their problems away, believed this one-two punch would do the trick. The specifics of what happened at the motel are nonexistent. If I am the sole survivor of the explosions, I will be the only witness able to provide information.

"You're here to get information about the bomber?"

"You seem to know a great deal about him," Vance replies.

"I know enough."

"And how did you come by this information?"

"To be honest, he was a client of mine."

"Amy survived, you piece of shit. We know you did it. You can't blame someone else."

Vance shoots a look of frustration at Officer Rittwell.

That news concerns me. Amy surviving makes me feel better about what happened, but now I've lost a considerable amount of leverage.

"How is she?" I ask, knocking back the remnants of tequila in the measuring cup. "Hopefully, not too bad off?"

"She's all in one piece and ready to testify—"

Vance places his hand on Officer Rittwell's shoulder. He quiets immediately.

"Did the man survive?"

"No." Vance's tone turns somber. "He wasn't as lucky and took the brunt of the blast. I've heard there's not much left that's recognizable."

"The man on the cake hired me to get Amy in that room. I'm sure you noticed my car in pieces around the parking lot."

"And here you are unscathed."

"There's a little bit of scathing on my arm. Harold tried to kill me twice. He ran his SUV into a car while trying to run me down."

"Are you referring to the Explorer?"

"Yes."

"The owner reported it as stolen yesterday."

"Interesting."

"We need you to come with us."

"Why?"

"As Officer Rittwell explained, Amy survived and informed the police of how you lured her to the motel and blackmailed her into compliance."

"The man who hired me provided all the information about Amy you could ask for. And Amy showed up willingly when I offered her two thousand dollars for an hour of her time."

"Do you still have this information?"

"No. It was in my car on top of a briefcase Harold gave me. He told me the briefcase held a recording device for a camera he placed in the motel room. When the bomb went off, the papers I had inside went up in smoke."

"We should have this discussion somewhere else."

"I want to help find this guy."

"Right now," Vance says, "you are a witness, a person of interest, a suspect, whatever you'd like to call yourself. Unfortunately, you are not a police officer."

Officer Rittwell grins from ear to ear.

"That's fine. I'll go with you. I have no motive and absolutely no bomb-making skills to speak of. You'll be wasting your time."

"Time is inconsequential when hunting for the truth."

Vance should write that on a sandwich board for the world to see. That lackadaisical attitude to finding Harold is on par with his efforts to find Lily. After Lily disappeared, all relevant information filtered through Vance on its way to the right people. Adding a middleman to any process splits it at the seams, creating holes for information to fall through. Adding Vance created more than holes; it left the police bare-assed in the wind. In the end, the glory and accolades fell in his lap. Vance may be intelligent and capable, but his only use to authorities in this matter is to convince me to come along without a fight.

At this stage in an investigation, quiet is the name of the game. Keep me quiet, and the police control the narrative. It's easy to paint me as the villain with Amy as a witness. From there, being railroaded is the obvious next step, which will be exponentially easier the second I end up in handcuffs.

"You need me to help you with this."

"We don't need help from a piece of garbage like you." Officer Rittwell has a dash of fuoco in his voice. "You're acting like you don't feel the least bit of remorse for taking that man's life."

"I don't. Remorse is a sign of guilt. I'm not guilty of taking his life."

"There's a man dead and a witness pointing at you."

"We die for nothing, Rittles. We kill for nothing. It's true whether or not we want to admit it. I don't know why he died. I feel bad if that makes you feel better. It doesn't help me any. It sure as shit doesn't help him. The fact is, someone wanted him dead. It was only a matter of when and how. You can call me a fatalist if you'd like, but I'm not his killer."

"A prison cell is the perfect place for a fatalist."

"That's true. However, a cell is not in my future. I'll go with you. Before I do, I want two things. The first is that I leave here without handcuffs. I don't like them and don't want to wear them. You can lock me in the back of the Rittlemobile or whatever you call your car, but no handcuffs. The second is that I need to go to the hospital to get checked out."

"I'm denying both requests," Officer Rittwell says. "How's that?"

"That's a terrible idea. It's funny how the mind works. I was eating a piece of Harold's face cake after the press conference, and something started brewing in my brain. The cake was delicious, by the way. If you'd like to have some, I'm sure Misty'd cut you off a chunk of hair or chin. So, I finished my piece of cake, and then I was sitting here drinking tequila and eating these incredible cupcakes when it hit me. The man Harold blew up—I know who he is."

"And who is that?" Vance asks.

"That is my little secret until I get what I want. I will give you a bit of a tid if you'd like. He's a bigwig in Jacksonville. Quite wealthy and highly regarded."

"You'll tell us everything you know or—"

"Here's the thing, Rittles. My head hurts. I've also got some cuts that need tending. Either I go to the hospital, or you get nothing."

"We'll find out who he is."

"That'll take time. This'll only take a little while. As a sign of good faith, I'll give you this," I say, pulling a business card from my pocket. A handwritten phone number is on the back. "This is the only thing Harold gave me that I still have. He told me to call this number if something went wrong. I'll also let you know that the man in the room arrived in a new Cadillac."

"A Cadillac?" Vance asks.

"That's right, a Cad-ill-ac-ac-ac-ac-ac-ac you shoulda found by now."

"Stop acting like an idiot," Officer Rittwell says, slapping the measuring cup out of my hand.

"There was no Cadillac in the parking lot."

"Well, then, Harold took it. He could have hot-wired it or gone into the room and taken the keys from the dead man. Did the victim have a wallet?"

"What?"

"A wallet? Did he have a wallet when you found him?"

Vance looks at Officer Rittwell, who shakes his head.

"Then he either left it in his car or brought it into the motel with him. If he brought it with him, then Harold, or whoever, took that along with the keys. Can I go to the hospital now?"

Vance exhales and makes a whistling sound.

"I think I have a concussion, and concussions are super-duper serious," I say. "And I'm feeling mighty drowsy from the tequila. I could fall asleep and never wake up."

"And the world would be a better place."

"Probably. But you would lose your job, Rittles, and I know how much this all means to you," I point to Rittwell's badge on his chest. "You will end up unemployed and homeless, all because you are too stubborn to take me for the medical treatment I need."

I stand up and pocket Misty's cell phone off of a nearby table.

"I'm ready to go if you are."

"Dammit. I'll call it in. Will a doc in the box work for the princess?"

"No, squire. Royalty deserves the hospital."

Chapter 13

Flynn

"Ma'am, what the hell are you talking about?" Officer Rittwell shouts, pointing to his chest. "Do you see the badge?"

Rittwell's badge does not impress the woman behind the non-emergency check-in desk in the hospital's waiting room.

"Linda."

"What?"

"My name is Linda."

Linda tosses her long black hair behind her shoulder, clearing the area as she points at the nametag on her multicolored scrubs.

"That's fantastic, Linda. I need your help."

"And so does everyone else in the waiting room. This is a hospital."

"Yeah, well, this man was involved in the bombing tonight at the beach. He needs medical attention."

"And I need a raise," Linda says, her uncompassionate brown eyes trained on me. "He's a terrorist or something?"

"I was nearly blown up by someone," I chime in.

"He's a person of interest," Officer Rittwell says.

"That's only because he finds my pillow talk interesting," I say, drawing Vance's eyes away from the TV in the waiting room and back in my direction.

"Shut up, or I'll smother you with a pillow," Rittwell says.

"Is that how concussions are treated, Linda, with a smothering?"

Linda ignores me and focuses on the computer screen in front of her, typing away with red nails long enough to click and scrape across the keyboard. Each nail has a different white flower painted on it. The time and effort she puts into her nails doesn't surprise me. People who are confrontational and outspoken tend to overcompensate with appearances. A nice jacket, fancy shoes, perfect hair—for Linda, it's nails. The part of her that wants to express love is reaching out with a flower, telling the world that Linda is more than an overflowing pot of bubbling rage and discontent.

Then again, there's a possibility I'm wrong about Linda. She could be a gentle and caring woman, a nurturer at heart, and we walked into her waiting room on the wrong day. For this to be the real Linda, I have to make assumptions. And I love to assume. I love to put thoughts in heads and imagine lives, but seeing Linda in this light feels like too great of an assumption. To make the caring Linda a reality, I would need to fill her life with love and happiness. And that I can't do. From what I've seen, there is no hope for this Linda. There is no gentle soul. I can only see the Linda before me, an angry woman in a job she hates with a playful side blossoming to the surface in the form of tiny white flowers on red nails.

"Are we going to see a doctor anytime soon?" Officer Rittwell asks.

"What in the hell do you think I'm doing right now? Typing 'cause I like the sound of it?"

Classic confrontational Linda. I shouldn't be judging her. I'm just as bad, possibly worse, hiding behind my hat and glasses like the Unabomber on vacation at the beach. Few people are willing to put themselves out there for the world to see. At least Linda is more open about who she is. I know I'm not. The only person who knows my motives is little ol' me. And I like it that way. If people could read my intentions at a glance, then I'd lose my advantage. That advantage is how I plan on getting out of this mess.

"I'd be more than happy to go nap in the back of the car while you two argue," I say.

"You think you have a concussion," Linda says, staring straight at me. "What are you, stupid?"

"A little. You see, sugar keeps me going when I'm nervous, and alcohol takes that bouncy edge off of the sugar. So, I've been eating cake and cupcakes and drinking tequila for a while since the explosion. Now that the sugar rush is over, I'm kind of tired."

"You're dumb." Linda's bedside manner is like an icy hug from an iron maiden.

"Thank you," I reply, smiling. "I like your nails."

"Would you two shut the hell up? Linda, get me a doctor now!" Officer Rittwell shouts.

Linda leaves through an open door behind the desk. As she walks away, I hold my hand out and shout, "Can you do mine?"

"Where in the hell did she go?" Officer Rittwell asks, looking back at Vance. Vance lost interest in our conversation at some point. The siren song of the TV in the corner was too much.

Officer Rittwell slams his hand onto the small bell at the desk. No one responds. He continues to hit the bell until Linda shows back up and takes it away.

A man in scrubs and a white jacket walks up to Officer Rittwell and me.

"Y'all need to calm down. You're upsetting people."

No one in the waiting room is paying any attention to us. There are upset people, but the stacks of hospital forms are the source of their ire.

"This man with a badge thinks he can jump ahead of people who've been waiting for over an hour," Linda says, flipping her thick hair back off of her face.

"This man is a suspect—"

"I was just a person of interest a minute ago, Rittles. I'm actually a witness," I say to the man in scrubs.

"What's wrong with him?" he asks, looking to Officer Rittwell instead of me.

"I was nearly blown up today, and I feel like I have a concussion."

The man in scrubs looks at me.

"You feel like you have a concussion?"

"You know, sort of floaty."

"Follow me."

Officer Rittwell calls out to Vance. We all follow the man in scrubs to a room just past a pair of doors leading to a long corridor.

I sit down on the rigid, paper-covered bed.

"You're a doctor?"

"You can call me Todd. I'm a registered nurse."

"Are you allowed to wear one of those, Todd?" I ask, pointing at his white jacket.

Todd grabs the stethoscope around his neck. "It's something we all carry around."

"No, I mean the white jacket. Isn't that for actual doctors?"

The comment is intentionally mean. I know I hit a nerve when Todd turns red in the face. That frustration works in my favor. Todd's opinion of me doesn't matter, but I need him to leave us for a while. A clean bill of health provided by a professional will spoil all my work.

I've set the table for an escape with my erratic and flighty behavior, but the banquet can still go to pot. It is imperative for Rittwell and Vance to consider me less of a threat. They can blame my erraticism on the tequila or the head injury; either is fine as long as they let their guard down.

"I am a registered nurse—"

"I know. You said that already. Listen," I say with nonchalant venom, "is the hospital going to charge less since I'm not being seen by a doctor? Also, is the term 'murse' for male nurse what I'll be seeing on my bill?"

Todd is displeased. All I can do is hope I crossed the right line.

"I'm gonna need you to take off your clothes. I'll be back in a moment."

I act surprised and stand up, turning to Officer Rittwell and Vance, who both watch Todd leave the room. "You need to get out."

"What are you, shy?" Officer Rittwell asks. "Because you're gonna hate it in prison."

"As a matter of fact, I am shy. And it's a good thing I'm not going to prison."

"Well, I need to look around the room first."

"Fine by me," I say, standing near the door.

Officer Rittwell inspects the room and walks back out, poking me in the chest three times before leaving.

I smile wide, close the door, and release a sigh of relief.

Everything feels like it might work out. Todd will deliberately leave us alone for another ten minutes. He'll come back and claim he had to finish paperwork on another patient or something along those lines. The truth is, I made Todd angry enough to need a break. Hopefully, he grabs a cup of coffee and takes extra time to ponder with each sip.

All I need to do now is distract Rittwell and Vance long enough for me to slip past. It's a terrible idea to run from the police, but the fear of going to a jail cell and staying in a jail cell is more powerful than common sense.

70

Several plans of escape bubble in my brain. The first plan is to request a bathroom break and then make a run for it. Without a solid idea of where the bathrooms are relative to the exits, I'll probably have to do something drastic to get away. The last thing I need is a charge for assaulting a police officer added to my current list of crimes. The second plan is to pretend I'm going into shock or a comatose state. Maybe they'll wheel me away. Once Rittwell and Vance are at a safe distance, I can make a break for it. While this idea percolates, Linda's lovely voice reappears.

"Which one of you dumbasses left their car parked right out front of the hospital?"

Officer Rittwell throws in the towel. "I'll move my vehicle," he says politely.

The sound of Rittwell leaving makes me want to kiss Linda on my way out of the hospital. With time wasting, I make my move by falling against the door. The fall produces enough noise to pique Vance's curiosity.

"Hey," Vance says, knocking.

Vance struggles to open the door with my limp body pressed against it. To add extra flair, I tip over and land facedown on the linoleum. Vance tries shaking me back to life. My eyes remain shut tight. Saliva drips from my mouth to the floor.

"Shit," Vance says. He runs out of the room, shouting for a nurse.

I shoot out the open door and into the waiting room, slowing down enough to watch Rittwell's police cruiser pull away and drive toward the parking lot. The poorly lit road leading back to Third Street is a short distance away. In no time, I'm running down the road toward the beach. It will take them five minutes at most before they discover I'm gone. If they search the parking lot, then I should have five to ten extra minutes to get away.

After a minute of running, I spot a kid no older than fourteen riding his bike in the opposite direction. He has pegs on the back of his bike. The small metal pieces protruding from the frame should support my weight and make my escape a little quicker. I haven't ridden on pegs since the last time I rode on the back of Thomas Dorchester's bike at age sixteen, and I can only hope my moderate weight gain in that time won't be too much of a problem.

"Hey kid," I shout as I run across the road. I take off Mordecai and wave him at the kid before placing him back on my head.

He stops, startled by the sight of me. He might have turned around and pedaled away if I hadn't managed to get so close so quick. A bearded man wearing a baseball cap at night under terrible road lighting makes everything all the more terrifying.

"Yeah," he says.

"I'll give you a hundred bucks to take me to the beach."

"What?"

"A hundred bucks for a ride to the beach."

"You serious?"

"Yes," I say, pulling out some of the money Harold gave me earlier in the day.

"I can't. I promised my mom I'd be home in the next ten minutes."

I pull out two kite-flyers and hold them up in front of my face. "There's an extra hundred in it for your mother."

"Get on," he says, grabbing the money. "Name's Kevin."

"I'm Flynn. Thanks for the ride."

I climb on and place my hands on Kevin's shoulders. The pedaling starts slow as Kevin struggles to balance his bike with the extra weight. Kevin picks up enough speed to make me hold on tighter.

I howl into the night air. Kevin follows suit. No sirens sound behind us. No lights flash.

Chapter 14

Flynn

The lack of police activity emboldens me enough to have Kevin stop at the nearest gas station. The beer section beckons. A six-pack of Natty glistens under the fluorescent lights, calling my name. Kevin wanders for a moment and settles in front of a collection of the saddest flower bouquets ever assembled. Kevin picks one out and stands in line behind me.

"Who're those for?"

Kevin keeps his voice low and lets me in on the secret. "My mom."

"I'll buy them," I say, holding out my hand. "You hold on to that money."

"I want to buy 'em myself."

"Well, kiddo, that's quite noble of you."

Instead of leaving after my beer purchase, I stand by in case the cashier gives Kevin any trouble for using a large bill. Kevin receives his change. We leave the gas station. Before Kevin can ride away, I hold out another kite-flyer.

"Here you go."

"What's that for?" he asks.

"I figure you'd put it to better use than I would."

"No, thanks," Kevin replies. "You should use it to get a haircut."

We part ways. Streams of cars and trucks force me to take my time crossing Third Street. Traffic evaporates on the last stretch of road to the beach. Light restrictions turn some beach-adjacent residential areas into ghost towns at night. These homeowners keep their yard lights off and their blackout curtains drawn. It's a mix of peaceful and eerie with one end of the street desolate and the other bright.

Alcohol use is a big no-no on the beach. Those rules exist thanks to the general belligerence of Americans one drink deep. The added problem of visitors treating the sand like a garbage dump creates a situation where an alcohol ban makes sense. As a responsible drunk that believes in recycling, the laws are silly. The police, however, lack a sense of humor and enforce these laws across the board. Getting dinged by the cops for drinking a beer is the least of my worries. But I'm not on the beach looking for trouble. I'm trying to vamoose to familiar ground. The less I stand out, the better. Carting around a six-pack stands out, which is why I stick five cans of Natty in the pockets of my cargo shorts. The sixth can is too tempting not to crack open.

It's a beautiful night for a walk on the beach. The earth has taken a small bite of the moon, like a child nibbling on a cookie. Its light paints the sand and surf in more shades of blue than Crayola can name. The ocean breeze slings riggings into hidden flagpoles with a tinny, rhythmic clanging. The languid beat rings out in the night while the stars flash above like sheet music in the sky.

Nights like this remind me of how massive something small can be. In the past, when the moon lit up the beach, I wanted nothing more than to be on the water. Lying prone on the vast ocean, the surfboard underneath me rocking back and forth, I would stare into the sky and observe the celestial play for as long as I could. Looking up provides the most dramatic example of perspective. Points of light small enough for the tip of my finger to remove them from my vision are all that represent something as grand as a galaxy. On those nights when I looked up, I thought about my problems. The pulsing lights gave me hope. They reminded me that even the biggest of objects seem tiny when looked at from the right perspective.

It was during one of these affirmation sessions that Lily disappeared. My parents went to dinner and left me to babysit. Saddled with problems, and upset that my parents added Lily to my load, I left her alone inside to go clear my head on the water. Instead of protecting my little sister, I laid back and thought about my life and my problems. When I came back to shore, Lily was gone.

Life lessons often come at great personal cost, and the hardest lessons to learn come with a crash course in perspective. A whole lot of crashing taught me that perspective exists because we need objects to appear small. If we could comprehend how big everything is, not in size but in implication, how every action we take adds to something more substantial than us, how the tiniest cog in the clock can make time stand still, then life would be a terrifying experience. Perspective keeps us alive. And if I had understood this simple fact, Lily would still be alive.

On that day, if I had stayed inside, the stars would still shine with hope. If I had stayed inside, I could say her name and not feel shame. But I went outside. I went into the water. I blotted out the light with the tip of my finger. When I realized Lily had disappeared, I called for her. With every ounce of air in my lungs, I shouted her name. Lily didn't answer. In a panic, I ran up and down the beach screaming. No one ever answered.

At my father's insistence, Curtis Vance walked me through what happened that night, over and over. Vance wanted me to show him everything. Show me. Show me. Show me. I tried and failed. And it wasn't from a lack of effort. At the time, I couldn't comprehend what it meant. Everything still felt so small. The sky was still full of hope. The day Vance caught his suspect, hope faded into darkness. My father, blind and bloodthirsty, wanted someone to pay for the crime. Vance made sure that happened.

But it was my fault. I should have known better. I was born after Etan Patz went missing in New York and became the first child to have his face on a milk carton. By the time I came around, society saw fit to serve children a reminder of mankind's evil for breakfast. My parents contextualized this evil with safety talk and buzzwords. Regardless of the amount of preparation, a child is still a child. Just because you realize the impossibility of Santa Claus doesn't mean you're ready to face things head-on. I did my best to grow up, to act the part. What no one ever tells you is that it's impossible to steel yourself to a world where mistakes are so severe. Saying 'I wish they took me' is silly. That's survivor's remorse talking and nothing more. Knowing that others wish it had been me—there's no way to prepare for that as a child or an adult.

A ringing phone interrupts my train of thought. I stop for a second, confused because my phone burned up in my car, and then remember that I took Misty's cell from the bakery. It was a selfish thing to do, a spur-of-the-moment act caused by necessity. Not only will I need a phone in the immediate future, taking Misty's makes it easier for me to contact people without the police being able to follow.

According to the caller ID, Tin is calling.

The phone continues to ring. It is unconscionable to drag more people into this mess. If my releasing the image of Harold to the media backfires, Misty and my mother could be in danger. Picking up the phone and talking to Tin puts her on the wrong side of the law. The police frown upon chatting with escapees.

Tin goes to voicemail, and the phone goes back in my pocket. Before I can pull my hand out of my pocket, Misty's phone rings again. The caller ID flashes 'Tin.'

Tin will not stop calling until I pick up. If anything, the woman is tenacious. That tenacity was one of the many things I noticed when I first met her at Metro. Misty dragged me there after her previous girlfriend dumped her. Metro is a club made up of several rooms with bars and multiple dance floors. Misty stayed downstairs to watch some woman who called herself Spikey Dykey dance in some show on their main stage. I went upstairs to a smaller and quieter bar where the only open seat was next to Tin, who looked adorable with her platinum pixie cut and retro eyeglasses. The bartender ended up being a woman I took an American Sign Language class with at the University of North Florida. The two of us started chatting in ASL, which prompted Tin to join in. She worked a part-time job at a small school for the hearing impaired. When Misty came upstairs after the show, the two of them hit it off. Misty was reluctant to wind up in another relationship. Tin kept pushing and pushing until Misty agreed.

Reluctantly, I take the call.

"Hello. Misty's phone speaking."

"Flynn?"

"Hey, Tin. Quick question. I'm on the beach, walking on the hard sand next to the water. Is this area called the littoral?"

"What?"

I'm hoping the odd question temporarily distracts Tin from the actual purpose of the call. It is the longest of long shots, but a distraction might keep Tin from delving into why I have Misty's phone. Resolving that issue without a lot of ancillary questions prevents the conversation from reaching the point where Tin could end up in trouble for knowing too much.

"I'm not sure why, but the correct term is slipping my mind. It's the area where the sand is all packed down."

"Why do you have Misty's phone?"

Swing and a miss. It bothers me when people can see through my bullshit. It bothers me even more when people can see through my bullshit over the telephone. Tin being able to tell what I'm doing with no visual cues means that either I'm slipping or she knows me too well.

"I'm borrowing it for a little while."

"Misty doesn't know that. She had me call while she searched in her car for it."

"If you could, let her know that I have it. I'll bring it back to her in a day or two."

"What happened to your phone?"

In a matter of seconds, Tin has sprinted across the nice fluffy sand and ignored the beautiful pond of ignorance to reach one hell of a line. Across from us is a rocky trail leading to the bubbling thermal spring of truth. Those bubbles are too tempting for Tin. She is the kind of person who has to test the damn water even if it scalds her.

"Mine got blown up earlier. I figured I would need another phone, and I was right because I just escaped from the police." Tin wants the truth. All I can do is give her what she wants and act like it is business as usual. "Oh, and it's better for the police to stay in the dark about me having Misty's phone."

"Misty told me that the police carted you off. Why would you escape from them?"

"If I hadn't, they would've looked at me as the sole suspect and let the actual bad guy go free. I need to find more information about him. Then, I'll turn myself in."

"Flynn," Tin says in a concerned tone. "I know you like to play games. This isn't the time. You need to turn yourself in and hope they're lenient. Let the police do their job and find this other guy."

"Tin, you know I love you, right?"

This is how Tin and I end all of our conversations. When I say, 'I love you,' it's a signal that I am done talking. It started because one night I drank too much and told Tin that I loved her. It was awkward, but the truth often is. The next day we all laughed about it. From that day on, it has been our discussion ender.

"Flynn?"

"I need to do this."

A person with a flashlight pops up from the dunes and starts walking toward me. People jogging on the beach at night are commonplace. Some wear hands-free flashlights around their neck or head. The first time I saw one of these flashlights, it looked like a will-o'-the-wisp bobbing at a distance as it bounced my direction. This person's light shines much brighter than the others I've seen.

"Hold on," I say into the phone before pressing it against my chest.

Acting like a weirdo while walking alone at night is a useful preventative measure for keeping other weirdos at bay. Singing out loud forces a person to reevaluate whether starting a conversation is necessary. Belting out "Take My Hand, Precious Lord" in my best Elvis voice is an adequate first line of defense. My mother is a big Elvis fan, and I grew up listening to his gospel records, so the words come easy and fast.

The person behind the light is undeterred. Instead of continuing to walk straight, I turn and walk toward them. We meet where the compact, damp sand gives way to the soft, white sand.

"Hey, buddy," a male voice from behind the light says. "You look familiar."

Elvis leaves the building, annoyed that this stranger did not get the hint.

"Is that right?" I ask. Misty's cell phone works as a shield to keep the man's flashlight from blinding me.

I'm not too worried about him spotting me from a police bulletin. The police will not alert the media to me being a threat. They mishandled the situation by allowing a family friend to bring me in for questioning. For now, the average viewer of the nightly news will see my face and connect it to the bombing only because of the press conference. When the police announce that I'm missing, they will call me a person of interest and leave out the fact that I was in police custody. Anyone who sees me on the news should assume the police have questions they need to ask, not that I'm a suspect. Everything would be different if I stayed in police custody. My title would be suspect, and the prevailing assumption would be that I'm guilty.

"Yeah, you look just like the man that's about to give me everything he's got."

"Are you serious?" I ask, cursing my luck.

My father always said birds shit in threes. A mugging, a bombing, and an attempted hit-and-run complete the turd quota for the hood of my car. Surviving the mugging means it'll be clear sailing and mixed imagery ahead.

"Empty your pockets," the man says, moving the light on his chest to show that he has a folding knife in his right hand. He opens a three-inch blade and points it toward me.

I bring the phone back to my ear. "Tin, I've got to go. Some man has a knife."

Tin shouts something that ends when I turn off the phone. I drop my beer and pull a fresh can out of my pocket. With the unopened beer in hand, I dig the tip of my sandal into the soft sand beneath me and kick it into the man's face. The sand stuns him long enough for me to hurl the can of beer at his head. It ricochets off of the mugger's forehead with enough force to knock him back onto the ground.

"I will admit that my actions were a little unsportsmanlike."

The mugger's knife is in the sand next to him. I'm able to pick it up before he realizes it is missing.

"I'm gonna fucking kill you," he shouts from the ground, holding his head.

A kick to the ribs reduces the mugger's enthusiasm regarding my demise. It also rolls him onto his side. A second kick provides enough encouragement to leave him facedown on the sand.

"What the fuck, man!"

He tries to stand up. I place my foot between his shoulder blades and push him into the sand.

"What's your name, buddy?"

"Falkyoo." A face full of sand muffles his reply.

"Falkyoo? Is that Eastern European?" I ask, laughing. "Empty your pockets, Falkyoo."

Falkyoo looks over his shoulder. I'm gingerly pointing his knife back at him. It is a safe distance away in case he tries to reach for it.

"Fuck you," he screams. Spittle shoots from his mouth.

While Falkyoo breathes heavily underneath my foot, I wonder how many other people he has looked down on from this same position. I lean over and place the blade on Falkyoo's cheek, applying pressure and moving it until he screams.

79

"Empty your pockets, or I get stabby."

Falkyoo reaches into his pockets and pulls out a wallet, a set of keys, and a cell phone. He places the items in the sand next to his pockets. Falkyoo's hands then return to protect his face.

"Get off me! Fight me like a man!"

The comment is ludicrous. The cocky idiot appears out of nowhere with a knife and threatens me. And he wants me to fight fair? If it were up to me, I wouldn't be fighting at all. Instead of learning martial arts as a child, I took ballet and ballroom dancing classes. I'd be a pacifist if the world would let me, but everyone sees this antiquated notion of nobility in fighting. The only thing I know about martial arts comes from Bruce Lee flicks. And the only reason my mother let me watch Bruce Lee movies as a kid was because she knew he had won ballroom dancing championships before becoming a movie star. My mother and I would watch his movies together. She would never talk about how he was hurting people, only about the choreography and his movements. Even today, when I see a Bruce Lee film, I still can't separate what's on the screen from my mother's discussions about the fluidity and beauty of how he moved.

"I hate sounding like a dick, but who's on the ground right now? I could dismantle you like a Lego set if I wanted."

"Would you shut the fuck up and let me go!"

"No," I say, replacing my foot on Falkyoo's back with my knee.

He groans when I adjust my weight and reach for his cell phone. I select 'Mom' under the contacts and then hit call, handing the phone back to him.

"Who the fuck is this?" he asks. "Who did you call?"

"Your mother."

"What? Why?"

"When she picks up, you need to tell her you love her."

"Please don't kill me," Falkyoo says, his voice tremulous. I press the knife to his throat.

"It's ringing. I can hear it."

The ringing stops.

"Mom? It's me. I know it's late. I'm fine." Falkyoo pauses while his mother speaks. "No, I don't know when they moved *Becker* reruns to. Listen, Mom. I just wanted to call and tell you I love you… I told you I'm fine… I don't need money. I just called to tell you that… Uh-huh. Yup. I'll talk to you again real soon. Bye."

Falkyoo drops the phone onto the sand. The call disconnects. The screen goes black.

"Your wallet is now my wallet," I say in a raspy voice close to his ear. "I can use your ID to find you whenever I like. I'll be keeping an eye on you over the next couple of weeks. A nine o'clock curfew should suffice. If you aren't in bed by then, I'll make sure no one ever finds the pieces of your body. And since I'm keeping your driver's license, you should get another one from the DMV 'cause driving around without one is illegal."

Both the can of beer I pelted Falkyoo with and the can I dropped are nearby. Karma is proving to be quite the bitch tonight, which makes it the worst time to face comeuppance for littering. Falkyoo remains on the ground as I take the cans and go. He isn't worth any more of my time. Hell, he isn't worth much at all based on how few bills he keeps in his wallet. Those bills make friends with the other presidents in my pocket. Leaving Falkyoo penniless on the beach to think about the failures in his life is an adequate punishment. Being humiliated and robbed during a robbery should force him to call it a night. At the very least, his next victim won't have to contend with a knife.

Falkyoo's only weapon, the knife he pulled on me, ends up in my back pocket. My only weapon, the beer I threw at Falkyoo's head, ends up spraying like a miniature fountain when I crack it open. A celebratory beer hits the spot as I continue walking along the beach toward my home. The police are, without a doubt, rummaging through everything. Shivers run up my spine at the thought of someone moving anything in Lily's room.

Another sip of beer puts a pep in my step and Elvis in my heart. My Elvis impersonation returns along with "Take My Hand, Precious Lord."

Chapter 15

Stephen

"Stephen?" Helen cries from the other side of the front door.

My key is in the lock. The door opens before I can turn it.

Helen welcomes me back to our home by wrapping her arms around me. Silence hangs between us. She refuses to ask about my inflamed eyes and bloody face. It looks worse than it is. The dried blood is menacing. The rust-colored streaks running down the front of my dress shirt make it appear as though I require a transfusion.

"We need to go."

"Is it over?"

I shake my head.

"What happened?"

"You packed the bags?"

Helen nods.

"Bring them downstairs. I'll get cleaned up."

Helen runs upstairs. Cold water from the kitchen sink brings much-needed relief to my eyes. The impact of the crash caused the airbag to inflate with the subtlety of a shotgun. My face slamming into the bag forced my eyes open. The white powder felt like acid. By the time I came to my senses and climbed out of the Explorer, Flynn had disappeared and my nose was bleeding everywhere.

"Are you hurt?" Helen asks, walking up behind me with a clean shirt in her hands.

"I'm fine."

The blood-stained towel in the sink indicates otherwise.

Three suitcases sit in the middle of the living room. The largest is Helen's. The smallest is Jack's. Before I met with Flynn this morning, I asked Helen to pack a bag of clothing for each of us because we might not be coming back.

Jack's birth brought joy to my life in amounts I never thought possible. His arrival made us a family unit. And then the doctors told us about Jack's disability. I thought they were lying. Five fingers. Five toes. All smiles. Every bit as perfect as the last. It took time for me to believe them. When I finally accepted the truth, I knew what I had to do. A boy needs his father. A boy like Jack needed me even more. I left the Navy to protect my son, and I will protect him, whatever the cost.

Helen wipes away tears as she hands me the clean shirt.

"What else can I do?"

"Get my duffel from the closet."

There was always a chance something would go wrong tonight. No plan is perfect. All anyone can do is prepare for failure. Over the past two days, I have liquidated every account and pulled out as much cash from our credit cards as possible. I bought a second gun for cash off of a collector to avoid the background check and waiting period encountered with a dealer. The gun, the money, and all of our essential documents are in that duffel.

My boss introduced me to a man that creates new identities. He can help us disappear. All of his contact information is in Lou's office at work. With that in hand, I'll be one step closer.

Helen returns with the bag. She holds it with both hands and struggles to keep it off the floor.

"I've got it," I say, throwing the duffel over my shoulder. "Let's go."

We leave our home with what remains of our lives shoved into four suitcases. Helen locks the front door behind us. She sees me loading the bags into the Cadillac and asks, "Where did you get this car?"

"It doesn't matter. Get in."

We enter the car in silence. The GPS lights up when I push the keyless ignition. GPS will be a problem in the near future. The next step is to drive downtown. I'm confident I can find another car in one of the unsecured parking lots that will be harder to track.

Chapter 16

William

Memories of my childhood are hard to come by these days. I've been someone else for too long. Acting has always been a part of me. That much I can remember. In a different life, I could have won a mantel full of Oscars. Faint memories of performing in school plays linger in the back of my mind. My father made me stop. He beat me real bad while raving about honesty. Acting is all about pretending, and pretending is just another way to lie, so I guess he might've had a point. That acting bug has been with me since before I can remember. It's that little lying piece of me that puts on the grand show of William. Before I let the show begin, I sneak up on the SUV parked in front of Flynn's house.

The curtain falls fast when the man calling himself Harold ends our conversation. Something doesn't feel right about him. His eyes are open wide. People that squint look honest to me. It comes from working outdoors for so long. I've met a lot of honest people on the job. We spent our time together outside in the sun. Squinting comes naturally in Florida on a sunny day. There's something that bothers me about people who keep their eyes wide open. It's unsettling to see someone look at you with open eyes during the day. And Harold's eyes don't squint a bit.

After talking to Harold, I walk back to my garage and start mulling over ideas for additions to Lily's memorial garden. Whatever I come up with needs to be something she'll like. Lily loves the color pink. It's her favorite. Pink makes her happy. All I want is to make her happy.

My life nearly ended when Lily was reborn. A single man living alone next door to a family with a missing child is the obvious suspect. The investigators dug into my life and alibi. I've heard that 'alibi' is Latin for 'elsewhere.' I couldn't prove that I was elsewhere the day Lily went missing. Then a man, one sent from a being who understands my purpose, came forward and confessed. He begged for a trial and an execution. And the state agreed. And the people agreed. And the world forgot.

Everyone except Flynn.

The guilt of losing his sister destroyed him like the loss of Lily destroyed his family. It hurts to see his torment. The distraught teenager inside still tries to drink himself to death night after night. But he knows he can't die. He has to find the man who took Lily. And I can't let him. Not for my sake. For Flynn's sake. Chasing that tiny light at the end of the tunnel keeps him holding on to this world.

Hours of hard work deserve hours of peaceful relaxation. A canopy I created with creeping vines covers most of my back yard. Flame vine, crossvine, and trumpet creeper all weave their way in-between the loose wooden thatch and keep it shady even under the brightest sun. The shade makes it a perfect place to enjoy the day. I lie down on a rattan chair overlooking the beach and watch a family play in the waves. The kids run back and forth in the water while their parents relax on towels. All that running tires me out. Their innocent voices fade away as I doze off.

A dog barking in the distance wakes me up. My nap stretched into an afternoon-ending event. The sun has set. My growling stomach says dinner is past due. Treating myself to a meal turns second fiddle when I can't remember closing the garage earlier. The door is wide open. A police officer leads a dog past my driveway. The officer looks at me carefully before continuing down the road. Police cars line the side of the road in both directions. With a click of the switch, the garage door rumbles closed. The garage light stays on when I go back into the house. Lily is afraid of the dark.

The picture on the frozen chicken dinner whets my appetite. Hunger pangs kick in, winding my gut tighter with every rotation in the microwave. Unable to endure seven minutes of spinning, I take my rumbling belly to the den for a distraction. The shag carpeting and wood paneling in my house were once a beach standard. This day and age, everybody modernizes and takes away the charm. They turn their homes into bland magazine-inspired lookalikes. Back when I was landscaping, people used to show me pictures of mature gardens and expect me to replicate them with some green-thumbed miracle. No one ever stops to consider how plants grow. The longer they live, the more beautiful they become. In my book, the same goes for homes. The longer they exist and gain charm, the more beautiful they become.

It takes me a minute to find the TV remote on the floor next to the sofa. An actress chokes out half an emotional plea before the channel cuts away to a local news bulletin. The microwave's timer buzzes as the reporter starts talking.

The chicken dinner's plastic tray is scorching hot. I slide it onto a plate and return to the living room sofa. Flynn and his Asian friend are on the news. A chyron pops up underneath them. 'INFORMATION ON LOCAL BOMBING.' I pick at the creamed corn until Flynn's speech ends. The reporters speculate after Flynn disappears. I turn off the TV and move a chair to the front window. The chicken dinner tastes extra special with the show outside.

Police cars migrate toward Flynn's house, swarming the area over an hour after his appearance on the news. They make their presence known with sirens and lights. The hoopla disappears after inconsiderate police stomp all over Flynn's lawn for thirty minutes. Several police cars remain in the area, hidden in the voids between the streetlights.

There's a gentle knock on the sliding glass door at the back of my house. The police must be traipsing through my yard, sniffing where they don't belong. I turn on the floodlights to catch their privacy-violating shenanigans. Instead, Flynn stands there, drawing his hand across his throat as a signal to cut the lights. I switch the floodlights off and slide open the door.

"Thanks," Flynn says after closing the door and pulling the vertical blinds.

"What'n the hell, Flynn?" I hold my hands to my temples and bring them back down with my palms open to the sky. "I saw you on the news. What happened?"

"A man named Harold."

"I knew that cat was looking to scratch."

Flynn walks to the front of my house and closes the blinds.

"I should've known, but got distracted by money. Que sera. Now I need to find him and make sure he understands the meaning of comeuppance."

"I'm pretty sure I got a bat or something. Man, I know I've got some spare handles for shovels if you need 'em."

"I don't plan on hurting Harold. I plan on finding out who he is and why he did what he did. Then I'll turn him over to the police and hope he gets beat to death in prison."

"Yeah. Whatever you need."

"Can I stay for the night?

"No problem."

"Also, could you give me a ride somewhere tomorrow?"

"Sure. Whatever you need."

Flynn's near-death experience hits me hard. What would I have done without him? Shivers move through my body like ice in my veins. I'm never alone. My family is always with me, but Flynn is like my other family. He's my last living relative.

"You all right, William?"

My face regains a smile.

"Oh yeah. Fine. Let me get you some sheets for the sofa."

"Thank you."

I pull a flat sheet, a pillow, a pillowcase, and a comforter out of the closet. They smell a little stuffy, so I lay them on my bed and hit each one several times to knock the smell out. After finishing, I carry everything out and set it on the sofa.

Flynn is in my kitchen, pouring a glass of water. He drinks the water and refills the glass to the top.

"I've been thinking about adding some extra hydrangeas to your yard around Lily's memorial. But I wanna add some lime to the soil to make it more alkaline. That way, when they bloom, they'll be a nice pink."

"That'd be great," Flynn says, his face long and tired. "Did you know that Al Kaline had three thousand and seven hits in his lifetime?"

"No, but I know Roberto Clemente had three thousand and died in a plane crash."

"He's one of the reasons I'm not a big fan of planes."

"Sounds like you had quite the day. I'll let you sleep."

"I figured you might have some questions about the explosion and why I'm not with the police."

"No. Flynn, I'd prefer to stay out of it. You know, stay low key. Get some rest. I'll close my door. That way, my snoring won't keep you up."

"Thanks again, William."

"No problem."

87

Chapter 17

Amy

A burst of flame is my last coherent memory of the explosion. Blinding smoke fills every corner of my brain until I'm standing outside in only a towel. I don't know if the towel is from my room or if someone brought it to me. I'm cold. My head hurts. I'm shouting, screaming at the top of my lungs. My voice is dull in my ears.

A female EMT forces me to focus on her. A blinding light shines into my eyes. Her thin face returns with a smile, wrinkling her olive skin. "Miracle," she keeps mouthing.

Numbness dulls everything. My brain. My body. It's hard to focus. Strangers keep speaking to me. Everything tells me to leave, to get far away from here. A man in a suit shows me a badge. I beg him to take me away. The EMT nods. He listens.

Wrapped in a blanket, they seat me in a room with a table, two chairs, and no windows. The man in the suit sits across the table from me. "Detective Cousins," he says in a voice heavy enough to break a person.

Detective Cousins asks me questions until I can't take any more. He apologizes and leaves the room. The moment of peace feels foreign. Chaos is exhausting, yet normalizes with time. There is no way to tell how long this night has dragged on or how long it will continue. The room lacks a clock. The momentary respite breaks as an officer brings me a pair of pink cotton sweatpants and a matching jacket. My parents are here to help. They have to be. This clothing comes from my old dresser at my parent's house. I bought this outfit at the same time as my friend Marcia. I bought pink. She bought purple.

The clothes are as warm and soft as I remember. A knock at the door opens an emotional floodgate. My parents are here to take me away. This ordeal is over. The door opens. Detective Cousins enters. He smiles in the face of my disappointment and asks the same questions again. I repeat the same answers. He leaves for a while and comes back, looking upset. I want him to be happy, so I smile.

"Everything will be okay," he says. The weight of his words scares me. His eyes tell me he's lying. I've seen men lie so many times before. 'I love my wife.' 'I've never done anything like this before.' Why is he lying to me? What doesn't he want me to know?

"Please let me leave," I plead. "I've told you everything. I'm tired."

"It's not safe yet."

The word 'yet' intrigues me. 'Yet' makes it sound like it might never be safe. I stop speaking and sit in silence. I rub the soft cotton of my sweatpants back and forth until my hands turn numb. When I cannot stand another question being asked, Detective Cousins says, "You're free to go."

My parents greet me with a hug as I step out of the interview room. Their excitement is overwhelming. Every instinctual emotion telling me to fall apart in their arms falls by the wayside. We leave the police station together, calm and collected.

The rising sun is a surprise. An entire night disappeared in that windowless room. The invigorating morning air provides me a brief respite from reality. My parents keep talking to me, but their words dissolve in the chilly air and pass right through me. My mind is elsewhere as they place me in their car. The drive passes in an instant. With a guiding hand on my shoulder, my mother escorts me through their house and into my childhood bedroom. She closes the door behind me.

The posters, the books, the pictures, everything is as I left it years ago. I've been back here often, but something feels different about it today. My old alarm clock sits dead, unplugged from the wall, the hour and minute hands stuck at half past eleven.

A switch flips. Unexpected energy rushes through me. The clock may not be accurate, but the sun can't lie about it being early. Iain should be awake in Scotland at this hour.

Iain needs to know what happened. My phone wasn't with me in the motel room. It stayed in my car to charge, safely tucked away from all the damage. My car should be accessible. It was outside of the police tape when they escorted me to the ambulance.

Without second-guessing my decision, I leave the bedroom to find my parents. They are grinding coffee in the kitchen.

"What are you doing out here?" my mother asks, walking up to hug me. It won't help, but I allow it for her sake. "You should be in bed."

"Your mother's right, you know," my father says. He focuses his attention on pouring coffee grounds into the filter.

"I will not be able to sleep." My mother expects me to turn to mush and do as she says. I won't. "I can't. I need to go to my car."

"What on earth for?" my mother asks. Concern dances across her face with several brief twitches.

"I need my phone." My father is the one I'd typically ask for something like this. A smile and a tilt of the head helps create the perfect daddy's little girl look. Instead, my tone is flat and demanding. Regardless of how I deliver the news, they will look at me like I'm insane. Both jaws drop. They need me to justify my demand. "I need to call my boyfriend and tell him I'm fine."

"I didn't know you were seeing anyone, dear. We'd both love to meet him."

My mother always wants to meet the men I date. Polite refusals are my primary defense, used out of concern that she might learn more about me than she should.

"He's very private. I'm not sure if he'd be willing to."

"How about you call him on our phone?" My father uncrosses his arms to point at the phone in the kitchen. When he finishes pointing, he runs a finger over his mustache. That mustache reminds me of Paul in the motel. "It'd be a lot easier than going to get your phone right now."

"Like I told you, he's private. He won't accept any call from a number he doesn't recognize. I need my phone."

"Then how about your mother and I get it for you? You can stay here. We can bring your car back."

"We shouldn't leave her here alone, Tom. How about we all go and get it together?"

"Yes," I say, walking toward the front door. "Let's go."

"Now hold on a minute, Amy," my father says, following me. "How about we have breakfast first and then go get your car?"

"I can walk."

The comment startles my parents.

"There'll be no need for that."

My father grabs his car keys and walks outside to his car with me close behind. My mother locks the front door while I climb into the back seat. When my mother sits down in the front passenger seat, my father starts the car and backs out of the driveway. A marked police car follows our every move as we drive to the motel. The car is quiet. Even if my parents were talkative, I'd only be paying attention to the police car following close behind.

My father pulls into the motel lot and parks next to my car. The damage turns our silence into a moment of breathless shock. Flynn's car is a burned shell. Police filter in and out of the room I walked into last night.

My father's eyes are begging me to answer the question, *Why were you here?*

How are you involved in this? asks his furrowed brow.

What have you gotten yourself into? asks his tightened jaw.

But his lips, when they finally move, his lips produce three simple words. "We are here."

My car sits outside of the area marked by police tape. The back wheel well on the passenger side has an extra key hidden in a little magnetic box. After the fourth time of having to pay a pop-a-lock company to come out and open up my car, I decided to keep an extra key hidden away.

My father winces at the squeaking sound my car door makes as it opens. There's no doubt in my mind that he'll tell me what I need to do to fix it once things calm down. My cell phone is in the center console cup holder, where I left it. I ignore the voicemails and texts and skip straight to calling Iain.

Chapter 18

Flynn

An old pair of jeans and a t-shirt with the logo of William's former company, Flower's Landscaping, sit folded and resting on the top of the clothes hamper when I climb out of the shower. The clothes fit surprisingly well. I've never considered my size compared to William's. Maybe that's a male trait. I'm not sure. The last time I borrowed a piece of clothing from another man's closet was in college. One of my roommates, Henry, let me borrow a tie for a job interview. He wasn't around to teach me how to tie it, so I resorted to online advice. Robert, my other roommate, showed up after many failed attempts and fixed the tie for me. My father's spirit somehow inhabited Robert that day. It's the only explanation of why he tied a full Windsor around my neck. I'm hoping William doesn't follow suit and try to fix how his old shirt drapes. Not wanting to leave a mess, I ball up my dirty clothes and shove them under my arm before looking in the mirror.

It's been a while since I've seen my eyes. A thin coppery ring on the edge of my cornea creeps toward my pupil. The pale copper ring shouldn't be there.

"Flynn," William shouts, knocking on the door. "What's going on in there? Are you okay?"

Blue. Red. Yellow…

"I'm fine."

"That was a lot of shouting to be fine," William says, his voice muffled by the door. "You were cursing at the top of your lungs."

"Sorry," I say, opening the door. "I didn't realize I was doing it. I don't have my medication."

William stands with his hands on the doorjamb. His look is one a father would give a son in distress.

"I'm fine. You got any baby powder?" I ask while taking my balled-up clothing from underneath my arm.

"Nope, but let me get those," William says, taking the clothes. Before throwing them in the washing machine, he pulls out a wallet and a knife and holds them up for me. "You forgot your things."

"Those belong to a guy that tried to rob me last night." I take the wallet from William and throw it into the kitchen trash. "Some jackass came at me with a knife. I beamed him in the face with an unopened can of beer and took his knife and his wallet. I figured you only get so many chances in life to rob someone ironically, so I went with it."

"What should I do with the knife?"

"You can keep it."

"At least you didn't get hurt," William says while tossing my clothes into the washing machine. A mechanical clunking sound gives way to the sound of running water. William turns around and puts the knife in his back pocket. "I'll get 'em clean and bring 'em back to your place."

"Thanks," I say, holding Mordecai in both of my hands.

It's been a long time since I last went outside without Mordecai the Fourth adorning my head. Pictures of me on the news all have me wearing a Cubs cap. The last thing I need is more attention drawn my way.

"I'm gonna feel naked without Mordecai," I say, leaving him on the dining room table.

"I've got a hat you could wear instead."

William disappears into his bedroom and returns holding an old straw hat with a fraying brim.

"Don't you think it's a little conspicuous?"

"No. This thing is conspicuously inconspicuous."

It takes time to view the new ensemble at all angles in the bathroom mirror. A fading t-shirt and a pair of stained and torn jeans fit with the straw hat and rough facial hair. The clothes of a man waiting for work to come his way outside of Home Depot clash with my square-framed glasses. The outfit says, 'Please hire me,' but the glasses say, 'Will work for tickets to The Flaming Lips.'

"Yeah, I guess you're right," I say, rejoining William in the kitchen. "I'm sorta digging this migrant chic look."

William laughs.

"Does it have a name?"

"Does it need one?"

"It'd make me feel better," I say.

"How about Jimmy the Hat?"

Jimmy pops off my head and gets the once-over.

"I don't think it's a Jimmy."

"Hell, I don't know. How did you name Mordecai?"

"He's named after an old Cubs pitcher, Mordecai 'Three Finger' Brown. When I put a baseball cap on my head, I always have three fingers on the brim. The name fit."

"How about Sally the Straw Hat?"

"Quality use of alliteration," I say, putting Sally on. "Thanks for lending me Sally."

William grins in the way all people grin when they receive approval or congratulations for something they don't quite understand. There's an awkward pause while William's eyes wander. If he was a woman between the ages of fourteen and thirty-five, this is where he would snap his tongue against the roof of his mouth to indicate his desire to change the subject. But William is a man in his late sixties, so he shrugs his shoulders and changes the subject with no further indication.

"So, where am I taking you?"

"My therapist."

William looks straight ahead with no discernible emotion. He's either surprised by my request or lost in thought. William sometimes gets distant. It's a trait I'm sure is a direct result of spending so much of his life in the intense Florida heat around chemicals and pesticides.

"William?" I ask.

"You're going to your therapist? Is this for that medication you talked about?"

"No. I've had an issue with my insurance, so I've been without for a while. I should be fine until it's cleared up."

"Why then?"

"Seems like a decent time for therapy. It's been less than a day since I helped blow up a man and was nearly blown up myself."

"But you ran from the police. Shouldn't we head for the Keys or something?"

"That would prevent me from being able to find Harold. If he ends up in the Keys, then I'll ask you very politely to drive me there."

"That's fine. Whatever you want."

William walks out to his garage and opens the door. A flood of sunlight pours in. The heat of the previous day remains, and the warm days of winter continue. William saunters outside and down to his mailbox, opening the box and reaching his hand inside. After not pulling anything out, he looks up and down the street like a man in search of a delivery.

"Coast's clear, Flynn," William hisses as he attempts to both whisper and shout at the same time.

William gets in his truck and reaches over to unlock the passenger-side door. Sally stays on at an angle to cover my face as best she can. Once in the truck, I keep my head down as William backs out onto the street.

"Here we go," William says, putting his truck in drive.

I continue to hide my face and don't say a word for most of the trip. William has driven me to my therapist before. He knows where to go. When we reach Third Street, William taps me on the arm.

"It's safe now," he says.

The next hour might prove otherwise. Visiting my therapist is a calculated risk. The odds of the police knowing that I go to a therapist and knowing that I have an appointment on this particular day are slim to none. But there's always a chance, and that bothers me.

The same urge that sent me to the hospital last night is driving me to take the risk today. My therapist can help me stay hidden a little longer. Trying to scare her might work. Or it might be a waste of time. The office requires a twenty-four-hour notice to cancel an appointment, so they're sending a bill either way. If I make the appointment and put on a show, it could work out for the best.

William pulls into the complex of single-story professional cottages where my therapist has her office. The development is a miniature village of doctors, chiropractors, financial advisors, accountants, and real estate agents all in individualized alpine cottages plopped down among an asphalt parking lot. The coquina walls fit the area while clashing with wooden beams more suited to an environment well above sea level.

I'm running out of time to decide. Countless trivial things can derail my search for Harold in an instant. And if it all goes wrong, I'd rather not

95

have William caught up in this mess. By the time Doctor Leah's coquina-covered walls come into view, the only option is to go all in on this venture. I've already put William at risk by staying the night at his house. There needs to be some payoff for what we've done.

"Park on the side of the building. You'll see the blinds close in five minutes. Fifteen minutes later, have your truck outside the front door."

William pauses and nods before responding. "Sure thing."

A soft electronic doorbell rings when I enter the office. Kim, the lovely brunette secretary, smiles at me. I flirt with her every time I'm here. She knows better than to date a client. It reeks of poor decision making. Kim's perfect hair and conservative clothing indicate she has enough sense to make an intelligent decision. But I still flirt because it's more fun than reading their lackluster magazine selection.

"Good afternoon, Mr. Dupree. How are you today?"

"Doing well," I say with a smile.

"I like your hat," Kim says while marking my time of arrival on a piece of paper.

"Twelve fifty-eight," I reply, pointing at the clock on the wall before tipping Sally. "Always fashionably early."

With two minutes until my appointment, the usual chit-chat ends up shelved. There's hardly enough time for me to get my charm engine started.

"Have a seat. Leah will be right with you."

Leah Marshall. Doctor Marshall. Doctor Leah. Leah. These names are all appropriate in this office. That was the first thing I noticed when starting therapy. Leah allows people to pick their level of familiarity. At first, I thought it sounded awkward. Soon, all the conversations felt friendlier and less tempered by the continual reminder that she is a doctor, and I'm the broken goods she's trying to fix. Something about saying Dr. Leah or Dr. Marshall sounds too formal. It makes me less open. But I have a distinct feeling that, after today, Leah will no longer want me as a client. I don't want to drag Leah into this. I need to. Someone believable offering information, someone with degrees and an established practice, means infinitely more than anyone else I know coming forward to send the police in the wrong direction. Manipulation and misinformation are the two keys to my survival.

"Leah's ready for you, Mr. Dupree."

"Let's hope so."

The door next to Kim leads to an office with two sofas and two plush chairs, all in a neutral sandy color. Leah is in a chair with the back facing her desk. I take a seat in the chair opposite, facing Leah's desk and a window looking out onto the parking lot. William is in his truck outside of the window, waiting for my signal. Every three weeks, when I come to this office and relax in this chair, the blinds are open and the light reflecting off the windshields of vehicles parked outside distracts me. My standard reaction is to move my chair to keep the sun from shining into my eyes. This time, instead of moving, I shield my eyes to make it obvious that the reflected light is bothering me.

"Oh, I'm sorry," Leah says. She stands up and walks over to the window, lowering the blinds and closing the slats. "Is that better?"

"Much. Thank you."

The fifteen-minute countdown begins.

Leah sits back down in her chair and crosses her legs, placing both hands on her knee.

"And how are you doing today, Flynn?"

"Could be better. Could be worse."

"Still living in that gray area you enjoy talking about?"

"Yup."

"I notice you have a new hat?"

"Mordecai is staying at a friend's place. This is Sally the Straw Hat."

"Change is good."

"I guess. Mordecai is my thinking cap, so I feel a little off."

"Sally looks like better sun protection."

"That's a fair point. Always looking on the bright side. And it is sunnier outside than I thought it would be."

"It's hard to believe Thanksgiving is two days away, isn't it?"

"Sure is," I say with a calm chuckle.

"What's the genuine reason behind the new hat?"

"Change is good."

"It's fine if you don't want to tell me."

"I do have a question. It's something you might be able to clear up for me."

"How can I help?"

"I've been thinking about how people deal with chaotic situations."

97

"Chaotic in what way?"

"General."

"Sure," Leah says, shaking her head.

"People waste a lot of their life trying to organize the world. We keep calendars and clocks and filing systems. And what is it all for?"

"You're not an organizer—at least not in that regard. You miss appointments on a semi-regular basis. I'm going to assume you're talking about someone else."

"Is it possible to fool ourselves into believing we have the least bit of control over our lives?"

"I don't know if 'fool' is the word I would use. People find comfort in control. Chaos exists around us whether or not we want to admit it. It makes us feel small and weak. Part of being human is learning to navigate the chaos. Many accomplish that by controlling the little things. If they concentrate enough on what they can control, then what they can't slips the mind."

"And when they lose that control?"

"It varies."

"It varies? I'm not sure what that means. Some go crazy, and others are fine? If I live my life by a plan and life sees fit to take that plan away, leaving me the emotional equivalent of being alone in the wilderness, am I going to go crazy?"

"It's impossible to tell. There's not a definable line for 'crazy' when we look at ourselves. We save that judgment for others."

"Which reminds me of a quote from Einstein, 'A question that sometimes drives me hazy: Am I or are the others crazy?' It's something my mother used to say a lot after my sister disappeared."

"You seem scattered today."

"A million things are happening at once, and I'm not a hundo on the sure scale how long I can hold it together."

"What happened?"

I stay silent and look around the room to avoid direct eye contact. Hopefully, my reluctance to talk about this subject piques her interest.

"Flynn," Leah says, saying my name in a sympathetic tone. She's trying to form a connection by starting what she has to say with a direct address. "We don't have to talk about this. You can spend your time here however you want. But getting this out in the open might help you feel more comfortable about your situation. You may end up feeling like you have more control."

Leah is trying to make it my decision to talk about what's bothering me. Talking to someone who's trained to be manipulative differs from talking to people manipulative by nature. A truly manipulative person would have understood that I'm trying to pull her from the water. Leah's too nice. She doesn't feel the hook in her cheek or see the rod and reel in my hands.

"That's a magnificent idea." I stay silent and wait for Leah to initiate.

"Flynn?"

"Yes?"

"What happened?"

"Oh, you're ready?"

"Yes."

"For starters, Curtis Vance showed up at my friend's bakery yesterday."

"We've spoken about Mr. Vance before."

This is an understatement. Every time a new novel of Vance's hits the shelves, I pick it up and dismantle it like a British critic. Armed with a checklist of things I feel are problems, I bitch to anyone who will listen. Everyone else tells me to shut up. Leah's job is to put up with it. But, as a direct result of my diatribes, we spend multiple sessions targeting my obsessive nature and discussing why I lash out in such ways.

"Those times were different. This time he was accusing me of some things."

"Did it have to do with your sister?"

"No. But my drinking may have gotten me into some trouble."

"Two weeks ago, you said you were going to stop drinking."

"Two weeks ago, I said I would start drinking less. Big difference."

"You've been a vegetarian for how many months?"

"Four."

Leah believes minor changes in habits can lead to significant changes in attitude. She's been encouraging me to change my diet and drinking habits since the day I started coming here. According to her, they are the easiest life changes to make. I disagree. I tried being a vegetarian, and still call myself a vegetarian, but I eat meat. By my calculations, if seven-tenths of my diet is vegetarian, then I can round up and still count myself as a full vegetarian.

"You can last four months as a vegetarian, yet you can't stop drinking for two weeks?"

"Yeah, I'm putting a hold on the vegetarian thing for a while. I'll be hitting up a steakhouse or two as soon as I leave here."

"You're willing to give up on all the progress you've made?"

"I'm worried I may never have the opportunity to eat a good steak again. I'm planning on living it up while I can. You smoke, right?" This is a question I know the answer to without ever having seen her smoke. The tobacco stains on her fingertips and the fact that she touches her lips far too frequently are dead giveaways. On top of that, there are Nat Shermans on her desk. The distinctive mini cigar box shape of the packaging is something I became familiar with when I used to frequent a cigar shop in Ponte Vedra before they went out of business. "Do you know where I can buy some Nat Shermans? I'm craving a quality cigarette right now."

"Wait, why won't you be able to have a good steak?"

It's entertaining to keep intentionally changing the subject. Being a bit of a space cadet forces me to go off on unintentional tangents all the time, but being in control of the tangents is entertaining. On top of the entertainment factor, a confusing environment is the best way to work toward what I want to accomplish.

"I was nearly blown up yesterday."

"What? What do you mean blown up?"

"The explosion in the motel at Atlantic Beach. I was there."

"You were there?"

"Yeah. An explosion went off in a motel room. I ran toward the room. Then a bomb went off in a car nearby."

"Are you hurt?"

"I hit my head and got some scratches, but that's all."

"It's a miracle you weren't seriously injured."

"I know."

"This is why you were talking about chaos earlier?"

"It didn't upset me as much as make me think. The bomb goes off, right? I hit my head." To boost the theatrics, I slap the arm of the chair.

"Everything goes black. It was like my brain shut down and rebooted. I can only remember one other time in my life that I've had that feeling."

A proper story always draws in the listener. The easiest way to tell if a story has legs is to provide someone a hook and then stop. Not a simple pause. The story needs to stop. If the story is compelling, then the listeners will want it to continue. The stop not only tells you if it's compelling, but it can also inject artificial suspense.

"Are you all right? You've been stopping mid-thought. Did anyone check you to see if you had a concussion?"

Leah not taking the bait will not distract me from my story. I know how I want this to play out. The timeline I'm on will not change.

"I'd only been surfing for a month and a half. This one day, I rode a wave outside of my comfort level. Everything started great. The board shifted when the wave crested, which caused me to slip and fall. Somewhere along the way, the board clipped my head. Everything went black. I sank like a stone. The world was spinning around me. The leash started pulling at my leg. That was my only link to the world, and then it slipped off my foot. When the leash disappeared, I disconnected from everything. My body couldn't function. My mind still worked. All I had was darkness. I didn't know what would happen. The darkness clung to me until this electric current started running through my body. My eyes opened. The salt water burned like I was staring at the sun, but I kept my eyes open because I could see light. And this light made me feel like everything would be fine."

I pause because I want Leah to want an ending.

All she does is look at me like I have a gaping hole in my forehead. If she thinks I'm injured and unbalanced, that could play into my hand better than planned. Leah knows me well enough at this point. I'm not a violent person. I'd been counting on certain variables to convince her otherwise. A head injury is an excuse Leah could use to explain why I might not act normal. That could be the detail that drives her over the edge. It's like Edith and Jason. The result of the physical abuse was for Edith to end their relationship. It took Jason becoming mentally unbalanced in addition to being abusive before she called the police.

"My neighbor William was watching me from the shore. He pulled me out of the water. I ended up fine. Yesterday, I didn't have anyone to save me. And I didn't come back to light. I came back to fire."

"Fire?"

"My car was on fire."

"Your car was on fire?"

"I didn't mention that before? My car was the one that blew up."

Leah's surprise shows. She composes herself by staring down at her skirt while straightening it. Once the fabric flattens appropriately, her eyes return to me.

"Someone tried to blow you up?"

"Yeah. Is it cool if I live with you for a while?"

"Flynn, that's inappropriate."

"That's beside the point. I need a place to crash. Is your pool house suitable for someone to stay the night?"

"How do you know I have a pool house?"

Part of Leah making people feel comfortable and friendly comes from her decorating the room with pictures of her and her family. I know most of these pictures and can pull ideas from them to use as I see fit. Pictures of Leah and her husband with their two dogs out by the pool show the exterior of the pool house. Another photo of the couple enjoying a glass of wine with company shows the interior equipped as a recreation room for some event. A final picture of the same room from an alternate angle shows Leah's husband motioning toward the pool with one hand while looking back at the camera. Rather than telling Leah how I know about the pool house, I elect to be coy because I need her scared and angry. I'm banking on this combination tossing confidentiality out the door. Leah needs to call the police and tell them every word I've said. If I tell Leah the truth, that I know about the pool house because of the pictures she keeps in her office, then she might not feel pressured enough to call the police.

"Why do you ask?"

"It's never come up before in our conversations."

"Are you sure?"

"Yes."

"Can I stay there?"

"Why?"

"It'll only be a day or two. I'm trying to avoid the police. They think I caused the explosion in the motel."

"Did you?"

"Sort of."

"You can't sort of blow something up, Flynn."

"Yes, you can. So, are you and Greg—Your husband's name is Greg, correct?—amenable to my staying with you? I promise to keep the area clean."

"How do you know I have a pool house?"

I'm surprised that my dropping Greg's name didn't cause Leah to flinch. She often brings him up in conversation. It concerns me that she's cognizant of what information she lets out. This gambit can only work if Leah doesn't scan the room and have a Chazz Palminteri epiphany where she pieces together how I know about her home.

"Is that a 'Yes'?"

"You are avoiding the question."

"You're avoiding the issue. I need your help."

"You cannot stay with my husband and me."

"We're only friends when I pay you by the hour?"

"That's not it."

"You know what that makes you, right?"

"This session's over."

My voice deepens into an ominous rumble as I lean in closer to Leah. "You will regret not letting me stay with you."

I leave the office looking angry and follow the hallway out into the waiting room with a smile on my face. If my ploy works, Leah will call the police and report everything I've told her. Instead of using their manpower to search for me, they'll spread out to keep watch over any place I could use to hide. They might even try monitoring steakhouses and smoke shops. All of this will provide me additional freedom in my movements.

"That went fast," Kim says. She removes a plastic container from the desk and places it in her lap. "Should we book your next appointment?"

"I'll call to schedule it. Have a great day."

William positioned his truck for a perfect escape. I'm in the passenger seat before Doctor Leah's front door closes.

"Drive," I say.

"Where to?" William asks, putting his truck into drive.

"We're going downtown. JTB to 95 to Main Street."

Chapter 19

Flynn

Fear of bridges should be universal. We begrudge and deny the efficacy of science across the board, yet, somehow, when engineers use science, everyone gives it a pass.

Scientists engineering a vaccine with a proven track record of success? That's all make-believe nonsense.

Engineers using science to allow bits of concrete and steel to float? I'd like to drive my family over that.

People must have faith in engineering because they see it in use so often. That's why schools need to make the video of the original Tacoma Narrows Bridge collapse mandatory viewing. That'd etch fear of bridges into our collective psyche.

The workers building the Tacoma Narrows Bridge nicknamed it 'Galloping Gertie' because the wind moved it with ease. Gertie swayed in the breeze until its collapse sixth months after opening. Sure, that accident happened in the 1940s, and we've learned a lot about bridge construction since then, but human fallibility has yet to change. More recently, engineers had to rework the Wonderwood Bridge out in Mayport during the construction process because it didn't meet the height requirements set by the Coast Guard. Though not as dramatic as swaying in the wind, it provides me supporting evidence that bridges are not trustworthy.

My fear of bridges is not crippling. It's a reasonable fear. Humans make bridges, and humans make mistakes. Mother Nature does not make mistakes; she exploits them. The last thing I want is to be in that final car on the next Tacoma Narrows Bridge as it sways back and forth in the wind before collapsing in a pile of debris and pieces of steel torn like ribbons.

Living at the beach can make life relatively bridge free. There's plenty of flat land and stores to provide whatever I might need. Living bridge-free is easy as long as I don't need to cross the ditch into town. Driving to Jacksonville requires crossing one bridge. Driving to downtown Jacksonville requires crossing at least two.

Crossing a bridge on my own requires me to focus on driving. That's easy in Jacksonville. Everyone drives like maniacs having seizures. Bridges are a minor inconvenience compared to Bubba trying to run you into a light pole. Not focusing on the road is asking for an accident. Riding shotgun in William's truck opens up the outside world. The freedom is all well and good until the Main Street Bridge comes into view. To reduce my stress levels, I clench my fists and hold my breath until the whizzing sound of tires driving on the bridge's hollow and airy grates ends. My breathing returns to normal, but my hands stay clasped until William's truck stops at a red light at the base of the bridge.

The only reason I'm willing to subject myself to the possibility of being on one bridge when it collapses, let alone two, is for something valuable. Right now, the most precious commodity in my world is information on Paul Mahoney.

If someone asked me two weeks ago, "Who is Paul Mahoney?" My response would be, "I don't know or care." Paul's mustachioed face first entered my consciousness via the local news. Everything I know about Paul Mahoney comes thanks to a bout of insomnia that kept me awake till the crack of dawn. With little else to report, the morning news spent ample time covering Mahoney's campaign for mayor. Following that spot, the kind-looking man picked up a broom for a commercial emphasizing his promises of cleaning up the city of Jacksonville.

Paul Mahoney was a respected journalist who grew up in the Jacksonville area. After moving on to New York City, he acquired a considerable amount of friends in high places. He teamed up with one such friend to create an online news website as the Internet became a cash cow. When the site sold at the top of the bubble, Paul Mahoney returned home to Jacksonville with an estimated fifty-million-dollar nest egg.

After many years of retirement, Mahoney tossed his hat into the political ring. In no time, he became a member of the Jacksonville City Council. After setting his sights on becoming the next mayor, he spared no expense in launching his campaign months before his competitors.

One of Paul Mahoney's major campaign promises, according to the local news, was to reinvigorate the downtown area by bringing in new businesses. The reporter covered how Mahoney took an abandoned bank off of Main Street and turned it into his campaign headquarters.

Downtown Jacksonville is full of buildings in various states of disuse. There's been a revitalization effort in recent years—or at least an attempt at a revitalization—intended to spur a downtown renaissance. The city spent years dangling financial incentives to lure new businesses into these empty spaces without realizing that only life breeds life. Artificial sparks to a city's necrotic tissue create a Frankenstein's monster bound to succumb to taxpayers with pitchforks.

The last time I visited downtown Jacksonville was a night trip to The Landing, which is an unremarkable mall downtown on the river. When I walked back to my car, the only three people I encountered were three different homeless men roaming the streets like the onset of a zombie apocalypse. Lucky for me, they were craving cigarettes instead of human flesh. With the downtown nightlife being minimal, you can't blame a person for wanting to set up shop anywhere else in the city. After all, what fun is work with no play? The downtown nightlife, outside of performances at the Times-Union Center, is nonexistent. And I doubt most people consider performance art a way to blow off steam after work.

According to the news report on Paul Mahoney, he, as one the renaissance men of Jacksonville, would fix this problem. He promised the downtown area would be his pet project, and he started leading by example. The bank he took over for his campaign headquarters is on Main Street, which makes it easy to find. The windows filled with signs saying 'Vote for Mahoney' make it even easier to find. William circles the block and parks in an open spot on Monroe Street, about a block from the bank.

While the outfit William provided me fits in at the Beaches, an old t-shirt and pair of jeans stand out in downtown Jacksonville. If you roam the streets during the day in anything other than office-appropriate attire, you will draw attention. Sally the Straw Hat stays in the truck. The attention she could draw my way might bring the police down around me in a matter of minutes.

William and I both climb out of the truck. Sally remains on the seat, and I go sans hat for the first time in a long time.

"I'll be back shortly," I say.

William nods as he puts coins into the parking meter.

The tinted glass of the bank's front door prevents me from seeing much of the interior. The door won't budge.

It's not the worst idea to keep your doors locked downtown. Every metropolitan area has its problems with the homeless, but, in Jacksonville, that problem stands out to a much higher degree. The number of people downtown in an average metropolitan city will overshadow the number of homeless people making a scene. In Jacksonville, the homeless can outnumber the employed on any sidewalk. This crapshoot adds to the general unease felt toward anyone in less than business casual attire.

A backlit button stands out on an intercom next to the door. I push the button. Nothing happens. No noise. No response. Instead of trying the button a second time, I knock.

A frail man arrives at the door. The man's polo shirt accentuates the thinness of his arms. He pushes the door open enough for the Florida sun to reveal the telltale look of a sleepless night. His glazed eyes blink slowly. There's a possibility this man might fall asleep standing up. His messy blonde hair and lack of a shave make it look as though he's been at the office all night.

"There's a buzzer to your left. It's a lot easier to hear."

He points to the intercom with the lighted button. It must not be loud if he didn't hear it the first time.

"It's shiny to boot."

"And how can I help you?" he asks.

"I'd like to speak to the man in charge."

"If you want to speak to Mr. Mahoney, then you'll have to schedule an appointment."

"I'd like to speak to the man next in line after Mahoney."

"Why?"

"I have some questions for him."

The thin man pulls a business card out of his pocket and hands it to me. The name on the card is Philip Blanchard.

"There's a contact number for the press on the bottom. Please call for an appointment."

"Are you Philip Blanchard?"

"Yes," he says before closing the door.

I push the buzzer on the intercom. Philip turns back around and, perturbed, opens the door.

"How else can I assist you?"

"Are you the man in charge when Paul Mahoney isn't here?"

"Yes. And I'm quite busy, so I must be going. If you would like to speak to Mr. Mahoney, please call the press number on my card. An appointment can be arranged."

Philip tries to close the door, but I grab the handle and pull it open, surprising him.

"It's gonna be hard for him to call me, seeing as he's dead."

Philip's jaw tightens; his eyes open wide. The gauntness of his face makes every tic all the more cartoonish.

"You found his car? When we called the police... I didn't think they'd be able to find it so quickly. They said it would take some time to track the car's GPS unit."

"I'm not with the police. I don't know if they've found his car."

"Who are you?"

"My name is Flynn Dupree."

My wallet is a mess of bills, receipts, and assorted debris. One of my business cards sticks out from within the folded corner of a burned photograph. Philip's tired eyes scan the card.

"You're a consultant? Is that like a private detective?"

"No. I'm a consultant performing an investigation."

"Then what's the difference?"

"Licensing."

"You're trying to track down Paul's car as well?"

"I'm investigating something independent from the missing car. Paul Mahoney died in an explosion last night."

"The thing at the beach?"

"You heard about it?"

"You were on the news."

"Yeah. I was in the parking lot when it happened."

"How did the police not know it was Paul?"

"According to an officer I spoke to last night, all the identification was missing."

"Come in," Philip says, locking the door behind us. "My office is over here. Sorry, I thought you were a reporter who caught wind of Paul going missing. As you can see, I've sent everyone home to ensure there aren't any leaks of his disappearance."

Philip escorts me across a high-ceilinged room full of unoccupied desks popping up like islands in an ocean. The building's age is in the air, which hangs thick with damp and dust. The sounds of work silenced, our footsteps clacking on the tile ricochet across the room. Once in his office, Philip takes a seat at his desk while I stay standing.

"Why was he there?" Philip asks.

"No idea. I was hoping you could tell me."

"I have a copy of his schedule. Nothing was on it for last night."

"Did he keep track of his infidelities?"

"No. Paul didn't have any. His life was squeaky clean. It made my job much easier."

"Do you have any idea why someone would want Mr. Mahoney dead?"

"Average voters liked Paul, but some businessmen and politicians strongly disliked him."

"Any reason why?"

"Paul wanted to clean up the city. In his mind, the only way to accomplish that was by digging through every elected official's past and present to unearth any interests conflicting with their duty to the people."

"He wanted a full investigation into everyone working for the city?"

Philip nods.

"But why kill him?" I ask. "He was with a hooker. If they had that on video, it would have been enough to ruin his political career."

"Knowing Paul, he wasn't there for sex. He was likely there for information."

"What information?"

"I have no idea."

"Paul said nothing to you about this? Not even an offhand comment?"

"Unfortunately, no."

"Does anyone stand out in your mind as a threat to Mr. Mahoney?"

"Lou Brombacher, Paul's primary competition for mayor. He's a shady man with plenty of well-hidden connections."

"Would he be willing to kill Paul?"

"No. But I know he's willing to be violent."

"How so?"

"We had a small dinner for our largest supporters recently. Some thugs showed up and tried to make a scene. We had to call the police. We couldn't prove it was Brombacher, but Paul and I both agreed it fell in line with his petty tactics."

"Did either of these thugs resemble the man on the cake?"

"I'm sorry. I haven't slept since last night after Mrs. Mahoney called me when Paul didn't come home. Did you just ask me about a man on a cake?"

"Oh, I thought you saw the news conference I held. A likeness of the bombing suspect was drawn on a cake."

"I caught a bit of it when they replayed it today. I don't remember cake being involved."

"Here," I say, pulling out Misty's phone. I bring up a picture she took of the cake and hand the phone to Philip.

Philip puts on a pair of glasses from his desk.

"Oh my," says Philip. "I know this man. His hair is a little different. It looks like Stephen Collins."

"Who is he?"

"My equivalent for Lou Brombacher."

"The second in command for your opponent?"

"He's his campaign manager. He used to be in charge of his personal security. When Brombacher decided to run for mayor, he promoted Stephen. It sounded like an odd choice back then. I've met him three, maybe four times. He's a pleasant man with a wife and a young son. I was surprised he worked for a man like Lou, but hey, in this economy, a job is a job."

"He's involved in the bombing."

"Are you certain?"

I nod.

"I suppose a bomb would make sense if he were involved," Philip says. "From what I've heard, he was a munitions guy, or whatever they call them, when he served in the Navy."

"Could you provide me with Lou Brombacher's address?"

"I have his campaign address if you'd like that?"

"Yes, please."

110

While Philip writes down the address, I pick up the business card I handed him earlier and write Misty's cell phone number on the back of the card. We exchange the phone number for the address.

"I'm really sorry for your loss. I'd prefer it if you didn't tell anyone we spoke. Call me at that number if you can think of anything else."

Philip remains seated at his desk, dazed.

Chapter 20

Flynn

William parks his truck outside of a renovated jewelry store. The small window display cases that used to show off their wares now have pictures of a man smiling in front of an American flag. I don't bother looking at the address Philip gave me to confirm if we've arrived at the right location, as a banner above the two glass doors reads, "A Vote for Lou is A Vote for You. Vote Brombacher."

"Be back in a few," I tell William before exiting the truck.

The glass doors refuse to budge when I pull on their handles. The doors emit a buzzing sound and open without a hitch when I try again. Unlike the empty bank, here the desks are full, the copiers are copying, and the phones are ringing. What stands out most is the staff of ladies under twenty-five. Every single one of them wears an outfit stretching the boundaries of business casual to the limits.

"Sir," says a gorgeous dark-haired woman with a Germanic-sounding accent. "How can I help you today?"

The distractions kept my eyes elsewhere, so it's impossible to say how long she stood there before grabbing my attention.

"Sorry," I point around the room, "scenery. I'm here to speak with Lou Brombacher."

"Mr. Brombacher is busy."

"Is he here?"

"Yes—" She stops herself, looking frustrated. "How can I help you today?"

"I need to speak with Lou Brombacher."

"He's busy."

"Yeah. You said that. I need to speak to him. Let him know a man with some juicy information about Paul Mahoney feels like talking."

"Please sit." The woman points to a chair alongside a desk. Another woman in her early twenties sits at the desk, typing away on a laptop. I smile when she looks up at me and then continue watching all the other women go about their work. The typing stops as I ponder the good and bad of hiring an executive assistant of this caliber for my business.

"I'd recommend not even thinking about it."

"Hmm. You can read my mind?"

"No need in this place. Any man who walks in will think the same. Believe me. You want nothing to do with them."

"How about you?"

"That's cute. I bet you got a pickup line to go with that. Go ahead. I've heard them all."

"I'm not a pickup line kind of guy. But you could do me a favor and tell me the worst one you've heard. That way, if I become a pickup line kind of guy, then I have a baseline."

She looks around and makes sure no one is too close.

"Some fool told me he was as thick as a brick."

"Here in the office?"

"No. At my father's club. I bartend there."

"Really?"

"It's funny because I thought he was making a joke. So I said, 'You must like flute solos.' He didn't laugh."

"Wow. That's the first time I've heard a Jethro Tull joke. Kudos on going one step further and hitting it with a saucy dash of masturbatory humor."

"Thank you."

"You're a fan?"

She shoots me a sideways look.

"I meant of Tull," I say, coughing. "Not… you know."

"Yeah," she says, smiling. "I know. Anyway, I'm a fan of all kinds of music. My mother brought my brother and me up right. I play the piano when I'm not otherwise indisposed."

"My name's Flynn."

"Nice to meet you, Flynn."

"No name?"

"I'm not a big fan of giving out my name. I usually tell people asking for it that my name is a two-letter word expressing perfection. If they get it, I'll talk to them."

"Nice to meet you, Emma. You expect a lot of people to be Jane Austen fans?"

"You got it."

"My mother is big on music like yours. My father made me read and reread the classics."

"My father gave me a hundred bucks for every book I read over a hundred pages."

"Really?" A hint of jealousy raises the pitch of my voice. I can't help but wonder how much I would have read if my father provided monetary incentives.

"He'd sit down with me while I told him everything I remembered about the book. Once satisfied that I had actually read it, he'd give me the money."

"Must've been nice to have that money as a kid."

"I saved it. That book money bought my condo."

"If I ask you to marry me, is that too forward?"

"So that's your pickup line?"

"That's my inner monologue escaping."

"That's tempting, Flynn, but I have to get back to work."

"Type away, Emma. Let that proposal mull."

"Don't worry. It's mulling."

"Type and mull. Type and mull."

The woman with the accent reappears from behind a door with a man, the only man I've seen since entering the 'Brombacher Election Headquarters,' which I'm just now seeing painted in big red, white, and blue letters on the wall. This man is in his fifties with graying hair slicked back. His pinstriped suit and wingtips make him the perfect Scorsese flick extra. The gangster look-alike dismisses the woman escorting him and beelines it to me.

"The name's Lou," he says, his hand outstretched. Lou is wearing enough gold to make a conquistador jealous. The rings on his fingers, the bracelet on his right wrist, the watch on his left, the tie pin with diamonds, and the chain around his neck all make me wonder if he tells his dentist that silver amalgam is not good enough for his fillings.

114

"Flynn Dupree," I say, standing up and shaking Lou's hand. "Nice watch, Lou."

"Thanks." Lou looks down at his watch and does not debate its quality. "I hear you have some information for me."

"Yes. Can we speak in your office?"

"Right this way," Lou says, placing his left hand on my back and pointing to a door with his right.

When we enter the office, Lou points to a chair. I take a seat. Lou sits down on top of his desk and hands me three letters.

"Just a quick opinion on these if you don't mind. My right-hand man has been incommunicado for the past two days. I'm firing him. He handles this sort of thing, so I'm not sure which to give him."

The penmanship borders on art. This quality of handwriting is rare and resembles old documents kept in the National Archive in D.C. or the Karpeles Museum in downtown Jacksonville.

"You wrote these?"

"Yeah."

"You have beautiful penmanship."

"I like a personal touch, you know. I'm that kinda guy. It's wrong to send someone an email or a text telling them they're fired."

The first letter details the time missed from work as the principal reason for Stephen's termination. The second uses apologetic language to inform Stephen his services are no longer necessary. The third simply says, "I am so sorry."

All three letters show that Lou Brombacher either has no idea where Stephen Collins might be, or he's trying his best to keep up appearances.

"I like the second one," I say with a smile.

"You said this Stephen didn't come in for two days straight. Is this Stephen Collins?"

Brombacher reaches over to a picture frame on his desk and hands it to me. The picture is from a golf tournament. Brombacher is shaking the hand of an austere gentleman holding a trophy, while the man I know as Harold stands at his side with a giant novelty check.

"There he is," Brombacher says, pointing to Harold in the picture. "I've been trying to call him for days. He's the reason I'm here now. I'd rather be out courting new constituents, if you catch my drift."

"If you mean what I think you mean, you don't have to travel far. Where did you find them?"

"An old friend has a temp business. He sends me the cream of the crop when they apply."

"There's a nice friend."

"It's good to have friends. All right. All right. Enough chat. I was told you have some information about Paul Mahoney."

"What I'm wondering is how much you're willing to provide me for this juicy bit of a tid?"

"Anybody ever tell you you're a bit of an odd duck? You're a little spastic and—"

"Yeah. I suffered some brain damage as a teenager."

"Sorry. Meant nothing by it."

"No one to blame but genetics and copper. How much are you willing to pay for information?"

"Right now, nothing."

"Gonna need you to raise your offer."

"Five bucks."

I take out one of my business cards and scrawl Misty's cell phone number on the back.

"Call me when you're serious."

I turn around to leave. Lou grabs my arm.

"Come on. You can't just leave like that. What do you expect me to do, write you a check? That's not how these things work."

"How do these things work then?"

"You gonna vote for me?"

"Why is that relevant?"

"It's preferable to be among friends."

"You're running preference is Republican, right?"

"Is that a problem?"

Lou's party affiliation covers the office walls. A variety of posters plastered haphazardly feature Lou Brombacher's face with the color red and the word 'conservative.'

"I'm just not that political. It's like a geriatric circle jerk. Wait— Scratch that. Let's go the other way. Politicians are infants swaddled in the American flag. They laugh. They cry. They shit themselves. Other than that, they do little else."

116

"That's what you think?"

"Yeah. It is worse being a voter. That's like whispering into a toilet and wondering why the plumber can't hear you."

"Come on. Voting is your civic duty."

"So is paying taxes. And I doubt anyone has ever sent the IRS a thank you note that wasn't full of a mysterious powder."

"Voting doesn't cost you anything."

"It costs us a lot. People hate each other for nothing. And politicians foist their bullshit on everyone under the guise of patriotism. Don't get me wrong, patriotism is great. Loving your country is great. But politicians aren't patriotic. They're nationalistic. They don't want a better country or a country others can look up to. They want to dig in their heels and say that America is better than everyone else. They think America doesn't need to change because America is too good to change. And that's dangerous, plain and simple. It's a foundation of bigotry, and I don't want to be a part of it."

"If you'd like some literature, you'll find out I'm not just about party lines."

"Just to confirm, you disapprove of gay marriage?"

The wheels in Brombacher's head are turning. He has to decide where I stand on the issue.

"I," he says with hesitation, "believe that marriage is a sacred bond between one man and one woman."

"Fair enough."

"You agree with me?"

"No. But I'm happy to know you believe in something."

"I don't believe in party lines. I believe in beliefs."

Lou Brombacher has a ring on his ring finger. There's a picture of him with a woman his age next to the phone. She pops up three more times in photos throughout the office.

"How many of the beautiful ladies sitting outside have you involved in this sacred bond with permission from your wife?"

"I never said I was a good Christian man. I said I didn't vote along party lines."

"There's nothing quite like a man who understands his weaknesses."

"Well, I appreciate your honesty. It's not what I'd like to hear... It's refreshing."

"All this political talk has given me an idea for a campaign ad. You're in a Technicolor dreamcoat—something flashy, but not too gaudy. 'Goodbye Horses' starts playing. The coat comes off. You dance like Ted Levine in *Silence of the Lambs*. Don't worry, a sign saying 'Believes in Beliefs' is covering what naughty bits aren't tucked away. You say to the camera, 'Would you vote for me? I'd vote for me. I'd vote for me hard.' You can then change your slogan from 'A vote for Lou is a vote for you' to 'It puts the ballot in the box.'"

"You're a funny guy."

"Thanks."

"Do you have information on Paul Mahoney, Funnyman Flynn, or are you just wasting my time?"

"If you're done trying to sell me on voting for you, then maybe you should start trying to buy my information."

Brombacher pulls out a gold money clip and counts out five kite flyers, placing them next to him on the desk.

I reach for the money.

"No, no," Brombacher says, stopping me from reaching. "First, I get a taste."

"A taste? Did we just step into an eighties movie?"

"You're a prodder, right?"

"I'm not sure what you mean. I'm not opposed to Prada, but I can't even afford Cole Haan."

"No, prod-der."

"Oh yeah. I'm definitely one of those."

I need to tell Brombacher the truth and see his reaction. How he reacts to finding out that Paul Mahoney died while in a motel with a hooker will tell me more than asking any question could.

"Fine," I say. "Paul Mahoney was in a motel at the beach with a prostitute last night."

"Oh, my," Brombacher says, his face lighting up. "This is wonderful. The election isn't until March, but this'll bury him long before then. Here you go, my friend." Brombacher hands me the five kite flyers.

"You're right. He will be buried long before March."

Brombacher laughs. "You have more? Pictures? A testimonial? What?"

I stay silent.

118

Brombacher pulls a bottle and two glasses from his desk drawer. He pours about two ounces of amber liquid into each glass.

"Drink," he demands, handing me a glass.

"Scotch?" I ask, smelling the glass. It has a peaty scent with a hint of charred oak.

"Single malt. Only thing I drink."

Brombacher takes a sip of his drink. I follow suit. He pulls two more kite flyers from his money clip, knocks back the rest of his scotch, and hands me the cash.

"Thank you," I say, putting the money in my pocket. "Mahoney died in the motel room."

Brombacher laughs hysterically and chokes out a sentence through the laughter. "The man finally goes and gets himself a hooker and then dies 'cause his ticker couldn't handle it."

Brombacher continues laughing. It's becoming clear he has nothing to do with Paul Mahoney's death. A man involved would play it much closer to the vest and not make an absolute ass of himself by being this overjoyed. It's time to release the most crucial piece of information I possess.

Brombacher points at me and holds up another two kite flyers. "You have something else, don't you?"

I nod and take the money.

"Mahoney didn't die from a heart attack. He was blown up by your soon-to-be-former campaign manager."

"What?" Brombacher asks, suddenly serious.

"Stephen Collins killed Paul Mahoney with a bomb."

The news stuns Lou. He looks down at the three dismissal letters and stands up from his desk. He stumbles into his chair and takes a seat. Brombacher places the letters on the desk and then puts his face in his hands before pulling them back through his slick hair.

"Why on earth would Stephen do that?"

"You tell me."

"I don't know."

"You can't think of any reason that your subordinate would kill your chief competition?"

"No, I cannot. And I do not like your insinuations. I run a tight ship. I may pay a person here or there to disrupt this or that, but I would never harm the man."

"You just spent a solid minute laughing about Paul's death."

"No. I was laughing about how he died. The prostitute was funny. A bomb is… less so."

"I'm glad you find bombs less humorous. Stephen tried to blow me up as well."

"Why would he try to kill you?"

"To tie up loose ends. You're going to tell me where Stephen lives and where he could be hiding, or I will go to the press and tell them you were behind this."

"All right," Brombacher says, reaching into his desk to pull out a Rolodex. The address tech is retro but fitting. "Hmmm…"

"What's that?"

"What's what?"

"That sound you made. Is something off?"

"No. Someone else opened my Rolodex."

"How can you tell?"

"It's open to a man I haven't spoken to for a while."

"You sure you didn't just forget where you left it open?"

"Stephen's information should be on top. I opened it before I left yesterday to make sure I had his address in my records."

"Can I see it?"

Brombacher pulls out a card from the Rolodex and hands it to me. The information is all handwritten. The name on the card is Joseph Prince. I pull out a pen and a small notebook from my pocket and write the name, phone number, and address before returning the card.

Brombacher places the card back into the Rolodex and searches for Stephen's information. He pulls out another card and hands it to me. I copy Stephen's home phone number and address into my notebook.

"Any idea where else he might be?"

"No. He keeps to himself. When the rest of us go out for a drink, he goes home to be with his wife and kid. I just, for the life of me, do not understand what he was thinking. Are you planning on releasing this information to the press?"

"Nope," I say, shifting in my chair. "But they will find out sooner or later."

"Vultures always find a carcass to nip at."

"Do you have any idea where Stephen might have disappeared to?"

"None."

"Any family or friends that live nearby?"

"No idea."

I laugh and finish my glass of Scotch.

"What's so funny?"

"You're hiding something."

"I have no idea what you are talking about."

"See, that's it right there. The way you speak changes depending on the questions I ask. You take more time to answer and lose the contractions."

"What does that have to do with anything?"

"You remember *Schoolhouse Rock*?"

Brombacher looks puzzled.

"Contraction faction, what's your action?" I'm not singing so much as speaking playfully to the bewildered mobster wannabe who's becoming angrier by the second. "Pinpointing liars and tellers of truths."

"What?"

"Sorry, I tried to do a play there on 'Conjunction Junction.' It was spur of the moment and didn't work as well as I thought it might."

"You think I'm lying because I'm not using contractions?"

"Oh, so it worked. Also, you used two there, so it makes it odd when you don't use any. You see, people who think too hard are typically lying. The extra time and conscientious use of language can indicate that someone is fabricating the truth. It could also indicate that you're nervous or well-trained in responding, which is something I might expect from a politician."

"What you're saying is that it means nothing?"

"Pretty much. I wanted to see how you'd react."

"How'd I do?"

"I'd say you have something to hide or protect. Then again, so does everybody else in the world." I stand up from my chair. Brombacher looks at me with a sneer. There's no point in trying to get any more information out of him. If I was a cop, and this was an official interview,

Brombacher would be at the point where he'd refuse to speak until his lawyer shows up. "No need to get up. I can find my way out. Also, make sure you don't tell anyone you ever saw me."

"Ditto," Brombacher says, leaning back in his chair and not bothering to follow me out.

Chapter 21

William

Flynn opens the passenger door of my truck and scares the hell out of me.

"Were you sleeping?" Flynn asks.

"Nah," I reply, wiping my forehead. "All these people, I'm just not used to it. I like our quiet street."

"Me too."

"How'd it go?"

Flynn hands me a small notebook opened to a page with the name Stephen Collins and a familiar address. I stare at the street name and then lay my head back on the headrest. I close my eyes to visualize where I've seen this address before. There were children in the yard while I worked. The family had three children of their own and two foster children. Their house looked out onto the marsh. The smell bothered me. It made me miss the clean smell of the ocean. That terrible smell of sweet decay overpowers everything.

"This is the address of the guy who tried to blow me up."

I open my eyes and turn to Flynn.

"I know where this is. It's off Penman near the marsh."

"You know the house?"

"No. I know the area. I used to have some clients back there. Nice places. Older with great trees."

"Do you mind driving by and pointing it out to me?"

"Sure thing."

I head over the Mathews Bridge and make my way back toward the beach. Flynn looks nervous when we go over the bridge, but calms down once we reach solid ground. The second bridge is over the ditch, which means we're close. A slow drive down Penman helps establish my bearings. My internal compass points us in the right direction. Stephen

Collins lives on one of the back roads off of Penman. It's a bit of a maze, but I find the simple two-story home Flynn wanted. The yard needs an afternoon of rain, and trimming the shrubs near the house would allow more light to come in through the windows. That's the meticulous William coming to the surface.

Flynn motions for me to speed up.

"Keep driving. Just go slowly."

"Don't you want to go up there?"

"Not yet. I've seen enough," Flynn says, turning to me. "Could you take me to Diggity?"

"You want to go drinking?"

"I always go there on Tuesdays. There'll be trivia and darts if you're interested."

"I'll pass."

I'm tired and could use some relaxation time in my back yard looking out at the ocean.

Chapter 22

Flynn

Haute Diggity is a modern bar within a piece of the beach from the seventies. Weathered and sun-scorched, the stucco facade has seen better days. The front door is a collection of wood planks thick enough to fend off a battering ram. Someone, somewhere covered the wood in successive coats of varnish until the grain became indiscernible. The heavy door connects to a weight via a pulley system that ensures it closes on its own. One of my college roommates, Henry Cooper, owns the bar. It specializes in craft beer and designer hot dogs. I'm here often, rarely missing a Tuesday night. Henry takes time off to throw darts and play their Tuesday trivia game. Our other college roommate, Robert Beednow, completes the team.

The fact that I show up to Haute Diggity every Tuesday might bother me if I paid with a debit or credit card, but I've always paid my bill in cash when Henry doesn't comp me. I'm not a fan of plastic. Something about everyone being able to follow a trail of money bothers me. Ironically, my distrust of financial institutions pays back dividends in the long run. With confidence oozing from my pores, I stroll across the wooden floors, confident the police aren't waiting for me.

Robert is alone at a high top table near the dartboard. He finishes the last of his beer and then waves at the bar in a desperate plea for another.

"Bee," I say, tapping my watch. Bee is a nickname Henry and I gave Robert back in college. We've always told him it's just a play on his name, but it's also because he enjoys riding the line between annoying and hilarious. Sometimes, all you hear from Robert is 'Buzz, buzz, buzz.'

"It's not even five yet. I thought for sure I'd beat you here."

"Market hours, bitches," Bee shouts, following the outburst with a quick dance involving his fists punching up into the air. The dancing stops with a double take. "No hat?"

125

"No hat."

"Damn." Bee leans in for a better look at my head. "I owe Henry five bucks."

"Really?"

"We haven't seen the top of your head in a while. I bet him you were going bald."

Robert Beednow is a hard man to avoid. His rotund form and love of drawing attention fuels his nights spent drinking after hours of sitting at a desk for a financial advising and analysis firm. Most people look at him and see a man lacking control. Bee's company sees his analytical mind and overlooks his eccentricities.

Tuesday trivia starts at seven and lasts for about two hours. We show up early and play darts at the bar's single dartboard. I take a seat next to Bee at the high top table and watch a group of four people as they finish a game of cricket. After the last bullseye, the couple on the winning team erases the chalkboard to start another game.

"What the fuck?" Bee shouts.

"Bee, calm down. So what if they're playing again?"

"I'll tell you what. I've been here for what seems like an eternity, waiting for them to stop playing. I asked if I could have the board next, and they agreed. You don't just back out of an agreement. A verbal contract holds up in the state of Florida."

"You've done a lot of research into darts law?"

"Don't go being a smartass. That's our board. And if this were taken to court, the judge would tell them to go fuck their face, their couch, and their mother. In that order."

"Bee, calm down. We've got a while till trivia starts. They'll get tired of playing. When that happens, we'll grab the board."

"Don't worry. I got this. You get me another beer." Bee walks over and asks the man on the winning team, a man no older than twenty-one with long, curling sideburns, "How much longer are you guys gonna be on the board?"

"We're done when we're done," the man with the sideburns says with a smirk.

"Yeah, well, that's not what ya said last time I asked."

"I changed my mind," he says, looking back at his girlfriend and the other couple. All of them look uncomfortable with the large, angry Bee standing nearby.

Bee's initial intimidation tactic involves his right index finger making the trip from the edge of his mouth to the bottom of his chin over and over again. The intent must be to draw attention to his goatee, which rises to his lips like the tines of a trident. During the intense caressing, Bee stares at the entire group like they just walked into his house without being invited.

"Well, here's hoping you tire yourself out after this game, 'cause otherwise I'm gonna get all up close and personal on you with some man dancing. And if you've never been ground on by a heavy man with little to no boundaries, then you're in for a whole new world of hot and unpleasant sexy." Bee moonwalks backward three steps, licks his fingers, and makes a hissing noise as he places them on his shirt where his nipples would be. "You ever had a man get all kinds of intimate with your leg before? Lucky for you, I'm wearing boxers today, so my grapes'll be like doorknockers on your knee."

"Fine," says curly sideburns. "We wanna play one more game. Then the board is yours."

"See, I don't believe you because that's what you said last time. And right now, you're the smoothie, and I'm the banana," Bee says, thrusting toward curly sideburns. "You're the smoothie, and I'm the banana. You're the smoothie, and I'm the banana. Do you get my drift?"

"No," he says, looking confused.

"He's doing the soup and noodle thing again?" a deep voice asks, drawing my attention. Henry Cooper takes a seat at the high top.

"No," I say. "He switched it up to smoothie and banana."

"That's weird." Henry pauses and looks at my head. "No hat?"

"No hat."

"Bee owes me five bucks."

"I heard."

"I'll add it to his tab."

Henry and Robert were my college roommates back when I attended the University of North Florida. While both Henry and Robert graduated with finance degrees, only Robert works in the corporate world. Henry worked as a cook in a restaurant during college and then started a small

127

catering company after he graduated. It took close to two years, but he saved up enough money to open Haute Diggity. Along the way, the catering business sparked an interest in the movie industry after Henry provided food for some local artists putting together films. Now he runs Haute Diggity and works on movie projects with the remainder of his time.

It's become standard to see Henry in some form of altered appearance. In the past few weeks, he's been experimenting with makeup and fake mustaches to boost his skills for future projects. He won't say where he learned how to paint his face. After hours of speculation, Bee and I came to the conclusion that he secretly went to clown college and double majored in face painting and juggling. The juggling part is an assumption based on how he maintained his regular life and kept the clown college hidden so effectively. According to Henry, the discovery was out of necessity; being his own makeup artist saves money that can then invest in other areas of his films. Today, he's wearing zombie movie makeup. Makeup caked on the left half of Henry's face provides him with a death mask look. The scars and sores of a budding zombie cover the right half. A neutral zone exists above his lips where he's applied a fake mustache.

"You missed the moonwalking."

"That sucks," Henry says, waving at the bar to bring someone over to our table.

"Nice 'stache," I say.

Henry nods. The mustache is thin and looks like something you might find on a dashing movie star filmed in black and white.

The partner of curly sideburns, a tan woman who speaks with her hands, grabs his shirt. "We'll be done after this game. I promise."

"Then we've reached an accord," Bee says, his arms outstretched. "Ho-ly shit!" Bee shouts. "Henry Mother Fucking Cooper!"

"How's it going, Bee?"

"Not too bad. I've got a joke for you," Bee says to Henry as he sits down.

"Does it involve a black man walking into a bar?"

"You know it does. It's how I announce your presence."

"I'd prefer a 'ladies and gentlemen.'"

"Ladies and gentlemen, Henry Cooper," Bee shouts while clapping his hands.

128

"That's better."

Henry is almost a head taller than Bee but still puts up with his ribbing. His ability to stay calm and collected is legendary. The only time anyone has ever seen Henry the least bit riled up was during a UFC fight where George St. Pierre nearly ended up being knocked out.

"What the fuck?" Bee asks, looking at the table with confusion. "You didn't get me a beer while I was handling business?"

"The waitress hasn't come back yet," I say with a shrug.

"You are literally three feet from the fucking bar."

"Yeah, and we're at a table with a waitress. If we aren't ordering from her, then we're costing her money being here."

Henry nods.

"Don't worry about it. We won't be here much longer. The board'll open up in about ten minutes thanks to my superior negotiating skills."

"I enjoyed watching you use those smooth negotiating skills," I say. "Well done."

"I'd prefer it if you don't rub up on my customers," Henry says.

"People show respect to 'The Doorknocker.'"

'The Doorknocker' is a dance in Henry's series of YouTube videos, *When White People Dance.* It involves thrusting awkwardly while fully clothed and in close proximity to someone. If given a chance, Bee will go on a fifteen-minute rant about how he was the inspiration for the dance. Not wanting to endure another lengthy explanation, I'm tempted to snap my tongue to indicate a change in the subject.

"It looked like you half-raped the guy's leg," Henry says.

"It's better than a full-rape of his leg."

"How about neither?"

"How about I shout 'Spring break!' before I do it. That way, they should half-expect a full-rape."

Henry shakes his head and looks back at the bar. There's no way to win an argument with Bee. It's best to move on. I take the initiative and change the subject.

"Have either of you watched the news lately?"

Henry shrugs his shoulders.

"Local? No," Bee says. "Financial? Yes."

"Oh. Never mind."

When the waitress shows up, all three of us order beer. I haven't eaten, so I order a 'Fish in the Garden,' which is a fish hotdog with homemade kimchi on top. The beers show up fast, and we drink in silence, waiting for the people on the dartboard to finish their game. It's clear to me that the couples playing are awful at darts. It takes several minutes for them to close out each number and then slows to a standstill when the bullseye is all that remains.

The pain of watching the terrible darts puts my head on a swivel. The bar is empty. No one other than the bartender is there to catch my eye. Overhead lights hit the Ben Franklin quote on the wall. The metallic letters shine "Beer is proof that God loves us and wants us to be happy" upside down on the wooden floor. A trio of broskies with their hats askew walk in and remind me I'm without Mordecai. It's a shame I left Sally the Straw Hat in William's truck. She would have made an interesting topic of discussion. Instead, I start a different conversation to distract from the dartboard.

"Would either of you ever sleep with a prostitute?"

Henry shakes his head.

"Pay for one or just have sex with one?" Bee asks.

"If given the opportunity, would you have sex with someone who works as a hooker?"

"I'm guessing this would be a freebie. If so, yes—depending on the whole cleanliness factor."

"She looks clean."

"Damn. You know a hooker?"

"I met one through work. It's strange because I've never met one until now."

"You're right. Working in Ponte Vedra, I've met plenty of women who will fuck a guy for his money. But none that I'd officially call a hooker. Is she hot?"

"She'd fall in that category if I didn't know what she did to make money."

"Done deal. I say do it."

"There's no chance of me getting back into her good graces."

"What did you do?"

"Nearly got her blown up."

Henry raises an eyebrow but remains quiet.

130

Bee's hysterical fit of laughter rolls through the bar. "You are shittin' me!"

"Nope."

"That is one big ass hurdle."

The man with the curly sideburns approaches our table.

"We're all done."

"About damn time," Bee says, walking over to the dartboard as fast as his legs will carry him.

"Thanks," I say to curly sideburns, adding a nod and a smile for good measure.

Chapter 23

William

The garage door opens. Something's not right. The door leading into my house is open. My memory is getting fuzzy in my old age, but I clearly remember Flynn shutting the door before we left earlier in the day.

"Dammit, William. What's going on?" My brother James is lying on the ground, unable to move.

"Did you see anything?" I ask James.

"I did," Lily replies. "Someone was here."

"Are they still inside?"

"I don't know."

I help James to his feet and place him back where he belongs. Then I grab the fourteenth shovel, the clean one, off of the wall before closing the garage door.

"Everyone, stay here and be quiet."

The light switch for my kitchen is right next to the door leading inside. I turn on the lights and enter, ready to swing at anything that moves.

Nothing moves. It's clear someone was here. The kitchen cabinets are open. Several broken dishes and glasses litter the ground. The living room has chairs knocked over, and the wall is spray-painted. 'U WILL PAY' stands out in big black letters that still smell like fresh paint. The sliding glass door leading from the living room to my back yard is wide open. There's no damage to the door except for a spot of black paint on the interior handle. Little swirls in the paint tell me someone forgot to wear gloves and now has stained hands. The only way spray paint comes off is with paint thinner or time.

My house only has one bedroom and two bathrooms. It's easy to check and make sure no one is hiding. The intruder pushed in the screen on the window in my bedroom. I leave windows open all the time. I'm so rarely not in my house, that when I'm out, even for as long as I was today, an open window doesn't keep me worrying.

The real questions are: Who will make me pay? And for what?

I've done things that would inspire revenge. No one is perfect, but I am careful. People don't know who I am or what I've done. I'm confident in that.

It's hard to remember the last time someone got angry at me. I had some words with a cashier when she rang me up twice for the same loaf of bread. I know she didn't get angry enough to follow me home and break into my house. But that silly idea of following someone makes my head tingle.

Flynn told me he was mugged on the beach last night. He turned it around on the robber and took his wallet. That's something worth getting even over. Last night, the moon was bright enough for someone to follow another person at a distance. Flynn is smart and quick on his feet, but he's not always careful. If the man followed Flynn, he led him to my back door.

The only positive of this fiasco is that I should still have his wallet. Flynn threw it in the trash before we left. In the kitchen, shards of glass and plates cover the linoleum. The trash can sits where it was earlier, the lid still on. Pushing the foot lever opens it up. I can't see the wallet. There are some plate scrapings and plastic bags and some rotting vegetables. I move the trash around, searching with my hands until I feel something hard. It's the wallet.

The driver's license inside belongs to Durrell Span. An odd name. Or at least it sounds odd. There was a time when parents only named their children after family or famous people. Nowadays, that's not enough. It seems like everyone has to make their names more original than they actually are. Instead of Darrell, this kid is named Durrell. And if he is the man who invaded my home, then there's little chance he will name a child of his own.

Durrell is not my type. The man is in his thirties and robbing people for a living. He's even dumb enough to break into my house while the police are watching the house right next door. Someone is bound to do the world a favor and kill him during one of his robberies. But he came into my home and left a mess. I can't even be sure what sort of irreparable harm he did to my family until I examine each one.

133

For now, I have to meet this Durrell. The address on his driver's license is only five minutes away. The street he lives on is behind a liquor store off Atlantic. I'm not planning to hurt him in his own home. The apartments in that area are too close together.

My favorite pair of leather gloves is in the bedroom closet. Thin and made of softened deerskin with a pebbled palm, the gloves are perfect for jobs requiring a soft touch. They've served me well for the last thirty years. The gloves slip on my hands like neither of us has aged a day in three decades. Their buttery feel reminds me of days long gone.

In the kitchen, I grab the essentials: a beer from the fridge and some rubber bands and a black permanent marker from the junk drawer. I towel off the beer while entering the garage.

As the garage door opens, I inspect my family for damage. James lost bits of dried dirt when he fell. It doesn't look like Durrell disturbed anyone else. I drop the supplies onto my truck's passenger seat before checking the mail. I take the three pieces of junk mail and leave the credit card statement in the mailbox.

It's a quick drive to Durrell's. I'm not even leaving Atlantic Beach. The acting bug in me takes over when I park down the road from the address on Durrell's license. It's an entire row of rundown townhome apartments. I leave my gloves behind and walk up to the door. There's a bay window in the front of the apartment, providing the perfect view of a man in another room watching a big-screen TV.

I don't see a doorbell, so I bang on the door.

"Baby, shut the fuck up!" I can hear a muffled voice shout from behind the door. "I'll be back in a minute. Someone's at the door."

The locks turn. It's time to act.

The man on the driver's license opens the door. The first thing I do is look for his hands. Durrell's left hand hides behind the door where he's holding the doorknob, and his right is on the doorframe. His right hand looks dirty. It could be black paint residue. It could also be a lot of other things. Spray paint is a bitch to get off, and this man may have a small amount where I need it to be. That's enough for me to push forward with my plan.

"What the fuck do you want?" the man asks. A cut on his cheek stands out like a bright red smile on his pale skin.

134

"I'm a pastor that's gonna be opening up a new church right around the corner. We have a small congregation and are looking for—"

"Are you fucking serious?" Durrell asks. "You're interrupting dinner with my girl for this?"

"You're telling me your stomach is more important than your soul?"

"Yes."

"You should pray for the Lord's mercy."

"Dear Lord," he says, putting his hands together and revealing his left hand has paint stains on the tips of his fingers, "please remove your penis from my ass. And by that, I mean this fuck from my door." Durrell leans out close to my face. Veins throb in his neck. I want to grab his throat and squeeze. He says, "Go to hell."

Durrell leans back to close the door in my face. "You first," I say, relishing my response.

The closing door opens a window, providing me an unexpected opportunity. It's not in my wheelhouse, but exceptions are a part of life.

Back in the truck, I put on my gloves and drive down the street into the liquor store parking lot. The three pieces of junk mail lack identifying marks on the interior and exterior. A generic insurance company blanketed the entire area with advertising. They provided the perfect envelope addressed to 'Dear Future Client' with enough space for me to add a note.

Dear Durrell,
This is the first of many. Payback is a bitch.
XOXO
The Man Who Stole Your Wallet

The beer can's condensation holds the envelope in place while I secure it with a rubber band.

Circling the block, I slow to a stop at Durrell's. No one is around. The timing is perfect. I get out of my truck and hurl the can of beer at the bay window. The can breaks through the window and slams into the wall, exploding upon impact. A geyser of foam shoots all over the room. There's no time to savor Durrell's reaction. I climb into my truck and drive off.

The message sent, Durrell will come after Flynn. Instead, he will find me.

Chapter 24

Flynn

My night at Haute Diggity ends early. Despite Bee's protestations and appeals for one more round, eleven feels like the right time to get gone. We all exchange a hearty goodnight, and I leave heading north on First Street. The lack of a police presence surprises me. Police officers normally patrol the streets outside of the beach bars, waiting for people to screw up enough to prompt their involvement. The police are busy elsewhere tonight, possibly looking for me. Such an honor makes me smile until the guilt overwhelms me. There is a chance someone ends up hurt at a beach bar because the police aren't there to keep order.

All I wanted was to distract the cops assigned to look for me, not have others pulled from their duties and added to the search. That isn't part of the plan. Then again, I'm not the best at making plans. I can't even keep a calendar organized for more than an afternoon. Plans can be essential. The problem with planning is that spontaneity is sacrificed on a concrete base. Even notes on paper feel oppressive. A general idea of what to expect at the goal line is all that's necessary. Finding Stephen Collins is the goal. The rest of the plan is like a nebulous cloud dampening the surrounding air. It's blurry, ill-formed, a wee bit questionable, but it's keeping up and in a constant state of wondrous change.

According to Doctor Leah, people find comfort in plans. She didn't specifically refer to it as a plan. She called it control. It's essentially the same thing. A plan is an attempt to exercise control of both the present and the future. If some find comfort in control, others find comfort in chaos. Every positive has a negative. For every yang, there is a yin. And that makes me a yin. Personally, I'm far more comfortable yinning it up.

Order has its place. It's simply not as normal as people want to believe. Life wears khakis and pretends to be bland. It's not. There's an unlikelihood to life that we ignore. Trillions upon trillions upon trillions upon trillions—let's just say lots of factors over billions of years have led to our species. Our existence is a mathematical improbability. Our lives are a gift from chaos. We're a flash of light—an anomaly of atomic arrangement. Leah was right. Chaos makes us feel small. Because we are. Order is not the norm. Order is a way to inflate our sense of self. We individualize and structure our lives one piece at a time, feigning control, navigating the chaos, building ourselves up to escape the inevitability that one day time will run out and control will disappear.

This only matters because I know my plan, as nebulous as it may be, is subject to countless things going wrong. I wouldn't say I'm navigating chaos, merely limiting its reach. It's the same thing except my way has the possibility of chaos having arm tats.

The next tangible step is to borrow Misty's car and head to the home of Stephen Collins. This can change. Anything could happen. Narrowing my options limits the possibilities. As I see it, two specific problems could surface and force me to reevaluate.

Problem number one. Misty has two cars: one for general use and another for deliveries. I spend several hours a week helping Misty with deliveries. The only payment I've received is a key for the hearse. The hearse is a useful advertising tool. That's why it sits outside of the bakery with its electronic billboards running all night. Some days, Misty picks up necessary supplies in the morning. If this is the case, her car for general use will be at the bakery. I don't have a key for that car.

Problem number two. The trick I played on Leah could backfire. The goal was Leah reporting my crazed outburst to the police. If this occurred, it should thin the police coverage on my family and friends. The time at Leah's office felt well spent, but I have no idea if it worked. The lack of police outside Haute Diggity could be for a different reason. Or Leah reported what I said, and the police increased the number of officers waiting outside of my home, my mother's condo, and other places I might frequent both day and night. Hopefully, the water is muddier, and the police aren't spending their time watching an empty bakery all night when they could be out trying to find me eating a steak dinner or buying cigarettes.

If these problems pop up, I know that the plan I have is malleable enough to form new permutations.

Atlantic Boulevard is dead on weeknights. I keep to the sidewalk opposite the bakery. There's no rush in my step or concern in my mannerisms. My head stays forward even as Seminole Boulevard comes into view. Misty's hearse is in the parking lot. The billboards flash the same information from the previous night. The pulsing red light is creepy at night. It lends the parking lot the allure of an unsavory hotel. My steady walking continues past the bakery. The stoplight at Penman, the first light after Misty's bakery, is where I cross the street into the old Pic 'n Save parking lot. From there, I have an unobstructed view of the area behind the bakery. While pretending to walk toward an Irish bar called Flies Ties, I keep an eye out until I'm certain no one is hiding near the bakery.

There's a small alleyway behind the bakery that opens up into a parking lot. No one is in the lot. A part of me expected to see at least someone watching the area. It's not even a challenge at this point. Instead of sneaking around like a real-life spy fantasy, I stroll through the lot, spinning my keys. With the smoothest movement I can muster, I saunter toward the hearse, unlock the door, and hop in. When my hands hit the steering wheel, I let out a deep breath.

The billboards keep flashing in red. To prevent the red-light district from becoming a mobile eyesore, I reach back and find the remote. The billboards power down. A turn of the key brings the hearse roaring to life. I pull through the parking lot out onto Atlantic Boulevard. It takes fifteen minutes of trial and error to reach the backroad William showed me earlier. Despite the incessant red light no longer flashing, a hearse attracts attention wherever it's parked. It could draw a lot of attention in a quiet neighborhood. Stephen's home is the only one on the street with lights on. I park on the road near the end of their driveway.

Misty's black collar is sitting on the passenger seat. Misty must have taken the collar off earlier in the day while delivering a cake to someone she thought it might offend. The sight of the collar inspires me to modify my plan. The initial plan of knocking on the door needed amendment anyway. It's rather direct and uncomplicated. If anyone were to approach me, I would just wing it and hope for the best. The collar gives me an out. With a dog collar in hand, I can wander as I see fit and tell any nosy neighbors that I'm looking for my daughter's lost dog that ran away. No one will question a father on that mission.

Putting the collar in my pocket turns into a terrible idea when the spikes dig into my leg. Instead, I wrap the neighbor-deterring dog collar around my right hand. The lights inside the house allow me to see the interior through the sheer curtains. The outside lights are off, which leaves me wondering if they skedaddled during the day. A small porch surrounding the front door is dark. I knock and prepare to punch whoever might open the door. Nothing happens.

The front door is locked. It doesn't budge as I turn the handle and give it a quick nudge with my shoulder. I leave the front porch and head around the house. The open curtains reveal an immaculate dining room. Four chairs sit equidistant from a table covered in a white embroidered tablecloth. A hurricane glass surrounding a candle sits as centered as possible on the table. Several family photos adorn the walls. One particular picture of the smiling family of three bothers me. Something about seeing Stephen happy is irksome. Anyone can walk by the Stephen in that picture and never suspect he's capable of blowing up several people. What would the neighbors think if I told them about how I survived a bomb Stephen Collins gave me under false pretenses? I can say with near certainty that each neighbor would dismiss me and laugh at the mention of their happy family man blowing up innocent people.

Chopped wood sits organized into multiple piles along the side of the house. The size of the pieces in each pile shrinks until the piles turn into seven five-gallon buckets in a perfect row filled with kindling decreasing in size from one to the next. The extent of this order is incredible. It must have made Stephen uncomfortable to sit in my house and see how I live. It's a shame I didn't provide him the grand tour. The pyramid of PBR cans and the pile of clothes atop my dresser would have sent him running, ensuring I wouldn't be knee-deep in the mess I now find myself.

Wishful thinking carries me to the back yard. A massive oak tree dominates the area with one substantial branch reaching out to a second-story window. The manicured grass is devoid of any toys. A ten-by-ten shed with a padlock on the doors near the other side of the house stands out. I stay away from the creepy shed on account of Stephen's recent love of explosions. The blinds covering the sliding glass door on the back of the house are open. The OCD feng shui continues into a living room clean enough to manufacture microchips.

139

The back door is locked. From the base of the oak, I can see through a dormer window on the second floor. One of the oak's branches reaches out over the roof and above this window. I've seen everything else I can from the ground. No one is on the bottom floor. However, there is a chance someone is upstairs. The window is prime for peeking. It's been years since I've climbed a tree, and I've never heard anyone say that climbing a tree is like riding a bicycle.

The first attempt is a learning experience. I leave the dog collar at the base of the tree and grab hold of a branch. While hanging from the branch, I realize that sandals are cumbersome. I kick them off and start again. This time, I grab onto the branch and wrap my legs around it. With my legs holding on, I inch toward the house. There are several budding branches broken on the way to the window, a sign that someone recently climbed this tree. I pull myself onto the top of the branch and then look toward the window mere feet away.

Inside, dinosaurs cover the walls while toys stand at attention in various parts of the room. Chaos reigns closer to the bed. Sheets are on the ground. Toys are scattered willy-nilly. It looks like a struggle has occurred. Everything else in the house is ordered, even the majority of this child's room is in order, but this small area is the exact opposite.

The roof near the window isn't slanted enough to keep someone from shimmying from the tree branch to reach the window. The branch almost touches the roof of the house, making it even easier for someone to have entered this child's room. Swinging down onto the roof would allow me to inspect the window. It's unnecessary. Everything points to a grim reality for Stephen's son. Damage to the window lock won't change my mind. Whether it was through the window by some stranger or out the front door by a father who knew he needed to run from the police, the boy is gone.

Shit. Now I might have to sympathize with a murderer.

Chapter 25

Flynn

The Cake Mistress Bakery parking lot is empty when I return the hearse. The lack of police presence means I can rest easy. I climb into the back. It takes two seconds to turn the electronic billboards back on. I've been using the remote control for the screens since the day Misty's father delivered the hearse to the bakery. I update the information scrolling across the signs more often than Misty. It's simple enough. The control is a small keyboard device behind the front seat. It can publish whatever messages need displaying on either or both of the billboards. The entire setup runs on an array of rechargeable batteries Misty's father installed. To make it cost-effective and green, Leslie integrated a set of solar panels into the roof.

Misty's father is a Navy veteran who opened up an auto shop after he retired from the service. Over the past several years, he has invested time and money into turning his home green by adding solar panels and opening up the house to more natural light. His new passion is trying to incorporate green technology into cars. According to him, integrating the solar panels into the classic hearse was a no-brainer because, when the sun shines down directly, the ground receives approximately one thousand Joules per second per square meter. The efficiency of solar panels is low, so most of that energy isn't used, but the energy received by the rooftop panels throughout a sunny Florida day is enough to run the billboards and charge the batteries for use over the entire next day.

The flashing red lights of the billboard lend the interior of the hearse a shady motel room vibe. I'm tired enough to stretch out on the rough carpet and stare at the headliner. The entire day has given me too much to process. It's not the most comfortable place to sleep, but tonight it will have to suffice. The lack of comfort and the red light do not stop me from falling asleep in a matter of minutes.

A stifled scream wakes me up. Misty is at the rear door holding a cake while I try my best to sit up. After adjusting my glasses, I wave to Misty and hold my index finger up to my lips like a teacher asking for silence. Misty slides the cake into the back and secures it with a series of belts her father installed to make sure nothing moves during transit.

Misty closes the door and walks around the car. She leans over the driver's seat and then reaches into the back to slap me. I move out of her reach and hold my finger back up to my lips. After Misty closes the door, I tap her on the shoulder.

"Would you mind grabbing your cell charger? Your phone is dying."

Misty turns around and gives me a death stare appropriate for being in the back of a hearse.

"It's not the only thing," she says in an ominous tone.

Misty exits the car and comes back with the charger. She plugs it in before holding up her hand. I place the cell phone in her hand. She connects the phone to the charger before putting the car in reverse and heading north onto Seminole Road.

"Where are you taking me?" I ask.

"I could drop you off at the police station up here on the left. I'm sure they'd love to speak to you."

"Yeah, I'm not ready to speak to the police."

"How about the fire department next door? There are a bunch of burly, muscled men that would love to talk to you about a certain fire they had to put out."

"I'll just stay in the back here, thanks."

"If you must know," Misty says, as she stops at an intersection shared by both the Atlantic Beach police and fire departments, "I'm delivering a cake to Selva Marina."

"Someone is that lazy? Selva is right there."

"A lovely old couple is paying me to bring it to them. It's for their sixty-fifth wedding anniversary. Considering their age, they didn't feel too comfortable bringing it themselves."

"Fine. I'll get out there. I needed to go speak to my mother anyway."

"Good. Because I don't know how comfortable I feel having you in the car."

"Is it the whole aiding and abetting thing?"

"Exactly. See, I'd rather not go to prison for a long time."

"Me neither. I escaped from the police to find the guy responsible. That way, he can go to prison instead of me."

"Do you realize how worried I am about this—about you? They think you blew someone up. You're lucky they aren't shooting to kill."

"You really are a buzzkill. You know that, right?"

"I think I'm somewhat decent in the grand scheme of buzzkilling. I saw you being hauled off by the police, and I wasn't a buzzkill. You stole my phone, and somehow I still maintained a low buzzkill status. Then you escaped from the police and told Tin that someone was about to stab you. See, that's when I started to be a buzzkill. But no. You weren't done yet. You followed that by turning off my stolen phone and never calling back to let us know you were safe. It's been a whole new and unpleasant experience for me, which is why, right now, my feet are planted firmly in the buzzkill camp."

"Sorry about that. I guess I didn't want to get either of you any more involved than you already are."

"So you spent the night in the back of my bakery's hearse?"

"Those two words together always sound so odd. I guess I thought over time I'd get used to it—"

"Shut up."

"Is this a bad time to mention that I borrowed the hearse for some investigating last night?"

Misty stares ahead. A stony silence fills the air.

"If it makes you feel any better, I found out the name and address of the man who tried to blow me up."

"It doesn't make me feel the least bit better."

"I have one more favor to ask of you."

Misty doesn't say a word as she pulls into the Selva Marina Golf and Country Club and parks in a small parking lot near the back door to the kitchen. I've helped Misty deliver a cake to this location before, and they prefer cakes delivered like any other food product.

"I may not be able to come to Thanksgiving dinner at your father's tomorrow. Can you make sure my mother makes it there? I'd hate for her to be alone on Thanksgiving."

Misty climbs out of the hearse and opens up the back. She leans in and nods her head to the left.

"A police car followed us here," she says while staring at me. "They parked in the other lot. And I'll pick up your mother."

"Thanks," I say with a smile.

"Also, you reek."

"I hope you mean I reek of class."

"There's an old saying about hoping in one hand and shitting in the other. You smell like the other hand."

Misty leaves the hearse open and walks up to the kitchen door. Before she knocks, I climb into the front seat and grab her cell phone from the charger. Trying not to draw the police's attention, I open the passenger door and stay low as I crawl out. I shut the door and then dash around the corner when the kitchen door swings open. I saunter toward the pool area and then back out into the parking lot. Halfway through the parking lot, Misty's cell phone rings.

The phone lights up with a number I don't recognize. Masking my voice, I take the call.

"Hello," I say in a high-pitched tone.

"Yes, hello. My name is Philip Blanchard."

"Philip," I say, clearing my throat. "I'm surprised you called me so soon."

"Yes, well, how is your investigation going?"

"Swimmingly." I pause and cringe at my word choice. "I'm close to wrapping things up."

"I spoke to the police after you came to my office yesterday. They told me some interesting bits of information about you."

"Such as?"

"That you are currently a suspect in the bombing at the beach."

I walk out onto the road and look back at the parked police car. "About that…"

"I found it fascinating that they still didn't know Paul was in the explosion."

"Yeah, I didn't let them in on that piece of information."

"Well, I did."

"You had every right—"

"I also let them know that you were working for us to investigate some threats against Paul."

"You did what?"

144

"I told them you are one of Paul's employees. One hired to ferret out some people who were making threats against his life. I told them that this was all a ruse we allowed to go too far."

"Why would you do that?"

"Because I need your help. Paul was investigating something I'm certain led to his death. I want you to assist me in finding out what happened."

"You plan on working with someone running away from the police?"

"I spoke to the police already. If you turn yourself in today and your story pans out, they promised me they would forgo additional charges for fleeing."

"How is our story going to pan out when it's a lie?"

"I'm a lawyer. When you turn yourself in, make sure you call me. I'll do all the talking for both of us."

"Um, thanks."

"You're welcome. Turn yourself in as soon as you can."

Philip disconnects, leaving me standing on the side of the street dumbfounded. I feel the urge to run back to Misty and let her know everything will be roses from this point on. Instead, I watch as the hearse leaves the parking lot with the police car following close behind.

Chapter 26

Flynn

Philip expanded my limited options. Before his call, finding Steven Collins and turning him over to the police was the only resolution to my current predicament. That plan ended with me clearing my name and living happily ever after. Now I have Philip offering me a lifeline. It sounds like he's already made headway in clearing my name. Despite sounding genuine on the phone, there is a possibility he's working with the police. Something about the situation feels off. The police informed him I killed his boss. Why would he keep me from looking guilty? And, on top of that, why would he lie to help a stranger out of a jam? For all Philip knows, I could have killed Paul Mahoney willingly.

Philip mentioned that he needed my help. Why me? What's so important about me? Twenty minutes of brain racking, and I can't pinpoint why I'm needed. My mind is numb by the time I reach the reddish brick walls surrounding the Viveza Community.

The brick wall separating the Viveza condos from the road is not high. Anyone in decent shape can clear it with little effort. I, being in decent shape, place my hand on the top and propel my body over. Once inside, I beeline toward building two, where my mother lives. Something about these condos bothers me. During the day, everything looks normal, and people all appear happy. At night, the towering oaks with tendrilous beehives of Spanish moss make it look like something out of a horror movie. Every time I stay too late, I expect someone to come lunging at me from behind a car parked in one of the many carports.

At this moment, the best part of these condos is how spread out they are. The entire complex of eight three-story buildings covers close to a square mile due to the parking spots and grassy lawns. The condos surround open-air courtyards. Every unit has a patio facing either the parking lot or some of the surrounding green areas. Cautiously, I approach my mother's building and take the time to observe the surrounding area before making any sudden moves. The only police car I can see is a cruiser parked in the spot right in front of the building. If they positioned a cop out front, then there should be one stationed inside the courtyard to catch me using the other entrances. That makes accessing the building through the front, back, and side entrances difficult.

My mother's condo is a corner unit with one patio facing the front of the building and the other facing the side without direct access to the courtyard. There are plenty of cars parked in the open lots. Any of them could be an unmarked police car. It takes five minutes to rule out hidden cops and reach the building. My mother's condo is on the second floor, which might be a reason the police are ignoring this side of the building. The ground-floor patios are all surrounded by an eight-foot-high brick wall with perfect handhold spaces. I remove my sandals and toss them up onto my mother's balcony before climbing up the brick wall. As I ready myself to jump the three feet to the balcony, a woman's voice stops me.

"Hello, Flynn."

Mrs. Pence, my mother's friend and downstairs neighbor, waves at me from her lawn chair on the enclosed patio. I take a seat on top of the brick wall.

"Hello, Mrs. Pence. How are you doing today?"

"I'm doing well. It's a lovely day out, isn't it?" Mrs. Pence is wearing cataract glasses around her regular glasses. The dark lenses reflect me sitting on the wall like a budget Spider-Man.

"It sure is."

"Did you forget your key again?"

"Yes," I say, lying with a smile.

"I can bring you my copy if you'd like."

"No, thanks," I say, standing back up. "I'm already here."

"Tell Barbara I'll be up to see her in about an hour."

"Will do," I say, not looking down. I leap from the top of the wall to the balcony and grab hold of the thick concrete railing. The edge of the balcony facing out is more than enough for me to find footing and jump over the railing.

The noise from tossing my sandals must have grabbed my mother's attention because she pulls open the curtains before I can knock on the sliding glass door. Instead of being surprised, she's elated at seeing me on

147

the other side of the glass. She unlocks the door and opens it wide, walking out onto the patio for a hug.

Sunlight is not my mother's friend. She spends much of her time indoors, locked away in the moody semi-darkness of her condo. Harsh light at the wrong angle leaves her a cadaverous shell of the woman I knew. A complimentary angle allows her pale skin to radiate with a ghostly glow and adds a sparkle to the ample gray encroaching on her light-brown hair.

My mother kisses me on the cheek and then returns to the dim lighting. I follow her inside, closing the door behind me.

"Did you find that picture? The one from Christmas?"

"No, Ma. I didn't."

"Please keep looking."

"I will."

"It's so nice of you to show up. And out of the blue—Do you remember why I named you Flynn?"

My mother does not allow me to answer.

"Because you always liked to make an entrance. The doctor who delivered you said you were the quickest delivery he had ever seen. He said it was like the doors of this world just opened right up for you. 'In like Flynn,' your father always used to say. It's from the actor Errol Flynn. He could get into anywhere and always knew how to make an entrance. Just like you. And to this day, you still make things interesting."

"I try to keep everyone on their toes."

"Do you remember how much Lily loved saying your name? I remember she used to sing songs with your name in it when you were sad, and it cheered you right up. Flynnie the Pooh," my mother starts singing. Lily found great joy in switching up lyrics to suit the moment. It amazes me that my mother can remember altered lyrics to songs Lily sang so long ago. This particular song is an insinuation that my allegiances to the Phillies run deep. Lily thought it was hilarious. I thought it was tantamount to blasphemy. "Silly Philly billy, it's Flynn."

Lily loved Winnie the Pooh. She'd cart a two-foot-tall stuffed Pooh bear around and sing songs to me when I was a pouty teenager. My mother forgets how much those songs pissed me off. I used to chase Lily around the house to make her stop. About half of the time, we would end up sent to our rooms until we calmed down. After Lily disappeared, the

148

sight of Winnie the Pooh made me cry. Tears would fill my eyes and fall like a sun shower, unexpected and unwelcome. The guilt was overwhelming. Like a voracious demon, it ate and ate and ate until I was hollow. On that day, the tears dried up. And then I understood loss. I realized that humans persist. Our bodies control our lives like ink on paper. We live in the finite. After death, we enter the infinite. Our bodies lose control, and others carry us forward, nestled in the abyss created by the guilt of living.

Lily persists for me differently than she persists for my mother. For me, Lily lives on as the girl I knew. For my mother, she has become a tainted memory—a fish tale in an unfamiliar language.

English is beautiful and intricate, but sometimes it's too succinct. In other languages, words can contain loads of emotion, so much so that an English translation is difficult. *Saudade* is one such word. There is no simple definition or translation of *saudade* because it's hard to define. It's a word described to me by a Brazilian girl I knew in college as 'the festering love within.' *Saudade* changed how Lily persists within my mother. A melancholy adoration taints her memories. The positive comes to the forefront, and the bad disappears into a background of charming idiosyncrasies.

The abyss is real for my mother. It's all around her. What I carry inside, she has hanging from the walls and adorning nearly all the shelf space in her condo. Lily's pictures are in simple frames to not distract from the moment caught on film. Most include others in the shot, but Lily is the focus. Each picture is in its own frame and in its own place, ordered in a way that only my mother understands.

Lily is perfect to my mother. Everything she ever did is precious and performed out of good intent. All she has to hold on to are these fragile shards of a broken life. I don't have the heart to say an unkind word or let her know that my memory differs from hers. I'm afraid that anything could upset this delicate balance she has found.

Lily's disappearance sent my mother into a catatonic state. The initial course of treatment did nothing. Out of easy answers, the doctors experimented with medications, mixing one pill with another and a new drug with another, and nothing changed. One day she woke up and was never quite the same. It's like she processes the world surrounding her

149

through a sieve. One minute she's able to hold an intelligent conversation. The next minute, she's lost.

"Do you remember why we named you Flynn? 'In like Flynn,' your father always used to say."

"Yeah, Ma. I know the story."

"I figured you could use a reminder. Do you remember the entrances you used to make dressed like Superman? The only difference is that all you had was a cape. You used to run around naked all the time with a towel tied around your neck, pretending you could fly. You know I think I still have some pictures of you dressed like that."

"They call that child pornography these days, Ma."

"That's the problem with the world. Everybody thinks the worst. That's why I pray every day for God to take me to a better place."

"You know I don't like you talking like that."

"Like what?"

"Nothing. Anything interesting happen since I was here the other day?"

"Well, we had a meeting for everyone in our entire building. We were discussing this additional fee of one thousand dollars—can you believe that, one thousand dollars—for work on the roof and repaving the roads in here. I was upset, because that's a lot of money, and I started yelling at them. And I kept yelling at them, 'This is my money! This is my money!' And they all looked at me like I was crazy. Can you believe that? Crazy."

"The whole world's crazy. We're doing our best to keep up."

"The nerve of these people. Grace was the only person to stick up for me. It's wrong for them to rob us like that."

"They aren't robbing you. It's maintenance. Did they provide you with something showing the expected costs?"

"I don't know. I stormed out."

"You should've stayed till the end, got the full picture, and then stormed out."

"That's what your father said."

"You talked to him about this?"

"He calls me every week. I told him about it. He offered to pay the fees for me. I said no."

"Do you need the money?"

"I don't need your money, either."

"You gave me the house. It's the least I could do."

"The house? No. I don't want it back."

"No, Ma. I was saying I could pay you—"

"I can't go back."

A moment of terror grips my mother. Her features turn blank as her mind wanders to the past. She hasn't been in our house for years. It reminds her too much of the bad times. Her soft smile returns as she approaches the living room wall. She takes a picture down and sits on the sofa.

"Do you remember this day?"

She won't hand me the picture. I have to sit down on the sofa next to her to see. In the photo, I'm standing to the right of a sandcastle as Lily stands to the left. We were bored that day and annoying our father while he tried to work. He bet us ten dollars apiece we couldn't work together and build a sandcastle that reached four feet tall. The picture captures our collective euphoria at proving him wrong. I remember being proud that day because we won the bet and made something impressive enough to photograph. Now that I look at it, it's nothing more than a mountain of sand without purpose. There's nothing special about it. It's sloppy and only reaches four feet because we piled up so much sand. But there I am, smiling. And that mountain of dirt will last forever, despite the fact I kicked it down right after the photo.

"Yeah, I remember. It took us a while."

"Lily used to hop like a bunny when she got excited. I remember her hopping into the kitchen, telling me I needed to bring the camera."

My mother looks at the photo, holding the frame in both hands.

"Such a good builder. It's a shame you can't fix the roof."

"Sandcastles and roof repair are a little different."

"I know. But it'd be nice if you could." My mother pauses, possibly to imagine the world where I can fix the roof. "Lily would have made an incredible architect."

My mother is right. Lily loved to draw and make pictures out of construction paper. She called it 'constructing worlds.' Plenty of these worlds occupy the walls in this condo. They're framed like the pictures and stand out because they vary in size. Triangles with crisp lines defined Lily's worlds. She could have turned her love of triangles into a career constructing things in the real world.

One of Lily's constructed worlds hangs on the wall behind the sofa. It's my mother's favorite. Lily gave it to her for Mother's Day. In this world, our family is together and happy. There's a sun made of multiple interlocking triangles shining down on our triangular faces, which hover above our triangular bodies. We're all holding triangular hands and smiling triangular smiles. Lily's favorite color was pink, but she often added white and yellow when she depicted herself. She made me pinky swear not to tell anyone else why. It will always be our little secret.

"Are you ready for Thanksgiving?" I ask. I'd rather not address Lily's architectural prowess with my mother. Doing so could result in a long and depressing conversation spiral that lasts for hours.

"Oh. That's tomorrow, isn't it?"

"Yes, Ma. I may not be able to pick you up. Misty agreed to come and get you if that's the case. She will probably call you tonight to set up a time."

"I'm looking forward to it." My mother stays quiet as gears turn in her head. Suddenly, the gears stop. She chimes back in. "When are you and Misty going to get married?"

"When she develops a preference for men."

"Such a handsome boy. But you need to shave. You should do that for tomorrow. Do that for me, will you?"

"If I get a chance, I'll shave."

"It's good to look your handsomest around the holidays."

"I need to get going."

"You just got here."

"I know," I say, standing up. "I have to take care of something."

"Make sure you lock the door," my mother says, refusing to look up.

"Mrs. Pence said she's stopping by in a little bit."

"Then leave the door unlocked."

My mother stays on the sofa, entranced by the picture she's holding. It's best for me to leave. She loses time when she looks at pictures. Hours pass yet, for her, it might as well be a minute.

The front door closing reverberates across the courtyard. An open-air garden radiates from a birdbath in the center. There are no police in sight. Second-floor landing? No police. Stairwell? No police. Front door of the condo building? One officer sitting inside a cruiser. It makes me feel a little less special to know that they sent only one officer to my mother's house. To top it off, the officer isn't paying any attention to me as I approach him. I knock on the passenger-side window. The officer steps out of the vehicle.

"How can I help you, sir?"

"My name's Flynn Dupree. I'm guessing you're looking for me. Should I get in back?"

The officer reaches into the cruiser and pulls out a piece of paper. He looks at it and then at me before sliding the paper over the car.

"This is you?" the officer asks incredulously.

There's a picture of me from my driver's license on the paper. The officer's questioning look is the same one bartenders give me after seeing my license. When it came time to renew, I made the mistake of renewing it online. The picture is of me at age seventeen and looks like a different person. Sinatra was wrong. Age seventeen was not a very good year. I'm wearing a petulant grin and a pathetic peach fuzz 'stache.

It looks like the police decided not to print a screenshot from the news conference and decided instead to use something they had on file. The problem is that the only two pictures they should have on file are my driver's license and the photo taken for my DUI arrest. In the DUI photo, I have six months of beard and about eleven inches of hair curling around my face. It's for the best they didn't use that photo. The homeless at the beach are harassed enough without my adding fuel to the fire.

"Seriously? This is the picture they circulated?"

"If it's you, get in the back. Door's unlocked. I'll call it in."

The officer doesn't take the time to escort me to the back of the car. He starts up the engine, eager to find something more entertaining than watching old people enter and leave a building. The back of the cruiser is a cage. Closing the door seals my fate. I'm now in Philip's hands. His incoming call is the last one on record in Misty's phone.

"You ready?" the officer asks.

"Let's get gone," I reply.

Chapter 27

Amy

"Responsibility," Marty says, pointing his sausage of an index finger at me while taking a long sip of soda out of his favorite cup. I can't help but stare at Marty's nails. He's always chewing on them like he hasn't eaten in a month. All that's left are nasty nubs with ragged edges. The pause from the drink and the straw in his mouth adds an awkwardly dramatic effect to him saying, "No call. No show."

Responsibility is a word he throws around all the time. To Marty, the world needs more responsibility. Being late is punishable by a tongue lashing. Missing a shift is a mortal sin. An appeal to common sense never enters the equation.

Marty's work life is the only time he abides by his ideal of responsibility. The lack of responsibility in his personal life is what's left him the fat mess he is today. The straw that broke the camel's back for Marty's wife was when she discovered him using their children to get his hands on pills. He'd been taking their ADD medication and grinding it up so he could snort it like a poor man's cocaine. The next day she moved in with her mother and filed for divorce. Marty, never one to take responsibility for any personal issue, told everyone that his wife took their children to find a better educational system than Duval County. The owner of the diner, who is a gossip of the highest order, tore this claim apart. She dug up the truth along with the divorce decree and made sure that the information found its way through the diner grapevine. The hole in Marty's life became filled with food and constant overtime. Those long hours added up to a managerial position. Marty referred to this promotion as God's will. In time he sobered up and started preaching life lessons.

"I already told you I was nearly killed in an explosion."

"Looks like yer fingers're workin'. Phones're easy enough to dial."

"Are you serious?"

"Honey, you plant in spring 'n harvest in fall."

"What the fuck does that mean?"

Marty wants to be a motivational speaker. Everyone who works with him knows this. He tosses out bits of wisdom and tries to sound intelligent to the best of his abilities, but all he does is look more pathetic.

"Means you needta think 'bout plannin' for yer future in the present."

Marty considers his rise from addiction to be an inspirational story, something that should lead to people admiring him and trying to follow in his footsteps. Sobering up after a life-altering event can be inspirational. However, his replacing an addiction to drugs for an addiction to food falls a little short. The biggest hurdle Marty faces in becoming an inspiration to anyone is his lack of charisma. No one wants to follow a person whose only goal is to look better by making everyone else look worse.

"You know what, Marty? You're right." The comment makes Marty smile. The smug spreading across his face slows down only when he leans in for a drink from his favorite faded red cup. "You're right about me needing to plan for my future."

"You've just gotta work hard. Someday, you'll be like me." Marty raises an eyebrow and takes another pull from the straw.

Only weeks ago, Iain told me he wanted to take care of me for the rest of my life. Iain is my future. *Painting is now my second love*, he told me before leaving for Scotland.

"I never want to end up like you," I say, allowing the comment to stew. "If I end up like you, then I'm going to kill myself. And the problem is... I like me."

"So, what're you sayin'?"

"I quit."

"You can't just quit. You're on the clock."

"I was on the clock. Now I'm not. I'm on my own time."

"Fine. We're better off without you. Wendy's half-retard and she does twice as good a job."

Marty finishes his comment with another smug pull from the drink. Before Marty's lips leave the straw, I grab the cup from his hand and smash it against the sink. The lid blasts off the thick plastic base. Soda flies across the kitchen. The cup doesn't break, so I bring it down again on the edge of the sink. Each time the cup connects to the metal sink, it makes a loud echoing boom. The thick plastic endures four hits until it cracks.

Marty stands shocked at the mess of soda covering the floor and walls. The broken cup hits him in the chest before he can react.

"You're buyin' me another," Marty shouts, flinching when I stop and glare at him.

"You might want to ask Wendy to come in here and clean up this mess."

Chapter 28

William

"My room's a mess," Lily says. She bends down over a pile of clothing and pokes at it.

"Don't worry. We'll clean it up."

The police left the room a shambles. Nothing's broken, but everything stored away is now on the floor. Despite being mindful of my feet, I almost step on four candles in the shape of cartoon characters. The burned wicks reach down enough to distort their features.

"Those go on my dresser," Lily says.

We return the candles to their proper place on top of the dresser.

"Who did all this? Was it the guy that hurt James?"

"No. The police did this."

"Why would the police be in my room?"

"You'll have to ask Flynn about that."

"He never talks to me anymore."

"He's swamped."

"I'm glad I have you, William. You're always there for me."

"And I'll always be there if you need me."

"Hey, what's that?"

There's a pile of clothes in the center of the room. The police took everything in the dresser drawers and unceremoniously dumped it on the ground. Sticking out of this pile is a set of pictures.

"What are they?" Lily asks.

"I'm not sure. Let's take a look." I open up the envelope and take out the pictures. "They look like pictures from the zoo."

"I remember that day."

"Do you?"

"Yeah. I saw a giraffe."

"Here's the picture. He looks nice."

"I named him Norman."

"That's a wonderful name for a giraffe."

"Look at the monkeys," Lily says, pulling at my hand so she can have a better view. "They're so cute."

"They sure are."

"Who's that man?"

"What man?"

"The one right there." Lily points at a man in the background. The sight of his face stops me dead. I squint to make sure. It is hard to believe he is there, all alone in the crowd. I rifle through the other pictures and find a total of six photos with him in the background.

"Who is he, William?"

"A brother of mine from a long time ago."

"You have another brother?"

"Not by blood. His father made me the man I am today."

"Well, then who is he?"

"He's the son of God."

Lily is quiet.

"Don't worry about it," I say, stuffing one of the photos into my pocket and leaving the rest on top of the dresser. "Let's finish cleaning up here. Then we can go home."

"Sure."

I fold all of Lily's clothes and put them back in the dresser while she puts all the knickknacks back in place. Lily lies down in her old bed after she finishes.

The room is dustier than I remember. It's been over a month since we've come here. Flynn's schedule is erratic. The keys I have to the front door are only useful if he's gone. It'd be hard to explain what I was doing inside his house. He wouldn't understand about Lily. No one would.

Sometimes, Lily gets sad and needs to come back to her old life. She can't go back permanently. This is the next best thing. We both come to her room and spend time together until she gets tired. Then we head back home.

"Hello?" shouts a voice from downstairs. "Is anyone here?"

"Uh oh," Lily says.

"Don't worry, dear. Everything'll be all right."

Chapter 29

Flynn

The ride to the Atlantic Beach Police Department is brief. It feels like only a minute passes before I'm brought into an eight-by-twelve room and asked to have a seat.

"Cousins will be here in a minute," an officer who never introduced himself says. His name badge says, 'Darling.'

I wait as Darling requested. Over a minute later, a sizeable man sets a sizeable box of papers across the table from me.

The smile on my face widens at the sight of someone new. The man takes off his suit-jacket and ignores me while shuffling through the papers in the box. Frustration gets the better of him. He takes a seat and pushes the box toward me.

"You know what's in there?" he asks in a voice deep enough to collect rainwater.

"Looks like paper to me," I say, without looking through any of it.

"It's evidence against you."

"All of that is evidence against me? For what?"

"You know what."

"I'm sorry, Mr.—"

"Detective Cousins."

"I'm sorry, Detective Cousins, but I don't know—wait. Is this about the pen I took from my bank a couple weeks ago? I'd be more than happy to give it back. Unless you all removed it from my house. That'd make you thieves by proxy."

"We both know you were involved in the explosion."

"Oh, that. I've been instructed by my lawyer to not speak about that."

"You're invoking your right?"

"I guess." An awkward silence fills the room while we stare at one another. Pointing at my watch, I add, "Philip should be here any minute."

"I guess we'll have to wait."

"Sounds like a plan."

Detective Cousins stands up and walks out of the room with his box, leaving me alone. It's close to twenty minutes before the door reopens. This time, Philip Blanchard accompanies Detective Cousins. Detective Cousins takes a seat on the adversarial side of the table. Philip sits next to me.

"Thanks for showing up."

Philip looks better today. A nap, a navy suit, a shower, and a shave turn him into a new man. His face is still thin, and his protruding cheekbones are more evident when he leans in and whispers, "Tell them only what they need to hear." Philip pulls back and then says aloud. "I've told them everything, Flynn. Please fill the detective in on what you have discovered."

"Well, I don't know precisely what Philip filled you in on, but the man that set up this entire thing is Stephen Collins."

"He's my equivalent for Lou Brombacher."

"That's true. But Brombacher had nothing to do with this."

"And how would you know that?" the detective asks.

"It's just an assumption. He smiled and laughed when I told him that Paul Mahoney died in a motel room with a hooker. We're talking schadenfreude to the max. That joy dissolved into terror when I told him that Stephen Collins blew him up. He's got something illegal going on, but he has nothing to do with Mahoney's death."

"Would Mr. Brombacher's illegal activities be another assumption?" the detective inquires.

"When I walked into his office, I thought he must have hired a significant portion of Jacksonville's strippers to work for him during the day."

"That's not illegal."

"I know. It's suspicious, though. Best guess? Iffy people are lining his pockets."

"Flynn," says Philip. "Please continue with Stephen Collins."

"Lou Brombacher provided me with an address for the casa de Collins. I went there. The place was immaculate except for his son's room. The area near the bed was a mess. Someone might have taken his son and forced him to do this."

160

"Why would you make that assumption?" Detective Cousins shifts in his seat and leans back in his chair.

"His life looks orderly. Even his plan had an order to it. The execution was sloppy. It ended up being traced back to him too easily. But he was on a forced timeline. Otherwise, I think there wouldn't be a trace of evidence leading back to him. I hate saying it because he tried to kill me, but I think he was being pressured by someone else to commit this crime."

"If you would like Stephen's address, Mr. Dupree would be more than happy to provide it for you. Otherwise, I believe Mr. Dupree would like to go home and rest."

"Hold on there," the detective says with a laugh. "He's not getting off that easy. He was involved with a plot to kill your boss."

"Flynn was roped into this scenario by Paul's curiosity, which ended up killing him and nearly costing Flynn his life."

"Solicitation charges. And assault on Amy Wright."

"I doubt Ms. Wright would admit she was there for sex. Mr. Dupree offered to pay her to arrive at a location, nothing more. And as for assault, Stephen Collins is responsible for the explosion."

"We have more questions for Mr. Dupree."

"Shoot," I say.

Detective Cousins leaves the room for ten seconds. He returns with Alien in an evidence bag in his left hand and a quarter of an ounce of pot in an evidence bag in his right.

"We found these in your residence," the detective says. "This will be enough to hold you for a little while."

Philip exhales deeply and then massages his temples.

"As you can see from your lawyer," Detective Cousins smirks as he speaks, "we've got you."

"Where did you find those?" Philip asks.

"The majority of the marijuana was hidden in a large mason jar of popcorn-flavored jelly beans in Mr. Dupree's pantry. The rest was on the kitchen counter right next to the pipe."

I open my mouth to speak. Philip stops me.

"Flynn, keep quiet," Philip says as he shakes his head. "So, Detective, I can only imagine that your search warrant allowed you access to the kitchen?"

161

"We didn't need a warrant. We had permission to search from the owner of the residence. Your father saved us some time and hassle, Flynn."

"The pipe's name is Alien," I say, smiling.

"You're admitting it's all yours?"

"The funny thing is, I honestly didn't know that I had pot in the jelly beans. It sounds like a place I might hide it when I have people over. Seriously, no one will ever go looking for popcorn jelly beans. I mean, they're disgusting. You'd have to hate yourself or be some weird sort of food masochist to put your hand in that damn jar. I only keep them because they're a reminder of how awful they are. Is that a thing? A self-referencing reminder? Really, though. It is a fantastic hiding place."

"Flynn," Philip says brusquely.

Detective Cousins laughs. His laugh is as deep as his voice. It sounds like the strum of a bass guitar.

"Yes, Flynn. You are making this too easy on us."

"No, I'm not. I have one question."

"And that is?" Detective Cousins asks.

"How did my father give you permission when I own the house?"

Philip lights up like a tree at Christmas.

Detective Cousins' smile turns to a snarl. He walks out of the room, taking the pot and Alien with him. Indistinct sounds carry through the door for about a minute. The detective comes back in holding a notepad and a pen.

"I take it you've spoken to whoever is out there, and they now want Flynn to sign something. You can keep it, whatever it might be."

"Flynn doesn't need to sign anything. I do, however, need to inform him that his father may now face an obstruction charge for lying to us about owning the house."

This is a low blow. They must think threatening my father will make me confess. What Detective Cousins doesn't realize is that my father is a prudent man. I can guarantee that, even if they recorded him giving permission, he used misinterpretable language.

"I'm sure you may think you have my father or me, but I doubt it."

"Think about it, Flynn. All he would have to do is make a single mistake. Now that's an easy thing for a father to do. Trust me."

"He doesn't make mistakes. And he's an attorney. So, if he did, he'd be able to defend himself vigorously in the courts. All I want to know is if I can get Alien back?"

"No, Mr. Dupree. You cannot have your paraphernalia back."

"That's a shame. I mean, you guys can keep the pot. Consider it a gift. But Alien has a good amount of sentimental value."

"Detective Cousins," Philip says, rolling his eyes at my insolence. "You're wasting our time. The search of Flynn's house was, by your admission, illegally conducted. I've told you everything pertinent to the situation with Paul, and Flynn has provided you the only solid lead you now have in this case. We are officially done for the day. You have my contact information. Please call me with any additional questions."

"I don't think you understand—"

"I don't think *you* understand. This *will* be national news. I *will* have the eyes and ears of reporters across the nation. The police can be depicted as either useful or bumbling. Flynn has no more information for you and is guilty of nothing other than following the orders of a man who willingly put himself in danger."

Detective Cousins does not respond. A vein in his forehead pulses into life under his skin.

"Any contact with Mr. Dupree without me present will be treated as harassment. If any additional statements indicate—hell, even hint—that Mr. Dupree is a suspect or a person of interest, I will file civil suits for both defamation and false light."

A beautiful woman enters the room. Her charcoal pantsuit with subtle pinstripes says she means business.

"You are both free to go."

The woman returns Philip's smile with a scowl. The tension in the room speaks to a past between the two. Maybe they travel in the same Jacksonville lawyer circles or have faced-off in court before.

"Ladybug. Nice to see you."

"Hey there, Ladybug," I say. She folds her arms and looks at Philip like he let out the world's biggest secret. The look and cute nickname indicate their relationship went beyond a courtroom to something intimate.

"I'd prefer it if you didn't use familiarities, Philip."

"Well, Marie, you have my number if there are any additional questions."

"We will contact you," she says, nodding in Philip's direction, "with any further questions we may have."

"I want that address." The detective slides his notepad and pen across the table.

I write down Stephen's address and then stand up. Marie escorts us to the front door of the Atlantic Beach Police Department.

"Flynn Dupree," I say, sticking my hand out for Marie to shake.

She looks down at my hand and crosses her arms. "I know who you are. You are lucky Philip is on your side."

Marie shoots Philip a look and uncrosses her arms before walking back into the police department. I follow Philip to a parking lot in front of a nearby park less than a block away. We don't speak until we are in Philip's car with the doors closed.

"Eyes and ears of reporters across the nation?"

"Sometimes, histrionics pay off."

"Who exactly is Marie?"

"The woman who would have crucified you if I hadn't shown up."

I raise an eyebrow.

"She's a prosecuting attorney."

"Thanks," I say.

"You're welcome," Philip says, putting his car in reverse. "I'd hate for you to think you owe me, but you do."

"Very blunt. I like that."

"Yes, well, I will have some work for you. I imagine you're tired and need some rest. I'll take you home."

"You know where I live?"

"I performed a little background research on you, and, yes, I have your address. With tomorrow being Thanksgiving, I want to spend time with my family. I'll contact you Friday with the details on how you will be assisting me."

"Shore nuff."

"What?"

"Sorry. Sure enough," I say, in my best non-southern beachspeak voice.

"Oh. Well, if anyone asks, I told the police you were working with Paul. I told them that when Stephen hired you, he provided information on both Paul and Amy. You came to us because you recognized Paul as a public figure. We found your information interesting because Paul received a phone call asking him to appear at the same address you were hired to observe. Paul told you to continue and hire Amy as you were directed. He showed up as planned. When the explosions went off, you ran for it because of all the confusion."

"Got it. What's 'false light'?"

"A type of defamation."

"You threatened them with defamation and defamation?"

"False light is rarely used and typically incorporated into defamation here in Florida. Most lawyers don't care to learn about it."

"Is it valid?"

Philip looks at me and smiles.

"Of course. They're trying to portray you as something you are not. We're surrounded by false light every day. Some bad. Some good. The bad is what they are trying to do to you. The good is how humanity copes with shortcomings."

"Why help me?"

"I used to have my own law practice. Even before that, I dealt with criminals. When I went out on my own, I preferred criminals. The pay was great. The majority of the time, all I had to do was ask the court to reduce a sentence in exchange for an admission of guilt. I've known many criminals. Criminals run."

"I ran."

"They all tried to run away from their problems. You ran toward them. You have been looking for the truth. And that's because you don't know the truth. Criminals run from the truth because they're guilty and they know it."

Philip parks in front of my house. A police car sits parked at the driveway's end with a classic Corvette parked in front of the garage. I climb out of the car and look back at Philip.

"A police car will remain outside until they find Stephen Collins," Philip says.

"Thanks again," I say, closing the car door.

165

Philip drives away. I dig my house keys out of my pocket while following the paver stones to the front door. The yard still looks beautiful, and the front door remains intact. The front door not being broken is a pleasant surprise. I expected the police to have knocked it in so they could search the premises.

William opens the door before I can reach it.

"William?"

"Hey, Flynn. I hope you don't mind. I've been cleaning up the mess the police left."

"Thanks. That's nice of you."

"No worries."

William stops and stares at me. I can see he wants to say something but doesn't know how.

"What's up?" I say to urge him on.

"I'm sorry, Flynn, but your hat—Mordecai got stolen. Some kids broke into my house and trashed the place pretty good. They took it."

"Are you okay?"

"Yeah. It happened while we were downtown. You don't need to worry. I'll buy you another hat."

As annoyed as I am about losing Mordecai, it's comforting to know William wasn't there when the break-in occurred. William is the kind of person who leaves windows open and doors unlocked. That's the beach he wants. William's beach is full of neighbors you can trust and people respecting other people's property. That's not the beach we have. Our beach is like the rest of the world. If somebody wants something you have, they will try their hardest to take it. There is no room remaining in the hearts of mankind for respect. Grown adults practically run each other over in cars and SUVs to get the best parking spot. It is a stretch to think children and teenagers will grow up to value another living being or their property.

"No need to worry about buying me another hat. I have a fat head. I'll have to special order one that'll fit right."

"Let me know if you change your mind."

"Will do."

Not knowing what to expect inside, I enter my house. Since the front door is undamaged, one of the other entrances is sure to be broken. If that's the case, I will have to board it up until I can find someone to fix it.

166

There's an unexpected lack of mess inside. The foyer is clean. Some of the small items I keep on a table next to the door are gone, and the shoes and sandals I leave near the door are not in the right order, but it still looks clean. When I walk into the kitchen, Curtis Vance is relaxing at my grandmother's old mahogany dining table.

Vance's orange Hawaiian shirt with khaki slacks and boat shoes add an extra layer to the relaxation. Leaning back in a chair, he smiles at me while I try to return the favor.

"What are you doing here?"

"Cleaning. Or at least I was. I'm taking a break."

"It looks great."

"They left quite a mess. I've been working on the living room and kitchen. Now that you're back, I'll leave the other rooms for you."

"Thanks," I say reluctantly.

"You're welcome."

The kitchen door is undamaged. That leaves the French doors at the back of the house as the police's entry point. Discovering the French doors intact, with zero damage to the glass and the locks, leaves me confused.

"What're you looking for?" Vance asks.

"I'm wondering how the police got in. I don't see any broken doors."

"After you gave us the slip on Monday, we came back here to wait for you. You left the side door unlocked. We let ourselves in. More specifically, I called your father and asked if we could enter."

"You're the one he spoke to. Fortunately, this is my home. Not his."

"Your father still owns it. Your mother received the right to live here from the divorce. I think it's called being a 'tenant for life.' That way, your father still pays all the taxes on it."

"Is that what he told you?"

"Yes."

"He lied. I own this house. He pays the taxes for me. It's in my name."

"Why would he—" Vance laughs. "Your father allowed us to enter and search because anything found would be illegally obtained."

"It looks like my father tried to protect me."

"Fortunately for Herman, I've heard they found nothing of interest. Some pot and paraphernalia, but that's not too big of a deal. If they found

167

something substantial and had to throw it out because of an illegal search, he might face obstruction charges."

"Good thing I'm not a criminal."

"Yet Philip Blanchard, a criminal attorney, is fighting on your behalf."

"What can I say, I'm a likeable guy. How did you find out about him helping me?"

"Officer Rittwell has been kind of enough to keep me apprised of the situation. I guess we both are likeable."

"It's nice to see you and Rittles hitting it off."

"He's a good kid. Reminds me of myself at that age."

"Is that right?"

Vance laughs. "From what I understand, there's a history between you two. He said he arrested you for a DUI, and then you stalked him for a while."

"There's a little more to it than that."

"You're the one who went out drinking. Whether you were driving a car, riding a bicycle, or bouncing around on a pogo stick, he was doing his job. You can't fault a man for doing his job."

"I suppose you'd tell a Holocaust survivor that German soldiers were just doing their job."

"It's sad to see you act like the petulant sixteen-year-old I remember."

I'm tired and don't feel like arguing. The worst part is Vance is right. Even now, mere seconds after I made the comment, I know that the Holocaust comparison is pathetic. I should have thought of something witty. Instead, all I did was ham-fistedly trip and fall into the realm of Godwin's Law. And now I can't think of anything to say back other than an obvious statement.

"Yeah, well, people like me keep therapists busy."

"I don't doubt that for a moment."

To keep Vance from pushing the topic any further, I move on. Vance knows almost everybody in Jacksonville, and I'm confident he can satisfy my curiosity about Philip. I'm still confused as to why he dug me out of the crater. He wants me to help him, but I want to make sure he's a person worth helping.

"What can you tell me about Philip?" I ask, pulling a Pabst out of the refrigerator.

168

When I open the can, Vance gives me a sideways look. My response is to take out a second can and hold it up. He shakes his head.

"I met him and Paul Mahoney through their work with the Southeast Cancer Research Fund. I spoke at a fundraiser for them. They're pleasant people."

"Anything else? Philip specifically."

"He collects records. That's pretty specific. We chatted about vinyl for a good fifteen minutes once."

"Less specific. Go broad."

"He was a defense attorney who inherited some money after his father—who was a circuit court judge—died of cancer. Philip established his law firm after and was quite successful. When Paul Mahoney established the Southeast Cancer Research Fund three years ago, Philip made a sizeable donation. They met at a banquet and hit it off. I think it was only months later that Philip left his firm to work full time for the SCRF. When Paul made the decision to run for mayor, he asked Philip to work on his campaign."

"Is that all?"

"All I know. I told you I've only met Philip a couple of times. And the rest I know from the newspaper."

"Very concise. Thanks."

Curtis Vance looks at me while I take a sip of beer. The look is one a father aims at his child when something bad happens and they want the child to broach the subject first.

Vance exhales deeply, looking annoyed by the standstill. "Do you realize how close you came to going away to prison for a long time?"

"The only way that would have happened is if people hadn't listened to what I was saying. I was manipulated."

"You were greedy. Plain and simple. You did something you shouldn't have for money."

"I was in a bind. I needed the money."

"No one in your situation is this desperate for money."

"You don't know me, Vance. You don't know my life. We're not buds. We don't call each other up and gossip."

"That's true. I'm friends with your father. I helped you on his behalf."

"Helped? What help? Cleaning up my kitchen? You put away the mess the police made after you let them in my house."

"That's all I've done here. Before I came here to help clean up the mess in your house, I was working on cleaning up another mess. I met with a gentleman in Ponte Vedra who claimed a man pretending to deliver a package assaulted him in his own home while shouting out the names of presidents. Oddly enough, he believes he saw his attacker on the evening news later that night and again and again over the past couple of days."

"Shit. I was shouting out the presidents?"

"Supposedly. Not all of them, though."

The internal list must have slipped out of my head. It's probably best to find another way to keep calm. If Doctor Leah lets me come back, maybe she'll have some better way for me to relax and focus other than counting to ten.

"Well, that wasn't intended."

"You didn't consider that, did you? You wanted to create a spectacle and get your face on the news, but you didn't think about the repercussions of your actions."

"I did it to protect my friends and family."

"And who were you protecting when you beat Jason Daniels?"

I don't respond. Vance deserves an answer after helping me out, but I don't want to tell him unless he wants to know enough to push me.

"The other night, I was amazed that you could sit around drinking tequila and eating cake like it's your birthday, preoccupied with yourself and showing a complete lack of sympathy for Paul Mahoney. The callousness you displayed reeks of narcissistic personality—"

"I was protecting a client," I say, tired of listening to Vance talk about me like he's a therapist. The best he can expect is for me to hand over a nickel and call him Lucy. "Jason Daniels was harassing his ex."

"I suppose all the police in St. Johns County were busy?"

"She tried to talk to them. They couldn't do anything."

"Did you try talking to Mr. Daniels? Did you ask him if he was harassing her?"

"Why would I? He's not going to tell me the truth."

"You believed in her story unquestioningly?"

"Yes."

"When you protect people, you end up with a blind spot. It was true back when people hid behind shields, and it's true today. People lie. We do it even more when we want something."

"She just wanted him to leave her alone."

"So you took her word that the police wouldn't help and then went to his apartment and beat him?"

"No. I tried to talk Edith into another course of action. She declined, so I went there and did as she asked."

"Vigilante justice?"

"If that's what you want to call it."

"What I'd call it is poor judgment. It's something that appears to plague every decision you make."

"I did what I thought was right under the circumstances."

"If you think that's right, I think you have a hard time telling the difference between right and wrong."

"The police couldn't help her. Their hands were tied."

"It's not about that. It's not about her. It's about you. And you need to think before you act."

"Don't you dare come into my home and tell me I didn't think this through. I did what my client wanted. Attacking him was the only option she considered viable. If I didn't do as she asked, she would've taken it into her own hands or found someone else. And I'm certain Jason Daniels is a lot better off thanks to my being there."

"Yes. I'm sure his thank you card is in the mail," Vance says slathered in sarcasm. "Who knew you could provide such a delicate beating? It looks like he slipped and hit his head. The damage was so minimal, and his story so unbelievable, that the police dismissed his claim. It's interesting, though. He never blamed his ex for hiring you to attack him."

"They dismissed his claim?" I ask, surprised. "I can't tell if you're serious because most of what you just said could've been with air quotes."

"Shortly after he called them. When I found out about him trying to push the police to investigate, I went to his apartment. We chatted for a while. During that discussion, I persuaded him to stop pestering the police with spurious claims and accusations."

"You threatened him?"

"In the right way. I let him know that monetary repercussions can be great in situations like these."

"You sound like Philip."

"Great minds think alike."

"Thanks for the assist."

"Flynn, I know I'm not a person you probably ever want to see. There's no excuse for my behavior toward you when we were looking for Lily. It's something I've thought about often... I feel ashamed. I took some of my frustration out on you because I got so wrapped up in Lily's disappearance that it was like my own daughter was taken. I never told you this back then—and I know it won't mean a thing to you after all these years—but you deserve to hear me say it. Lily's disappearance wasn't your fault. You were a kid. A kid with more problems than I could've known. And I'm sorry for how I acted."

I stay silent and take a swig of beer. Vance continues.

"That said, at some point, you'll have to stop feeling guilty about the wrong things and start feeling guilty about the right ones. Otherwise, you'll never move on. Lily's gone, Flynn. We all know that. Whether or not Jonathan Heath killed her, that doesn't change the fact that she's gone. The past is the past. We have to accept it and move on."

"I can't. In my dreams, Lily begs me to find her. In my nightmares... In my nightmares, I find her. She died screaming. Alone. I carry that everywhere with me. It's my yoke, binding me to this cart of shit I call a life."

Silence floods the kitchen. This is a conversation neither of us wants to have. I've been leaning against the kitchen counter, trying my hardest to move away, hoping that Vance doesn't notice my unsteady hands and uneven breathing. Vance has been leaning forward in his seat, his hands on his knees and his legs nervously twitching underneath. If this were any other situation, he'd have finished standing up and walked out of the door. The two of us still being here shows that somewhere deep, we both know this discussion, any discussion between the two of us, is necessary and long overdue. Some might even call it cathartic. The problem is, I don't know if I can handle the purification of this relationship. I've disliked Vance for such a long time that I need him as a villain.

Vance stares down at the tile with eyes open wide between slow blinks. I've heard that those attuned to the language of eyes can read

172

blinks and eye movements like a facial semaphore. To me, a person with wide-open eyes tries to take everything in and process it. A person with narrowed eyes hides or shields themselves from the world. I've read that someone looking to the left while speaking may be lying, while looking to the right can indicate that they are telling the truth. The problem with the eyes is that they may tell a great story, but they aren't the first to write it down.

Vance wants to leave. That's obvious. The only thing his eyes might tell me is when he plans on leaving. Something is holding him back. Maybe his mind is processing all that's transpired. Maybe he's trying to think of the right thing to say when he leaves. Maybe he's waiting for me to make a move, to throw him out of my house, to break the silence with another emotional outburst. It's impossible to tell. No one can predict the length of silence or how it will end, but it's best if it's ended by the truth.

"I needed the money for my medication," I say. "The price of my meds went up. My insurance dropped me."

"They can't do that."

"That's what I thought. I did what I did to Jason Daniels because I thought it was the right thing to do. I took the job from Stephen Collins because I didn't have a choice."

"How long has it been since you last took your medication?"

"I can't remember. Two months. Maybe more. I tossed the empty bottles because seeing them made me sad. A lot of useless facts pop up in my head, but trying to remember the last time I took my medication brings a whole lot of nothing to the surface. It's like years blend together. I've been taking them so long I can't pinpoint a time."

"How are you feeling?"

"Some days are better than others. One minute, I'm fine. The next, I have to be asked to calm down in a grocery store because I wasn't simply reading the label on a jar of peanut butter, I was shouting at the jar of peanut butter. In my head, everything feels logical and ordered. It just doesn't always translate to reality that way."

"Flynn, you need to get a lawyer or talk to your father. He could help."

"He's got a new life with a healthy son. He doesn't need us. And he's already paying for my visits to my therapist. Even if I get my medication, I'll never get better. I'll only not get worse. It'd be better for him if he just let me and my mother go."

173

"You know he'll never do that, right?"

"Shore nuff."

"I need to get going," Vance says, standing up from his seat.

"Thanks for cleaning."

"Call your father some time."

"He could call me."

Vance waves his hand in the air—not as a gesture to say goodbye, but as an indication he has no desire to continue discussing this topic. He leaves through the side door toward the garage.

I knock back my beer and grab another from the fridge. With a fresh PBR in hand, I walk through the house from room to room to observe the mess I now need to clean. The amount of damage the police did to the rest of the house is minor compared to my father's old office.

The light switch near the office door lights up four torchiere floor lamps, one in each corner of the room. The floor is a sea of loose paper, manila folders, and pictures. Dozens of numbered boxes rest at various angles against the walls. Floating among the mess in the center of the room is a blue beanbag chair. A bear with a bat branded onto the fake leather stares back at me. Saving the cleanup for later, I cross the debris on the floor and sit down.

The four lamps light up a map of the southeast United States positioned in the center of the ceiling. Pins riddle the map, marking the locations of child abductions. Strings connect to the pins and run off the map to a numbered picture. Each number once corresponded to a box, which represents all the information I could find on a particular child abduction. Close to sixty abductions dating back decades cover the ceiling. Thousands of pages now need sorting and filing.

Lily's picture is the largest of the bunch, and the only without a number. I take a sip of beer and sink into the beanbag. Lily's playful brown eyes are wide and expectant. Something off-camera caught her interest. Another part of the mystery. Another page on the floor.

Thanksgiving is tomorrow. Misty will want to know I'm able to attend. As I pull Misty's phone out of my pocket, my notebook comes out along with it. The notebook's top page contains the contact information for Stephen Collins and the mystery man from Lou Brombacher's office. I send Tin a simple text: *Tell Misty I'll be there tomorrow.*

"Joseph Prince," I say aloud, reading the mystery man's information. "Let's see what you're up to."

Curiosity drives me to make this call. Without a landline on the desk, I'd call it a day. But businesses need a point of contact, and mine is this landline. To use Misty's phone on this hunch would be unduly stupid on my part. It's bad enough that I've given Misty's number to Philip and Lou Brombacher.

This is the last lead. I've made some cash and cleared my name. After this call, I'm on to better things. The phone rings twice and sends me to voicemail. "You've reached the offices of Parker Shipping." The voice is a female, not a Joseph. "Our offices are currently closed. Please leave a message or try again later."

"Hello," I say against my better judgment. "My name is Flynn Dupree. I'm calling about a waylaid shipment and spoke to a Mr. Prince last time I called. Please call me back any time after noon at ..." I provide my home phone number and hang up.

I lie back on my beanbag chair and look up at all the pictures on the ceiling.

The lack of office hours on the recording is odd, but not odd enough to be an issue. Someone opened Lou Brombacher's Rolodex to this person's information. At the time, it sounded like something to do with Stephen Collins. It doesn't appear that way anymore. There's no reason a man on the run would call a shipping company.

Cold beer passes my lips. I'm content.

Chapter 30

Flynn

With my car destroyed and my mother not owning a car thanks to the massive amounts of medication coursing through her body, Misty has to leave the kitchen at her father's home in Mayport to chauffeur us to their Thanksgiving celebration. The look on Misty's face is a subdued version of Munch's *The Scream*, a sign that family time has been a little tense.

"That good?" I ask while helping my mother into the back seat of Misty's car.

"Yup," Misty says, throwing it in reverse before I'm buckled in. Misty glances at me while putting the car in drive and then turns back to me again with a smile. "Your face looks like your Halloween costume was a baby's ass. Pardon my language, Mrs. Dupree."

"He looks adorable," my mother says.

"Just the cutest baby on the block," Misty says in her best goo-goo ga-ga voice with an accompanying slap to the left side of my baby asscheek face.

"Who wants to change the subject?" Misty ribbing me about shaving for Thanksgiving was inevitable. My hair is still the same length, but I shave infrequently enough for it to qualify as a topic of discussion.

"You know I do," Misty replies. "But I don't think you'd be a fan of my next question."

Misty knows me well enough to not upset my mother by asking how I made it out of jail. I stay quiet for the rest of the car trip while my mother and Misty converse and catch up.

When we arrive at Leslie's home, he's sitting on a lawn chair in the front yard, smoking a cigarette and drinking a beer from a longneck bottle. Leslie has a habit of peeling the label off of any beer he drinks. He told me that the urge is so strong he never drinks cans because they don't feel right. Misty pulls her car into the driveway. Leslie stands up and

176

walks over. Leslie was a Navy man for two decades before settling down with his family in Mayport. The naval base nearby makes him feel at home, and his background in the armed services makes his auto shop one of the most successful in the area.

A long-sleeved dress shirt and a pair of jeans replace Leslie's typical wardrobe of dirty sleeveless shirts and dirtier jeans. The dress shirt is a demand Misty made of me as well, but I'm also required to wear khakis.

Leslie holds out his hand for me to shake. Handshakes with Leslie are a reminder of how comfortable a life I've lived. Leslie's calloused and rough hands make mine silky and soft by comparison.

"Barbara, it's been a while," Leslie says, hugging my mother. "You look great."

My mother blushes. She wore one of her brunch outfits to dinner, a red and black skirt with a matching top and coat. Yesterday she made a trip to the salon with her downstairs neighbor Mrs. Pence, where she had her hair trimmed and permed for dinner.

Misty, in her usual black attire, ushers us all inside. Before I can comply, Leslie grabs my shoulder and holds me back.

"We'll be a minute," Leslie says, watching Misty and my mother walk into the house.

Leslie turns around and walks into his garage, where he picks up a chair identical to the one on his front lawn. Leslie walks back to the lawn chair he had been sitting in and places the other one next to it. After he takes a seat, he taps on the armrest of the second chair. I sit down.

We look out across the street at the neighboring houses. Leslie reaches down and pulls a bottle of beer from a cooler on the ground between us. He offers me the beer. I take the bottle and twist off the cap.

"How're things?" Leslie asks.

"Not too bad."

Leslie lights up a cigarette, inhales deeply, and does his best to release the cloud of smoke away from me.

"With the girls around, I can't even smoke in my own house."

Misty is the oldest of five at age twenty-eight. Her brothers Tyler and Aaron, twenty-five and twenty-four respectively, followed in their father's footsteps and enlisted out of high school. With both currently deployed, Leslie is now outnumbered. When Cherie, twenty-two, and Heather, twenty, moved out to go to college, Leslie started smoking inside. Any time his children return home, they force Leslie and his cigarettes back outside.

"Misty told me you ran into a little trouble the other day."

"Yeah. I found my way out of it."

"She said it was pretty big. That you might not make it today."

"I was involved in the explosion at the beach."

Leslie blows out a cloud of smoke and almost drops his cigarette. "Seriously?"

"Misty didn't tell you about it?"

"Not that."

"We both ended up on the news."

"Misty was involved?"

"No. I went to the bakery after. We both ended up on the news in front of the bakery."

"I heard someone died. Is that true?"

"Unfortunately. Paul Mahoney."

"Paul Mahoney…" Leslie takes a drag and thinks for a second before exhaling and turning to me. "Paul Mahoney? The Paul Mahoney? The local millionaire, Paul Mahoney? The man who announced he was running for mayor, Paul Mahoney?"

"The one and only."

"Shit. I donated fifty bucks to his cancer group last year. How did you end up in that mess?"

"I got roped in by a client."

"You're lucky you aren't in jail."

"My car blew up as well. I'm lucky to be alive."

"They tried to kill you?"

I nod.

"At least you got rid of that shit car."

"And now I don't have a car."

"Didn't your father leave you his Golden Hawk?"

"The Studebaker? Yeah, but it's been sitting there for a while. I don't even know if it works."

"I can take a look under the hood."

"No, you don't have to do that."

178

"It's no problem. I'd be more than happy to come over and check it out. I'm a little busy the next couple of days. It'll have to be later at night."

"You don't have to rush anything. Any time would be great."

"The sooner, the better. That way you'll have a car. And it's no problem. I enjoy working on cars at night. It helps me sleep."

I take my keys out of my pocket and pull off a ring holding two keys.

"Here you go. One is for the side door to the garage. The other is the side door to the house. Thanks for checking it out."

Leslie takes the keys and places them in the pocket of his jeans.

"No problem."

"Oh, and if you park in front of the house, William will probably stop by. If he forgets who you are, just remind him you've met before."

"Will do. I'll have it up and running in no time."

"The only problem then is that I'm not a fan of driving stick."

"Don't you drive Misty's hearse around?"

"Yeah. It's just a lot of things all at once. I already miss my automatic."

"You'll get used to it."

"I hope so."

"Well, shit, now that I know you were nearly blown up, it's even better you made it. Miracle of miracles, right?"

Leslie stands up and tosses his cigarette to the ground, where he crushes it with the tip of his oxford.

"Let's head on in," he says, urging me to walk with him. "My new girl is here tonight, meeting everyone for the first time."

Leslie introducing his new girlfriend to everyone at once sounds like the beginning of a holiday disaster. Since his wife died, Leslie has lacked any ability to commit and spends his time bouncing from one woman to the next. The situation can be awkward, but Leslie often adds to the awkwardness by dating women his children deem subpar.

"She's smoking in the bathroom," Misty says, confronting her father at the front door.

"Who is?"

"You know."

"This place already smells like shit, and now she's making it worse. People will need to use the bathroom."

179

"I'd prefer you not say my house smells like shit."

"Well, it does because you always smoke inside. We should have had it at my place like I wanted."

"This feels more like home. We got memories here."

"And the smoke makes them cloudy."

Tin walks up behind Misty and silently motions to a colorful banner hanging over the entrance to the kitchen. There's a sense of pride in how she's pointing it out to me, like a masterpiece unveiled for the first time. The banner has 'Thanksgiving Spectacular' written in an ornate script with drawings of various foods dotting it from end to end. Tin finishes pointing and taps Misty on the shoulder. "I need you in the kitchen. I don't know what I'm doing. Hey, Flynn."

"Hey, Tin. Misty's got you working?"

"Me and Cherie. But I'm lost." Tin smiles. I love that smile, so orderly and kind, and the platinum pixie cut hair and retro cat eye glasses make her even more adorable. "You should head into the living room. Heather and your mother are in there watching football."

"Thanks," I say before Misty pulls Tin back into the kitchen.

"I'll be in the living room in a bit," Leslie says before walking off. "I'll go speak to Ginny about smoking inside."

A conversation between Heather and my mother ends abruptly when I enter the living room. Both turn and focus on me. Heather, who I've not seen in some time since she's been away at FSU, immediately draws my attention. Misty always shelters Heather. She never says a word to anyone when Heather comes to town. I've known the entire family since I was a child, and I only ever find out about Heather's visits after she returns to Tallahassee.

Heather stands up and hugs me. The last time I saw her, she seemed shorter. When she hugs me, there is only an inch or two difference in height.

"Wow, you look great," I say.

"Thanks," Heather says, sitting back down. "Long time, no see."

"It's only been about a year or so."

"She's grown up so much. Look at her," my mother says to me. "You look like a dancer," she says to Heather. "Did you know that my Flynn can dance like a dream?"

"I didn't know that," Heather says, smiling.

180

"You should see him foxtrot."

"Yes, Flynn," Misty's voice says from behind me. "Show us your foxtrot."

"As long as Heather is willing to participate."

Heather stands up.

"Heather, sit back down," Misty says, scowling at me. "I just wanted you all to know that we'll be eating in five."

Misty punches me in the arm, a demand for me to follow her. In the kitchen, Tin is flustered by last-minute string bean toppings as Cherie mashes potatoes in a pot. Cherie looks almost identical to Misty, without the black clothes and piercings. Although, where Misty is a petite woman, Cherie is a little more round. Her roundness is neither unhealthy nor unnatural. Life wears away at everyone's edges. Modern life rounds us off sooner than people would like. Despite her youth, Cherie's edges have all softened, eroded like sea glass by the constant ebb and flow of an office job that keeps her tethered to a desk too many hours a day.

"Hey, Cherie," I say, walking over for a hug.

Cherie hugs me and goes right back to mashing potatoes. Misty takes me by the arm and pushes me out of the way.

"What was going on there with Heather?"

"Nothing."

"Stay away, Flynn."

"I don't know, Misty," I say with a laugh. "We're friends and all, but that doesn't take her off the table."

"You've known her since she was a child."

"I've known you since we were in middle school."

"If I see your wolf eyes look in her direction again, I will end you."

"When do I get to meet this Cubs fan?"

"Really? That's where your head is now?"

"Why not? Any time seems like the appropriate time."

"Maybe you should stop by the bakery. I can introduce you now that the police are no longer up your tailpipe."

"Always making up plans for my tailpipe," I say. "I'll make sure I add that to my schedule."

"For now, go schedule yourself a seat at the dinner table."

My mother and Heather follow my lead to the dining room. My mother takes a seat next to me, while Heather sits directly across the

181

table. Cherie brings out the mashed potatoes and sits at the end of the table next to Heather and me. Leslie enters the dining room hand-in-hand with a woman wearing a pink top and a pair of pink shorts made for someone thirty years younger. The woman's blonde hair frizzes out and frames a narrow face accentuated by an abundance of bright makeup.

"Barbara, Flynn, this is Virginia," Leslie says.

"Nice to meet you," Virginia says. The bright pink clothes overcompensate for her rough and deep voice. Cigarettes have done a number on her vocal cords. "You can call me Ginny."

"Nice to meet you, too," I reply.

My mother watches Ginny with muted interest. I've seen that look before. It's the one she wears when she needs to understand something. The look continues as Ginny takes a seat next to Heather.

Misty brings the remainder of the food out and sits down at the other end of the table. Tin takes the last seat between Misty and my mother.

"I'd like to say grace if you don't mind," Leslie says.

"That would be lovely," my mother replies, her head nodding.

Everyone bows their heads, and then Leslie begins.

"Dear heavenly Lord, I thank you for this bountiful feast before us and for bringing together our family and friends. I thank you for watching over my boys and keeping them safe, wherever they may be. And I would also like to welcome Virginia," Leslie stops mid-sentence due to a loud cough from Cherie. "I would like to welcome Virginia to dine with us under your light. Amen."

Piles of mashed potatoes, turkey, ham, green beans, sweet potatoes, and stuffing end up strategically placed on plates around the table in less than a minute.

Tin glances at me over and over again as I eat. She puts her fork down before asking, "Weren't you a vegetarian not too long ago?"

"Yeah."

"Really?" Heather asks.

"Actually, Tin, I still am. I'm just not a very good one."

"It's silly," my mother says, stating it as a fact. "People are made to eat meat. End of story."

"But not everyone thinks that way, Ma."

"I swear, Flynn. You're always trying to not be you. Swearing off meat. Letting your hair grow out. Growing a beard? Why a beard?"

182

"I shaved it, Ma."

"It's like you're trying to hide."

She's right. I try to hide. The beard, the hat, the glasses. These make me feel more comfortable. Something about having one more layer makes life move a little more smoothly.

"At least he's not wearing his hat," Misty says.

"Misty's right about that old thing. My son, always wearing hats. I hate those dirty things. They cover up your eyes. And those awful glasses. It's like you hate a gift from God."

"Your mother's right," Heather says. "I had the biggest crush on you when I was younger. The eyes were a big part of that."

A warmth creeps across my face. It's a telltale sign I'm blushing. I'm missing Mordecai and my beard now more than ever. Right now, I'd prefer to hide.

Misty starts turning red. The black makeup and piercings highlight her growing rage.

"Are you single?" my mother asks Heather.

My eyes focus on Heather, who smiles and lowers her head, and then to Misty, who places her elbows on the table and stares at me.

"There are a lot of guys at FSU. I try to focus on studying."

"That's a no," my mother grabs me around the neck and pulls me close to her. "A perfect match."

I force an uncomfortable smile and take off my glasses, using the sleeve of my dress shirt to wipe my forehead.

"There they are," my mother says. "The eyes have come out to play."

I put my glasses back on and stress-laugh, knowing my face is now turning a darker shade of red. Everyone except Misty and Cherie laughs.

"You all right, Cher?" Leslie asks.

"I'm fine, Dad."

"You're just a little quiet is all."

"I speak for at least forty hours a week. My jaw is tired."

Cherie's job is in a call center. Some days she talks so much her voice is shot at the end of her shift.

"Doesn't look like it's stopping you from eating," Ginny says with a smile. The comment was, I'm sure, meant as a lighthearted joke about her jaw currently being used to eat food. It's not being taken that way around the table.

183

When their mother died, all the children took the loss hard. Leslie associating with different women off and on throughout the rest of their childhood didn't make it easier on them. To those lonely children, each new woman could have been the one to take their father away. This made any woman who came through the door a potential threat, and that feeling still lives on.

"So, you're saying I'm fat?" Cherie asks.

"No, I was just saying that you were eating—"

"Cherie, she didn't mean it like that."

"No, Dad. It certainly sounded like that's what she meant."

Cherie is fuming at this point and looks like she might throw a plate across the room. When she picks up her fork and knife and places them onto the plate, I feel a tug on my khakis right around the knee. Cherie stands up and puts both of her hands on the table.

"The nerve," Cherie says, "to come to the house we grew up in dressed like a bleached-out whore." I look to my mother, who is watching with a smile. The rest of the table is in shock, waiting for Cherie to finish her thought. I feel an urge to cover my mother's ears because I know something big is about to come out Cherie's mouth. "We've opened up our house, cooked for you, and this is how you act? What I'd love is for you to walk out our front door and go back to blowing sailors and fishermen for beer and loose cigarettes."

Cherie speaks in such a calm and sober tone that it takes everyone by surprise. Ginny's face runs in streaks of makeup as tears pour from her eyes. Leslie escorts her to the master bedroom at the back of the house.

At the same time everyone sits staring, the tug on my knee grows into a foot on my thigh. The initial shock almost sends me into a standing position with both hands in the air. Instead, I try to remain calm and act like nothing is happening. Heather stares at me with a wry smile while I try my best to shake my head with no one else noticing.

Cherie's knee hits Heather's leg the instant she sits back down.

"What in the fuck is that?" Cherie asks, looking under the table.

Misty sticks her head under the table and then bobs right back up.

"Flynn," she shouts.

"Yes, Misty," I say, eating a forkful of turkey.

"Don't blame Flynn," Cherie says. "It's not like it's his foot inching toward her crotch."

184

"Am I the only one who realizes my mother is sitting next to me at the table?"

Misty practically jumps up from the table. Tin follows in unison.

"Sit down," Tin says to Misty.

"I told you to stay away."

"I didn't—"

Heather stands up from the table and looks defiantly at Misty. "Last time I checked, we're both adults."

"Oh, shit," I say, standing up. "Can we all go talk about this somewhere else?"

"That's a magnificent idea," Tin says.

"You can't tell me what I can and can't do," Heather says.

"So, what, you're going to go and do Flynn?" Misty asks.

"If that's what I want, yes."

"He's eight years older than you for chrissakes! That's nearly half your age."

"And if I were eighty and he was eighty-eight, it wouldn't matter as much."

"No. The thought of you two together, even old, would still bother me."

Heather walks away from the table and back to her bedroom. The slamming door reverberates through the house.

"All of this food has been delicious," I say to break up the awkward silence.

"Shut the fuck up, Flynn," Misty says.

"Heather's not a child." Cherie points a finger in Misty's direction. "You're not our mother. You're our sister. You forget that too often."

The ring tone for a new text message goes off in my pocket. The sound happens again and then dies down.

"Was that my phone?" Misty asks.

"Probably not," I say, pulling the phone out of my pocket and unlocking it. A text message opens.

If I want to fuck Flynn, you can't stop me.

"Nothing on here," I say.

I lock the phone and put it back into my pocket. The ring tone for a text message goes off again.

"Give me my fucking phone!" Misty shouts.

185

I reluctantly slide the phone across the table to Misty. Tin snags it and places it in her pocket.

My mother grabs my arm, prompting me to turn to her.

"Flynnie, what's the name of that song? It goes 'Do dooo do doo do do do.'"

Sometimes, I wish I could tune out everything like my mother. Reality approaches quickly and can turn to violence at the drop of a hat. In her mind, she finds peace in something as simple as a song playing over and again.

"I'm not sure, Ma. Let's go watch more football."

"Don't worry," she says to me while standing up from her chair. "I'll think of it before too long."

Chapter 31

Amy

Thanksgiving for my family is a minor occasion. It's always been that way. As an only child, the Thanksgiving family get-together has always been a work of fiction. None of us place a lot of stock in the holiday. We eat food together and then go about our business. My parents decide this Thanksgiving deserves special attention.

My mother cannot cook. This is part of the reason Thanksgiving never mattered in our family. The only time she cooks is when she pulls something from a package and follows the instructions. She spent the last twenty-five years of her life working as an accountant. Numbers and instructions are something she can understand, but the best kinds of food come without an instruction manual. Fixing this is no easy feat. The only way for us to have a special Thanksgiving meal is to buy it. A grocery store in Ponte Vedra provides these meals to the hopeless cooks of the world for a hefty price. The desperate pay for the entire meal, all the way down to tiny packs of butter for the rolls.

Dinner starts at five o'clock sharp. Stress shut down my appetite at some point during the past week. The smell of the food unknots my stomach, telling me it's open for business once again. My mother bought enough to feed a family of eight. That abundance makes it a perfect time to play catch up and put some necessary calories back in my body. The turkey is a little dry and bland, so I smother it in gravy and add some stuffing to each forkful. Sweet potato casserole is new to me. The toasted marshmallows on top put the dish in a category that's both dessert and savory. There is little to no discussion at the table other than the food itself. "This is delicious." "That seems odd." "What exactly is this?" Twenty minutes in, my stomach reaches its limit.

After dinner, when my parents are both in the kitchen, I decide to let them know I'll no longer be staying at their house.

"I know you're both concerned about my safety," I say to my parents. My mother stops washing the dishes. My father sets down his cup of coffee. "But I'm supposed to be house-sitting for my boyfriend while he's away on vacation."

This is a half-truth. Iain never asked me to house-sit for him. He did, however, provide me with a key and ask me to check in occasionally and make sure the mail doesn't pile up too much.

"That's not something you should worry about, dear," my father says. "He'll understand when he gets back and you tell him the circumstances."

"The problem is that he's paying me, and I'm also supposed to be taking care of his dog. That's where I've been disappearing to. It'll all be easier if I stay there." This is all untrue, but I know these lies will make my parents feel guilty about trying to prevent me from leaving.

"Well, where is this house? Your father and I can come with you. That way, we'll know where you are. And we can stop by and make sure you're—"

"No. He wouldn't appreciate me bringing people he doesn't know into his house. Even if those strangers are my parents."

"It sounds like you're taking this seriously," my father says with a stern look. "I'm proud of you for being so strong despite all that's happened."

I blush. My father's kindness makes me feel like my lies are much more significant.

"And you don't have to worry about my safety. It's a nice, big house in Ponte Vedra with a gate and a security system."

"Weren't there some robberies in Ponte Vedra not too long ago? A woman was killed, I think," my mother says while drying off a newly cleaned dish.

"I'll have the dog there. It's a Siberian Husky, so it'll keep me safe."

"I always wonder why people buy dogs like that for Florida. It just doesn't make a whole lot of sense considering the coat."

"I couldn't agree with you more, Dad. I thought it was weird myself."

"Stay here a minute before you leave," my father says, sprinting out of the kitchen. When he returns, he's holding a black gun box in his right hand and a box of bullets in his left. "I want you to take this with you."

188

I'm surprised, but I understand. My father and I used to go to the shooting range twice a month. The Colt Cobra .38 Special inside the box is something I've practiced with for years.

"What a great idea," my mother says. "I didn't even think about that."

"Just remember everything I taught you," my father says with a hug before handing me the gun box and the bullets. He escorts me to the door. "And don't forget to call us if you need anything."

"Thanks, Daddy." I give my father a peck on the cheek and leave.

Chapter 32

Stephen

The air conditioning is broken in the Taurus wagon I hot-wired after we ditched Paul Mahoney's Cadillac. In fact, the only thing that works in this god-awful, ramshackle, piece of shit station wagon held together by duct tape and Bondo is the engine. The windows are manual, and even they start popping as soon as you roll them down more than an inch. The sad thing is, the car, as terrible as it may be, reminds me of better times. We bought a used Taurus wagon like this after our wedding. "The smart choice," the salesman told Helen. She smiled. It stank of soccer dad. I still bought it for her. It lasted until I could afford to trade it in for something better.

Today would be our fifth Thanksgiving together as a family. It has only been days since the dream of turkey dinner at the dining room table felt like an undeniable reality. Helen bought both a turkey and a ham at the store because the ham was only fifty cents per pound when purchased together with a turkey. This year was meant to be a feast. It was meant to be a time for family—a time for our family. Now it all feels so far away. Turkey dinner is only a dream. Canned chicken in a station wagon is our reality.

Curled up into a ball, Helen is on the passenger-side seat sobbing. She refuses to eat. I don't blame her. The chicken tastes more like salt than chicken. It was the only thing in the gas station close to turkey. Even the turkey sandwiches—the there every day rain or shine sandwiches—were missing from the cooler. Our gas station meal is chicken in a pop-top can, two bottles of water, two old apples waxed to a mirrored finish, and a bag of Bugles. Deep down, I had hoped the Bugles would remind Helen of little cornucopias. They did not.

When Helen speaks, it is individual words separated by choking sobs to form the same shattered question: "What—have—we—done—to—deserve—this?"

Every time I tell her, "Nothing," she takes a labored breath and continues to cry.

The truth can hurt. This might be the first time in Helen's life that she has truly felt like things are out of control. We have always been able to overcome any wall that stood in our way. This time that wall feels insurmountable. I have tried to keep a brave face while near her. The calm facade is nothing more than a lie. She knows me too well.

Chapter 33

Flynn

The Thanksgiving Spectacular ran shorter than expected. Leslie dropped my mother off at her condo and me at my house. It's not even four o'clock, and it feels like bedtime. Emotional roller coasters tire me out. A Pabst from the fridge accompanies me up the stairs to the office. The answering machine light is flashing. Bypassing the Cubs beanbag chair, I continue to the flashing red number two. I'm reluctant to push the button.

There's a chance Misty left me a message explaining how to fit various objects in various orifices. Tongue lashings are best taken all at once, ensuring tomorrow will be a better day. I push the play button.

"Hello, Detective Dupree. My name is Maura Danes." The only Danes I know is Edith. This voice sounds older, so I'm reasonably sure this is Edith's mother. She's speaking carefully, as though she rehearsed this message in her mind before calling. "You are one of the last people Edith called. She did not show up for Thanksgiving. Please call me at …" I jot down the phone number Maura recites on a piece of paper nearby. "We are concerned."

The message concerns me, too. Vance said Jason tried to appeal to the police, and they turned him away. This could be how he got back at Edith.

A second message plays.

"Flynn. This is your mother speaking. I remembered that song. I thought you would like to know."

The voicemail ends with her leaving me in the dark about the song's title. I delete my mother's message and dial the number Maura provided. The phone rings once before being answered.

"Hello?" The voice is Maura Danes.

"Mrs. Danes? This is Flynn Dupree."

"Oh, Detective Dupree. You received my message. I'm sorry to call you, but we already called the police. They said they couldn't help us until Edith was missing longer. I thought that since you're a detective, you might help us."

"I'm not a detective, ma'am."

"Edith has you as Detective Dupree in her phone."

"I'm a private consultant. What happened? You said she's missing."

"We don't know what happened. Edith hasn't been returning our calls. Today, she didn't show up to help cook. It's not like Edith. She's not at her apartment. There is a mess here, and she left her phone behind."

"When was the last time you spoke to her?"

"Edith spoke to Daphne on Monday. That's my other daughter. We both tried to call her Wednesday, but she didn't pick up. She told Daphne on Monday that she met someone. They were going to dinner on Wednesday."

"What's the last call she made with her cell?"

"I don't know. Let me give the phone to Daphne."

"Thank you, ma'am."

"Hello." Daphne sounds like she has a cold or has been crying.

"Daphne, my name is Flynn Dupree. Who was the last person Edith called, and when?"

"One second," Daphne says. Thirty seconds of intermittent noise passes as she searches the phone and speaks to her mother. "The last person she called was Brian. It was Monday at about seven."

"Your mother said that you called me because I was one of her most recent contacts. Did you call Brian?"

"Yeah. Brian said he hasn't talked to Edith. They were supposed to go out Wednesday. She didn't show up or call to cancel."

"You're at Edith's apartment, right?"

"Yeah."

"What's the address?" Daphne provides me the address. "I'm coming over. My car isn't working, so it may take me a while. I'll be there as soon as possible."

"Do you think everything's okay?"

"I'll see you soon."

I hang up and rifle through my desk for Curtis Vance's phone number. Nothing. All of my notes are gone. I'll have to remember to ask the police for everything back.

Vance is one of the few people I feel comfortable enough to call in this situation. My issues aside, he has plenty of connections. Things might go smoother if he comes along. Plus, I can't think of anyone other than William who might give me a ride somewhere on Thanksgiving. William can rub people the wrong way when they first meet him. I'd rather not create roadblocks when meeting Edith's family.

Vance's phone number isn't something I've ever considered remembering. I doubt he's listed, which makes the white pages useless. The other option is my father. The two of them talk all the time. He's bound to know the quickest way to get in touch with Vance.

My father's phone number is one I have committed to memory. I think about calling it often but rarely do. He has specific times during the day when he picks up the phone. An unexpected call from eight to four will go to voicemail. During those hours, he's working and does not appreciate disruptions. He used to get upset when I'd interrupt his workday. In his world, the law is a burden we all bear. The only way for him to reduce the burden is to limit his exposure. He does that by only working during specific times of the day. Any interruption forces him to refocus, adding extra time and effort to his work like penalty minutes.

The one benefit I have over other callers is that I don't call without reason. If he's paying attention and sees my phone number calling, he picks up. This holds true when he picks up on the second ring.

"Flynn? Happy Thanksgiving."

"Happy Thanksgiving, Dad."

"I was wondering if you would call."

I don't know how to respond.

"How was Misty's?"

"How did you know that's where we went?"

"I know you can't cook. Neither can your mother. Misty can. And she's like family. Also, your mother told me you were going there."

"Oh."

My parents separated ten years ago and divorced a year later. I was old enough to understand why it all fell apart, but no one is ever old enough to accept their world ending. Our lives had been picture-perfect before

Lily's disappearance. One blow after another pounded the foundations until they crumbled, destroying everything we built. My father returned to Chicago, where he was born and raised, and moved on with his life. He remarried and started a new family. I've only met his son, Francis, once. Right now, he'd be about four. My father moved on to a whole new life, leaving the rest of us to figure out what to do with the rubble.

"Misty's was great. Loads of fun. Dinner and a show. How was yours?"

"Great. Francis is getting to the age where he can partake. He doesn't like turkey or ham. He had a peanut butter sandwich with mashed potatoes on the side. Slightly unorthodox. Highly entertaining."

"Listen, Dad. I need to get in touch with Curtis Vance."

"Does this have to do with what he's been calling 'The Great Unpleasantness'?"

"Not really."

"The last time I saw something called 'The Great Unpleasantness' it was referring to the American Civil War."

My father probably read that in a book. All I have to do is ask if I want to know where. He can tell me the book, the author, the context, the page, and probably even provide me a word-for-word quote.

"Flynn, I know you're old enough to make your own decisions—you need to be more careful. What happened is coming back to me filtered through Curtis. He's made it sounds like it's all a big misunderstanding. Considering the circumstances, that's unlikely. I wish I could protect you, but wishes won't make me anything more than flesh and blood."

"You prompted an illegal search of my house to ensure all evidence was unusable."

"Did I?"

"What bothers me most is that the only reason you would do something like that is if you thought I was guilty."

"Did I ever tell you the story about Santo in Philly?"

"Probably."

My father loves telling stories about the Cubs. He's passed along life lessons through Cubs stories for as long as I can remember. Years ago, my mother secured him a spot at the Cubs fantasy camp in Arizona. That camp provided him access to a lot of the players he had known from a distance for so long. The stories they told were the same stories he had been recounting all of my life. Ron Santo, arguably one of the greatest third basemen to grace the game, was my father's favorite. So much so that I used to jump in the air and click my heels together whenever the Cubs won a game because I knew it would make him laugh. For my father, a Santo story is suitable for any occasion.

"The Cubs are in Philly. Santo hits a three-run blast in the eighth. To his surprise, the Philly crowd gives him a standing ovation. Santo comes into the dugout and says to Glenn Beckert, 'I've never had anyone give me a standing ovation on the road.' Beckert responds, 'You still haven't, Ron. Take a look at the scoreboard. A man just walked on the moon.'"

The phone is silent. I can't tell what he's thinking, but I know what he's implying. Not everything is as it seems. Sometimes in life, we need to look up at the scoreboard to understand what's going on.

"Thanks for the advice."

"You're welcome. And if you need money, all you have to do is ask. I know you get kicks out of the whole private eye shtick. It's dangerous, Flynn. There are a lot of dangerous people out there."

"That's why I need Vance's number. One of my clients may be in trouble. I need his help."

My father provides me Vance's cell and home phone numbers. His mind is like an encyclopedia, and his ability to recall information is something that makes me jealous. I remember studying for tests when I was younger, and he could answer any question I might have without having to glance at my textbooks. His eidetic memory allows him to recall almost every moment of his life in detail. He once described it as a placid lake stretching into the distance with buoys as a guide. My memory is like looking out at the ocean during a storm. The cresting waves are all I see. For my father, there are no waves. Every inch is visible, but only if he's willing to take the time and look.

"Thanks, Dad. Enjoy the rest of your Thanksgiving."

"You too. Be careful."

I disconnect with my father and dial Vance's home phone.

"Curtis speaking."

"This is Flynn. I need you to come over to my house as soon as you can."

"Is everything all right?"

"The client I told you about, the one who dated Jason Daniels, is missing."

"Are you sure?"

"Her mother called me. The last time she spoke to anyone was on Monday."

"You think Jason Daniels had something to do with it?"

"I don't know. Did anything seem out of the ordinary to you when you visited him?"

"No. He was dressed for a night on the town, which was odd because he said he didn't have any plans. His apartment was cleaner than most single men keep their space."

"I need you to pick me up."

"It's Thanksgiving. I'm getting ready to have dinner with my family."

"A woman's life is on the line. I'd drive myself, but my car is a burned husk."

"Let me call you back."

Vance disconnects. The dial tone fills my ear. Numbing silence erases the sound of the dial tone from my memory as I spend the next fifteen minutes waiting for the phone to ring. It never does.

With the callback in limbo, I get ready in case Vance is on his way over. An old houndstooth blazer with suede patches on the elbows suits the occasion. I'm still wearing the khakis and dress shirt Misty required for Thanksgiving. The jacket completes the casual professor look. It's something that might prove useful when I meet with Edith's family. I corrected them about my being a detective. This little touch might help them feel more at ease when we speak.

The doorbell rings before I can make it back to the office to continue staring at the phone. It can't be Vance. Twenty minutes isn't enough time for him to explain to his family why he's missing dinner and make it across town to my front door. On the other side of the door, in a pair of cutoff jean shorts and a black shirt with the word 'Safari' in neon yellow letters across the front, is Officer Rittwell.

"Nice jacket. I like the patches."

"Nice shorts. They accentuate your hairy thighs in ways that make me wish I could erase my memory."

Officer Rittwell is silent.

"What are you doing here? Out on a safari?"

197

"Curtis called me, and Safari is a Journey tribute band."

"Less interested in Safari and more in why Vance called you."

"To help you out."

"That's just rude."

"What?"

"I asked him to come over."

"He asked me to come over."

"So, he did."

"I can leave."

My preferences no longer matter. Edith is in trouble. Every second I spend being selfish could cost her.

"No. I need a ride. Let's go."

Officer Rittwell drives a red Jeep when he's not in his squad car. The missing soft-top tarp that covers the bulk of the seating space allows me to climb in rather than use the door. I use the roll bar to lift myself and then slide over the door.

"Head to Ponte Vedra, I'll shout directions as you need them."

Rittwell drives down Third Street without ever saying a word. The sound of the wind sweeping into the Jeep is enough to fill the void of silence between us.

The wind dies down, and the awkward silence returns as we reach a stoplight. A homeless man with a sign sits on the median only a few feet from the Jeep. The man stands up and approaches us holding a sign reading: *Out of work. Please. Anything will help feed my family.*

I shout at the homeless man, "Come on over."

Officer Rittwell looks perturbed as the man approaches. I hand Rittwell a crisp kite flyer. It's one of the bills I received from the artist formerly known as Harold.

"You gotta be kidding me."

"Give it to him."

Rittwell gives him the money. The homeless man's repeated shouting of, "Thank you," fades as we drive away.

"Why on earth would you give that bum a hundred bucks?"

"It's Thanksgiving, and he had a sign saying it was to feed his family."

"You know it's gonna be smoked or drunk away, right?"

"He could spend it on booze or drugs. It doesn't matter to me. But there is a possibility he spends it to help his family. That does matter to me."

"What in the hell? You're willing to give a hundred bucks to some piece of crap on the side of the road, but you don't feel even the least bit of remorse for killing a man."

"As cliché as it may be, the world isn't always black and white. We spend most of our time in the gray."

"Black, white, or gray, you're still an idiot for giving a bum that much money."

"It's from the money Stephen Collins gave me."

Officer Rittwell looks at me and says nothing. We ride the rest of the way to Edith's apartment with the silence only being broken by my providing the occasional driving direction.

Edith lives on the third floor of a three-story building. That explains why she was adamant no one entered her apartment through her windows. It's also good to know that Edith shares my fondness for living on the top.

An older woman opens the door.

"Detective Dupree?" she asks. Based on her voice, she is Maura Danes.

Rittwell raises an eyebrow and shoots me a look.

"Flynn Dupree, ma'am. I'm not a detective."

"That's right. You told me that over the phone. Who is this gentleman?"

"Leonard Rittwell. I'm with the Atlantic Beach Police Department. I'm accompanying Mr. Dupree as a personal favor."

"Thank you. Come in."

We both enter the apartment. Edith's trap for her ex is a paintball gun mounted on a pedestal secured to the floor. Wires coil around the base, connecting to two nails hammered into the baseboards four feet from the front door. Orange spots cover the white walls around us.

How much time we lose to fear? Is it a day, a week, a month, a year? It's hard to say and even harder to know what we fear. We all hide behind locks and dogs and guns and pepper spray and time-tested nuggets of wisdom like 'better safe than sorry.' But how useful is it? If we spent a minute trying to understand our evil inclinations for every hour we spend trying to protect ourselves from the evils of the world, then we all might

199

be better off. Instead, we hide behind locked doors and fear the unknown. Because it's easy to fear. It's easy to turn a key and separate ourselves from the savages lurking outside. Such a simple act makes us feel good. It makes us feel safe. The lock and key mark us as one of the civilized. But that civility comes at a cost. Locking ourselves away prevents us from understanding what waits on the other side. Keyholders can only prepare by looking at the dark corners of their own souls.

Edith counted on a lock to protect her. If Edith stopped to think about how far she would chase a desire, then she might have understood that a lock is just an object, and a door is only a speed bump along the way. Whoever took Edith was in this mindset. They entered the apartment and, despite a paintball pelting, remained undeterred.

"Is he okay?" a disembodied voice asks.

"Flynn? Flynn?" Officer Rittwell grabs my arm and shakes me. "What's wrong with you?"

"Nothing," I say, collecting myself. "Must've had too much turkey today."

Two women walk toward us. One of the women, a blonde in a form-fitting black dress, approaches us with her hand outstretched.

"Stephanie Rausch," she says, shaking my hand and then Rittwell's.

I don't see anyone else in the apartment, so I assume the other woman is Daphne. She's wearing jeans and a t-shirt. Her hair is a vibrant and unnatural shade of red that settles my curiosity as to what a troll doll would look like if they were the size of a human and living among us.

"Daphne?" I ask to be certain.

"Uh-huh."

"Stephanie is the manager of the apartment," Edith's mother says.

"Yes," Stephanie adds. "Maura contacted me after she called the police. I'm here to help."

"Thanks," I say, walking back to the door and looking at the locks. There's a simple lock on the door handle and a complicated lock for the deadbolt. There isn't a single scratch on or around the locks, which is a sign no one has tampered with either. "These look new. Edith told me these were changed recently."

"Yes," Stephanie says. "Someone broke into Edith's apartment. We changed them out for her."

"How many people have keys to this apartment?"

200

"Whoever she's made copies for and us."

"What do you mean by 'us'?"

"The office has a couple sets for every lock. The maintenance group should have a couple copies as well."

"So, several exist?"

"People lose their keys. For the sake of convenience, we have copies just in case."

"When were the locks changed?"

"After the break-in."

"Day of? Day after? When?"

"Monday. I put in the work order Monday."

"Could I talk to you outside?"

The request confuses Maura and Daphne. They voice their opinions to Officer Rittwell as Stephanie obliges and follows me outside.

"Did Edith tell you about her ex?"

"I didn't know her that well."

"What did she say after the break-in occurred?"

"Someone else in the office spoke to her. They brought it to my attention once the police were involved. One of our employees changed the locks. Only he didn't believe anyone broke into her apartment."

"Why?"

"The locks weren't damaged, and there was no damage to the door or the frame."

"What do they think happened?"

"He thought she left her door unlocked. Then someone played a joke on her. It's possible. I've accidentally left my door unlocked before."

"Was the deadbolt unlocked when she came back home that night?"

"Why does that matter?"

"If it was someone randomly stumbling across an unlocked door, then they couldn't have locked the deadbolt when they left unless they had a key."

"I don't know. Maybe she left a set of keys inside or gave a key to someone else."

"Edith mentioned her ex had a key. She also said she had the locks changed after they broke up."

"I could check on that and see."

201

"No need. I don't see why she'd lie about changing the locks. Could you put together a list of everyone who's worked since they installed the new locks? Try to include when they worked."

"Why?"

"You said everyone here has access to apartment keys. I'd like to know who's had access recently."

"How soon do you need the list?"

"As soon as possible."

Stephanie gives me a questioning look. It's the look a camel gives when their load of straw is reaching max capacity. I can't blame her. It's Thanksgiving. If Misty's Thanksgiving Spectacular had gone smoother, I would still be at her father's house enjoying a beer. Nothing ever works out as planned. We're all here right now for a reason. Stephanie needs to understand that.

"Someone has taken Edith. That's a guarantee." I could be wrong, but I need to start strong. Any doubt in my language can create doubt in Stephanie's mind. "The woman lived her life by a schedule. She would not miss Thanksgiving with her family. It's not something Edith would have overlooked. That means someone has her. I don't know what he's doing to her. I don't know what he's done to her. All I know is that she is gone. And we don't even know for how long. Imagine yourself in that situation. How long would you like someone to dawdle?"

"I can have it ready in an hour."

"Thank you. Instead of waiting here, I'll go speak with Edith's ex."

"I'll be in the front office. Come there when you finish."

"Thanks."

Stephanie walks down the stairs as I return to Edith's apartment. Everyone stops and stares at me.

"Is Stephanie gone?" Maura asks.

"She's getting some information for me. She said it'll take her a little while."

"What are we supposed to do?" Daphne asks. "You want us to stay here and wait?"

"That's not a bad idea. Someone might call or show up."

"What are you going to do?"

"Speak with Jason."

"Is he involved?" Daphne asks.

It's best to conceal my feelings. I could say yes and cause them to panic, but that won't benefit anyone. Lying could have the same effect. The common-sense approach is hiding how I feel and moving forward.

"He knows Edith. He might be able to provide us something to help find her."

"Will you come back here?" Maura asks.

"Stephanie said she'll have information for me in about an hour. I'll be back after that. Don't worry if I don't come back immediately. There's a good chance I might follow up on her information before I come back here."

"You're just going to leave us—"

"We'll wait here, Mr. Dupree," Maura says, looking at her daughter. "Please come back when you find something."

"I promise."

Officer Rittwell exits the apartment. I follow. He looks over his shoulder as though someone is following us. After climbing back into his Jeep, Rittwell turns to me.

"They think someone took her."

"So do I."

Chapter 34

Flynn

The exterior of Jason's apartment is as I remember it. Nothing about it has changed, yet it seems like weeks have passed since I sat in my car and watched the front door, waiting for the right moment to attack.

This time is different. I don't sit and observe or wait for the right moment to strike. I climb out of the Jeep and walk right up to the front door. Rittwell follows and stays to the side of the door while I knock.

No one answers.

Showing up here could be a waste of time. I've assumed that Jason will be home. He's a single man living alone. He could be out of state visiting family for all I know.

I knock again. No response.

Rittwell shrugs his shoulders.

"I wouldn't open the door for you either," Rittwell says, laughing at his own joke.

The laugh ends when the sound of a turning lock begins. The door creaks open halfway. No one sticks their head out. Several seconds pass with nothing else happening.

"Hello?" I say, pushing the door. There's no resistance other than the weather-proofing on the bottom scraping across the doormat. The door comes to a stop at the wall. No one is in the foyer.

"Hello?" I say louder than the first time.

No one responds. Fairy tales begin when magical doors open themselves. Fairy tales go wrong when the eager stumble through those open doors. I enter the foyer with an ounce of caution.

Whoever opened the door is coaxing us inside. The only reason to coax someone inside is to gain the upper hand. The only reason to need the upper hand is if you are planning on attacking. As the dots connect, Jason comes around the corner with a baseball bat.

Owning a Louisville Slugger is a sign that Jason can make proper decisions. There's a certain class in a Louisville Slugger that you won't find in an aluminum bat. There's history in that wood. But history and class don't translate well when the bat becomes a weapon. In this instance, the bat is no better than the bone of an animal, and the only way it's of any use is if the person swinging it around is of equal or greater intelligence than the missing link at the beginning of *2001: A Space Odyssey*. Jason's first swing misses and connects with the wall. The bat goes through the drywall, forcing Jason to struggle with pulling it back out. In that instant, Officer Rittwell's training kicks in. He pushes me aside and tackles Jason to the ground. Jason performs a spot-on impression of a wet noodle and submits immediately.

"What're you doing in my house?" Jason shouts at the top of his lungs.

"Keep him still," I say to Rittwell. "I'll go search."

The apartment only has one bedroom. It takes less than a minute to determine Edith is not here. There's no clothing covered in paintball paint and nothing to indicate that a woman has ever set foot in this apartment. The immaculate interior makes me wonder if he's hiding something.

"Where's Edith?" I ask, walking back to Jason. I kneel so he can see my face. "Where's Edith?"

"Why would I tell you?"

"Because it's the right thing to do."

"Says the guy who assaulted me."

"You assaulted both of us with a baseball bat." Rittwell twists Jason's arm behind his back. "You're lucky I don't arrest you right now."

"You're not a cop."

"Actually, he is. He's off duty, though. Tell us what you know about Edith."

"If you're a cop, you need to arrest this guy. Look at what he did to my face."

Jason has a black eye and a split lip. They are minor injuries that have all but healed.

"You came at us with a bat. He didn't touch you."

"He attacked me the other day. You pigs wouldn't listen to me and arrest his ass."

"Edith is missing. Do you know anything about what happened to her?"

"No. I haven't talked to her in months."

"You haven't been stalking her?"

"I'm not wasting another minute of my life on that bitch. She's had it in for me since the moment I dumped her list-making ass. First, she burns my fucking clothes. Then, she tries to get the police to arrest me. And now, you assholes."

"You haven't been calling and leaving threatening messages?"

Jason's eyes and facial expressions are as sincere as a man pinned to the ground by another man wearing jorts could ever be.

"I went crazy when she burned my shit. The police told me to leave her alone or end up in jail. I've left her alone. I don't want any more trouble. Please leave me alone."

"Let's go," I say, standing up.

Rittwell releases Jason and walks over to the Louisville Slugger. He picks up the bat and puts it over his shoulder before walking away.

"Oh, come on, man. That thing was expensive."

"It's either this," Rittwell says, holding up the bat, "or I arrest you."

"Enjoy the bat," Jason says from the floor.

We leave the front door open for Jason to close. I follow Rittwell back to his Jeep. He tosses the bat into the back seat and then climbs over the driver's side door.

"I took it to keep him from using it on anyone else."

"What?"

"The bat. I'm not stealing it. He shouldn't have it right now."

"I'm not judging."

"Where to?"

"Let's head back to Edith's apartment complex. We need to see what Stephanie found."

Chapter 35

Flynn

The leasing office door says closed, but it opens when I turn the handle.

"Stephanie?"

"I'm in here," a voice echoes through the building.

The leasing office is furnished and decorated like something I'd expect in a mansion on TV. It has vaulted ceilings and dozens of trees and plants. Paintings cover the walls, and marble-topped tables hold knick-knacks next to tasseled chairs and sofas. Windows on the far side of the office overlook the pool. Its rippling light comes in and casts shadows on the ceiling. The only part of this office resembling an office is through an opening that leads to a set of six cubicles. The area is mundane, and where we find Stephanie sitting at a desk.

"How's it going?"

"The guy we spoke to tried to attack us with a baseball bat."

"Really?"

"Officer Rittwell tackled him."

"I wish I could have been there to see that."

Rittwell cracks a smile.

"What did you find here?" I ask.

"The information you wanted. I just have some reservations."

"Such as?"

"I can't give you employee information without first speaking to an attorney. Our corporate legal department is closed today. A personal contact promised they will call back with a decision."

"I need that information."

"I need to make sure that I can provide it to you."

"Ma'am, you spoke to her family," Officer Rittwell says. "You know how concerned they are."

"I could lose my job."

"Edith could lose her life."

"This isn't something I want to do," Stephanie says, her face devoid of emotion. "This is something I have to do."

"None of us want to be here. I'd rather be at home relaxing and imbibing. I'm sure you'd rather be at home in the tub with a glass of wine. Rittwell would rather be at home listening to hair bands on cassette and waxing a Trans-Am."

"I can't help you."

I miscalculated in thinking a little humor might work in our favor. Now, all that remains is aggression.

"You're going to let me see the information."

"I can't until I hear back from—"

"Do you know the term 'pariah'?"

Stephanie is silent.

"The modern meaning is a social outcast. That's what you'll become if you don't help us."

"Don't threaten me. I'm trying to do what's best for everyone."

"You're trying to protect yourself by protecting your company. You know that someone working here taking Edith will reflect poorly on you and all the properties your bosses own. Your company will fire you because you are the manager. You are the face they chose to run this particular location. The only way to keep your job is to give us that information. If you do that, then you were part of the solution and not part of the problem. People will see you as a caring individual who did the right thing. Even if you lose all your tenants, they will respect you for trying to help. If you don't give us the information, then you were only trying to help your company. They will hang out to dry and, if Edith dies and it was someone in those files, then you'll forever be associated with her death. And I'll be the first to testify for the Danes family when they file a civil suit against you and your employer. We both know that your bosses will put all the blame on you."

"You don't understand—"

"Uh-huh, pressure and all that. Blah, blah, blah. Give me the fucking files."

Stephanie sulks as she hands over a clipboard. The top page is a spreadsheet of nineteen different names and the hours they have worked.

"This is a lot of people."

"You asked for everyone with access to Edith's keys that's worked since the lock was changed. We have office staff, leasing agents, and maintenance."

Next to each name on the list is a breakdown of the week by day and then by start and end times. Some people have regular hours, typical eight to five, while others have irregular hours. Their times start randomly during the day or night and end randomly.

"How accurate are the times on the spreadsheet?"

"Everyone has to scan in and out with a badge. The system we use is accurate to the second, but we always round down to the minute."

"That's generous."

"Standard procedure."

"It looks like some people are full-time, and others are part-time. Some part-timers have strange hours."

"Maintenance. People call at odd hours with emergencies, so we send people out at odd hours to help them out."

"The maintenance crews only work part-time?"

"We have two that work office hours. The rest are available as needed."

"Do you know if any of them have been hanging around when they weren't needed?"

"I don't know. My staff might have seen something. I haven't."

Each employee listed on the spreadsheet has a single sheet of paper dedicated to them. Among the information is a black-and-white picture that I'm sure is on the employee badge Stephanie mentioned earlier. Everyone shares the same annoyed and disgruntled grin. Stephanie probably had them stand against the wall and force a smile to take the snapshot that is now a permanent part of their work attire.

"There's a lot of people here," I say, flipping through the pages one at a time and skimming their information. On its own, the paper is useless. I can guess whether or not they are guilty, and that's about it. Besides the picture, all I have is an address and length of employment. "Is there anybody on this list that you consider suspicious?"

"I'm their boss, not their therapist."

"Do any of them act strangely around women?" Rittwell asks.

"Not in the office. They're all trained in sales or customer service. I've never had any serious complaints."

"You made your office employees sound professional and then bring up complaints. I'm guessing some people have complained about the maintenance workers?"

"There've been some incidents with two employees where misunderstandings have occurred."

"Misunderstandings?"

"As I said earlier, some of our employees are available if there are problems during non-office hours. People wear less clothing at night. Some women felt uncomfortable about the way they looked at them."

"They were leering?"

"If a woman shows up at the door falling out of a tank top, wouldn't you?"

"What are their names?"

"Durrell Span and Chip Walters."

The names on the spreadsheet are in alphabetical order with Charles 'Chip' Walters last on the list. Durrell Span's name is three spots above. I flip to Chip's information. He looks like an average guy annoyed at having his picture taken. He lives in Ponte Vedra and has worked for this apartment complex for three years. Durrell Span's photo lacks the clarity found with the others. The person with the camera must have moved while taking the picture. The name Durrell doesn't sound familiar, but the picture looks like someone I've met before. His address is in Atlantic Beach. He's been working here for six months.

"This Durrell, does he still live in Atlantic Beach?"

"If that's the address he has on file, then it's current. We send a pay stub every two weeks to that address."

"Is it normal for your part-timers to not live in the area?"

"We pay twenty an hour for the time he puts in from midnight to eight and fifteen for the rest. That's good money."

"Yeah, but he only works for an hour or so. Is it worth the inconvenience and the drive?"

"It must be for him."

I keep Durrell and Chip's information and hand the clipboard back to Stephanie.

210

"You can't have those," Stephanie says, reaching out for my hand.

"They're just copies." I pull my hand away in time. "And I won't tell if you won't."

Stephanie stays silent.

"We'll look into these two. Can you go back to Edith's family and let them know I'll call with any updates?"

Stephanie lets out an annoyed exhalation.

"Thanks," I reply.

Chapter 36

Flynn

Chip's home is on the way back to Atlantic Beach. We stop there before going to Durrell Span's home. Chip lives off A1A in a stretch of about two dozen houses on a street where every building looks like a shoebox. They're all lined up alongside the road, each almost identical to the next. The only difference is the paint.

Each house has a small porch out front. At Chip's address, a man is relaxing on the porch in a faded blue Adirondack. He stares into the distance, ignoring us as we approach.

"Hello, Chip?"

The man stops staring at the distance and starts staring at us. He's silent as I hold up the piece of paper with his picture on it.

"Mr. Walters, do you know Edith Danes?"

He continues to stare.

"She disappeared from the apartment complex you work for—"

"You the police?"

"I am a police officer," Rittwell says, "but this is nothing official. We just have some questions."

"Don't know her."

"The manager, Stephanie—"

"She a bitch. She send you?"

"There were some complaints about you and Durrell Span from some tenants."

"Nah uh. No way. Don't put me with that man. You come to my house and tell me I'm like Durrell. That man crazy."

"I didn't mean to offend you. How's Durrell crazy?"

"Listen," Chip says, leaning forward in the Adirondack. "If I tell you, you can't tell nobody it came from me."

"That's fine."

"We got called into work on this lady's kitchen sink. Garbage disposal was leakin' everywhere. We fix it. He start goin' through the house like it his. He come out holdin' some unmentionables."

"Lingerie?"

"Yeah. He pull out a knife. Said I better not tell nobody. I didn't."

"What color was the lingerie?"

"Black… I think. He stick it down his drawers like he crazy."

"Thank you."

"That it?"

"Shore nuff. Enjoy the rest of your Thanksgiving."

Chip stands up and walks inside. Rittwell and I walk back to his Jeep.

"I hope you're up for an awkward conversation with Durrell."

"Stealing underwear is a long way from kidnapping."

"I know. But Edith told me that the person who broke into her apartment left her a black camisole and matching pair of underwear. It sounds like he might've done his shopping while at work."

"You think he stole underwear from someone else's apartment to leave for Edith after breaking into hers?"

"Or he's a creep who stole underwear for less savory purposes. Either way, it's something to ask him about."

"Less savory?"

"Don't get me started."

Chapter 37

Flynn

The picture of Durrell Span sticks in my mind. His face is blurred, but some part of his ill-defined mug is bothering me. He's about my age and lives in Atlantic Beach, so our paths must have crossed. It could've been at a bar or even Misty's bakery, which is only a stone's throw from where he lives.

"What's the address again?" Officer Rittwell asks.

"One sec," I say, reaching into my pocket to pull out the sheet of paper with Durrell's information on it. Rittwell took one look at the address after we left Chip's and drove here with no additional directions needed. From what I remember, we're on the right street.

We both look at the address while I hold it underneath the dome light in his Jeep. Rittwell inches down the road, stopping in front of a row of townhouses. They've seen better days. The moon lights up the night enough for the pointed roof and eaves to glint like a knife slicing into the sky. Pale yellow lights above the doors warn those approaching to slow down while revealing damaged siding and dead shrubs. Rittwell comes to a stop and turns off the engine. After looking at the address once more, he turns off the dome light.

"There it is," he says.

The light of the moon is the only illumination hitting the paper in my hand. The white background rises in a ghostly pale while the ink on the paper settles into dark pools. Durrell's face comes to life like a spirit from the beyond.

"You all right?" Rittwell hits me in the arm harder than I'd prefer. It reminds me of Misty's penchant for hitting people. It doesn't make sense to me, but if the world made sense, life might be less interesting.

"I'm fine," I say. "This guy's picture reminds me of someone."

"Who?"

"No idea."

Rittwell looks at the picture of Durrell.

"Maybe a thinner Fatty Arbuckle."

"Would that make him a Regular Arbuckle?"

"I don't know. This picture is awful."

Rittwell hands the paper back to me. I put it in my pocket.

"I'm gonna go knock on the door."

"Wait," Rittwell says, keeping me from getting out of his Jeep. "The last time we knocked on a door, a man came at us with a bat. Let me make a call. I'll have some officers here in a minute."

"Go ahead and call them. I promise I won't knock on the door."

Rittwell pulls out his cell phone and starts speaking to someone. I take the cue and exit the Jeep. Durrell's townhouse has a bay window with a piece of cardboard taped over a hole from the inside. No curtains or blinds cover the window. Anyone walking by has an unimpeded view of the living space. A TV is on, and the volume is loud enough to hear through the cardboard. The place is a mess. On the other side of the window is a dining room. Beyond that is a living room. A light illuminates a narrow set of stairs leading to the second floor. A jacket, dappled with distinct orange spots, hangs from the banister, five feet from the front door.

What Rittwell said prevents me from trying to kick the door down. If a man with nothing to hide is willing to come at us with a baseball bat, what will Durrell do if we walk through his front door?

"There's a jacket with orange paint on it."

"Like the paint on the walls?"

I nod.

"Shit. They said they'll be here in a minute."

"Is it enough to get inside?"

"I don't know."

Atlantic Beach is small. The police department is less than a mile away. It takes three minutes for a squad car to arrive. The headlights turn off as the driver pulls up behind Rittwell's Jeep. A female cop exits the driver's side, and a male cop exits the passenger side. Rittwell walks over to them.

"Gabby. Hal. Thanks for huffing it down here."

"It's Thanksgiving," Hal says. "One of the few days we're slow."

"We're lucky we don't have to put out fires. The fire department had four fires today. People never follow instructions on frying a turkey."

"Is that who I think it is?" Hal asks with a finger pointed at me.

"Flynn, this is Gabby and Hal." Rittwell introduces both, but neither will shake my hand.

"Lenny," Hal says. "This guy is a suspect in one of the biggest murders I've ever seen around here."

"He's a person of interest," Rittwell says in my defense.

"We all know what that means," Hal replies.

"I'm guilty until proven innocent?"

They all ignore me. Gabby stands by while Hal puts his hand on Rittwell's shoulder and turns him away from me. Hal is in his fifties, and I'm sure he's been a mentor to Rittwell at some point. He's acting like he's a father trying to teach his son right from wrong.

"You can't be associating with people like him. It'll destroy your career."

"That's beside the point. A woman's gone missing. There's a strong possibility she's been taken by a man that lives here."

"And why do you think that?" Gabby asks.

"This man works where she lives. He has a jacket inside with orange paint on it. The person who entered this woman's apartment was shot with orange paintballs."

"C'mon," Hal says. "I go paintballing with my nephews once a month. That paint gets everywhere. It doesn't mean a thing."

"Hal," Gabby interjects.

"What, now you think we should trust this guy?" Hal says, pointing at me.

"I don't trust him. I trust Lenny."

Hal points at Rittwell and speaks to him like he's a child. "You know if you're wrong on this—"

"Hal," Gabby says, demanding his attention. "All we're doing is knocking on someone's door."

"All right," he says, relenting and following Gabby to the front door.

Rittwell and I stand back and watch as they knock on the door and wait for a reply. After five minutes, they walk back to us. I run toward them with Rittwell close behind.

"What're you doing?"

"Nobody answered," Hal says. "It's all we can do."

"What about the jacket?"

"What jacket?"

"The jacket inside! This guy has something to do with Edith's disappearance. Just look through the window on the left. It's on the staircase."

Hal and Gabby look at me. Rittwell walks up to the window and looks inside. His eyes wander until they focus on the jacket.

"He's right. It's hanging from the handrail. That's the same color paint on the walls we saw earlier."

"You expect us to kick in his door because of some paint?"

"I expect you to do your job and look into it," Rittwell says, walking right up to Hal.

"Don't you dare tell me how to do my job."

There's only one viable option on how to proceed. The police can handle it their way, by standing around and bickering with one another, while I handle it my way, by slamming my heel as hard as I can near the lock. The door doesn't give. The sound breaks up the argument. Everyone comes rushing at me. I kick the door again and, despite my leg feeling a whole lot of impact, nothing happens. Rittwell stops Hal and Gabby from pulling me away from the door by standing behind me and blocking their access.

"Dammit, dammit, dammit!" Rittwell shouts.

"This is prime gray area," I say to Rittwell.

Before I can try forcing the door again, Rittwell's leg shoots past me like a horse reacting to a pulled tail. His foot slams against the door. The wood splinters near the lock yet remains intact. I shoulder the door once. It budges. Twice. It opens wide.

There is no turning back. The worst that can happen is we find nothing, and I get arrested for breaking and entering. There's limited time before Hal and Gabby make it past Rittwell. I run up the stairs three at a time. There are two doors at the top. One door is open, leading to a bathroom. A sparsely decorated bedroom is behind door number two. The room contains a bed and a lamp on the ground near a closet with closed sliding panels. Legs and arms extend beyond a bedsheet tossed haphazardly over a body. Whoever it is doesn't make a sound. Before I go to the bed, I slide open the closet doors to make sure no one is hiding inside. There is a single pair of shoes and some clothes on hangers with an additional pile on the floor.

The body on the bed is moving by the time I turn around.

"Edith," I say, prompting the sheet to rise and fall. A voice trying to break free of a gag accentuates the motion. "It's Flynn, Edith," I say, pulling back the sheet and exposing her face.

The order Edith wore like a shield the other day has been stripped away. Her hair is a tangled mess. Someone with a shaky hand applied makeup to her face. A piece of fabric fills her mouth and wraps around her head, tied tightly from behind. The knot is too tight to untie, but I manage to pull it down enough to free it from her mouth.

"Flynn?" Edith's voice trembles.

"Don't worry. You're safe now. The police are downstairs."

"He said you were dead."

"What?"

"He killed you and your father."

"I'm fine."

"But your hat," Edith says, pointing down with her right index finger. On the right side of the bed is a Cubs cap. But it's not just any Cubs cap; it's Mordecai the Fourth. I pick him up to make sure there's no mistaking. Mordecai fits like a glove.

"Flynn," Rittwell says, looking into the room from the door. "Is she? Oh, God—"

"Do you have a knife or anything to cut her free?"

"What in the fuck?" Hal says, sticking his head into the room. "Jesus Christ. Gabby," he shouts down the stairs, "call an ambulance."

Hal pulls a Swiss Army knife from his pocket and cuts at the straps holding Edith's feet in place. Edith does her best to sit upright, but the bindings on her legs keep her in place as Hal works to free her legs. The sheet slips down to reveal Edith's torso. Carved across her body, just below her breasts, the name Durrell stands out with bloody vibrancy. The name is in all block letters. The wounds are various depths. She must have fought back while Durrell cut into her.

The sight of Durrell's name is too much. Did the monster who took my sister brand her as well? This is all too real.

"I'm sorry for getting you killed," Edith says, dazed.

218

Durrell told Edith he killed my father and me, using Mordecai as proof. William said teenagers broke into his house and stole Mordecai while we were downtown. That was Tuesday. That means William was wrong about the teenagers, and Durrell broke into his home. If he was stalking me, then he should know that I don't live at William's. The only way he would think I live in William's house is if he watched me enter it and stay put. The only time I've spent the night at William's since I was a kid was on Monday night.

Falk me sideways.

"Durrell is Falkyoo," I say in surprise.

"Fuck you too, pal," Hal shouts.

"Durrell is Falkyoo. He's the man on the beach."

"The man on the beach?" Rittwell asks. "What are you talking about?"

"Durrell Span is the man on the beach." I take off Mordecai and point to him. "He took my hat, Mordecai."

"You're not making any sense," Rittwell replies. He takes Mordecai out of my hand. "You can't take evidence."

"It's my hat. He attacked me."

"You know him?"

"No. Durrell attacked me the other night. He came out of the dunes with a knife."

"You're sure it was him?"

"Almost positive."

"Why would he attack you?"

"I don't know."

This is beyond a coincidence. The odds of Durrell having attacked me and then turned up as a suspect in the disappearance of a client I met earlier that day are infinitesimal. Edith's stalker wasn't her ex. It was Durrell. His part-time job allowed him the freedom to follow Edith around. Durrell must have seen me meet with Edith and then followed me that entire day. He chose his moment and came after me on the beach. At least, that's the only way this all makes sense. Nothing else fits.

Considering that, my humiliating him on the beach might have been the absolute worst thing I could have done.

"One of you needs to give me a ride."

"We don't need to give you anything," Hal says while cutting the ropes tied to Edith's wrists. "What you need to do is go downstairs and stay put."

"My neighbor could be in trouble."

"What does that have to do with anything?"

Chapter 38

William

The deluxe frozen turkey dinner fills the house with a Thanksgiving aroma. A hint of salt in the ocean breeze rolling through the open back door adds an extra pop to the turkey and fixings. The oven kicks off heat as I wait for the timer to count down. It's amazing how time slows only when you want it to fly. The smell of dinner in the oven reminds me of my first Thanksgiving.

What was I thankful for then? Being born anew.

God came to me in my time of need and brought me back into this world a changed man. Bits and pieces of my previous life come back to me now and then. It's like having a ghost follow me around. Sometimes, that ghost tells me a secret, filling me in about what I once was.

Every time the ghost whispers to me, it's something that makes me unhappy. All that matters is God opened his arms wide and accepted me. I became a part of his family. And Thanksgiving is a time for family.

The kids fill the house with life. Ethan, James Jr., John, and Rita play a never-ending game of tag, darting in and out of the open door, circling around the trellises and then back inside and around the living room furniture only to start all over again. Emma, Isabelle, and Lily use the dice and cup from a Yahtzee set to coordinate the movements of green army men in a game with ever-changing rules. Poor Walter isn't having any fun. He's pouting on the sofa because there's only a cobbler for dessert and not a pecan pie.

The adults are ready to eat, sitting at the table in anticipation. My father, Martin, sits at the head of the table with my mother, Beatrice, to his left. Susan is next to my mother, talking about the previous year's Thanksgiving with our parents. On the other side of the table, my siblings Emily and James are deep in conversation about global warming.

"I'm so glad you could all join me," I say, my hands outstretched to those I love.

Everyone stops and turns to me, smiling as they all say, "It's great to be here."

"I'm so glad you could all make it. I know you're all busy, and it's just great that you could find the time. Because family is the most important thing in the world."

"Hear, hear," my father says, standing up from the table clapping. Everyone else follows suit and claps along. The attention is more than I'm used to. Not wanting anyone to see me blushing, I turn away from my family.

"No need for that, dear," my mother says. "You've done us all a great service…"

A burning smell hangs in the air, distracting me from my mother's voice. It doesn't smell like dinner is burning; it smells like smoke rolling off a log fire. *A great service.* The phrase echoes in my mind, carried up into the air on the thick smoke of smoldering green cedar. My clothes disappear. Damp earth replaces the floor. The smell of nature and burning cedar fills my nostrils with every breath. The walls fade into a lattice of young pines with the spaces between covered by chicken wire. I try to reach out. The sap from the pines sticks to my hands. *A great service.* The phrase echoes once more from my mother. Smoke curls from her lips. She comes close to me and exhales a cloud of smoke. It smells of burning herbs. I try not to inhale, but the smoke billows from her mouth until I can't hold my breath any longer. The smoke burns as it forces its way into my lungs. It burrows into me with every inhalation and steals pieces of me as I exhale. My past floats away, dissipating in the breeze. One stubborn puff of smoke gathers others into a cloud. The cloud builds and builds until a deluge pours down upon my pine cage. Lightning strikes, setting off my nerves in an electric flurry. A rolling thunder echoes until it fades into a ghostly whisper. *Jimson—*

"James, son," my father blurts out. "Could you help William and pull the turkey from the oven?"

"I've got two working arms and legs," I say. "No need for anyone else to get up."

Smoke rolls out of the oven into the kitchen. Buttered herb stuffing fell from the tray down onto the heating element. The smoke continues to curl as I turn off the heat and turn on the fan. With great aplomb, which is a word I learned from a TV cooking show, I present the turkey dinner to my family. The oohs and aahs are overwhelming. Everyone is digging in and chatting by the time I stop serving and find time to sit down.

"Mother, the turkey is wonderful," Susan says.

"Thank you, dear," she replies, adding a smile for good measure.

"She does a wonderful job, doesn't she?" my father asks the table.

"Except for, what was that, fifteen years ago?" James has brought up the time the turkey came out way too dry every year since it happened. It was only once, but he always brings it up. My mother blushes every time.

We all laugh. It's perfect. Everything is perfect. And then someone knocks on the front door. Everyone goes silent in an instant. Forks and knives fall onto the plates in a clatter. The food disappears, taking the joy of the occasion with it. The knocking begins again. Everyone disappears. I'm alone at the dining room table with a turkey dinner for one.

Chapter 39

Flynn

"William?" I shout, knocking on his door. I keep knocking until William opens the door. He smiles as soon as he realizes it's me.

"Flynn?" William brings his hands up to his head before pointing both of them at me. "Happy Thanksgiving. I've got an extra frozen dinner I could heat up for you if you're hungry. They had 'em BOGO at the store. I picked up four."

"No, thanks. I'm still full. I just want to make sure you're safe."

"Safe?" William asks, confused.

"This is gonna sound crazy, but the guy that attacked me on the beach is the one that broke into your house." I wish I had Mordecai to show him, but Officer Rittwell was adamant that they need to keep him as evidence. "He was stalking a client of mine. He ended up kidnapping her."

"That does sound crazy. I'm fine."

"I'm afraid he might come back."

"Don't worry," William says. "I'll be fine."

The officer Rittwell introduced as Gabby walks up behind me. She was kind enough to drive me back here, but she seems ready to leave.

"Sir," Gabby says to William. "Do you need any assistance?"

"No," William replies.

"Sorry to have bothered you, sir," Gabby says to William.

"Call my landline if you need anything," I say. "Be safe. And Happy Thanksgiving."

"You too," William says. "No need to worry about me."

William closes his door. Gabby gets back in her police cruiser and rolls down the window when I wave goodbye.

"Flynn," Gabby shouts from inside her car. "You need to come back with me."

"Listen, I'm tired. If you need me to fill out paperwork, I'll gladly do it. But I don't want any credit."

"What?"

"Three police officers were there. You don't need me to add anything. If you do, just ask. Give all the credit to Officer Rittwell."

"Are you sure?"

"Shore nuff. Do you have a pen?" I ask. Gabby pulls a pen out of her pocket and holds it up. "Not for me. Have Rittwell call Maura Danes. You can contact her at—"

"Hold up," Gabby says as she catches up. I provide the name and number again. "Got it."

"Please have Officer Rittwell call her as soon as he can. He met her earlier. He'll be the best person to explain what happened."

"You want to give up all the credit for this?"

I nod.

Gabby waves and says, "Goodnight." She rolls up the car window and waves once more before driving away.

With all the distractions, I failed to notice the cherry red classic Mustang parked in my driveway. The lack of light outside my house prevents me from seeing the depth of the color, but I'm about ninety-five percent certain it is Heather's car. I was there on her seventeenth birthday when Leslie gave it to her as a gift. Leslie made Heather drive a clunker until he was confident she wouldn't destroy all of his hard work. The big surprise took place after the birthday party. When Heather hauled the party trash out to the garbage can, the Mustang was in the driveway with a makeshift bow on top. Leslie couldn't find a big enough bow, so Misty made one out of a roll of paper towels and a lot of hairspray.

The lights inside my house are on. The front door is still locked. I unlock it and walk inside.

"Surprise," Heather shouts, jumping out from behind some boxes in the hallway. The TV is on in the living room. She's been here long enough to make herself comfortable.

"Hey," I say, trying to act casual and not let the awkward come through my voice. "What are you doing here?"

"We had a lot of leftovers, so I thought I'd bring you a plate."

"Thank you. That's very thoughtful."

"I waited till you got back. I'm watching a documentary on the Red Beach in Panjin, China. You don't mind, do ya?"

"Of course not," I say as politely as I can muster. It's frustrating when people ask questions like that. Anything less than affirming their behavior turns you into an asshole. "How did you get inside?"

"You gave my father your house key," Heather says, walking into the kitchen and pulling the keyring I gave Leslie earlier in the day out of a shoulder bag with a floral design. She puts the keys back into the bag and pulls out a movie. "I thought you might want to watch this together."

"I, um..."

"It's *Love Actually*. You ever seen it?"

I'm trying to hide the fact that I'm excited about her choice in movies. It's one of my favorites. I'm sure she doesn't know that. I can't remember a time I would have brought it up in front of her. Her bringing the movie isn't important; I have a copy of my own. Her being here is what matters.

Durrell's bloody name comes back to me every time I close my eyes. I'm tired, physically and emotionally, but I don't want to sleep. If I stay awake long enough, then maybe the inevitable nightmares about what happened to Edith might not be as bad. Heather being here will keep me awake. Watching a movie I like might be enough to soften whatever nightmares come my way. Hell, if I concentrate enough on Liam Neeson, I may hit the jackpot and end up dreaming about taking a bath to get all the coarse sand off of me while a Force ghost Qui-Gon Jinn watches approvingly.

Chapter 40

Flynn

When the doorbell first rings, I think it's a dream. Instead of waking up, I roll over in bed and keep my eyes closed. The second time the doorbell rings, I know it's for real. The clock on my bedside table shows the time as nine-twenty. I crawl out of bed like a spry turtle and put on a shirt and a pair of shorts from the pile of clothing on my dresser. While I'm walking to the door, the doorbell rings again. Before the echo of the bell stops, I open the door to find Philip Blanchard standing there in a navy blue suit with a briefcase in hand.

"Good morning," Philip says, smiling while he looks me up and down. "I see you've shaved."

"Seriously," I say, holding onto the door, "it's nine o'clock."

"I know."

"In the morning."

"You didn't see my press conference?"

"You had a press conference on Thanksgiving?"

"No. I had one this morning."

"How early do you wake up?"

"How late do you go to bed?"

"Touché."

"I tried calling the number you gave me, but a woman picked up and said she wasn't your fucking secretary." Philip emphasizes the last two words by making a quotation mark in the air with his left hand. "Her words, not mine."

"Yeah, that's Misty. I borrowed her phone for a while."

"Wait. Is Misty a stage name? I haven't been calling a stripper's phone all this time, have I?"

"No, she owns a bakery. Misty's mother named her after one of her favorite songs."

"That's fine. I tried to call you to set up a time for me to deliver this."
Philip brings the briefcase in his right hand to his chest and taps it with
his left hand.

"The last time someone gave me a briefcase, the thing exploded."

"I'm only giving you the documents inside. In my experience, paper
rarely explodes."

"Come on in," I say, motioning for Philip to enter. I direct Philip
toward the kitchen, where we both take a seat at the kitchen table.

Philip sets his briefcase down on the table and pulls out a stack of
papers, photographs, and a handwritten journal.

"This is the job I have for you."

"What is it exactly?"

"I think this is why Paul was killed. He'd been looking into something
for a little while. I don't know what it all means or why someone would
have killed for this information, but it's all here for you to figure out."

"Why is this not going to the police?"

"Paul never told me what he was looking into, but he did tell me he
was on the trail of a story that would win him the election."

"It's information about Lou?"

"I don't know."

The diary might cause some problems. The writing is a grab bag of
simple words mixed with symbols and shorthand that I will need to
decipher.

"Do you know what some of this shorthand means?"

"No."

The last entry of the journal is in block letters: GF IR 630.

"Listen, you helped me out of a jam. I owe you big time. But if you
think this information resulted in Paul Mahoney's death, it should go to
the police."

"No. I need you to figure this out. After that, I plan on using the
information to shore up my campaign."

"Your campaign?"

"That was what my press conference this morning was about. I
announced that I will run in Paul's place. Paul was certain the results of
his investigation would guarantee him the election. He wanted to use
what political power he gained to change this city for the better. I still
believe in Paul's vision. And I also believe, come March, I could be

elected instead. To ensure that happens, I need to find out what he was investigating."

The prosecuting attorney, Maria Aceves, would have eaten me alive if given a chance. Philip protected me when I needed it most. Helping him is the least I can do.

The professor of the one economics course I took in college used to say, 'There is no such thing as a free lunch.' It sounded idiotic considering how much free food is given away across the campus, but I've come to understand the truth behind the statement.

"All right. I'll do it. But I will need something in return."

Philip nods. "Understandable. About how much will expenses run?"

"No idea. It could take me a while to figure this out. But on top of the expenses, I'd like a little more for my time."

Philip laughs. "Keeping you out of jail isn't enough?"

"It got you through the door. We both know I shouldn't be doing this. And because it could cost me, I'd like to get paid."

"How much?"

The best thing to do is name a high price. Philip has few places left to turn. And if I name a high enough price, he may scrap the idea altogether. But I also know Philip has connections. And he might be able to use those connections to help me find a lawyer to get my insurance coverage back.

"Zero."

Philip acts like I hit him in the face.

"What?"

"I need a lawyer for some medical issues. If you know someone who can help, then I'll take their help in lieu of payment."

"That's unique. I can call some people, but none of them will work for free."

"Why don't you pay them? I'm sure they'll give you a better rate than I'd get."

"I don't have that much money. Most of what I have is tied up in investments, and I've been working for a charity for a while. I haven't been making a lot."

"Well… shit. Then how about, as newly minted associates, you call them to see if they'll help me? And if you can't pay me in cash, then I guess we'll have to consider other options."

"What does that mean?"

"Do you have any kids?"

"What in the—"

"Sorry, that was bad timing for that question. I know you're not married right now. I was wondering if you have been married before or if you have any kids?"

"I've never been married, and I don't have any kids. I don't see how any of that is relevant."

"It's only relevant to me as far as payment goes. You're in your forties and still single. You haven't invested your time and money in building a family. People need something to drive them, something in the back of their minds to distract them from life, something to spend their money on. You've never had a wife or kids to burn through your paycheck. I don't see you as the type to blow all your money on women in clubs or bars. You're a collector. I'm not sure what you collect. What I do know is that you collect something as a hobby."

"Interesting assumption. Why couldn't I invest all of my money?"

"You could. You said you have investments. But someone already told me you collect records."

"You're right. I collect records and games. You're also wrong. I'm not in my forties. I'm in my late thirties."

"Games," I say, an eyebrow raised. "What kind of games?"

"Older video games and systems."

"I like it. I didn't see you as the type to collect video games. Great. I'll make a list of records and video games for payment."

"And if I don't have the ones you want?"

"You must have connections that can help find items. I'm fine with waiting until those connections find what I want."

"Provide me a list. I should have them for you by the time you finish."

"Wunderbar."

"There's something else I need to discuss with you," Philip says, looking relieved to be moving on. "Do you still have Amy Wright's contact information?"

"It all ended up incinerated in my car."

Philip pulls out a sheet of paper from his briefcase and hands it to me. A hastily written address follows two phone numbers.

"Here is her information. I want you to call her and try to apologize."

"What? Why? I mean, I'd love to tell her, 'Sorry I nearly blew you up,' but why would she even want to take my call?"

"You need to at least try. We hindered the police the other day. If Amy pushes for further investigation, then I'm almost certain they could go after you for assault. We can't have that happen. If you end up sidelined, then I might not find out what Paul was looking into. You need to smooth things over before it all goes wrong."

"Yeah," I say, looking at the numbers on the paper. "I'll call her today."

Chapter 41

Amy

An unfamiliar alarm wakes me up from a dead sleep. The only thing I'm sure of is that it's not my phone telling me it's time to wake up. The sound echoes into the bedroom from the living room in Iain's home. When the sleepy haze lifts and my mind focuses from the panic, I'm afraid it could be the fire alarm going off. Before I can climb out of bed, the phone on the nightstand rings.

"Hello?" My voice is panicked.

The calm voice of a man asks, "Ma'am, are you okay?"

"I'm fine. I was just sleeping and—"

"Do you know what set off the alarm?"

"No."

"Our system is showing that a door on the back of your home has been opened. I can send the police to you right away."

The police are the last thing I want to see. They followed me since the explosion and only stopped because I called Detective Cousins and asked him to leave me in peace. If the police show up, I could end up in trouble for being here.

I spent the night at Iain's home rather than my own without considering the potential for an awkward predicament. I wanted to sleep in his bed. The scent of the pillows reminds me of him and makes me feel like everything will work out in the end. Iain wouldn't object to me being here despite him never giving me explicit permission. And that's only because he isn't picking up his phone. The last thing I want to do is tell him I stayed the night in his house without asking first. That kind of behavior has stalker written all over it, and I don't want to scare him off.

"No," I say shakily. "I can see what happened now. The wind blew it open. Everything's fine."

"I need the security code, ma'am, to disarm the system."

232

I provide the number Iain gave me to turn the security system on and off with the keypad near the front door.

"Thank you. I will turn off the alarm right now." The ringing sound stops, and my heartbeat begins its gradual decline to a slower pace. "Be safe, ma'am."

"Thank you."

Next to the bed is my father's gun case and a box of bullets. I take the revolver out and quickly load it. I climb out of Iain's bed. The scent of his cologne follows me across the room. It's a woodsy scent that lulled me to sleep last night in a matter of moments. It made me feel so comfortable that it's almost a shock to the system to feel stressed while inhaling the same scent.

The belt of Iain's terrycloth robe dangles past my knees after I tie it around my waist. The robe is plush and heavy on my shoulders. Before leaving the bedroom, I roll up the sleeves so I can hold the revolver in my hands without the robe being in the way. The man on the phone told me that the back door was opened, which means it has to be one of three doors downstairs. The main room of the house is an open living room area with two-story high ceilings that looks out onto a pool and patio overlooking the ocean. Two glass doors lead out to the patio in that room. When I walk out to the landing leading to the stairs, I see that neither door is open. The stairs lead down into the living room, which I cross to reach the kitchen.

A teapot boils in the kitchen. The hissing whistle becomes louder and louder until someone removes it from the burner. Dishes rattle as cabinets open and close. I level my gun and enter the kitchen.

Standing next to the stove is a man wearing oversized sunglasses, a navy blazer, a designer shirt unbuttoned to his sternum, tight jeans, and a pair of cowboy boots. The collection of competing fashion statements pours water from the kettle into a teacup and then puts a tea bag into the steaming water.

"Don't mind me," he says, picking up some of Iain's business papers off of the kitchen island. "I'm just doing a little light reading."

"Who are you?" I ask, pointing the revolver at him.

"Would you like a cup?" The man holds up the teacup. I don't respond. He shrugs and takes a seat in the breakfast nook. "I hope you

233

don't mind. Iain has such excellent taste. He made me a pot before, and I could hardly wait to come back and try it again."

"Who are you?" I ask.

"You can call me The Sheik. Everybody does. I'm one of Iain's business associates. Would you mind putting that away?"

The Sheik points to the gun in my hand and makes a motion for me to lower it, but I keep it aimed at his chest. My father always said that the best place to shoot an attacker is in the chest because it's hard to miss. I take my eyes off of The Sheik to look at the kitchen door leading outside. The door is wide open with the wooden frame broken near the lock.

The Sheik opens his blazer enough to reveal a holster and the grip of a handgun.

"I'm a bit of a gun aficionado myself. And the gun aficionado inside of me is surprised to see you holding an old snub-nosed Colt. Production stopped on those decades back. It's sort of like being face-to-face with a cop from the seventies."

The kind of man who can identify a gun from a distance is not the kind of man you want showing up uninvited. I flinch and readjust the gun's position in my hand. My father bought this handgun used over twenty years ago for home protection. It's a Colt Cobra .38 Special. Before my father had this gun, he owned a single action for target shooting, but he got rid of it when he wanted something more suitable for home protection. A single action requires you to cock the hammer and then pull the trigger to fire, but it takes time, and merely touching the trigger can cause them to misfire. With a double action, all you have to do is squeeze the trigger. Double action revolvers are less accurate, but they are quicker to shoot and take a hard squeeze to fire.

"Don't be alarmed," he says at my reaction. "I'm not psychic. I saw the little shiny horse on the grip when you looked toward the door."

"Who are you?" I scream.

"I told you, I'm a business associate of Iain's."

"Then why did you knock in the door?"

"For effect. You see, I've had a man waiting outside of this house. He finally called me to let me know someone stayed the night. So, here I am."

"What do you want?"

"For starters, I'd like you to put that gun down before you end up hurt."

I lower the revolver and hold it at my side with my finger still near the trigger.

"Thank you." The Sheik takes a sip of tea and then continues. "I guess my question is: What exactly are you doing here?"

"House sitting."

"You don't know this, Amy, but I know you. I research the lives of all my business associates. The one thing I'm having trouble believing is that Iain is having his whore take care of his home and keep his bed nice and warm while he's in Scotland with his son."

"I'm not a whore. And I promised him I would do it."

"You realize his wife recently died, right? I know I just broke into Iain's home, but I still have to ask, 'What kind of person are you?'"

I say nothing.

"To make matters more interesting, Iain's wife died, what, a month ago? And now someone has tried to blow up his whore."

I recoil after hearing the word 'whore' a second time.

"Not a fan of being called the obvious? How about I call you Aldonza?"

"How about you leave before I call the police?"

The Sheik raises his voice. "Look at you—"

"I'm calling the police."

"Come on. Just because you don't understand the reference doesn't mean it's not great." He pauses and stares at me. I don't respond. "I'm willing to wager that you had a chance to have the police show up here already when the alarm went off. They should be here any minute. I'm guessing you told them not to show up. The same reason that stopped you the first time will keep you from calling them for seconds."

"Is that what you think?"

"It's just a guess. But I think you should also stay away from the phone because no one wants to be in a news headline, especially not one like: 'Aldonza killed with own gun!' It doesn't have a ring to it. Now, correct me if I'm wrong, but wasn't Iain's wife stabbed to death in this kitchen? Think of the irony of an intruder killing two different women in two different ways at two different times in the same kitchen. What are

235

the odds? It sounds like Iain might need to buy a stronger lock or maybe a stronger door to keep people like me out."

My grip tightens around the revolver. My instincts tell me to shoot this man. But if I do, will Iain ever speak to me again? He hasn't answered my calls in days. Now, this. Shooting someone he does business with might push him over the edge. Iain told me when we first met that he is an artist at heart and a businessman by necessity. He has moments where his emotions can turn on a dime. Losing his wife took a lot out of him. I know he will return stronger, but I'm afraid that anything else happening might tip the pot.

"It's a matter of being at the wrong place at the right time. Really, for both of you. If only Iain had been there to stop that intruder, his wife might still be here to come home to after he's finished fucking you. And now, if he were here, you would be in a much better situation."

"I still have a gun, and I know how to use it."

"But you won't. Most people have this strange disinclination when it comes to pulling triggers. It's hardwired into our brains or something. I can't say for sure. What I do know is that by the time you get over that fear and raise your gun, well before you ever fire a single round at me, I'll have already fired off a couple rounds Wild West style. Personally, I would hate to kill such a PYT as you, but a man like me will do what has to be done."

"What do you want with Iain?"

"What I want… What I really want… is to speak to Iain. That's all. He's not answering my calls, and that's starting to upset me. And when I'm upset, I overreact, which leads to events such as this."

"He's not returning my calls, either."

"Such a dick move on his part. I know if I had an Aldonza calling me while I was back in the old country burying my wife, I'd make every effort to pick up and schedule our next session."

This man is frustrating. There is a chance I can fire off a shot before he can reach his gun. But I'm not reckless enough to find out.

"It's not like that. I just wanted to let Iain know what happened to me."

"I read about your miracle escape from that motel room. You can tell we're in the South when preachers are saying that your life being miraculously spared is an act of God. I just wish they knew how you live that spared life. I'd bet they'd get as big a kick as I do. But when you

236

think about all this, there are a lot of interesting coincidences. Iain's wife dies, and he disappears into the ether. Then, after a prolonged period of not contacting his business partners, his Aldonza is nearly blown to pieces. It's almost like someone wants his attention."

"You're—" The gun in my hand begins to shake.

"I'm merely pointing out the obvious. I'm a simple businessman who wants what he paid for. What is it Iain told me the first time I met him? Ah, yes. 'I'm an artist at heart and a businessman by necessity.' It's amazing how similar the two of us are because I'm a businessman at heart and an artist when pressured. And right now, I'm feeling the pressure. Are you feeling the pressure?"

I nod.

"Good. Because I thought my barometer might not be working right. Here, I was afraid that the approaching storm was a figment of my imagination. It's good to know I'm not the only one concerned.

"What I need you to do for me is to get your pretty little ass in gear and call your boy. I need you to let him know that if I don't hear from him by eight tonight, the pressure might increase a little more. And to expect two miracles in one week is greedy even by Bible Belt standards."

I turn around and walk over to the portable phone sitting in its charger near the entrance to the kitchen. Iain is selective about whose calls he picks up. If he is answering calls, the phone in his home is one he's bound to consider. The Sheik watches me dial the phone from his seat at the table. The phone rings. It drops me into voicemail after the second ring. Iain's voice prompts me to leave a message. I turn to The Sheik.

"It went to voicemail."

"Then leave him a message."

"Iain. There's a man in your house calling himself The Sheik. He's demanding that you call him by eight o'clock tonight. He has a gun. Please call."

The Sheik stands up and claps as I finish the call and hang up the phone.

"Bravo. Thank you for your assistance. Quick. Concise. Everything I want in a message. And the part about the gun was a great flourish. If he doesn't call me now… well, let's not think about that."

"He'll call."

237

"Hope dies last, right? Honestly, the only way I'm certain he would call is if, instead of you, I found his son here alone. It would take a callous man to not make a call to save his child. Unfortunately for me, I will have to take what I can get."

The Sheik walks past me into the living room toward the front door. Instead of opening the front door immediately, he presses the button to open the gate at the end of the driveway and then walks out without taking another look in my direction.

I can't stand the thought of that man coming back inside. This isn't a place for him. This is Iain's home. And it will someday be mine.

The door has three locks. A deadbolt above the handle, a security chain, and a deadbolt at the top of the door Iain installed when his son began sleepwalking. I lock all three.

From a window near the door, I watch as The Sheik passes the front gate. I press the button on the intercom to close the gate behind him. In a single motion, he stops, turns, and points his finger at me like it's a gun.

Once the gate closes, I return to the kitchen to inspect the broken door. Fixing it will require calling a handyman. To keep bugs from getting in, I prop it closed with a chair.

The distant echoing sound of my cellphone keeps me from starting breakfast. My stomach is already in a knot from having to deal with The Sheik. The ringing phone makes it worse. There's no telling what it could be now. One thing after another keeps coming my way. I can barely keep up. I've already got so much on my plate that I'm having trouble keeping things straight. But it could be Iain calling.

I run up the stairs as fast as I can, picking up my cell phone without looking at the number.

"Hello?" I ask, winded.

"Amy?" a voice asks. I can tell it's not Iain's voice. It's softer and without an accent.

"Yes. Who is this?"

"Flynn Dupree."

I'm taken aback and do not respond.

"Are you there?" he asks.

"Yes," I say, trying to keep my calm. He knows something. Maybe he even knows about The Sheik breaking into my home. It's impossible to tell. "How can I help you?"

"I called to apologize."

"Really?"

"Yes."

"And that's all?"

"Yes. I wish I could do something more to make up for what happened. I didn't know what I was doing when I hired you. If I had known... if I had done... I'm sorry that all this happened."

"I was told that you were also nearly killed in an explosion?"

"Yeah. After the bomb went off in the motel, I ran to help. Then, one went off in my car."

"And you're okay?"

"A scratch here or there, but nothing too serious."

"How would you like to come over to my place tonight for dinner? We can compare war wounds."

There's silence on the other end of the line. I almost shocked myself when I asked. I want someone to be with me tonight. The Sheik set a deadline of eight o'clock, and I don't want to be alone. I'd call the police, but Iain has connections to the man threatening me. The last thing I want to do is cause him problems. Having Flynn nearby could solve this issue.

"Yeah," Flynn says. "I can come over. What time?"

"Will seven-thirty work for you?"

"Of course. I have a great bottle of wine I could bring."

"No, thanks." I'm inclined to ask him to bring whatever weapons he can get his hands on. That's too revealing. I want him to come over and not ask questions. That way, everyone involved will be safer. "Bring yourself. That's all."

"Got it. Leave the pants at home."

Being stuck between a rock and a hard place forces people to make decisions they would rather not. Right now, both the rock and the hard place are squeezing my head and giving me a headache.

"I'm sorry," Flynn says. My silence must have spoken for me. "That came out wrong."

"That's fine," I say, trying to sound chipper and optimistic. "Do you have something to write with?"

"Why?"

"I have some directions for you."

Chapter 42

Flynn

After calling Amy, I take everything Philip gave me and walk to The Cake Mistress Bakery. The pictures, documents, and notebook all fit into a canvas messenger bag I picked up on the cheap at a second-hand store. With the sun shining and the temperature in the low seventies, the walk to Misty's bakery is pleasant. The time provides me ample opportunity to imagine how angry Misty still might be from Thanksgiving. Tin escorted her away, and she came back much calmer, but Misty was still upset enough that Leslie had to drive me and my mother home. Now that the previous day has had time to fester, our interactions could be rougher. Regardless, I need to speak to Misty about the information I received.

Misty took journalism classes in college, and I suspect she might be able to shine some light on the shorthand Paul Mahoney used in his notes. All that I could gather by looking through all the pictures and information is that four people listed only as IR, TS, LB, and JP are working together. What are they doing together? I have no idea. The notes say nothing specific, and anything that might shed some light on the matter is all in shorthand.

It's a safe assumption that the LB mentioned in these notes is Lou Brombacher. There's a small notation of '100k' next to a set of numbers '1015' that could be a date. If I'm trying to interpret, it looks like someone paid a hell of a lot of money to Lou Brombacher on October fifteenth.

If Brombacher is involved, then the mystery man from Lou's Rolodex, Joseph Prince, could be the JP reference. It could also be a million other things. And why would Brombacher provide me information that potentially connects him further to what's happened? Brombacher could have flipped to the next name in the Rolodex, and I wouldn't have known. Joseph Prince could be the key to everything. The only problem

240

is that I'm speculating, and Philip will want more than speculation. Speculation may help you find gold, but it doesn't help you win elections.

The clock reads just after two when I arrive at the bakery. Misty is cleaning off a table in the back as the bells on the door ring. Her head pops up. She sees me and walks up to the front.

"Well, look who decided to show his face."

"For the record, I've got nothing to feel bad about."

Misty stares at me, raising an eyebrow but not saying a word.

"You know I'm not going to do anything with Heather, right?"

"I can't say that I believe you."

"You're right. My loins are en fuego. I both need and must do dirty things."

"I've got an itty-bitty space in the fridge. I'll gladly take a knife to your loins and store 'em in there. That should put out the fire."

"Ouch. Can't even make a joke, huh?"

"Did Heather go over to your place last night?"

"Yes. We watched a movie. Then she left."

"So you say."

"I promise you nothing will happen. However, I am still interested in an introduction to the Cubs fan you hired."

"She's already gone for the day."

"That's a real shame. I might have Heather's number at home."

"Ha, ha, ha," Misty says like a cough. "Is that why you came down here?"

"No," I reply, pulling out the documents Philip provided me and spreading them on the front counter. "Can you understand any of this?"

Misty picks up the journal and starts thumbing through the pages.

"Why would I understand this?"

"You took journalism classes, right?"

"Yeah. A couple. But that was a long time ago."

"Can you tell me anything?"

"Not really. Most of this is in shorthand."

"Yeah, that's the problem."

"It definitely is a problem. All this is nonsense. It's clear that when this person writes their notes, they write as little as possible."

"Is that normal?"

"I'm not an expert, but sure. They only write what they need to know to bring it up in their memory. For you to understand this pile of paper, you need this person's brain."

"And that's not going to happen."

"Then you need to speak to someone close to them. They might provide insight no one else can."

"Philip couldn't make heads or tails of this, and they spent a lot of time together."

"Is this Paul Mahoney's?"

"It was what he was working on when he died."

"Why did Philip give this to you?"

"He wants me to make sense out of it."

"Then I suggest you speak to Paul Mahoney's wife. She might provide you something to make this all come together."

"Dammit. I wanted to avoid that at all costs."

"Right now, you have nothing."

"I guess I'll need to clear it with Philip first. Can I borrow your cell?"

"Are you serious?"

"His number is in there, and the business card he gave me is back at home. I promise I'll commit it to memory, so I won't have to bother you again."

"Fine," Misty grumbles. She pulls out her cell phone and hands it to me. "Stay away from the text messages."

"Yes, ma'am," I say, saluting Misty.

Misty heads back to work while I search through the logs to find when Philip last called. A short call earlier in the day sounds like the one he described after waking me up. I select the number and hit connect.

The phone rings four times and then goes to voicemail. I disconnect and try again. Philip picks up.

"This is Flynn."

"Have you found something already?"

"All I've found out is that this will be more difficult than we thought."

"How so?"

"I checked with a friend of mine who studied journalism to see if she could decipher some of the notes. She told me that there's no way. The shorthand refers to a thing we know nothing about. When we have an idea, then I can proceed."

242

"How can we get this moving along?"

"I need to speak to Mrs. Mahoney."

"Right now?"

"You tell me. I'm doing this for you, remember?"

Philip remains silent for a moment. A scratching sound on the other end of the line makes me believe Philip is scratching something off a piece of paper.

"I'm free for the next two hours." Philip waits until I can get a pen before providing me an address and brief directions on how to reach the Mahoney home.

"About how many bridges will I need to cross?" I ask. "It sounds like two."

"Two sounds right. Is that a problem?"

"No. I'll be there in about thirty to forty minutes."

Philip disconnects. I wait for Misty to reappear into my line of sight before shouting.

"Misty, do you have any more deliveries today?"

"Nope," Misty says, walking back up the front. "The only delivery today was a cake for the cop who saved that woman."

"Really? I'm not too familiar."

"You need to watch the news. This cop from right down the road saved this kidnapped woman. They threw a party for him. I spent most of this morning making the cake."

"That's great."

"You need the hearse, don't you?"

"Yes."

"For how long?"

"I'd like it for the night."

"Why's that?"

"I've been asked to attend a dinner."

"Oh, a dinner with—?"

"Someone you don't know."

"Who's that?"

"I've got something on the back burner right now."

"No, you don't."

"How do you know?"

"Because you're a braggart. I would know if you had someone else."

243

"I met her while working."

"If this is the hooker, I'm gonna kill you."

"Well, she's really hot."

"What the hell is wrong with you?" Misty asks while hitting me several times in the left shoulder. "She sleeps with people for money!"

"First of all, my lawyer was the one who told me to make amends. I called her to do so. She invited me over. And as far as money goes, she knows I don't have money. So if she sleeps with me, then it has to be a matter of attraction."

"That's disgusting. You're disgusting, and there will be a matter of *contraction* of diseases if you aren't careful. Although, you were talking about your loins being en fuego. I'm sure she's got something viral that'll get you burning."

"I'm always careful."

"No, you're not. You nearly got her and yourself blown to pieces the other day after you basically blackmailed her into working for you."

"Yeah, that whole situation may put a damper on my trying something with her."

"You do what you want. Seriously though, be careful. Someone tried to kill you. You need to be thinking about something else right now."

I am. I'm thinking about how in the hell I'm going to be able to talk to Mrs. Mahoney.

Chapter 43

Flynn

Homes on the St. Johns River can vary wildly. If you search hard enough, you can still find little bungalows next to the water that look like something you might drag out onto a frozen lake for ice fishing. The majority of the homes are a decent size, the kind you think of when a family has two and a half children, a dog, and everything is still filmed in black and white. Then there are the enormous homes—the mansions. There's nothing as extravagant as you'd see in the Hamptons or some other tony address. These mansions are enormous, but not the size of a castle. Most people own a small amount of property and then build something as big as possible. The opposite could be said for Paul Mahoney.

Trees cover most of the land owned by Paul Mahoney and his wife. The continuous canopy reaches from the road leading to the property all the way to the river, with the only break being the area where the house sits.

A thick wall of shrubs separates the property from the road. After pulling the hearse into the driveway, I end up driving for almost thirty seconds before reaching where Philip's car sits parked in front of the house. Philip comes out through the front door and stops in his tracks as I exit the hearse. Philip holds his head in his hands, emphasizing the look of shock on his face.

"You drove a hearse here?" Philip asks. Removing his hands from his head seems to propel the words forward with force. "Are you insane?"

I turn around and look at the hearse. The sight is something I see regularly, so it takes a few seconds for me to understand how another person might view such an automobile.

"I wasn't even thinking about that. My car blew up. I borrowed this one from a friend. Let's keep her away from the windows. She'll never know."

"That's a brilliant idea. Or, maybe, don't bring the one and only type of car a person might associate with death."

"Next time, I'll know," I say, shrugging my shoulders. "Oh, by the way, I have this for you."

I pull a folded piece of notebook paper from Paul Mahoney's journal and hand it to Philip. He looks confused at the sight of the paper. I stare at him with wide eyes until he unfolds and peruses it. There's a certain amount of pride I feel in the list, and I want to see Philip's reactions to my work.

"This is what you want?"

"It's what I could come up with off the top of my head. Sorry about the handwriting."

"You have Sarah Vaughan's Mercury records underlined a lot. Original pressings?"

"Yes," I say quickly. Those are the most important to me. They are for my mother. Hers were damaged when she moved to her condo. "Original pressings in good shape. No remakes. I've looked before but can't tell one from the other."

"I'll find them."

"Do you need clarification for anything else?"

"No," Philip says, exhaling deeply. "I don't have all of this."

"You're the collector. I'll take whatever you can find in good shape and playable. And I don't want anything sealed. I plan on playing the records and games."

"The Tijuana Brass?" Philip laughs.

"Don't judge."

"Uh-huh. I've got an extra Virtual Boy and some games if you'd like."

"I'd rather not go blind."

"It'll take me a while to find all of this."

"Take your time."

"As much fun as it is to talk to you about a payment you've yet to deserve, we should go inside and see if there's anything Pat can clear up."

"Her name is Pat? Pat Mahoney?"

"Yes. Pat, short for Patricia. Why?"

"Nothing. It's just so close to almost being a dirty joke."

Philip puts his hand on my shoulder and faces me.

"You contributed to her husband's death. You need to stop acting so callous. Focus and try not to make an ass of yourself."

"Got it. I'm sorry. I'm psyched about handing you that list."

"It was a very nice list," Philip says in a tone most reserve for placating a child.

"Thanks," I say, taking in and releasing a deep breath. "I'm ready."

Philip opens the front door. The interior design resembles a deluxe log cabin. Roughly hewn wood covers the walls. Thick tree trunks act as pillars holding up the ceiling. The furniture reminds me of the handcrafted pieces sold at the flea market. The only difference is the quality. Flea market furniture looks like a man with an excess of tree branches and access to wood glue spent an afternoon being creative. The furniture in this house all qualifies as expertly built folk art. The last time I saw furniture like this was on a family trip where we ended up in Berea, Kentucky, wandering through the many small furniture shops around town.

A black cocker spaniel walks over to Philip and me and looks up with tired eyes. Its tail wags as it sniffs my leg. The dog loses interest and walks away with its head down. I've never had a dog, so I'm not sure if they can be depressed. This dog looks like it's carrying the weight of a lot of emotions.

A woman with long gray hair walks up to the dog and pets it on the back. The dog rolls onto its side and stretches out.

"Is the dog all right?" I ask.

"He's just a little sad. The poor thing doesn't know what to do. He'd get like this when Paul would be away for too long. I'm not sure how he's going to cope."

I take a knee and pet the dog. Its black fur almost feels like human hair.

"What's his name?"

"Talker. A cocker named Talker. Ever since he was a puppy, Paul used to talk to the dog, and the dog would respond with a bark or some other noise. For ten years, they've been inseparable. Sometimes, I think Paul loved the dog more than our children."

"I'm sorry for your loss, ma'am."

"You can call me Pat."

"I'm Flynn Dupree." I hold out my hand. Pat shakes it. She has a firmer grip than I would have expected.

"Philip tells me you're looking into Paul's assassination."

This is the first time I've heard anyone call Paul's death an assassination. Although it is the best term for what happened, the use of it adds gravity to the situation.

"Yes, ma'am. Um, Pat. Sorry."

"It's all right. No reason to apologize for being brought up right."

"Had Paul been acting any differently?"

"No. He's always been a hard worker, spending extra hours here and there on his projects. If I didn't know him so well, I'd think he was having an affair. He's always been the type to keep secrets."

"Can you understand some of this shorthand? Or do you know any of these individuals?"

I give the journal to Pat. The pictures are in the front of the journal. She looks through each one and then hands them back to me.

"I don't know any of them. Although the fat, bald one resembles a nephew of mine."

Pat skims through the journal and, after several pages, returns it to me.

"I have no idea what any of this means."

"There are several letters that keep popping up together: TS, IR, JP, and LB. My best guess is those are initials. Can you connect anybody to those initials?"

"I'd have to dig a lot deeper than I'm capable of right now. LB stands out because I know Paul was not the biggest fan of Lou Brombacher."

"Can you remember anything else that Paul might have done or said that could help clear any of this up?"

Pat doesn't say a word. She just walks away from us toward the kitchen and removes something from the fridge. She walks back and hands me a piece of paper torn from the corner of a newspaper.

"Paul always had a notebook on him, so it was rare that he wrote in anything else. I know he used to finalize his notes in journals like the one you have in your hands and then file the original notebook away. This is something he wrote the day he died. Paul left his cell phone in the kitchen overnight. It went off when he was making coffee in the morning. Paul seemed excited. For the first time in a long time, he didn't have his notebook with him. He wrote this down on the newspaper and then tore it off. When the call ended, he ran back to his study and prepared for work. After he left, I found this on the floor in the hallway. I put it up here in case he needed it."

"Thank you."

The corner of the newspaper makes little sense.

Talleyrand Dlux 9.3 1201 TS

Chapter 44

Flynn

Months have passed since I last stepped foot in Dean's Bar. It's not far from where I live. I've simply not been in the mood for Dean's. It's still the place full of life I remember, a landmark bridging the gap between young and old in a haze of smoke and years of accumulated dirt.

The only reason I'm here is to speak to Samoan Stan. Samoan Stan is a man I first met at a fish market in Mayport. At the time, I called him Samoan Stan because his yellow slicker had that written on the front. It turned out his coworkers lacked a certain flair when it came to nicknames. It was just an apt description. His first name is Stan. He has Samoan ancestry. Despite it being a bit too simple, Stan isn't one to fuss. He'd have been okay with whatever nickname they thought up.

The fish market is a part-time job for Stan. During the week, he works at the Talleyrand JAX Port terminal. I've never been sure what anyone does in those shipping areas. All I know is that's where he works during the week. On Saturdays, he works in Mayport and then comes to drink at Dean's.

Stan doesn't come to Dean's to play pool. He comes to watch people. It wasn't too long after I first met Stan in Mayport that I noticed him in Dean's on a Saturday night. I lost my table to some hustling cowboy and his friend after an embarrassing game of eight-ball. Stan bought me a beer, and we watched the two cowboys play each other for about an hour.

Stan's an entertaining guy. More importantly, he may be able to shed some light on Paul's notes. Stan's sizeable frame is identifiable from across the bar. Before I make it halfway across the floor, Stan turns away from the crowd and focuses on me.

"Flynn," he says, patting me on the back with his bear paw of a hand. Stan doesn't shake hands. He pats people on the back. He says it's cleaner. "It's been a while."

"It has."

"Life been workin' out for you?"

"There've been some high points."

"I got married."

"I thought you were already married."

"I was. Got divorced. Got remarried."

"Quick turnaround."

"Oh yeah."

"How's the scene so far?"

"Been dead. It's early. You come to play pool?"

"No. Just to see you."

Stan turns in his chair to face me directly. "Me?"

"You."

"I'm honored. Want a drink?"

"One can't hurt. I've got a date," I pause. "A thing tonight."

Stan's muscular arms shoot up like flares, signaling the bartender.

"A Five Jays for me and my friend."

"Really, Stan?"

"If you only have time for one drink, then you'd better make it one that lasts. Plus, it'll loosen you up for that date-thing."

Stan only has to call the drink a Five Jays when he orders it. The original name is Five Jays Down South Shooting Turkey. It is by far the most debilitating drink ever concocted. Stan provides credit for the drink's creation to a woman named Ciara. The cocktail is a mixture of Johnny, Jack, Jose, Jim, Jameson, Southern Comfort, and Wild Turkey. To make it tolerable, a splash of soda goes on top. The first time I drank one of these, I could barely walk after about fifteen minutes.

"If I'm drinking that, then I need to get some questions out of the way."

"Questions?"

"I've been hired by a man to investigate something that may have to do with shipping through Talleyrand."

I hand Paul's notebook over to Stan, who opens it in his giant hands and flips through the pictures.

"Does anyone look familiar to you?"

Stan holds up a picture of three men together in conversation.

"This is Joseph Parker, his son, and a man named Reid."

251

"Is that a first or a last name?"

"I've only heard him called Reid."

Stan picks out another picture and holds it up.

"This man is the head of night security at Talleyrand. Mike Holcombe. I've heard rumors about him taking bribes to look the other way on multiple occasions."

"Is that possible? I thought 9/11 changed shipping and made it tougher to sneak anything through."

Stan is silent for a moment. There's no reaction other than staring blankly ahead until he smiles as if he thought of something hilarious.

"I've got a joke for you."

"Let's hear it."

"What's the difference between a criminal and a businessman?"

"I don't know."

"Not even a guess?"

"Nope," I say to move him along. Stan is the kind of guy content to spend his entire night in one seat. He has all the time in the world. I don't.

"One gets caught."

I try to laugh convincingly while Stan laughs out loud and slaps his knee. Stan looks back at me when his laughter dies away.

"You ever fill up your hand with water before?" Stan asks, like hands are something only a select few have the authorization to use. "You know, cup it so you can drink?"

"Yeah."

"When you do that, the water will always find its way through the spaces between your fingers. All that's left is some in your palm. Now let's say you fill your hand up the same way and then make a fist. When you open up your hand, you'll have about the same amount of water left in your palm. The rest of the water finds its way out, just like the first time. With shipping, there's too much moving through to be a perfect system. There's always room for things to fall through the cracks. Tightening restrictions is like making a fist. It won't solve the problem. Stupid people will still get caught, while careful people with common sense will always find some way to beat the system."

"What safeguards are in place to prevent someone from bringing something through the port?"

"Customs checks your cargo a mile from shore, and there's an X-ray machine that checks the cargo at the port."

Stan finishes with the pictures and starts flipping through the notes. "This is all gibberish."

"I know. It's shorthand. Does this make any sense to you?"

I hand Stan the piece of newspaper I received from Pat Mahoney.

"Talleyrand? Not much there other than the port and parking for the Florida-Georgia game."

"That's why I came to you. Do any of the numbers make sense?"

"The last number there looks like a date. December first. Nine-point-three—not sure what that is. The same goes for 'TS.' Maybe it stands for 'tough shit.' D-L-U-X? If you say them together, they sound like deluxe. Other than that, nothing."

"How hard is it to find out which ships are coming in and going out on December first?"

"Do you know where it's coming from?"

"No idea."

Stan closes the notebook and hands it back to me. "I'm gonna seal my lips from here on about work."

"One more thing."

Stan looks at me disapprovingly. "Shoot, Columbo."

"You mentioned Joseph Parker. I received information about a man named Joseph Prince."

"It's the same person. Joseph Parker's nickname is the Prince of Philips Highway. He owns a lot of businesses out that way. But I know him because he owns a shipping company, and word spreads around work when he's looking to hire."

"By hire, do you mean recruit… for illegal…?"

Stan runs his paw over his face and then crosses his arms. Instead of speaking, he looks ahead until the bartender taps him on the shoulder. Stan takes the drinks and hands one to me.

"Before you down that, let's say a toast." Stan holds up his Five Jays. "To all the ladies who've left my wallet light and my balls blue: Stay out of my sight. This drink's 'cause of you."

The only way a Five Jays is tolerable is by drinking it as quickly as possible. The problem with drinking it as quickly as possible is that they serve it in a pint glass with only a couple cubes of ice. The second my lips hit the glass, I know I might be in for a rough night. After finishing half of the drink, I put the glass down on the bar. The alcohol sends a warm feeling through me as it burns its way down into my stomach.

"If I told you I was in AA, would you make me finish that?"

"I'd make you finish a second one."

"That's pretty harsh, Stan."

"I don't trust people who don't drink."

Despite Stan having told me this many times before, I'm sure he will start all over again. Before he can chastise me for not finishing my drink, I knock back the rest and set the empty glass back on the bar. Stan is polite and waits for me to finish before putting his glass down.

"You see," Stan says, his eyes focused on the other side of the bar where two women are conversing, "I can't trust a person without alcohol in 'em. Your true self comes through when you drink. If you're a scoundrel, you want to brag and fight and be noisy. If you're a good guy, you want to dance and sing and have a good old time. And if you're in the middle, well, alcohol makes you choose who you truly are. I can deal with scoundrels, and I can deal with good guys, but I can't handle not knowing someone's true nature."

"That's pretty deep, Stan," I say, hoping to put the conversation back on track.

"Deep thoughts fall into good guy territory."

"When you say people flock to Parker when he hires, are you talking about scoundrels? Is he looking for the rough and tumble type to do something illegal?"

Stan looks at me and then back to my empty glass.

"Well done, Flynn. Now this person on your date-thing will get to know the real you."

"I'm not sure she's ready for that."

"No one ever wants to reveal their true selves to a member of the opposite sex. It ruins things, which is why it's best to get that out of the way tonight. Her opinion of you can only go up."

"You don't know how right you are. I'm currently rock bottom. I'm surprised she invited me to her place."

"Nothing quite like a woman with an agenda."

My only response is a chuckle.

Stan continues to look ahead across the crowd. Nothing interesting is going on. It borders on amazing how he can entertain himself for hours watching people do nothing.

"Parker doesn't hire thugs." Stan doesn't turn to me. Instead, he keeps watching random people. "When people speak out loud, they talk about Parker's legitimate businesses. The illegal activities are all whispers. The benefit of someone speaking out loud is that they're confident about what they say. They speak out loud because they believe in their words. When a person whispers, they do so out of fear or shame. That's why they hide their words. Don't make me whisper about Joseph Parker."

"Understood. Thank you for all your help."

Stan puts his massive hand on my shoulder before I can turn to leave. His gaze returns from across the bar and focuses on me. The look on his face does not change. Although I'm within arm's reach, his eyes stare through me like I'm across the room.

"Remember," he says aloud, "fear or shame."

Chapter 45

Flynn

Amy provided me specific instructions on how to find her apartment and enter the gated parking lot. Apartment buildings on the beach keep their lots secured to prevent strangers from using the residents' parking and beach access. The only way for a visitor to gain entry is to use the call box next to the gate. Instead of providing me a code for the keypad, Amy told me to scroll to the name 'Wright' and hit the call button.

The phone rings once before a loud and continuous beeping sound goes off. The gate slides open. I take my foot off the brake. Misty's hearse lurches over a speed bump and rolls into the parking lot. The building reminds me of the older motels you see on the beach when driving down A1A. Off-white paint covers a cinderblock facade pockmarked by windows looking out over the parking lot. Covered entryways partition the building into three-story chunks of apartments identified by lettered placards. I drive until I find a door marked 'D.' Despite a pool and patio area limiting the amount of available parking, I land a spot in front of Amy's building. The hearse's flashing signs tint the surrounding area with their pulsing red lights. It would be polite to turn them off, but Misty needs the advertising.

Amy told me not to bring anything. It was odd. Most people want something. She even turned down my offer of a great bottle of wine, preferring me to come as I am. The 'no strings attached' invitation came as a surprise, considering the circumstances. It worked out for me since I lied about having a great bottle of wine and am terrible at picking out wine at the grocery store.

A carpeted stairwell, clean and protected from the elements, is behind the door marked 'D.' The enclosed area smells like someone is cooking something delicious. The bottom floor has two apartments. Neither matches the number Amy provided.

256

The second-floor landing has the same layout as the first floor. I know I'm where I need to be when I see the door is ajar, and the numbers above the peephole match what Amy provided. The door moves when I try to knock, reducing the sound to a gentle tap.

"Hello," I say instead of trying to knock again. "Amy?"

"Come on in." It's Amy. The soft Southern accent is a dead giveaway.

A short hallway opens up into the dining room. The kitchen is boxed in except for a single entrance facing the dining room and two cutouts in the drywall from waist to shoulder height that must exist to provide a bar feel. Amy leans down and waves through a cutout.

"Have a seat in the living room. I'll bring you out a glass of wine."

I'm not a big wine fan, but it'll be a welcome change of pace from the Five Jays. The remnants of Stan's favorite drink sit heavy. Plopping down on Amy's plush sofa sends the liquid sloshing back and forth inside my stomach. She's furnished the living room with a matching sofa and armchair. The sofa faces a fifty-inch TV on the wall. The armchair faces the sliding glass door, which leads out to a balcony overlooking the ocean. There's a single copy of *Ponte Vedra Living* among several copies of *The Economist* fanned across the coffee table. I pick up the *Ponte Vedra Living*. It's over a year old, whereas *The Economist* issues are all recent.

The cover article of *Ponte Vedra Living* is about some woman's roses. As I skim through, I come across an article about travel. Some PV residents went to Bolivia's Salar de Uyuni and took photos interesting enough to publish. The pictures are of a family in various states of pretending to be either terrified or astonished as the sky's reflection across the salt flat makes it look like they are walking on clouds.

"A little light reading before dinner?"

I put the magazine down. Amy hands me a glass of red wine. Classy people always whiff their vino. I give it a shot. It smells like every other red with an added hint of soap from the clean glass. Amy tips her wine back and takes a sip. I do the same. Instead of drinking, I let the wine touch my lips before setting it down on the coffee table.

"Do you like it?"

"Yup," I reply, not knowing what I could add about the wine to sound intelligent. "Tons of flavor."

Amy smiles.

"Please don't take offense," I say. "Why did you invite me over?"

Amy takes a seat in the armchair and sets her glass down on the coffee table next to mine.

"The police only told me you were released. Not why. I want to know what happened. And when you called me, I thought it might be nice to hear from you why you aren't in jail."

"I could have told you that over the phone."

"It's easy to tell a lie over the phone. It's hard in person. I wanted to see you tell me in person. At the very least, I deserve that."

"Yes, you do."

"So?"

"You're ready?"

"Not quite. First, what's up with your eyes? They're very odd. I don't remember them looking like that at the diner."

"Yeah, it's sort of a curse."

"How? They look like gold."

"It's an illusion caused by the light. My eyes are pale green, but I have Wilson's disease. It's genetic. My body absorbs too much copper. My irises are ringed with an accumulation of copper known as a Kayser–Fleischer ring."

"What does that mean?"

"I'm fine if I take medication."

"If?"

"My insurance cut me a while ago. I've been trying to fight it. That's the reason I took the job that… I needed the money."

"What happens if you don't take your medication?"

"My body will absorb copper until either my brain dies or my liver fails. When I was young, they didn't diagnose it until I already had some frontal lobe damage."

"That's strange. A genetic disorder doing that to your body."

"There are stranger genetic disorders. You ever heard of methemoglobinemia?"

"No. Has anyone?"

"It turns your skin blue."

"Like a smurf?"

"Sort of. There's an issue with the methemoglobin in their blood. Their body gets enough oxygen to live, but not a hundred percent. So a person with methemoglobinemia is naturally bluish."

"I'd rather have too much copper."

"They may be blue, but when they look in the mirror, they see a healthy blue person staring back at them. When I see my eyes, I see a slow march toward additional neurological problems or the eventual failure of my liver."

"Yet, you still drink?"

"I blame that on the frontal lobe damage."

"A crazy person doesn't know he's crazy."

"True. That's why I don't see any problem with drinking."

"Well, that was a much longer answer than I was expecting. Let's get back to you nearly killing me. If I don't like what I hear, I'll be kicking you out. Otherwise, I have food just about ready if you'd like to join me for dinner."

I'm shocked at her frankness. It's understandable, though. I'm sure the police have jerked her around since the explosion. She's probably desperate for some kind of answer about what happened.

"A man calling himself Harold hired me to hire you. He provided me information on you and told me not to take no for an answer. I did as he asked. Everything I told you before you went into that room is everything he told me. I thought we were recording that man who showed up. Harold never told me how he would use the recording, only that recording him was the intent. It all turned out to be a lie.

"Harold is actually Stephen Collins, an employee of Lou Brombacher. Brombacher is running for mayor against Paul Mahoney, the man killed in the motel room."

"So, this whole thing is connected?"

"Yes, but not in how it looks."

"But it looks like it's clear who tried to kill me."

"Yes. Stephen Collins tried to kill us both. But it all hinges on who hired him."

"And it's not his boss?"

"It could be. But I don't think so."

"Why not?"

"He had more to gain by humiliating Paul Mahoney. The two of you on video in a motel would be enough to take Mahoney out of the race. Killing him is too much. Which makes me wonder why Stephen Collins would have gone that far?"

"Maybe he snapped, like those people who shoot up their office."

"His actions say otherwise. He didn't stay and fight like a man who snapped. As far as I know, he didn't call anyone to take credit for what he's done. My opinion is that someone forced him into doing all of this."

"How could someone force another person into killing people?"

"By taking his son."

"Oh, my God." Amy reaches for her glass and takes a gulp of wine. Amy swallows and looks at me. "Are you not going to drink?"

I look down at the wine glass and shake my head.

"Honestly, I'm not big on wine. I'm more of a beer drinker. And a friend talked me into having a drink with him before I came here."

"You do smell a little smoky."

"Sorry," I say, taking a whiff of my shirt. "I was at Dean's. I didn't realize it would stick with me that long."

"Dean's? Interesting place to go before meeting a lady."

"Yeah. I had to ask a friend some questions."

"Does this have to do with this Collins person?"

"Indirectly. I have Paul Mahoney's notes. He was looking into something. I'm following up on it."

"That sounds fascinating. And now you've done what I wanted. Thank you for telling me your side and then some."

"You're welcome. I wish I could tell you more, but that's all I know."

"When you figure it out, let me know. Then maybe we can have dinner again."

A confused smile breaks across my face.

"Am I staying for dinner?"

"If you'd like," Amy says while standing up. "Would you like some beer instead of wine?"

"It'd be impolite not to finish what I've started." I look down at the wine glass and pick it up. Amy grabs it from my hand before I can put it to my lips.

"I'll drink this. I've got Chimay. Is that okay?"

"Red, white, or blue?"

"Blue."

"Sounds great."

Amy walks back into the kitchen with my full glass and her nearly empty glass. The muffled sound of a cork popping lets me know that Amy has experience in opening Chimay bottles. Amy returns with two wine glasses. This time, hers is full of whatever red wine she poured before, and dark-colored beer fills mine. Amy hands me the glass. I take a sip. The bubbles sliding down my insides make my stomach feel better.

"Now that you answered my questions, you can ask me one."

"I feel bad admitting this, but I know a lot about you. Stephen Collins provided me a file on you when he hired me. I read it. There was a lot of information."

"Really? Then I guess I'm an open book."

"Not entirely. I know you attended and graduated from college in New York. Why did you come back here? It's such a big difference."

"Exactly. I thought I wanted the big city. I didn't realize it can wear on you. When I couldn't find a good job in New York, it dawned on me how much I missed home."

This feels like a perfect time to ask Amy how she ended up in the world's oldest profession, but I haven't had enough to drink to lose my tact.

"I've never left the Beaches. I've gone on vacation with my parents when I was younger and taken trips out of town, but never stayed anywhere long enough for me to feel homesick."

"What was your last trip?" Amy asks.

"I headed down to Miami a while back to see the Cubs play."

"The cubs? Like at a zoo?"

"Oh, they're a baseball team from Chicago. It's where my father grew up, so I've been a fan since before I had a chance to decide if I wanted to be a fan or not."

"I've never been into baseball. It's too slow."

"That's why they serve alcohol."

Amy laughs. It's the first time I've heard her laugh. The sound is sharp and sweet, like a bird's chirp.

"Baseball's not for everyone. It looks like your interests lie elsewhere," I say, pointing to *The Economist* magazines.

"I've been trying to re-educate myself. It's funny how quickly you can fall out of touch with the world."

"I've never been into financial news and world events. They're a bit dry."

"That's why bars serve alcohol."

This time we both laugh.

A buzzer rings in the kitchen.

"Everything's ready. Sit at the table. I'll bring it out to you."

Amy plates the meals and sets them on the dining table before I can get comfortable in her dining room chairs. The plate has a burned-looking piece of meat, asparagus, and buttered parsley potatoes.

"Steak au poivre," Amy says.

"Ahh," is my only response. I'm not a gourmand, so that means nothing.

"It's steak crusted with peppercorns."

"Interesting."

The first bite is tasty. It's a unique blend of crunchy and earthy. The flavor turns bothersome after a few more bites. It's like steak with a side of charred sand. I try my best to scrape off the pepper without Amy noticing.

"I feel like I should let you know now," I say to distract her from me scraping off the pepper, "that I don't like potatoes."

"Most people like potatoes."

"Most people don't have neighbors tell them at a young age how potatoes, eggplants, and tomatoes are from the very poisonous nightshade family."

"Why would someone tell you that?"

"Probably just so I'd know."

"You don't eat any of those?"

"Not willingly."

"No french fries? No pizza?"

"No and no."

"That's almost un-American."

"Now might be a good time to mention that I don't like bacon."

"Childhood visit to a slaughterhouse?"

"Personal preference. Something about the smell."

"How strange."

"I know."

"So, you're afraid of being poisoned by potatoes, but you drink beer? Doesn't that destroy your liver?"

"I never said it made sense. And I know heat destroys what little poison exists in potatoes. They're just something I don't eat."

"I'm not judging you. It makes a girl feel inadequate when someone doesn't eat her cooking, that's all."

"I know. I'm starting to wish Hallmark made a line of apology cards for people like me. 'Sorry I didn't go on vacation with you. I'm afraid of planes.' 'Apologies for leaving food on the plate. Deep down, I'm concerned I might die.'"

"How about, 'Sorry I talked you into showing up at a hotel room rigged to explode.'"

"That one would be great. However, I feel like the market might be too slim."

"Is pepper poisonous? I notice you've been scraping it off the steak."

Damn. The surreptitious scraping did not work.

Amy is observant. That skill must be beneficial in her line of work. Part of me still wants to ask her why she does what she does. Unfortunately, there's never a right time to ask someone why they're resorting to prostitution as a source of income.

"No, not that I know of."

"Then why are you scraping it off. The peppercorn crust is the best part."

"I've never eaten peppercorn crust before." It's best to lie. I'm already not eating a significant portion of the meal. Saying the most integral part is gritty won't go over well. "I'm a little concerned about sneezing."

"You should never be concerned about sneezing. A doctor friend of mine once told me that sneezing is the rough equivalent of one-tenth of an orgasm."

"I can vouch for both sides of the equation. That's a pretty rough equivalent."

"It sounded like BS, but everyone has their own little pleasure scale."

"I suppose that's true. In French, orgasm translates to 'little death.' If we add the potatoes to this doctor's scale, I'd say you're trying to kill me."

"A+B=C, huh? Well, listen, Pythagoras, keep it up, and I will kill you."

"Yes, ma'am."

I cut off a piece of steak with the crust still on it and put it into my mouth. It tastes the same as before.

"What do you think?"

"It's nice," I say, swallowing the bite. "It's odd with the texture. I guess I'm just not used to it."

"Taste takes time to acquire."

"Shore nuff."

"If you don't like normal food, what do you cook?"

"Not much. I prefer food in boxes or things easy to put together. I'm big on cereal."

"What's the most complicated thing you've made?"

"A simple syrup."

"That's just water and sugar."

"It was a little more complicated. It was a special simple syrup."

"Special?"

"Yeah, I added powdered laxatives and stool softeners to it."

"I know they don't sell lettuce in a cereal box, but you may want to try some roughage instead."

"It was for some unscrupulous nurses."

"You poisoned nurses?"

"I didn't poison nurses. They stole food from my mother and made themselves sick."

"Why would nurses steal food from your mother?"

"She was put in a nursing home for a while under observation. Her favorite thing to eat is fresh fruit, so I'd bring it every day. She wasn't very responsive, so she didn't eat it. There was a stretch of days where I'd store her fruit in the fridge, and the next day it would be gone. After it happened twice, I asked the nurse about it. He said that I should've put my name on it. I thought that was silly, considering the person who ate my mother's fruit knew they didn't bring it or pay for it. They took it. So I made that special simple syrup, added it to the fruit, and left it in the fridge like normal. The next day I showed up with more special fruit and noticed that someone took what I left previously. I overheard one nurse talking about a stomach virus going around. It made me snicker. I kept

264

bringing the special fruit every day, and every day it disappeared. I had to stop after a week because more and more nurses were calling out sick from the stomach virus."

"They didn't suspect the fruit made them sick?"

"Not that I know of. It's strange, right? You'd think someone might have connected the dots. I felt a little bad about it, but it's not like I was forcing them. I left it there. They kept on taking it."

"They're like you."

"What?"

"Drinking alcohol and afraid of the dangerous potato. They probably suspected the stolen fruit was making them sick. They kept doing it because they knew deep down they deserved to be sick for stealing someone else's food. I guess you're good, after all."

"I don't follow."

"You drink out of guilt."

Good eye. Most people drink because it's social. I'm part of the self-destructive club. I've never thought of myself on par with those nurses, though. Amy is right to look at us side-by-side, thieves and flagellants with self-abuse as a means of recompense.

"And you're too polite to ask me about what I do."

I choke. "I'm sorry?"

"We both know what I do for money. I get this feeling that you want to ask me about it but are afraid."

"It felt inappropriate."

"You already know. There's no need to be coy. I do what I do for money, plain and simple. It's my decision."

"How did you get to this point? You have a degree, and you're sleeping with men for money."

"I don't sleep with men for money. I sleep with men because I want to. I run a business. And like any business, I have a varied clientele. Some pay me for massages. Some pay me to attend events as arm candy. They don't dictate the terms. I do. And they all pay. They pay me for my time, and I decide how that time is spent.

"It's all about independence. When I worked in New York, I hated it. I wasn't in control of my life. Now I am. It's that simple."

"Okay. Why do you work at the diner?"

265

"I don't anymore, but I picked up shifts there to keep the taxman from knocking on my door. I need to claim income from something. Now I have to find another something to keep me legitimate and busy.

"With that discussion out of the way," Amy says, putting down her fork and knife. "What is it that drives you? You may not want to believe it, but you and I are alike. We run our businesses our way. It's just a difference in services."

"I don't know. After hearing about what you do, I may have to change the scope of my work."

Amy laughs her bird-like laugh before placing a linen napkin over her mouth. When she stops laughing, she sets the napkin back onto her lap.

"You might need to clean up a little and head to the gym before you make the big bucks."

"I don't know," I say, rolling up my sleeve and flexing what little muscle I have, "the ladies melt like butter against this hot steel."

Amy laughs so hard she snorts and then reflexively sneezes.

"Stop it. You're killing me."

This causes me to laugh as well. We chuckle together until the moment passes, and Amy starts again.

"You never answered my question, Flynn. What drives you?"

Reluctantly, I remove my watch. The dial is still visible through the busted crystal. It's an antique Rolex watch with the date stopped on the sixteenth. I hand the watch over to Amy.

"A broken watch?"

"It's a watch my father gave me when I turned sixteen. He told me that, before I got a car, I needed to show him I could take care of something valuable. My birthday is in February, the eighth, and the watch lasted until June sixteenth."

"What happened to it?"

"On June sixteenth, I was supposed to watch my sister for the evening while my parents went out to dinner. The moon wasn't full, but it still lit up the sky. The ocean was like glass. I used to go out on the water and think on nights like that. Just lie on my board and look up at the sky. I'd been having some problems with a girl. I needed to think about my life more than I needed to watch my sister. And before I knew it, she was gone.

"When my parents came home, I was a wreck. They were shouting. I was screaming back. My father started in on responsibility and me being a failure. I snapped and took off the watch. I shoved it in his face before I threw it across the room. It hit the kitchen table and fell to the ground, where I stomped on it until my father pulled me away. I was so angry, angry at myself.

"So when someone asks me why I do what I do, I look at my watch. The day it stopped is the day I started trying to make amends. I guess I'm hoping someone I can save will walk through my door. Because deep down, I know that if I can save someone else, then maybe I can save myself. Until that day, I'll be spinning my tires, stuck at sixteen."

"I'm sorry."

"Me too."

Silence follows Amy handing me back my watch. As I put it around my wrist and tighten the band, Amy places her hand on mine.

"How about dessert?"

"I'm not big on sweets."

"I am. And remember, I dictate the terms."

"Yes, ma'am."

"Go into my bedroom and get undressed."

"Are you sure?"

"Yes. I told you. This happens only when I want it to."

The master bedroom is not what I expected. My pink and frilly imagination meets with varying shades of blue and gray stretching from the walls to the carpet to the sheets to the pillows. Flowers and accent pieces play a role in adding warmth to the cool colors. A blackout curtain partially covers a sliding glass door leading to the same balcony accessible by the living room. The beach is visible from the bedroom, which means the bedroom is visible to anyone on the beach.

Moonlight casts a ghostly luster onto the white sand below. The dark shapes of two people lurking on the beach stand out, their outlines discernible against the glow. One motions to the other. They retreat under a pier that juts out from the apartment complex yet does not quite reach the ocean's edge. I close the curtain and undress, making it down to my boxers before Amy enters the room.

"Stop," she says.

"Huh? I thought you told me to undress."

267

"I did. That's enough. At least leave me a little work."

Amy's loose-fitting sundress falls to the floor when she slides the straps off of her shoulder. She picks the dress up off the floor and sets it on her dresser before turning back around.

"Ta-da," she says after turning around. Amy is in ridiculous shape. If God could mine clay out of the cloudy fields of heaven and fire it in some celestial kiln, this is the figure He would create. But I don't even know if that grandiose thought does her justice. It's clear to me that Amy is driven. Her body is a testament to smart decisions, made day after day for years. The sight alone makes me feel inadequate.

I sit on the bed and applaud.

"Best magic trick I've seen in a while."

"One minute," Amy says, holding up a finger. She walks out of the room. The living room lights turn off. She walks back in and says, "I always forget to turn those off."

Amy jumps into the air and lands on the bed like she intended to drop an elbow on one of the pillows. It leaves her with her head propped up on one arm like a model waiting to have her picture taken.

Before I can pretend to take a picture with an imaginary camera, Amy grabs the back of my head and forces her tongue down my throat. I'm not sure why, but the aggressive nature surprises the hell out of me. I pull back out of instinct.

"Condom," I say.

"What?" Amy responds, sounding surprised.

"Do you have a condom?"

"Do you need a condom?"

"I didn't bring any. Is that a problem?"

"No," Amy says, rolling off the bed and walking to her bathroom. She searches through a drawer and returns with two in her hand. "One for now and one for just in case."

Amy hops back on the bed and picks up where she left off. Something still feels odd about the whole moment. I don't know if it's the fact that I've just been talking about my sister or a feeling like Amy is sleeping with me out of pity. All I know is it doesn't feel right.

Before things progress any further, splintering woods follows a pounding sound. Amy stops.

"I think that's the stairwell door on the balcony."

"What?" I say, looking toward the sliding glass door.

Amy looks to her bedside table and then runs from the bed to her dresser, shifting items and frantically looking for something.

"Shit," she says, looking right at me. "My phone and gun are in the kitchen."

My eyes open wide. "Gun?" I mutter.

"My father let me borrow his after the explosion. It's so I'd feel safer."

We both quiet down when footsteps on the wooden floor of the balcony move our direction. I walk to the bedroom door and crane my neck to look out at the balcony. Someone is peering in through the glass.

Amy sticks her head next to mine and looks out into her apartment toward the kitchen.

"Maybe I can scare them off."

"What?" I say. Amy inches her way out into the living room and turns on an overhead light. Before she can move any farther away, I place my hand on her shoulder. "No."

Amy turns to me with a look of anger in her eyes. Behind her, a figure emerges from the darkness with a chair. They lift the chair up and slam it down into the glass door. The chair's impact causes two distinct cracking patterns to begin on the glass. Instead of continuing to watch, Amy and I retreat into her bedroom and lock the door.

"What do we do?" Amy asks, her eyes looking back and forth across the room.

The sound of the chair hitting the glass door rings out again. The person breaking into the apartment will break through the bedroom door in less than a minute. We can hide under the bed, which will not work. Movies have twisted common sense when it comes to beds. Hiding in a prone position at the mercy of anyone with the seven shiny gray cells it takes to check under the bed is a terrible idea. The bathroom is a better option, but it's hard to hide or surprise anyone from a predictable enclosed space. Bathrooms come in all shapes and sizes, but they are all similarly wide open with small places for storage. Aside from a large hamper or storage bin, there's nothing big enough for one adult to hide, let alone two. And even if we could conceal ourselves somehow, the average person will find a hiding space in the bathroom in a heartbeat. We could escape through the other glass door, but I doubt we would get far half-naked and leaving the same way this intruder is coming in. That

269

winnows our options down to the closet. It's the same as the bathroom, with an added element of surprise. While every bathroom may contain the same basic components, each closet is unique. And Amy's closet goes beyond unique.

With the door open, it's clear she spends a lot of money on clothing. A fixture holding dozens of belts and hats hangs on the inside of the door. Clothing fills two of the closet walls while the third has a collection of work outfits to satiate a variety of fantasies.

"I've got an idea," I say, walking into the closet.

Amy follows me in. I close the door.

"What's your idea?"

"Help me put some of this on."

"What?" Amy looks at me like I'm insane.

"We don't have time. If I can put some of this stuff on," I say, pointing to the role-playing outfits, "then I'll be able to blend into the closet. The person breaking in will eventually open the closet door. This'll give me a split-second advantage I wouldn't have otherwise."

"You think it'll distract them?"

"It's worth a shot," I say, putting on a fuchsia-colored hat and a pink feather boa. Amy takes a pleather bustier and ties it around my back. I search through the belts on the door until I find one with metal studs that wraps comfortably around my hand. Before I can turn the lights out, Amy finishes my ensemble by securing a pink tutu around my waist.

"I'd prefer it if you never tell anyone about this."

"You look cute," Amy says.

"I look like I'm going to watch *The Rocky Horror Picture Show.* Hide behind that clump of dresses hanging over there."

Someone struggles with the bedroom door handle. I turn out the lights in the closet as pounding on the door begins. The closet door is ajar enough for the soft lighting from the bedroom to seep in. The light is barely enough to tell one piece of clothing from another.

It only takes two strong hits to the bedroom door for it to give. The sound puts me on edge, but I still have the element of surprise. The person should search the room first and then move on to the bathroom and closet. It surprises me when, only seconds after the doorframe yielded to the pounding, the door opens. A man's hand reaches in and begins feeling around the closet wall, looking for the light switch. After not finding the switch, he leans his body in. A gun precedes the man's head. Stephen Collins performs a double-take when he looks in my direction. The slow realization that the lump of random clothing is a person allows me time to attack.

I reach out with my left hand and move the gun up, away from my body and Amy's hiding place, while throwing a punch at Stephen's head with my right. The shot to the face lands hard. Stephen gasps as he stumbles out of the closet. Instead of letting him escape, I grab the gun and twist it from his hand. It falls onto the carpet with a dull thud.

Stephen remains in a state of shock as I continue lashing out at him. A hard shot to the face crumples him to the ground, where I kick him in the ribs.

Something hits me from behind hard enough to knock me forward onto the bed, leaving me helpless as the room spins.

Chapter 46

William

Some people consider me a nosy neighbor. I consider myself a helpful neighbor, considerate enough to keep an eye out. The problem with living on the beach is that anyone can come up from the sand onto your property. Attentive neighbors are the last line of defense against thirsty beach vagrants grabbing glasses of water from any beach home. That makes my watchful eyes a benefit my neighbors receive.

Flynn is at the top of my list when it comes to keeping an eye out. The last of my original neighborhood family, he understands the importance of having someone like me keeping watch. Flynn allows me full access to his property whenever I see fit. If I know the grass needs mowing or the plants and trees need some tending, I fix the problem without ever having to say a word. The same extends to keeping his property safe. I have a key to his house just in case anything happens.

Most of the time, I keep an eye on the back of the property to make sure no one comes up from the beach and starts snooping around. For the front, I keep my windows cracked and my blinds open. This way, I can be aware of strangers passing by. Lowering the TV's volume ensures all the goings-on outside can be heard inside.

While sitting around watching some reruns of *Law and Order*, headlights shine into my house enough to catch my attention. A car door opens and closes. That's enough for me to take a look.

From my front window, I watch a guy get out of a classic Chevy truck and pull a bag out of the truck bed. I'm not too good with cars, but the truck looks old and is well-maintained with a glossy shine that's reflecting the moon. This man approaches the police car parked in front of Flynn's house. The streetlights light him up enough to show me he's dressed like he's going out for a beer instead of a robbery. The police officer opens the car door and walks out to speak to him. They chat for a minute or two before the police officer allows the man onto Flynn's property.

The policeman doesn't seem to care too much because he climbs right back in his car. Knowing that the police are okay with the man allows me to relax a little. I return to my sofa and TV. Strange noises float in through the open windows, noises like machinery and random tools. All that racket convinces me to head back up to the front window. The view I have covers most of the street and the front of Flynn's lawn, but I can't see the man.

I grab my keys and head out to my garage. While waiting for the garage door to open, I take a trowel off of the wall and place it in my pocket. I remove the knife from my back pocket and leave it on my workbench. Ever since Durrell broke into my house, I've kept his knife in my pocket. It's important, for Flynn's sake, that I check out what's happening, but I don't want to bring anything too threatening. A trowel is small enough to conceal and strong enough to do some damage. The trowel's handle sticks out of my pocket and rocks back and forth along with my braid as I walk the short distance to Flynn's yard. The police officer doesn't pay any attention to me as I enter through the front gate and walk across the yard toward the noise coming from Flynn's garage. Light escapes from the open side door in a little line down the driveway.

Trying not to disturb, I peek inside. The front of Herman's old Studebaker is open, and the man is on the side of the car using an air compressor to re-inflate the tires.

"Excuse me," I say. The man doesn't respond. "Excuse me," I shout. The man keeps working on the tires and ignores my shouting.

I pull out the trowel and keep it in my right hand next to my leg while inching toward the man. He still doesn't realize I'm behind him as I reach out with my left hand toward his shoulder.

"Stop right there," shouts a voice behind me. "Put down the knife."

There's a police officer with his gun drawn as I turn around. I drop the trowel and put my hands in the air. The officer looks down and puts his gun back in his holster.

The noise from the air compressor stops.

"Sir, what are you doing here?" the officer asks.

"His name's William," a voice behind me says. "He's Flynn's neighbor."

I turn away from the officer and face the man who was inflating tires. He looks familiar. I've met him before but can't remember his name.

"I'm Leslie," he says. "Misty's father. Flynn's friend, Misty."

"Oh," is all I say. The face fits. I've only seen this man a handful of times and met him once, but I do remember him.

"William?" the officer asks, pointing to the trowel. "Were you planning on using that for something?"

"What is this, a trowel?" Leslie asks.

"I brought it for protection."

"You thought I was robbing the place, and you brought this?" Leslie hands me the trowel, which I put back into my pocket.

"It's small and kinda sharp. I thought…"

"No worries."

The officer walks into the garage and starts admiring the car.

"What do you think, Officer Rittwell?" Leslie asks. "It's nice, isn't it?"

The car is an old beauty with ridges and lines that carmakers run away from these days. Originality and inspiration ooze from its baby blue paint to its chrome accents, all the way down to the white-wall tires.

"It's nice," Officer Rittwell replies. "Wasn't Flynn driving a piece of shit when his car blew up?"

"Yeah, this is his father's. Or, I guess, was his father's. I remember this car from before Herman left. It was pristine. Flynn's lucky the garage is closed up tight. The salty air never got in. Otherwise, this would've corroded quite a bit."

"What does something like this go for?" Officer Rittwell asks.

"It varies on the condition and how original the parts are. It would probably cost about as much as a new car."

Leslie reaches into his pocket and pulls out his wallet. He takes out a business card and hands it to Officer Rittwell.

"Here's my information. If you're ever interested in fixing up an old car, or if you want me to find you one of these to fix up, I can do it."

"Thanks," Officer Rittwell says, putting the card in his pocket. "I'll call you next week."

"My hours are on the card. The only time you might miss me is during lunch. Just leave me a message. I'll call you back."

"Will do. You two try not to get into a trowel fight in here," Officer Rittwell says before leaving the garage. He only makes it three steps before stopping to stare at Flynn's house.

Conversing with Leslie about salt air corrosion might help slow my truck's rust problem. But that conversation can wait. Officer Rittwell's behavior holds my interest. Something in Flynn's house caught his attention. He holds up his hand to stop me from moving outside.

Lights in the windows shine sporadically. Not house lights or anything bright enough to fill a room, but flashlights. A little here and a little there. It looks like some people are moving through the house, looking for something.

"Go back in the garage," Officer Rittwell says.

I hand him my keys, drawing attention to one key in particular. "This is for Flynn's front door."

"Do you have a key to the side door?"

"No," I reply. The key could open the side door, but I've never tried. I return to the garage and close the door behind me.

"What's going on?" Leslie asks.

"I don't know. There're lights inside. Looks like flashlights."

Leslie walks toward the door. I put up my hand.

"The officer told us to stay put."

"I've got a gun in my truck. Considering the circumstances."

"No. We stay put." The look on Leslie's face says he doesn't want to listen, so I try my best to distract him. "Earlier, you were saying something about the salt air corroding this car. My truck is getting a little rusty. You think that's the problem."

Leslie shakes his head in disbelief, like I've gone crazy. It's a familiar look. I used to be a person with anger issues. In my twenties, I went to a retreat to rid myself of anger. This place broke me down and rebuilt me with kindness, love, and drugs. They taught me to never use my hands to destroy, only to create. The tattoos on my knuckles, LOVE and MORE, are a testament to me being a changed man. But they also draw a lot of attention. And the first time someone sees my tattoos, they take a step back and give me the same look Leslie is giving me right now.

The look disappears from his face when faint shouting precedes gunshots ringing out in the night air. Leslie dives to the ground and pulls me down with him.

275

Chapter 47

Flynn

Waking up to the disorientating effects of a spinning world has yet to be a positive in my life. It's usually as a result of alcohol or something harder. Instead of a 'Why, God? Why?' dull frontal lobe headache, I have a 'Who, God? Who?' pain radiating from a lump on the back of my skull. Despite the passing headlights and engines buzzing by, the spinning isn't bad enough for me not to recognize the back of Misty's hearse. I'm not a hundo on the sure scale about what happened. The last thing I remember was kicking Stephen Collins while he was on the ground. It's not the manliest of moves, although neither is dressing up in Amy's costumes.

I'm still wearing the bustier, tutu, and boa, but my glasses and the floppy hat disappeared somewhere along the way. There's a pair of handcuffs around my wrists. They aren't official police handcuffs. They're a pair Amy must have had in her closet. The insides of the cuffs are soft. They might feel kind of nice if they weren't being used to restrain me in the back of a moving vehicle.

The spinning slows to a near halt until several rounds of streetlights flying by kick-starts it all over again. Staring at the driver helps me focus. It takes time for Stephen Collins' face to stabilize. The only logical conclusion is that he's taking me somewhere to kill me. I'm not sure why he didn't finish me off at Amy's. The only reason would be that he thought it might attract too much attention. That doesn't entirely add up since he was willing to break into Amy's apartment despite neighbors living so close. His intention may not be to kill me, but I'm not ready to wait and find out.

Trying not to draw attention, I lift my head enough to see out of the window. We're heading south on Third Street. It's hard to say where Stephen is going. We haven't left the beach yet. Undeveloped land at the beach is scarce. If Stephen drives far enough south, we'll hit Ponte Vedra.

276

There are some parks near A1A that could accommodate a corpse. I'm not dead yet, but I doubt Stephen plans to keep me alive much longer. When we reach whatever Stephen deems an appropriate burial plot, he will pull me out of the hearse and leave me in a hole. Or he could just throw me off a bridge. That does sound easier than a burial. All Stephen needs to do is heave-ho me to a watery grave. Neither ticks my boxes for an enjoyable end, but, if forced to choose, I'd prefer the water.

At Amy's, Stephen had a gun. It's safe to assume that he still has one. If I try to attack him, he can shoot me. If I try to escape, he can shoot me. If I do anything he doesn't like, he can shoot me. My only option is a surreptitious escape. And the only way to pull that off is to force someone else to rescue me in a fashion Stephen will not see coming.

The handcuffs restrict me from struggling, but they hardly prevent me from moving. Instead of handcuffing me behind my back, Stephen handcuffed me around the front. Years of excessive drinking has taught me that it's easier to carry an unconscious person with their hands and arms in a more natural position. But this natural position will make it easier for me to get free.

Inch-by-inch, I move deeper into the hearse toward the control panel for the LED signs. The signs cycle through their messages, lighting up the sides of the hearse with flashing red advertisements. When I change them, Stephen will have to be paying attention to the billboards and not the road to realize what has happened.

The second I reach the panel, I delete all the current messages. In their place, I publish a simple plea on both billboards.

Call 911. Being held at gunpoint. No joke.

The instant I publish the message, I inch back to where I awoke. If someone pulls Stephen over, he will look back at me to see if I've moved. The less movement for me, the better. Stephen could dismiss any attempt made to impede his movements as the acts of an aggressive driver or something else. If I haven't moved, then the chances are minimal he will attribute any aggressive action as a by-product of my efforts.

The car comes to a stop. I cease all movement. It's now a matter of when the police will arrive. There are plenty of people on the road, and all it will take is one of them to make a call. The police will respond. I can only hope that Stephen doesn't turn around and shoot me before they show up.

The car moves again.

It seems odd that I'm still alive. Someone attacked me from behind in Amy's apartment. They could have smothered me or choked me or shot me—they could have done a lot of things to me and didn't. I'm still alive and in decent shape. But why let me live? Why take the risk of me escaping?

It only makes sense if they need me. And if they need me, then they'll keep me alive as long as I'm useful.

The car slows to a stop once more at another red light. Stephen reaches over to the seat next to him and holds up a wallet. He removes random debris. I can only see the shapes. The outlines of credit cards and business cards, receipts and pieces of paper, and then there's a shape I know all too well. That piece of debris only means something to me. Stephen looks at both sides before putting it back into the wallet. He leans over and rolls down the window. He's trying to throw away my wallet. It's something I can't let him do. A piece of me snaps.

Like an animal, I go for the kill. Both of my handcuffed hands grab the side of Stephen's head, and I use all my strength to slam him into the car's door. He swings his elbow back. It connects with my chin, knocking me down behind his seat.

The car rolls forward again and then stops. Stephen doesn't even bother to look back at me. He opens the car door.

"What the hell are you doing?" Stephen shouts, his body halfway out of the car.

"The police are on their way," a male voice shouts back.

A chill runs down my spine. A Good Samaritan is trying to rescue me. Shit. I didn't expect that to happen. The intent of the message was to push people into reacting. But it said that I was being held at gunpoint. I thought that would keep people from trying to be a hero and force them to call the police.

Car horns blare behind us. Stephen gets out. I sit up enough to see a truck blocking the hearse. Everything looks a little fuzzy without my glasses. Stephen walks toward the truck, which is blocking both lanes and preventing any traffic from moving. Stephen stops moving. A man holding a rifle to his shoulder walks around the car. Stephen holds up his hands and backs away. Without saying a word, Stephen takes off running between the cars and down the road.

The first thing I do is turn off the billboards on the side of the hearse. Next, I climb over the front seat and crawl out.

"Are you okay?" the man with the rifle shouts. He runs in my direction. The man stops in his tracks when I exit the hearse. "What the hell?"

"I'd prefer if you didn't ask," I say, walking over to him. I end up close enough to see the look of confusion in his eyes. "Do you have a bobby pin?" I ask, holding up my hands and shaking the handcuffs around my wrists.

Dumbfounded, he shakes his head.

"Thanks for helping me," I say, turning around to the traffic piling up on Third Street.

"The police are on their way."

"Thanks. Don't move your truck just yet." I walk down the median toward the cars stuck behind the hearse. The first car is a boxy old man's car with a confused elderly couple inside. The next car is a sedan with a woman on the phone. I walk up to her car and knock on the window.

The woman waves her hands as if trying to banish me with a magical spell.

I knock again and hold up my hands, trying to emphasize that I'm handcuffed.

"All I want is a bobby pin," I shout at her window. "I know you can hear me."

The woman puts down her phone and opens up her car's center console. She rummages and shifts some things before turning around with a bobby pin in her hand. She rolls the window down just enough for her thumb and forefinger to fit through the opening. I hold out my hand, and she drops the bobby pin into it.

"Thanks," I say, turning back to the hearse.

The man is still standing guard next to the hearse, waiting for me to return. While walking, I pull the plastic end off of the flat part of the bobby pin. When I was younger, I wanted to be a magician. My parents bought me an escape artist set with handcuffs and an instructional video on how to remove a pair of handcuffs without a key. It's easier than it looks. The handcuffs on my wrists are solid, but the lock isn't complex. The end of the bobby pin fits into the lock and easily bends back. I pull the bobby pin out and reinsert it, bending it once more. Reinserting the bent pin back into the lock, I slide it around until the cuffs loosen.

"You need to move your truck," I say to the man. He watches in amazement while I remove the other cuff and then toss the pair into the hearse. I untie the pink boa looped around my neck and the tutu around my waist, tossing them onto the seat next to the handcuffs.

"Sure thing, but the police aren't here yet."

"I need to leave now. Tell the police what happened. The man you chased off is wanted for the motel bombing that's been on the news."

"They're gonna want to talk to you," the man says when I climb into the hearse. He moves out of the way. The instant I have enough clearance, I turn the hearse around and start driving back to Amy's.

Odds are in favor of Amy being gone. Stephen's goal in coming there must have been to deal with both of us. Why else take such a risk? Whatever was supposed to happen after taking us is still a mystery. The beach traffic passes by as I speed toward Amy's. The sounds of angry horns fade into the distance.

Last time I came through Amy's gate, I called the name 'Wright' from the call box. This time I don't bother. No one will pick up. It's almost ridiculous how easy it is to get past gates like these. Every development like this has a set of easy access codes for mail delivery in addition to each renter being able to pick their own code. If #1111 doesn't work, try #1234 or #1212 or #6969. People love to choose something they won't forget. The gate opens when I type in #1111. I pull through and slow down close to the police cars in front of Amy's building.

Stephen kicked in the door to Amy's balcony and shattered the sliding glass door. That amount of noise is an attention-getter. The police come and go from the stairwell as one officer stands still near their vehicles. I take the time to undo the bustier before leaving the hearse. The police will already be wary of a man in boxers approaching the scene of a crime. A man in boxers and a bustier might get shot before he has the chance to explain.

The lone officer standing outside notices me from a distance and approaches as I walk toward the building.

"Can I help you, sir?" he asks, looking me up and down.

"Yes. I was here not too long ago. People broke in. Someone hit me in the head. I was taken."

"Sir, what's your name?"

"Flynn Dupree."

"I'm sorry."

"Flynn Dupree."

"Sir, where is your clothing?"

"It should be upstairs with my glasses."

"Let's get you dressed. I'll need you to come with me after."

"Why? What's happened? Is Amy Wright up there? Is she okay?"

"Sir, Ms. Wright isn't here. There's been a shooting at your residence."

Chapter 48

Flynn

Amy is in the back of an ambulance with a blanket wrapped around her like a shroud. An EMT speaks to a man in a suit while pointing surreptitiously back into the ambulance. Amy's eyes grow wide when she sees me. I wave. The blanket falls from her shoulder when she meekly waves back.

I've been a blight on this poor woman's life. Nearly blowing her up wasn't enough. I forced a trifecta with a break-in and a kidnapping. Somehow, despite all that, she's alive and well.

"Flynn," says a voice behind me. Officer Rittwell approaches. My officer escort returns to his car. "It's good to see you're in one piece. Amy said you were both attacked."

"By Stephen Collins and his accomplice. I know Stephen was there. But someone else hit me from behind."

"It was his wife."

"How do you know that?"

"Amy witnessed it happen."

"The officer that brought me here said there was a shooting. What happened?"

"Amy was taken at gunpoint and forced to come here." The distance between my house and Amy's apartment is an easy walk comprising homes and limited beach access. There is more than enough privacy to march someone at gunpoint. "Once inside, there was a struggle. The gun went off. Helen Collins was shot twice."

"She died?"

"Yes."

"How's Amy?"

"As good as she could be. It's tough to say. She killed a woman. Self-defense. But she killed someone."

"What were they doing in my house? Did Amy say why she was brought here?"

"Helen Collins told her to search for anything implicating her husband."

"What do we do now?"

"We wait. You're in for another late night."

Chapter 49

Flynn

According to Amy, Helen Collins force-marched her to my house via the beach. They broke in through the back door. Helen forced her to search for anything that might confirm Stephen's guilt. Officer Rittwell entered the house and surprised them. Helen Collins forced Amy outside at gunpoint. Amy fought back. During the struggle for the gun, it went off. Helen Collins died on my patio.

All that remains of the incident is a broken door, a bloodstain, and police tape. Coming home to find someone's blood on the patio is like the Spanish Inquisition, no one expects it. I also would have never expected to end up handcuffed and half-naked in the back of a hearse, albeit a familiar one. But familiarity means little. Events like this can change the meaning of anything.

My father used to say that objects were the best way for him to remember the past. He explained this tactile memory to me as a series of buoys across a placid lake. The touch of an object brings him to a particular buoy on the water where he can see memories from the surrounding time. He keeps these objects secret, allowing them to mean something to him alone. The only ones I know of are two pebbles and a piece of red sea glass he kept on his desk as paperweights, each from a distinct part of his life. One pebble brings back memories of his childhood growing up and the days spent with his friends and family on the rocky shores of Lake Michigan. The other pebble is from the coast of California and reminds him of the time he spent traveling there with my mother before I came along and forced them to settle down. The piece of sea glass is something he found on the beach after moving into our house. The opaque red glass is polished and the size of an eyeglass lens. My father took the two stones with him to Chicago, leaving the red glass in Lily's room.

I've considered that tactile memory to be the reason he left this house. Lily's room is a sad reminder for my family. One minute it was a location of comfort and utility, a bedroom like any other, and in the next it became something more. It evolved through grief. Lily's room became a shrine, a location of faith and disuse. Nothing changed physically. Its contents remained. We changed. Her bed is still a bed and her dresser is still a dresser, but emotion grew on the utilitarian shell like a cocoon. What emerged was a viable connection to the worst moment in our lives.

Whether this truly is the way my father accesses his memory or merely a story he told to keep me intrigued, I'll never know. All I do know is that I don't have this ability. I understand how memories can change inanimate objects into something of reverence. However, they are reminders for me. The impact of their meaning is not strong enough to pull me to another place in time. I understand that the bloodstain on my patio represents the loss of a life. But that dried blood does not control me.

I'm grateful it happened outside. As callous as it may sound, I'd rather not have another reminder of death inside the walls I call home. The police wouldn't have released the house back to me for some time if the shooting had taken place indoors. As it is, they only let me inside to go to sleep at four in the morning.

Deep beauty sleep is a welcome end to such an interminable day. That beauty sleep lasts until about two in the afternoon. My normal morning routines become normal afternoon routines. The feeling that something's not quite right hits me the moment I step foot downstairs. It's hard to explain. It's like how a TV left on, despite nothing being on the screen, still exudes enough energy for someone to know that it's on.

Peeking around the corner into my kitchen confirms this feeling. A man wearing a fuchsia blazer sits at the table. He holds a pair of big green sunglasses in place while sipping from a teacup. Uninvited visitors being in my house have become commonplace over the past week. I must've drunkenly taken an ad out in the newspaper advertising my home as a congregation point, or so it would seem since everyone thinks it's acceptable to be here without my permission.

"You know, Flynn, you should pick up some nice loose-leaf for company."

"I'm sorry, do I know you? How did you get in my house?"

"The policeman parked out front believed me when I said I was a friend of yours. He didn't pay too much attention to me. I went around back. Someone was nice enough to leave your broken door unsecured. I let myself in. And no, we've never met before. However, I have been informed that you're trying to find me."

"I don't know who you are."

"I'm called The Sheik."

Interesting. This man says I've been searching for him. To the best of my knowledge, I've never heard of anyone called The Sheik. However, he looks familiar.

"Do people call you The Sheik? Or is that something you call yourself?"

"People call me The Sheik because I'm a fashionable Muslim."

"You do look like the best-dressed pimp in Whoville. I'm guessing you spell fashionablc with a 'C' and a cedilla."

The Sheik stretches in a way to show he has a gun in a holster underneath his blazer. I'm guessing this man is violent and acts out often. Few people spend their days showing up uninvited and flashing guns. Fewer still look like they dress with a pin the tail on the donkey approach and believe they can effectively intimidate others. So either this man is deluding himself into thinking he's a tough guy, or he is a tough shit prone to acts of violence. Wait. Tough shit. TS. The Sheik? Did someone make it this easy to investigate? Is this a slip-up or a scare tactic? If I could look at Paul's notes and pictures, then I might be able to confirm why The Sheik looks familiar. I think he's the man Stan said was Joseph Parker's son.

"Okay," I say, hoping my theory is correct. "Why were you contacting Paul Mahoney?"

"Who said I was?"

"Paul left extensive notes. Some are more cryptic than others. Your name, however, makes some clear appearances."

The Sheik takes off his giant green sunglasses and sets them on the table. He takes a sip of his tea and holds the mug with both of his hands.

"If you don't want to answer, I can have the officer outside arrest you for trespassing."

"Come on now. We're friends here. It's the ones outside your door that want to get you. That officer is there to keep tabs on you until they pull

286

the trigger or put you in cuffs. If he was there to protect you, why am I here?"

"Excellent point. Better point: I don't know you."

"But the enemy of my enemy is my friend, or, better put," he says before continuing in a crappy Midwest accent. "The bomber and policeman shouldn't be friends. One man likes to light a wick. The other is a plain ol' dick—"

"You keep talking. I'll mosey on outside and get the policeman."

"Not a fan of my humor?"

"Just confused. Were you in contact with Paul Mahoney?"

"You need my help. You don't know it yet, but you do. This little," he says, while waving his fingers in the air, "thing is probably still a mystery to you. However, you are on the right track."

"And which track is that?"

"I can't tell you. I'm a representative of someone who is only willing to assist if the police stay out of it. They're trying to avoid all the trouble that might accompany their name popping up in this investigation."

"Trouble?" I ask.

"Here in the River City," he replies, the bass in his voice rising to the forefront. "That's a big ol' 'T' which rhymes with 'B' and ticks like a bomb."

"Let's rewind this all back to before you started threatening me. You were in touch with Paul Mahoney. He used to be a reporter and knew how to keep sources confidential—"

"Obviously not. Seeing as I'm here."

"You do know him?"

"This isn't going as planned. You see—"

"You thought you'd show up, flash your gun, and find out what little I know?"

"Something along those lines. Listen, I know where you live. I'll stop by some other time."

This guy is a pawn. My connecting him to Paul Mahoney is something he didn't expect. He's in a position where he has to speak to the person above him before making another move. That person could be his father. Or it could be someone completely different. That ambiguity is why I can't let him leave. I need to follow him and find out who is in charge.

287

The problem I face is not having a car. Without checking, I know Misty would have picked up the hearse. It's her work vehicle, not my personal transport. Honestly, whether it's there or not is irrelevant. It would be impossible to follow someone inconspicuously in an antique hearse.

"You have all your licensing for that gun, right?"

"Why do you ask?"

"You answered a question with a question. I'll take that as a 'Yes.'"

With no additional hesitation, I rush out the front door, arms waving above my head. The officer at the end of my driveway jumps out of his cruiser and runs across the lawn as I shout, "There's a man inside who's threatening me." The officer continues past me and into the house. Inside, The Sheik has his green sunglasses back on while his gun sits on the other side of the table with the clip removed. He doesn't move from the kitchen table, just calmly finishes his tea, and then holds his hands up for the officer to place handcuffs around his wrists. The look on his face is not of concern or rage; it's a look of absolute certainty that he will not be in handcuffs for long.

"Anything to add?" I ask The Sheik.

"I just hope I'm prisoner 24601."

Chapter 50

Amy

The police drop me off at my apartment after I finish making my statement. The apartment is a mess. It's been a long night. Instead of cleaning, I pass out. By the time I wake up, it's well into the afternoon. It's later than I wanted to sleep, but it was worth it. I wake up feeling like a new person. The first thing I do is check Delta's website to ensure Iain's flight is coming in on time. With the flight confirmed, I take a shower and then get to work on my hair to provide it the slight curl I know Iain prefers. After my hair is perfect, I apply a little makeup; nothing too fancy or bright because Iain prefers me to look natural. I spend too much time choosing an outfit, eventually opting for a simple jeans and t-shirt look.

My hands shake while navigating the tiny Atlantic Beach roads, but I settle down by the time I'm on the highway. Iain's flight arrives just after five o'clock. After navigating the minimal amount of Saturday highway traffic, I fight through the airport bustle and pull into a spot in short-term parking right at four. The first thing I do in the airport is find Iain's connecting flight from Atlanta on the arrival board. When I see it, this giddy feeling overwhelms my nervousness. I know I'm glowing. The smile on my face remains when I find a chair facing the exit for the incoming flights.

As planes land, waves of people meander their way into the arms of their loved ones. Each successive round further destroys Hollywood's depictions of photogenic people emotionally coming together at the airport. Overhead announcements of arrivals and departures supplant musical crescendos buoying emotional climaxes. Rippling collisions of bulbous bellies and red-faced lovers mashing their lips together replace enraptured models with hard bodies pressed against one another. Movie tropes drown again and again with each new tidal wave of reality.

Today will be the day Iain introduces me to his son, Benjamin. I've seen him before, not just in pictures, but in the flesh when I first met Iain. They came into the diner one day after spending time at some random beach festival. I'd never seen them before, and they weren't even in my section when Iain came up and provided me with his phone number. We spent a moment flirting until Marty started shooting me dirty looks. I promised Iain I'd call.

Iain is the first older man I've dated. I'd met several through work, some older than Iain, who is only in his forties, but he was the only one I've ever dated—or thought I was dating. It turned out he was married. I knew he had a kid because they were together in the restaurant on the first day we met, but he never mentioned being married. The way he described his wife gave me hope of a future together. He made it sound like, despite still loving her, he needed more from a wife. I know I can be what Iain needs, but I'm afraid I don't have what it takes to be a mother.

As an only child, the most experience I have with children is babysitting for family friends when I was a teenager. I know nothing about children or how to handle them. To make matters worse, Benjamin, at age thirteen, has lost his mother and will be introduced to the other woman in his father's life. Each new thought about what might happen makes me feel more and more nervous. If I could smoke in the terminal while waiting, this would all be much easier.

A caramel macchiato takes the edge off of waiting without cigarettes. Every five minutes, I check the arrival board until the plane lands. A quick look in the mirror of my compact reassures me that Iain will see me looking perfect when I welcome him back.

People keep on marching in small groups away from the terminal. My eyes never look away. Five minutes pass. I'm nervous. Ten minutes pass. I feel excited about them coming around the corner any second. Twenty minutes pass. I'm getting concerned. Thirty minutes pass. I'm feeling sick to my stomach.

The arrival board says the plane has landed. I've flown in and out of Jacksonville several times. If a plane has been on the ground for this long, they should be waiting for their luggage. The only thing I can do is call Iain. The phone rings once before going to voicemail. Being sent to voicemail is no big surprise. It's been happening for over a week, and, for the first time, there is a valid excuse. The phone could still be off if the plane is taxiing. Maybe some airline traffic is holding everything up. The only logical next step is to go to the baggage claim and see if people from his flight are picking up their bags.

Heels don't stop me from jogging through the airport. People stare and snicker while I make my way through the crowds as quickly as possible. The trip ends after I force my way down an escalator, followed by the awkward metallic clip-clop sound of my heels.

Iain's flight number shows up on a carousel to my left. The flight's information flashes while bags move through the area. Smiling, cheerful people pick up their bags and leave. Iain is not there.

I navigate around several small crowds until I end up in line at the Delta kiosk. The woman behind the kiosk calls me over.

"Are you okay?" she asks.

My concern must be showing. I force a smile.

"Yes, I'm fine. I was waiting for a friend, Iain Reid. Spelled I-A-I-N R-E-I-D. He never showed up. I wanted to see if he made his flight."

"Do you have the flight number?"

"He was coming from Edinburgh with a stop in Atlanta," I say, adding the flight number as requested.

The woman taps away at her keyboard for about a minute. She stops typing to check her watch. "No one by that name was on that flight. In fact, I'm not seeing anyone by that name having flown into Jacksonville today."

"Did he make it to Atlanta?"

"Not that I can see. Have you tried calling him?"

"Yes," I say, leaving my smile behind as I walk away. "Thank you."

Iain's not coming back. I try not to think about it, but all I can see are the warning signs I've ignored over and over again. There's no more pretending. There's no more lying to myself. After everything I've been through, now I know I'm alone.

There's an empty bench near the wall. I take a seat, wanting nothing more than to cry. After everything I've done for Iain—after everything I've done for us, he's abandoning me. He's leaving me alone like he left his wife alone so often. And it's a guarantee he's not alone. He found someone else. I should have let her live. If I hadn't killed his beloved

291

Rose, then he never would have gone back to Scotland. He never would have left me to take care of this business.

"You look lost," says a familiar voice. The man's baseball cap obscures his features.

"Fuck off," I say. "I'm not in the mood."

"Really," the man says, looking up and revealing his face. It's Stephen Collins. Anger has taken over his body. His fists clench like he wants to beat me. He's baring his teeth like he wants to eat me. And the veins in his neck are so visible he looks cartoonish.

"Well, if you're planning on killing me, you might as well go ahead. I'm not sure this day could get worse."

"Just give me back my son." Stephen looks like he wants to scream, but is stifling it for the sake of not making a scene.

I tap a spot on the bench next to me. Stephen sits down.

"What are you doing here?"

"I want Jack back."

"You'll get him back when I'm done with you."

"You've killed my wife. How do I even know my son is alive?"

"He's alive. Don't worry about that."

"Why did you have to kill her," Stephen asks, his eyes red.

"We broke into Flynn's place looking for whatever information he might have. A policeman showed up. Your wife tried to take the gun you gave me. I couldn't let her speak to the police. I will not go to jail for this."

"You're a fucking monster."

"If you'd done the job right the first time, then none of this would be happening. All of this is your fault."

"My fault? I didn't want any of this. I killed a man for you."

"You haven't killed anyone. I pushed the button. You told me what it would do, and I pushed it. Because of that, Paul Mahoney is dead. You did nothing. Now, listen to me. There are rules. And right now, you aren't following them. We can't be seen together."

"Did the rules include inviting over the patsy for dinner?"

"I did what I had to do. I needed information, and I got it. Then I tied him up with a nice little bow for you. Somehow, you still screwed that up."

"I didn't think he'd be troublesome."

292

"He's partially brain-dead, yet somehow he's outsmarting you. Where did you find him?"

"A business card left on my car. All of this will come back on us."

"On you. Remember, I still have your son."

"I should break your neck here and now."

"And then your son dies a slow and painful death."

"Bitch."

"Where's your phone?"

Stephen pulls out a small phone. It's a disposable cell. Perfect for keeping everything anonymous.

"Call your old boss."

"What? Why do you want to talk to Lou?"

"Just do it. And not his office number. We both know he has a phone for his mistresses and private dealings. I want you to call that number. The number he's guaranteed to answer."

Stephen dials the number. I hold out my hand. He gives me the ringing phone.

"Hello," Lou Brombacher says.

"Hiya, Lou," I say, looking directly at Stephen.

293

Chapter 51

Flynn

My first call after The Sheik's arrest is to Bee. He's always wanted to go on a stakeout, but I'm usually following people during the week while he works. He's excited and says his next call is to Henry.

There's a knock on my door about thirty minutes after the Sheik's arrest. It's Officer Rittwell wearing a button-down and khakis.

"Good to see you're dressed up this time," I say with sincerity. I'm not sure if I can handle seeing Rittwell in cutoff jorts twice in one week.

"Good to see you're alive. Can I come in? I brought a peace offering." Officer Rittwell holds up Alien.

I'm shocked when he puts Alien in my hands.

"You're kidding me. This isn't some kind of entrapment?"

"No," Officer Rittwell says, walking inside. I carry Alien into the kitchen, setting him down on the kitchen table. "We can't keep any of your stuff. It was illegally obtained. You'll get it all back in time, but I figured you might need to use this to take the edge off people trying to kill you."

"Thanks," I say. Seeing Alien on my table is a reminder that Mordecai is missing from my head. My selfish side pushes me to ask if and when they'll be returning Mordecai. Instead, I ask a question that few people other than Officer Rittwell could answer. "How is Edith?"

"She'll recover physically. But… I—I don't know how anyone can fully recover from someone carving their name into you. And that piece of shit is still on the loose."

"I thought I might stop by the hospital."

"Don't," he replies quickly. "I stopped by. Her reaction was… well… I was asked to leave. She's been moved to a facility. Baker Act."

"Shit."

"Yeah," Officer Rittwell says.

Awkward silence envelopes the kitchen.

"So," I say to break the silence. "When are the police releasing The Sheik?"

"Who's that?"

"The guy in my house this morning."

"From what I heard, you aren't pressing charges."

"True."

"Pretty soon, then. I know they had to confirm the registration on his gun and his concealed carry license are both valid. Do you know what he was doing here?"

"He wanted to chat. Sorry, I saw the gun and freaked. That's why I'm not pressing charges. An overreaction on my part."

"You're shit at lying," Officer Rittwell says.

I shrug my shoulders.

"Try not to get yourself killed," Officer Rittwell says in a severe tone. "You're not as useless as I thought you were."

"Thanks, I guess."

"That came out wrong. Edith Danes is alive because of you."

"You helped."

"Seriously. That fucker would have killed her."

"I know," I say.

The bloody name carved into Edith flashes through my mind. A scarlet smile emerges from her neck. Edith gasps for breath. She says my name. But it's no longer Edith. It's Lily.

"Flynn," Officer Rittwell says, pulling me back to reality. "I'm heading out."

"Yeah," I say, clearing my throat. "Thanks for stopping by. And thanks for bringing back Alien."

Officer Rittwell leaves through the front door. I head upstairs to call Bee again and let him know that he needs to get here as soon as possible.

Chapter 52

Flynn

Someone outside the house lays on their horn. It's Bee in his Lexus. I wave from the front door, hoping he stops before the neighbors get upset. Henry is in the front passenger seat. I hop in the back and scoot to the middle.

"Thanks for coming."

"Thanks for the invite," Bee says.

Henry waves, but says nothing. He's wearing a chalk-white handlebar mustache. His face paint splits down the middle with one half like a clown and the other half like a drag queen.

"That'll help us blend in."

Henry holds up a middle finger.

"I said the same fucking thing when I picked him up. Apparently, he's working on a psycho-clown killing drag-divas horror flick."

"Sounds watchable."

Henry holds a thumb up.

"Bee," I say, looking behind the car to make sure the street is clear. "Back up a little bit. We're following the Charger in front of my place."

"Got it," he says, backing up and taking a position down the block. After parking, Bee reaches over to the passenger side floor and picks up a soft-side cooler sitting next to Henry's left leg. "I brought steak sandwiches for the stakeout."

"For two vegetarians?" I reply with feigned disgust.

"Neither of you are vegetarians."

"We became vegetarians about three months ago," Henry says, breaking his silence.

"Bullshit. Henry, you own a hot dog restaurant. I see you eat them all the time."

"Quality control," Henry replies.

"Quality control doesn't prevent something from being meat."

"It does."

"I agree."

"Bullshit. Bullshit on you both. Flynn, we ate hamburgers together this month. Three months, my ass."

"That's different. I'd been drinking. That doesn't count."

"Like hell, it doesn't count."

"I didn't even think of alcohol," Henry says.

"I hate you both so much. Tell you what, I'll eat all three subs."

"We'll eat them," I say. "By objecting to eating meat, we can maintain our vegetarian status."

"It doesn't work that way."

"Do you still smoke?" Henry asks Bee.

"No. You know I stopped two years ago."

"But you smoke on occasion, right?"

"That's different. I smoke when I'm stressed out."

"It's not different at all."

"Fuck it. Flynn, you smoke too."

"I never said I didn't."

"How about everybody shuts up," Henry says, scratching his mustache. "We'll eat sandwiches and listen to music."

"Where are we going?" Bee asks.

"Here for now."

"Here? In front of your house."

"In all fairness, we're not exactly out in front."

"What the hell are we doing here, then?"

"The guy who owns the Charger parked in my driveway is being brought back here by the police shortly. We're going to follow him when he leaves."

"Fine. I guess I could eat a sandwich early," Bee says, opening up the cooler and passing the sandwiches out. Bee closes the cooler and hands it to me. "But I get to choose the music."

"Only if it's not Supp—"

Henry stops talking as "Supper's Ready" by Genesis starts playing.

There's only one drink in the cooler. Before I can open the bottle of water, Bee grabs it from my hand.

297

"Mine," Bee says. "I only brought one bottle, and I didn't bring it to share."

"It's fine. It's just odd that you brought three sandwiches and only one drink."

"We're on a stakeout, and I'm the only one who can hold his liquids. I'm not encouraging either of you to take a piss in my car. Plus, the other day, you were talking about hooking up with a prostitute. So that," Bee says, pointing to my mouth, "is going nowhere near this." Bee holds up the bottle of water and takes a sip. "If you want something to drink, go to your house and get something. It's right there."

"Gladly," Henry says, holding his hand out. I give him my keys. He leaves the car.

Henry takes his time getting the drinks. Every minute that passes is another minute I'm worried The Sheik might show back up. It takes Henry almost twelve minutes to walk three hundred feet and back again. He comes back to the car with the remainder of a case of PBR. Henry sits down in the car and shakes his head.

"How many are in there?" I ask.

"Nine," Henry says, handing me a beer. "I counted them over and over again, hoping to miss as much of this song as possible. How much longer until it's over?"

"About ten minutes," Bee replies.

"Fuck," Henry says as he opens a beer. Bee reaches for the beer. Henry slaps his hand away. Bee goes back to drumming on the steering wheel and occasionally taking a bite of his sandwich.

"Supper's Ready" wraps up as The Sheik arrives. An officer drops him off at his Charger. Bee puts his car in drive and follows. Henry unplugs Bee's phone before another Genesis song starts. Before Bee can object, "Get It Right the First Time" starts blasting on the radio. Bee seems content as he sings along and follows The Sheik at a distance. The drive takes us across the ditch and into Jacksonville. We head south on Philips Highway and keep going until we end up in a strip club called The Prince's Palace.

"Are you shitting me?" Bee asks. "This is working out way better than I thought it would."

We all exit the car and enter the strip club. The bouncer looks at Henry in his makeup, pauses to think, and then shrugs his shoulders and points to a sign listing the prices for various services. Bee happily pays the cover for us all before running through the smoky haze over to the DJ booth. Henry follows Bee. They end up sitting near the stage. I do my best to find The Sheik, but I can't see him anywhere. The next girl coming to the stage looks surprised and confused as "Counting Out Time" by Genesis plays. I want to ask how much Bee paid to have this song play, but I need to find The Sheik. Bee shouts and cheers as the stripper does her best to dance to a song she's clearly never heard before.

"Flynn," shouts a voice I can't quite place. I look around and then see a familiar face behind the bar. Emma waves at me. She's scantily clad compared to her attire in Lou Brombacher's office, but she's barely showing any skin compared to the rest of the women in the area.

"You said you worked at your father's club," I say, taking a seat at the bar.

"I do," Emma says, smiling. "I didn't expect to see you at a place like this."

"C'mon. I have a face made for this place."

"Maybe you did, but you've shaved."

"That's right," I say, touching my face. "I'm surprised you recognized me."

"I enjoyed our chat."

"Did you?" I say, a little surprised. "As did I."

"Well, then. What brings you here other than the obvious? And can I get you anything?"

"This will probably be a little awkward, but I think I'm here to see your father. He's Joseph Parker, right?"

"Yes," Emma says, suddenly stern. "Why?"

"Well, I'm an independent consultant. I've been looking into something for a client. It's led me here. More specifically, a man calling himself The Sheik showed up at my house—"

"You've got to be kidding me," Emma screams. "Follow me."

Emma storms out from behind the bar, across the club, and into an area marked 'Employees Only.' We pass by multiple doors before Emma opens up a door leading into a large, well-lit office. The Sheik sits across from an older man leaning back in his chair behind a desk. The man's turquoise golf shirt and khaki pants clash with the slick suit and unbuttoned dress shirt I have always imagined were standard issue for

299

strip club owners. He sits up straight as we enter. Emma makes a beeline to The Sheik.

"Oh shit," The Sheik says after seeing me. When he tries to stand up, Emma slaps him hard across the face.

"What the fuck, Clarence? Or should I call you The Sheik?" Emma shouts. The Sheik curls up into a ball while trying to deflect Emma's blows. "You're now following around the guys I meet?"

The man behind the desk stands up and bellows, "Emma!" Emma stops and takes a step back. The man continues, this time in a calm and deliberate manner. "Emma, dear, your brother did not go to meet Mr. Dupree on your behalf. He was meeting him because I asked him to. I was unaware that you two had ever met before."

The Sheik stands up and straightens himself out as he glares at Emma.

"Clarence," the man says, looking at The Sheik. "I told you to stop using that ridiculous nickname. I named you after my father because I thought you might care to wear the name proudly and act with a modicum of dignity."

"Dad," Clarence says before getting cut off.

"No," the man says. "Emma, I need you back behind the bar. Clarence, I need you to leave while I speak to Mr. Dupree."

"Dad," Emma says with a questioning look.

"Don't worry, dear. We're just going to talk."

The man behind the desk waits until his children leave before introducing himself.

"Joseph Parker," he says with his hand extended. I shake his hand. He motions toward the seat Clarence had occupied. "Please," he says as I sit down. "How can I help you?"

"Why did you send your son to my house?"

"I apologize for Clarence's actions. And I hate that nickname he's given himself. The Sheik? He grew up Baptist. It's killing his mother that he's converted. It doesn't bother me that he's become a Muslim. What bothers me is that I think he converted because he wants to call himself The Sheik. It's odd. And I'm worried that he might believe chic and sheik are the same thing."

"I'm not too worried about what he calls himself. Why was he at my house?"

"I am a businessman, Mr. Dupree. But I'm also a father. And although I may not be the best role model, some consider me a pillar of the community. These are all things I take very seriously. If an unknown factor that could disrupt my life arises, I look into it."

"Is this because I made that phone call before Thanksgiving?"

"That started it. It led us to look into you. That was when we discovered you were an investigator of sorts. We simply want to know why you are investigating us."

"We? Us?"

"Me, my family, my organization. Any of it."

"I'm investigating Paul Mahoney's death." Stretching the truth might be the best move. "His widow and some of his friends hired me to find out who killed him and why."

"How did you find my phone number?"

"Lou Brombacher gave me your information after I confronted him about his subordinate, Stephen Collins, blowing up Paul Mahoney. He noticed that his Rolodex was open to your information when it shouldn't have been. So, by any chance, has Stephen Collins contacted you?"

"Before I answer, I need assurances that my name and the name of my businesses will remain out of this. You didn't press charges against Clarence. You seem like the kind of person we can trust to not rock the boat."

"If you give me something useful, I'll keep your name out of it. But if you're telling me you're into something sketchy—"

"Fair enough. Let's just say that everything I say is hypothetical."

"Sounds good."

"Stephen Collins called me. He wanted some forged documents. I gave him the contact information of Iain Reid. He produces such things. That's the only contact I had with the gentleman. If I'd known what he did, I would've told him to take a hike. When he called, I assumed Lou needed something."

"What's your relationship with Lou?"

"He's a character, Lou. He wants to be everyone's buddy. You meet him once, and then he starts with the favors. He asked if I could help staff an office. I told him I wasn't a temp agency. He asked if any of the ladies working here either had or wanted office experience. I put the information out there. Emma volunteered first. After that, a lot of them went for it. You know, a lot of these ladies are smart. They know they can't do this forever. It's good to have office experience."

"That's it?"

"That's it. Listen, I don't judge any of these ladies if they moonlight. Lou spends money, and he's not a saint. But our relationship was just business."

"What was your relationship with Iain Reid?"

"Business as well."

"That's it?"

"Obviously, there's more. But this part is completely hypothetical. Let's say that you have an import business like mine. In that line of business, you meet art procurers like Iain. Someone like Iain can provide high-quality pieces with provenance to back it up. Hell, you even buy a Russian triptych off of him as an anniversary gift for your wife. His products are great, but, allegedly, they are not all legally procured. However, Iain can produce documents that allow it all to be sold in the States."

"Isn't that tracked?"

"Yes and no. Sometimes they salvage pieces from properties without the proper authorization. Let's say, a set of stained glass windows from an old church in the middle of nowhere. The person or persons those belong to would never be able to find them once they're gone. Other art, something from a known artist, for instance, can be tracked."

"Who buys this stuff? And wouldn't, in this hypothetical situation, Iain Reid and myself be in trouble if the buyer researches the art and finds out it was stolen?"

"You import products only with proper documentation. How it's procured is none of your concern. You only know that it is real and legal because the paperwork and provenance tell you so. And, honestly, there's a bad boy financial whiz born every day with more ego than common sense. They see these objects as a fitting display of their power and place. They spend whatever and never complain. All they want is something rare and real to show off to their friends how civilized they are. But, some time ago, Iain stopped providing you art. When you asked him about it, he said he was out of the business. Best guess, knowing Iain, is that things went sideways with his suppliers."

"How long has it been since I talked to him?"

"It's been quite a while. Iain contacted you out of the blue months ago. He was working with a partner here in Jacksonville and needed some seed money for a project. You provided Iain with a short-term loan and greased a few wheels at Talleyrand for a shipment he had coming into the country."

"Do I know what it is?"

"No idea. Iain wouldn't tell you. And now he's gone. His wife died recently. After that, he took his son and went back to Scotland. He cut off all communication." Joseph Parker pulls a notebook out of his desk and picks up a pen. He spends about a minute writing and comparing notes before ripping a page off and handing it to me. "This is the bill of lading reference information Iain provided for his shipment. It arrives next week."

"The only thing I understand about this is Iain's name. What is this?"

"It's basically a shipping contract."

"Why would you give this to me?"

"I've always had this foolish notion that humanity exists for one fundamental reason: progress. We are here to make the world a better place. There have been some hiccups along the way, but we've still marched toward a better future. And I feel like this day and age, no one cares about progress. All anyone wants to do is fight for their interests. When we start to only care about ourselves, then this whole house of cards will fall.

"Also, it's fake," Joseph Parker laughs. "I looked into it. I can't find any corresponding records. Iain wasn't the kind of guy to double-cross a partner. He was the kind of guy who liked to make money. With Iain gone, I'm out the money. If this shipment turns out to be real, I can't claim it. If the police claim it, I'm unaffected. If the container is full of art, I don't have Iain to provide documentation to sell it. It's worthless to me."

"What do you want me to do with this?"

"I don't care. But I will warn you that Iain disappeared for a reason. And my son provided some information to Paul Mahoney, and look at what happened to Paul. I don't know why these things happened. It could be because of that shipment. Tread carefully."

"Why did you give Paul some information, but not this bill of lading?"

303

"Paul Mahoney looking into Lou's background was an open secret. We reached out to Paul when Iain stopped returning our calls. He offered us a decent sum to help offset our losses. My son was supposed to provide him all the information we had, but he chose not to. I guess Clarence thought he might squeeze a little more out of Paul at a later date. That's why I'm passing that on to you. Since you are working on behalf of Paul's family, then I consider this information already paid for. My father used to say 'A-B-A-G.' Always be a gentleman. I try to run my businesses by that standard."

"He sounds like a principled man."

"Through and through."

Chapter 53

Flynn

Bee and Henry reluctantly leave The Prince's Palace after my conversation with Joseph Parker ends. I don't see Emma or The Sheik on our way out. Bee drives us straight back to my place and drops me off before they head to Haute Diggity. The garage is open. It's a surprise to see Leslie working on the Golden Hawk. Being almost involved in a shooting doesn't seem to have bothered him.

"Didn't think you'd come back," I say, withholding a handshake because oil is all over Leslie's hands. "Or that your daughters would let you."

"Well," Leslie says while rubbing his hands with a rag, "Misty said if I get shot over here, then I better survive because she wants to kill me for being an idiot. I told her I promised you I'd help."

"And I thank you very much for that."

"It's basically done. I've just been cleaning up some messes I made in here. I haven't had a chance to drive it yet. But it did turn over."

"Great. Sounds like it's good to go."

"Yeah. You said it's been sitting for a long time, but it was in good shape. Especially for having been kept so close to the beach."

"I've cleaned it up every now and then."

"The tires look new. That surprised me. When did you have them changed?"

"Not sure." I'm surprised because I genuinely can't remember when I had the tires changed. "I guess it was a little while ago."

"Flynn, are you okay?"

"Yeah. I'm a little tired. I was up late after what happened."

"That's understandable. It's been a long week for you."

"Did William stop by again?"

"No. He must've recognized me this time. We had a moment last night," Leslie says in a joking voice. "Well, I'm heading out. Enjoy the Hawk. She's a beaut."

"Thanks again."

"I'm just glad to see you out of that shit Camry."

"I'm the only person who liked that car."

Leslie hands me the keys I lent him and leaves. I lock up the garage and go into my house through the side door. At the fridge, the reality that Henry took all the beer for the stakeout hits me like a ton of bricks. Depressingly sober, I walk out to my back patio and look at the bloodstain, which is soberingly depressing.

William is in his back yard. It's dark, but his floodlights are on. He is gardening. I wave. He waves back and then takes a plant inside.

Chapter 54

William

My head buzzes like an egg is ready. I try to move but can't. My feet are duct-taped to the legs of one of my dining room chairs. My arms are behind me, bound at the wrists. In front of me stands one smiling Durrell Span. He wears a look of pride, staring intently as things focus for me. The smile matches the one on his driver's license, which makes me wonder what kind of photoshoot he might've had at the DMV.

"Hello there," Durrell says. "I guess I should feel extra bad about this, seeing as you are a preacher and all."

"I guess you caught me red-handed," I say, wishing my hands were free. Durrell taped my wrists together behind me, but I can still move a bit. It's hard to free myself with him watching. Instead, I stay still.

"I've been waiting for your son. You know, the asshole that attacked me the other night, and then brought the police to my place to take my girl."

"It's Saturday. I'm sure he's out enjoying himself at a bar. You should do the same."

"Nice try, old man. We're settling debts tonight, whether you two like it or not."

"Fine by me," I say, leaning forward. I put on the look of a thinking man involved in some math. "I'd say the damage to my walls and kitchen will set me back about two grand. You paying with cash?"

"Fuck you," he says, moving closer. He looks like he wants to hit me.

There's a bulge in my back right pocket. Durrell must not have bothered to search me after knocking me out. The knife slides out easy and opens quick. The blade makes a sudden 'click' sound when it locks in place. Durrell lunges at me. I'm able to cut the duct tape on my wrists, but the knife flies out of my hands before I can free my legs. Durrell is strong, and I can't run. As he grabs me by my braid, I grab him by his collar and lose my balance. We tumble to the ground. The back of Durrell's head hits the edge of the table with the full force of both our falling bodies.

The knife is within reach. I grab it and cut my legs loose. Durrell is on the floor, moaning like a dreaming drunk. I put the knife back in my pocket and run to the garage for a handful of zip ties. I bind Durrell's arms behind him and then his ankles before I use zip ties to connect both and hogtie him on my floor. A dish towel shoved into his mouth dulls the moaning.

Durrell is heavy. It takes almost everything I have to drag him across the floor. After a lot of effort to get him to the center of the garage, I leave him be and move my recliner back to a safe viewing distance. Then I use a ladder to string up a series of interlocking chains from reinforced hooks in the ceiling. The chains connect to a custom rig made of sturdy oak. I haven't used it in a while, so I lay it out before connecting everything. I drag Durrell into place and cut the zip ties on his wrists. Durrell unconsciously performs his best impression of a bird in flight while I strap him to the crossbar with three leather restraints for each arm. In addition to the restraints, two zip ties per arm, one near the wrist and the other near the elbow, ensure that Durrell cannot free his upper body. I cut the zip ties on his legs and attach his ankles to the lower portion of the rig with a leather strap on each, adding a zip tie to each ankle to be on the safe side. I connect the ends of the chains to the wooden rig and then thread the other ends through the steel rings secured to the wall. There's a hook just beneath each of the rings which locks the chains in place. Durrell is now secure.

I leave the garage and walk out to my back yard, which is silent except for the welcoming sounds of waves crashing on the beach. The sun has set. My house's floodlights fill the yard with bright light. I haven't looked at the clock and have no idea what time it is or how long I was unconscious. The lump on the back of my head is sore. It feels like it's pulsing. The last thing I remember is sitting outside underneath the canopy of vines, enjoying my afternoon. The bastard must have snuck up behind me and hit me with something.

Helleborus niger is tricky to grow in Florida. It takes a lot of effort to make it happen, but I've always found the effort worthwhile. I planted them close to the house, just underneath the canopy. Florida isn't known

308

for its shade, and the only place for them to thrive is away from direct sunlight. Clusters of green leaves line the back of my house about a foot from the siding. The scientific name is Helleborus niger, but most people call it the Christmas rose. The flower blooms sometime between December and March. Fortunately, I don't need the blossoming flower. I carefully pull up one of the clusters, ensuring the roots stay intact.

Flynn sees me pulling up the Christmas rose and waves. I smile and wave back. Normally, I would go over and say hello, but I can't risk Durrell waking up without me nearby. My wave is quick and neighborly before I head inside. A quick gander in the garage reveals Durrell is still out of it. I pull a pot out of a cupboard and fill it with some water. I clean the dirt off of the Christmas rose and then add it to the pot, putting it on the stove and turning up the heat enough to keep the water just shy of boiling. The water heats up quickly. It simmers for a minute before I turn the heat off. The pot cools while I go into the garage and pull down the stairs leading to the attic. At the top of the stairs is a green plastic kiddie pool. It used to be kept in my yard. I bought it intending to soak my feet in it on scorching days, but I only ever used it once or twice. Now I have a perfect use for it.

"Stop," Lily says suddenly. She shows up out of nowhere and surprises me. "William. Please stop."

"Lily?" I drop the kiddie pool onto the garage floor. "What are you doing here? You shouldn't be here. Not now."

"Please, William." Lily's soft and sweet voice turns harsh and strained. "You don't have to do this."

"I do. If I don't do this, then everything will go away. He's ruined everything."

"No. It's not too late to call the police. He attacked you in your own home. Just take those things off of him and call the police."

"I can't. This man came here to hurt me, to hurt Flynn. I can't let him do that. I can't let him hurt my family."

"But I'm your family, too," Lily says. "If you do this, I can't be a part of your family anymore. If you do this, I will have to leave."

"No, you won't. You'll always be with me. You can't leave."

"William—"

Durrell screaming a slew of curses in my direction cuts Lily off. She disappears instantaneously.

Durrell is officially awake and has dislodged the dish towel from his mouth.

"Do you prefer sugar or honey in your tea?" I ask politely.

"I'd prefer you fuck off and die."

I pick the towel up off the ground and shove it in his mouth. It quiets him down to a breathy whimper.

"I guess it's up to me," I say. "I've always been a fan of honey. And to make sure you don't get too bored while I'm gone..."

There's an old cassette tape player on my workbench. Next to it is a shoebox of cassettes Flynn found lying around and gave to me since he knew I had the player. I pull out a handful of tapes and decide on *Elvis' Christmas Album* over *What Now My Love*. The tape starts up near the beginning of "Blue Christmas."

"This is a good one," I say before returning to the kitchen to see if my tea is ready.

Helleborus niger has been used for centuries to purge toxins from the body. Steeping the plant is an essential step in unlocking its full potential. It takes a minute for the water to reach the desired color of green tea. The plant leaves behind a bitter taste, which is why I place a spoonful of honey in the bottom of an oversized coffee mug. Once the honey dissolves in the Christmas rose tea, I drop in four ice cubes to cool it down.

Durrell struggles against his bindings. The muffled screams and rattling chains make quite the racket. There is no chance for tea time if he's in this state. I set down the mug and unhook the top chain from its anchor point on the garage wall. As I pull down, the chains go taut and lift Durrell's upper body into the air. Durrell screams and struggles until he reaches about four feet off of the ground. After anchoring the top chain, I unhook the bottom one and pull it until Durrell's legs lift up almost even to his upper body. I secure the chain and return to Durrell. He swings back and forth until I grab him by the shoulders. When he's still, I place the kiddie pool underneath his body.

Durrell's eyes are as wide as hubcaps. His muffled screams turn to weak pleads. I remove the towel.

"Please," he says, tears streaming down his cheeks and into the kiddie pool. "Please don't do this."

I smile like the DMV says, 'Cheese!'

310

"Please," he says. "I'll do anything. I have a family."

"You know," I say. "There's been a lot of news coverage on what you did to that woman. I know you don't have a wife or kids. Only a mother. A mother that says you deserve what's coming your way."

"Right. Yeah. I deserve to go to jail. Send me there. Call the police. I'm sure there's a reward."

"There is a reward. But I'm not interested. All I want is for you to do something simple."

"Anything. I'll do anything."

The mug of Christmas rose tea is warm to the touch. I carry it over to Durrell.

"I want you to drink as much of this as you can."

"Fuck off."

"Don't worry. It's just tea. My Christmas tea."

"I'm not drinking it," he says, believing he has a choice.

"You'll either drink it like a human being, or I'll pour it down your throat with the funnel I use to put oil in my truck."

Durrell acquiesces. That's another word I like, acquiesce. It's not often I get to think about that word, let alone find a use for it, so I'm smiling while I put the mug to Durrell's lips. The first sip ends with revulsion, a sign the tea is bitter even with the added honey. He chokes with each gulp, spilling droplets of tea down into the kiddie pool.

"Try not to spill it," I say, slowing down how much I give him. I keep the mug tilted until it's almost empty. I tip the last bit toward him and offer some encouragement. "Live life to the lees, or so a wise man once said."

Durrell finishes the last bit of the Christmas rose tea. I put the mug down on the ground and pull my recliner closer to Durrell. I take a seat and lean back.

"You're gonna let me go now, right?"

Durrell's eyes are wide, expectant. I smile when I think of what's about to happen.

"You did what I asked of you. You drank my tea. And I will grant you freedom. But there are all kinds of freedom. And for the sake of argument, we're going with my definition of freedom."

"You son of a bitch!" Durrell spits at me, but it lands on the floor just before my chair.

"The tea you drank—hell, I don't know if you can call it tea if it doesn't have tea leaves in it—anyway, it was made with Helleborus niger. It's more commonly known as the Christmas rose. It purges evil. Some speculate that this particular plant poisoned and ultimately killed Alexander the Great."

"You son of a bitch," Durrell screams. "I'm going to fucking kill you!"

"When you think that this plant killed one of the greatest men to have ever lived, it's an honor to die like him."

"You can't do this! Please!"

"Please, what? You came here to kill my neighbor. Oh, yes. Flynn isn't my son. He lives next door. That means no one will be stopping by to interrupt us. Also, I personally soundproofed this garage. I can't say it's perfect, but it'll do. You'll just have to trust me. Screaming won't do a thing."

"Why? Why are you doing this?"

"You want freedom. That's my specialty. Now you can live forever."

I detach the chain connected to Durrell's arms and lower him until his head is about a foot above the green plastic of the kiddie pool. After securing that chain, I then detach the chain securing his ankles, pulling on it until his feet go all the way up toward the ceiling. He's now upside down like an animal in a trap.

It varies on how long it takes for people to get sick. Some get sick almost immediately. Others can take minutes. The pool is there for whenever it happens.

Durrell hangs there, looking sicker and sicker as Elvis sings in the background. When "I'll Be Home for Christmas" ends, I can tell he's at a tipping point. I go to the cassette player and turn the cassette over. "If Every Day Was Christmas" starts playing.

"What did you—?" Durrell stops talking and turns red. He retches. His body convulses. Finally, the evil pours out of him. The sickening sound of muffled choking follows each purge. It continues off and on for six minutes.

"Do you feel better?"

"Why are you doing this?"

"You look better."

"Let me go. Please…"

312

My fingers grip his neck. Whether he's exhausted from the purge or merely accepting his fate, Durrell doesn't struggle. The pulse under my fingers is faint and slow.

"Just so you know," I say, pulling Durrell's knife out of my back pocket. "That tea won't kill you. What it does is help purge the body. It also slows down your heart rate and lowers your blood pressure. And that's why I had you drink it. You see, I don't want your blood all over my nice clean garage."

Durrell looks down. It dawns on him why there is a kiddie pool underneath him.

"No," he pleads. "No! Please!"

"William, please," Lily says, appearing out of nowhere. "Please don't do this."

"Lily, I'm sorry. This is something I have to do."

"No. If you do this, I'll—"

"Who the fuck are you talking to?" Durrell screams.

"This isn't a conversation you need to hear," I reply.

"There's no one there."

Lily stands there plain as day. He's trying to trick me. I make a deep cut on either side of his throat. The blood spurts out, but the tea has done its job. Blood rushes from the cuts, pumping in steady streams timed with each beat of his heart, down across his face and into the little green pool. Durrell stops screaming. There is a peace that comes to him. His eyes gloss over. His breathing slows. The blood continues to run across his face into the pool, even as his last breath leaves him.

There's a choking sound to my right. It's Lily. Wounds on Lily's throat match Durrell's. She coughs up blood as she tries to speak. All that comes out are whimpering gasps.

"No," I scream, running to her.

Lily falls to the ground and disappears.

Chapter 55

Amy

The office for D-lux Casino Cruise is a hovel in Mayport on the water with a dock out back. It's for the best that the boat isn't here. I'd hate to change my mind this far in. I've done too much to give up. This was all going to lead to a business Iain and I would run together. With him gone, it's now my business.

According to the information Iain left me before he disappeared, the man who runs this casino boat will ensure my product lands stateside. All I know about our contact is that his name is Carlton.

The shanty is no better on the inside. The interior resembles a kitsch seafood restaurant. Old fishing poles, tackle, nets, model boats, and pictures of smiling people holding up their catch adorn the walls. Fake seagulls hang from the ceiling beneath tiles weighed down and discolored by water damage. A fake pelican near the door stands vigil for the dignity of a man dressed like a mixture of a pirate and a sailor from the '40s. He stands up from his seat behind the cash register when I enter.

"Hello and welcome to D-lux—"

"I need to speak to Carlton." I'm short with the man because I want to limit my time in the seventh level of Davy Jones' locker.

"And who's asking?"

"Amy. I'm Iain Reid's partner."

"Are you shitting me? I've been trying to call that asshole for over a week."

"You're Carlton?"

This man's involvement in something fishy doesn't surprise me, but it is surprising that Iain, a typically careful man, enlisted this sea clown for a business deal.

"Yes. Where's Iain?"

"He's indisposed. You'll be dealing with me."

"What the fuck does that mean? No. Iain needs to call me."

"Iain already paid you what he promised. You'll get the rest at delivery."

"It doesn't matter if he paid me, his cargo needs documentation. Otherwise, we all end up in prison."

"It's already been taken care of," I lie.

"I need him to tell me that."

"He's out of town, so I'm telling you."

"No offense, girlie—"

"You either go through with it, or I anonymously report your side business."

"Fine. I need the documents before I leave. My records going out need to match what's coming in."

"The package has all the documentation necessary." This is a lie, but I know I can figure something else out if I have to.

"How is that possible?"

"We have paid the captain of the ship in full. All you have to do is wait at the GPS coordinates Iain provided you. They will scuttle the goods in life rafts near your position. Just pick them up, and you're good to go."

"That's ridiculous."

"You agreed to pick up cargo at sea. This is what's happening."

"You've got to be kidding me? That is some spy-type bullshit. You need to rethink this."

"What do we need to rethink? The cargo will be in international waters, which you travel to every night to let degenerates gamble. Except this time, the degenerates stay on dry land."

"The odds of this working—"

"I don't care what you think the odds are. Just do your job, and you'll be perfectly fine."

Carlton looks dejected and depressed. I can't tell if it's because he's caving in to my demands or if he is recounting previous regrettable life choices in his head.

"We good?" I demand.

Carlton rubs his chin, staring at me as though he can see through me.

"Are we good?"

"Yeah," he replies. "We're good."

Chapter 56

Flynn

Officer Rittwell bringing Alien back is a sign the rest of my confiscated belongings are on their way. Until that happens, I will remain computerless. Researching Iain Reid requires a trip to the library. Leslie fixing up the Golden Hawk allows me to drive around town beholden to no one. The car lacks insurance, and the tags are so expired they belong in a museum, but I've had friends drive uninsured with expired tags for years without getting caught. A day or two shouldn't hurt.

It's been a while since I last used my father's old car. Years of driving the Camry leaves the Hawk feeling foreign. The Camry's pops, wheezes, bangs, and choking cries fade into the distant past. Leslie must have pumped the Hawk full of cheetah blood because it runs like a brand new car.

Some pit stops on the way to the library are necessary. First, I stop and fill the Hawk up with gas. The tank is near empty, and I'd hate for it to die on the side of the narrow beach roads. My second pit stop is at a corner store to pick up a cell phone. I need a phone right now and don't have the time or patience to explain to my carrier how my last phone died a fiery death. After I get the disposable cell on and working, I text Misty and Philip to let them know this is the number they can use to get in touch.

With the Hawk flying, I'm at the library lickety-split. The library is on a premium piece of real estate right off of Third Street. I park and go inside. It's been a little while since I've been to the library. It all still looks the same. I've never used their computers before. To ensure I don't commit a dreaded local library social faux pas, I go to the front desk and ask about proper protocol. A librarian helps me log on while explaining the rules and printing fee structure in excruciating detail.

The search for Iain Reid first takes me to a website for his business. The only mention of Iain is as a primary point of contact for anyone interested in 'unique artistic opportunities.' Joseph Parker told me a lot more about this business than I learn from his disclosures and mission statement.

A search of property records in and around the Jacksonville area produces nothing under Iain's name. This makes sense because it's hard to believe a criminal would allow themselves to be easily found. The *Ponte Vedra Living* website pops up in the search. The article is about Rose Reid's garden. Various pictures show sections of the house's exterior and the property's view of the ocean. There is a mention of Rose living with her husband, Iain, south of Mickler's Landing in Ponte Vedra. The spelling indicates it might be the same Iain Reid I'm trying to find.

The third read-through sparks a memory. Amy Wright had a physical copy of *Ponte Vedra Living*, featuring this article, in her apartment. I print out the article, including all the pictures, and go back to searching. This time I try searching for Rose Reid in the hopes that wherever they live might be under her name. There's nothing about their home. There are, however, plenty of articles about Rose Reid's death.

Joseph Parker said that Iain's wife had died recently, but I didn't realize her death was newsworthy enough for me to have heard about it. According to several newspaper articles, she was a victim of the Haiku Bandit. They all cite a source close to the family. That source went so far as to provide a copy of the haiku the bandit left behind. The bandit's haikus are part of his MO, but this was the first to be released to the public. I print out an in-depth article about the investigation into Rose's death and leave the library.

With Curtis Vance's cell phone number dialed and ready, I wait until I'm safely out of the library's 'hush or we'll shoosh you zone' before hitting call. He picks up and sounds perturbed.

"Hello?"

"Hey, Vance. It's Flynn."

"Oh," he says in a softer tone, probably pleased that I'm not someone trying to sell him anything. "I'm sure you're calling for help."

"Yup," I say, starting the Golden Hawk and exiting the library parking lot to head south. "You said you spoke to the police in PV to help me out

317

of that jam. I was hoping they might've said something about the Haiku Bandit killing Rose Reid."

"Why?"

"It's something I'm working on. Did they say anything?"

"No. A lot of us old guys still keep in touch, though, and this was a popular topic after it happened."

"Why's that?"

"The police don't think the Haiku Bandit killed her."

"Why not?"

"There were a lot of inconsistencies."

"Such as?"

"I don't have the time now, Flynn."

"Come on. It'll just be a minute."

"Fine," Vance says in a voice that doesn't sound fine. "For starters, the haikus weren't right."

"Really?" The article about Rose's death is on the passenger's seat. I pick it up and scroll down to the haiku. "The newspaper says there was a poem at the scene.

> *Accidents happen*
> *To the best of all people.*
> *Mistakes are easy.*

That sounds like a haiku to me."

"Yes, but the Haiku Bandit didn't write that."

"How can you be sure?"

"The Haiku Bandit wrote all of the other poems by hand, except that one. That one was printed. It doesn't match up. And the bandit had been entertaining until then. A buddy told me one—hold on for a second," Vance pauses. The line goes silent. "Oh yeah.

> *Plop, plop in water.*
> *Forgive me. I had to go.*
> *Don't worry. Flushed twice.*

I laughed real hard at that one."

"So that's it? Couldn't the bandit have not been humorous due to killing someone?"

"Flynn, I don't know. I don't have all the details. But it does seem strange to print a remorseful haiku ahead of time. And the bandit had been careful until then. They only robbed people who were out of town for multiple days. And the bandit always did something odd to the house, like rearrange furniture or, in one case, paint an accent wall. Things just didn't seem similar enough."

"Did they suspect the husband?"

"Nah. He was supposedly broken up about it. And he was out of town when it happened."

"Okay. Well, thanks for that."

"Anything else?"

"Nope."

"Have a good one. And you should call your father every now and then."

"Talked to him on Thanksgiving."

"He was probably real happy to hear from you."

"I bet. Thanks again."

It's rare that I venture this far south into Ponte Vedra, and I've only ever been to Mickler's Landing for a beach wedding. The turn off A1A goes right into parking. I find a spot, pocket the photos of Rose Reid's house, and make my way to the beach. The article says their home is south of Mickler's Landing. Wandering south, I compare every house on the beach to the one in the photos. It takes almost an hour to find the right one.

A blonde woman is in the yard watering the rose bushes. The house has direct beach access connecting to the side of the yard without rose bushes. To ensure I'm not seen, I run as fast as I can from the sand to the grassy lawn, past the pool to the side of the house. Once safe, I peek around the side of the house to get a better look at the woman. She finishes her work and turns around enough for me to see the side of her face. I stop dead, almost ready to fall over. It's Amy Wright. It's impossible to say why she's here as my mind struggles to make connections. She had the *Ponte Vedra Living* magazine featuring Rose Reid in her apartment, which means she might know the family. It all seems convenient. I want to ask her why she's here, but I can't since I'm trespassing, and because I've screwed her life up enough.

Amy finishes watering the roses and takes a seat on the patio overlooking the ocean. Where she's seated prevents me from leaving how I came in. There's no way she wouldn't see me if I walked back to the beach. In search of another exit, I walk around the side of the house to the

319

front yard. The fence separating the yard from A1A is a little high. Cars honk at me as I climb up and over. The best I can do is smile and wave at the traffic in the hopes they don't call the police to report a prowler. I walk north alongside the road toward my car.

After about fifteen minutes, my new cell rings. I recognize the number as Philip.

"How are you, Philip?"

"Well. Not well. I'm not sure how I feel."

"Why's that?"

"Have you seen the news today?"

"No. I got up and had some business to take care of."

"Lou Brombacher is dead."

I'm silent for longer than I realize.

"Flynn? Are you still there?"

"Yeah," I say, still shocked. "How did he die?"

"There's no official word. But I know a little birdy or two downtown. They're saying it's suicide. They said he downed two bottles: one was tequila, the other was unspecified pills."

"He didn't seem like the kind of guy who would kill himself," I reply. The bottle of tequila bothers me. He said he only drank scotch. "Did your birdy tell you anything else?"

"Yeah. Lou had a late meeting that wasn't on his calendar. No one on his staff was aware of it either," Philip says calmly. "I spoke to someone who has seen the security footage. A Caucasian woman showed up late. He welcomed her in. She was in his office for half an hour. And then she left. She was wearing a large hat and sunglasses at night, so she clearly tried to hide from the cameras as best she could. There's no camera in Brombacher's office. No one knows what happened, but according to some of his employees, it wasn't uncommon for him to have women stop by late after work."

"If they have this woman on film, then why isn't she a suspect?"

"He left a suicide note on his desk. It was short, but it was in his own handwriting. Lou appeared to be taking credit for—"

The apology letters to Stephen Collins flash through my mind. One was short and vague.

"Was the note addressed to Stephen Collins?"

"How did you—"

320

"Did it say, 'I am so sorry'?"

"Brombacher didn't kill himself, did he?"

"I don't believe so. Lou told me he only drank scotch. I doubt he'd be expanding his horizons with tequila for his last drink. And that note was something he wrote to fire Stephen. I read it the other day after I first met you."

"Well, this complicates things."

"Do you mean for you running for mayor? Because I doubt this has anything to do with that."

"Not to be callous, but every nutjob in the city will accuse me of orchestrating this. Even if someone else confesses, I'll still be guilty to them."

"At this point, it's more important that we catch whoever did this. Do you have any more information? All they told you is that he met with a white female?"

"I told you they're treating it like a suicide."

"You need to tell them what I've told you. My fingerprints will be on that letter. That should be enough to prove it was written prior. Give them my info if they want to speak to me. I'm not usually the voice of reason, Philip, but this is well beyond us."

"What else did you find out?"

"I spoke to some of the people in Paul's notes. They're not exactly the law-abiding type, but they put me onto a lead that panned out. A man by the name of Iain Reid. A lot of Paul's notes make connections between him and a person listed only as LB."

"So, Lou?"

"Best guess. I've been told that Iain Reid had potentially partnered with Lou on bringing something illegal into the country. Reid forges documents. Stephen Collins is less involved than I thought. I think he was supposed to be a patsy, just like me."

"Why would you think that?"

"It's a hunch. I think Lou offered seed money. Money which he would want back with a good deal of interest. While investigating Lou's questionable business practices, Paul stumbled upon this deal. He ended up being killed by Lou's right-hand man. I'm sure that even if the bomb got pinned on me, Lou would be dragged into it, and the scandal would

321

take Lou out of the picture. One less hand in the pot means more money for those that remain."

"You think this Iain Reid is responsible?"

"Not that I know of. His wife was killed. He went home to Scotland with his son. But a man I spoke to said he has another partner."

"Any ideas?"

"A wild guess. I found out where Iain's home is. Amy Wright is there. I'm not sure of their connection, but she has been a part of two deaths in this whole ordeal. Now you're telling me a Caucasian woman met with Brombacher before he died. It might add up."

"Okay. Your job is done. I'll get your payment as soon as possible. I need to process this. We can't just go to the police and blame Amy. She could cause us some real trouble unless we have evidence. Do you have anything concrete?"

"No. Most of what I've been told was hypothetical. An unnamed contact provided me a bill of lading reference number, which is supposed to reference Iain's shipment but is fake."

"I guess you can never trust a forger. What's the number?"

I provide the number to Philip. He reads it back to confirm.

"Another thing. Paul wrote GF IR 630 as his last entry. Iain Reid's girlfriend, maybe. It was the time of his appointment with Amy."

"That's not exactly solid."

"And I still don't know what Dlux 9.3 1201 TS means. It's what Paul wrote on that note his wife gave me. TS is The Sheik. He's someone Iain had worked with in the past. They provided Iain some seed money as well for this project, but it appears Iain cut them out."

"Okay. Please don't do anything else. You have to understand that this goes beyond me beating Lou. No more investigating. No more. We need to tread lightly. I have to make some calls. I'll get back to you in a day or two."

"Shore nuff."

Chapter 57

Flynn

A day without plans is the best kind of day. It's a day to relax. It's a day full of time to help put the past week behind me. The whacks I've taken at this Gordian knot have unraveled a thread or two. All future attempts are up to the police. As irksome as being relegated to an observer may be, Philip made it abundantly clear that it is for the best.

"No more," Philip said, his voice cold even by lawyer standards.

Philip is right. Involving myself over and over again is a mistake. Death keeps knocking on my door. He's an impatient bastard who cannot stand it when his signs go unheeded. A body on my patio is the best way to drive home the fact that even a supernatural entity's patience can run thin. This started with a simple job. Now there are three people dead and who knows how many more in danger. And then there's Edith Danes.

A shower is a peaceful place meant for quiet reflection. Closing my eyes allows my imagination to run wild. Nightmares that have kept me from sleeping more than a couple hours at a time return with Edith's pain-stricken face covered in blood. The warm water turns red, painting my body in sticky rivulets. The smell is invasive. A metallic taste fills my open mouth, bubbling, falling to the tile with a loud splattering sound. When I open my eyes, it's only water. But it was real. Edith lived through it all—the pain, the blood, the constant reminder of her attacker now carved into her body. There is solace in knowing that someday my nightmares will end. There is only guilt in knowing that Edith's never will.

Edith survived, but Durrell is still on the loose. No one knows where he is. No one has seen him since Thanksgiving. There's no telling where he is or what he's planning.

All of this has made me tired. I slept off and on for almost eleven hours last night. It's close to noon when I get out of the shower. The smell of blood leaves my nostrils, and all that remains is the fresh scent of soap. Heart shapes in the upper left and the lower right side of the mirror peek out through the fog. One of the countless police officers or random intruders that have been all over my house must have left me a reminder of their presence as a joke.

I get dressed and go downstairs to grab a bite to eat before taking a walk on the beach. The rhythmic roar of the waves will help clear my mind. All the fridge has to offer is beer and a jar of pickles. I pull a pickle from the brine and make a mental note that it's time to go grocery shopping for something more than PBR.

When I turn around, Stephen Collins is there with a gun in his right hand. I take a bite of the pickle and then hold my hands up. The pickle juice runs down my right thumb and onto my wrist.

"Listen," I say after I've finished chewing. "I had nothing to do with your wife's death."

"I know you didn't. That bitch, Amy, killed her."

"The police are saying it was self-defense."

"Bull SHIT," Stephen says through gritted teeth. "This is all her fault. But you, if you had died like I planned, everything would have been fine."

"Fuck me for living, right?"

"You are a drunk loser who, somehow, despite this useless veneer, fucked everything up beyond relief."

Stephen shakes as though a chill runs through his body. I'm not sure whether to run, beg, or negotiate. Instead, my mouth moves before I know it.

"Rude," I say, confusing Stephen. "Sure, I sleep in late and am eating a pickle for breakfast. And, yes, a lot of times I drink to excess, but I like to think I'm better than a drunk loser."

"It doesn't matter," Stephen says, his eyes beginning to water. He takes a seat and drops the gun on the kitchen table. Stephen uses his shirtsleeve to dry his eyes. He stares at me, red-faced and desperate. "None of this matters if I can't save my son. I need your help."

"What?"

Steven must have shot me. This is all a delusion caused by my brain processing the last remnants of oxygen coursing through me. The tang from a bite of pickle debunks this theory. I'm alive and breathing in this

324

vinegared reality, and Stephen's fingers are nowhere near his gun's trigger.

"I need your help to find my son."

"What do you need me to do?"

"I need to find Amy."

"Why do you need her?" I ask, despite knowing the answer. Stephen needs to confirm Amy is behind everything.

"She's the one who took him."

"You're full of shit. Amy asked you to blow her up?"

"No, she wanted Paul Mahoney dead. I convinced her that unwittingly being a part of the act would put her above suspicion. I needed her to point to you as the suspect. So I staged the explosion. She wasn't happy with the idea, but she went along with it because I promised it would work, and she'd be able to trigger the bomb."

"Let's say I believe you. Why didn't Amy give you back your son after you killed Paul Mahoney?"

"Because there were too many loose ends. You escaped and made me the suspect. If I got caught, then I could turn her in as well. She needs both of us dead. Why else do you think she invited you over for dinner? My wife and I were waiting on the beach for her to signal us. The entire night was a trap. She planned on drugging you, but you wouldn't drink the wine. When you went into her bedroom, she flashed the lights in the living room. That was our signal. We broke in. When you got the jump on me, Amy was the one to knock you out with some paddle she had."

"And your wife dying?"

"Amy said it was because Helen attacked her, that she went after Amy's gun. A lie, or possibly a half-truth. Helen knew what Amy looked like and where she lived. Amy thought I was going to kill you. If she killed my wife, then I would have been the only person remaining who could connect her to the explosion."

"Amy thought you were going to kill me?"

"She never said what she wanted me to do with you. I was going to leave you tied up. The initial plan involved killing you. Once that fell apart, there was no need for you to die."

"That's reassuring."

"I am truly sorry for dragging you into this. I only did this for my son."

325

"Give me the gun. Then I'll help you."

"Take it," Stephen says, pointing to the gun. "It's all yours."

Stephen allows me to pick up the gun. This could all be over. Common sense tells me to ignore what he's saying about Amy and run outside to the officer at the end of my driveway. Stephen will undoubtedly run away before the officer makes it inside. After that, he will leave me alone. Or I can believe that Amy has been pulling strings all along and take Stephen to Iain Reid's home. Amy relaxing at Iain's means there's a better-than-average chance she's staying there instead of her damaged apartment. And if she has Stephen's son, Iain Reid's house is big enough to keep him hidden.

The police may not believe that someone took Stephen's son, but I do. A puppet master has been cajoling us along this entire time. Lou Brombacher would be the obvious choice if he weren't dead. His suicide note was one that I know he wrote about firing Stephen, which means someone is trying to frame him.

"Fine," I say, handing Stephen back his gun. "I'm not doing this for you. I'm doing this for your son."

"Thank you," Stephen says.

"Follow me," I mutter while finishing my breakfast pickle.

We exit the house through the side door and enter the garage. Stephen ducks down in the passenger seat to keep the officer watching my house from seeing him. There's a familiar red Jeep parked down the road that follows us as we leave. Officer Rittwell must be keeping an eye on me in his spare time since he's not in his police car.

The trip down A1A is quick until we pass Mickler's Landing. It's hard to be certain how far we need to go to find Iain Reid's house. The long walk back yesterday has skewed my judgment of the distance. My only option is to take it slow and look at each home on the road. Our slow pace pisses off a number of other drivers. Each angry driver behind us exhibits their emotions through a unique combination of honking, flashing headlights, enraged waving, swerving, choice words, and what I can only assume is barking like a dog with its head hanging out of the window. One thing almost everyone has in common is that they slow down enough to provide me a clear view of their favorite finger as they fly by.

Once spotted, Iain Reid's house is a welcome sight. Officer Rittwell's Jeep follows my lead and pulls off onto the shoulder, which is the unofficial parking lot of A1A. Rittwell parks two houses away from us. That distance should keep Stephen from being suspicious. Unfortunately, that distance is also too much for anyone without a telescope to identify Stephen. That means Officer Rittwell won't be calling for help unless something goes wrong.

We exit the car and cross A1A when the traffic allows. Stephen looks over the gate blocking the driveway. I pull him down.

"Do you want her to know we're coming?"

"Her car is here."

"We could have found that out while being a little less conspicuous," I say, pointing to the left of the gate where several bushes are growing high enough to block anyone in the house from seeing someone coming over the fence circling the property. "That's inconspicuous."

"There is no inconspicuous," Stephen says. "We're right on the road."

Ignoring Stephen, I toss my sandals over the fence and climb over. Stephen follows as I retrieve my sandals. We rush to the side of the house and stay close to the wall, making our way to the patio and pool overlooking the ocean. Stephen looks out and turns to me.

"No one's out back. There's a door a couple feet over on the right."

Stephen leads the way. The door is broken near the lock. Without hesitation, Stephen pushes against it. There is a chair wedged underneath the handle on the other side, keeping it closed. The chair makes enough noise as the door opens for Amy to appear in the kitchen. Before either of us can react, Amy disappears back into the house. Stephen chases her, drawing his gun. Gunfire erupts when he exits the kitchen. Stephen staggers backward. He searches himself for bullet wounds and is elated to find none.

"This just got intense," I say.

"Do you think so?" Sarcasm flies like spittle out of Stephen's mouth.

"She might've only shot at you because you had your gun drawn."

"The fact that she has a gun on her means she's not playing."

"Maybe I should try to reason with her."

"Be my guest."

A metal spatula stuck to a magnetic strip over the kitchen counter is the closest thing to a mirror in the kitchen. Its polished surface allows me to peek around the corner and find Amy behind a bar near a glass wall looking out at the ocean.

"Amy," is all I can say before a shot rings out and a bullet whizzes past the spatula.

"Anybody coming out of that kitchen will be shot," Amy shouts. "I'm serious. The only reason I didn't hit you, Stephen, is because I wasn't able to aim while running. Well, guess what? I'm set now. I won't miss this time."

"Reasoning might have just come off the table," I say, peeking around the corner again with the spatula. Amy fires another bullet, missing the spatula. "Yep. It's a no-go."

"What's the plan?" Stephen asks.

"I didn't come here with one. Amy is behind a bar in the corner."

Stephen takes the spatula and kneels to look around the corner. He pulls the spatula back before Amy fires.

"She's pinned herself in there," Stephen says. "Her back is to a glass wall. I could go behind her and—"

"There's no way she doesn't see you coming."

"You think going head-on is better?"

"No. She could have a lot more bullets than you."

"I have nine."

"Seriously? That's it?"

"I had plenty. Those bullets are sitting in a car near Amy's apartment. We had to abandon it after what happened there."

"You mean causing a scene and knocking me out?"

"I already told you Amy knocked you out. She came out of that closet, swinging a big paddle."

"She's cute, but she really is a terrible person."

The view from the kitchen reveals a decent portion of the house's layout. Amy is in a wide-open living room with an enormous glass wall overlooking the ocean. Sofas, chairs, and a lot of knick-knacks on small tables and pedestals dot the space. Stairs on the far side of the room lead up to the second floor. A hallway stretches from the base of the stairs further back into the house.

"How many bathrooms do you think this place has?" I ask.

"Why the hell does that matter?"

"This house is a rich man's wonderland. But these high ceilings take up a lot of space. That side of the house is where they live. This side is for show."

"I'm confused."

"If I had your son locked up, I'd have him in a downstairs bathroom. Considering the size of the house, I'm guessing there are four bathrooms. There should be a half bath right there on the corner so people can use it during little parties they have. Farther down that hall should be a full bath attached to a bedroom. The downstairs bathroom probably doesn't have a window that opens. She could have your boy tied up in a shower or tub, so she doesn't have to worry about him soiling himself. It makes sense because it'd be easier to clean up."

"You think he's over there?"

"I'd bet my life on it."

"I can make it."

"You're going to run all that distance with only nine bullets for cover?"

"I can use that pillar over there to hide behind and then make a break for it."

Stephen points to a freestanding marble pillar near the front door. It reaches halfway to the ceiling and provides zero structural support. Iain's art importing background means it could be ancient. All that matters right now is it looks solid enough to stop bullets and is wide enough to hide behind.

"You'll get shot, and then I'll get shot because you have the only gun. Try to think unemotionally about this. What's the best way for one of us to get across?"

"If I fire three shots spaced enough to keep her head down, you should be able to make it to the pillar without her knowing you've made a break for it. Then I can fire at her again, and you should be able to make the rest of the distance with five shots. That would leave me one bullet."

"Good," I say, taking off my sandals and getting ready to run. "On the count of three?"

Stephen takes a deep breath and gets close to the wall. "One," Stephen says, readying himself.

"Two," I say, regretting having agreed to come here.

"Three."

Stephen leans out from behind the wall, taking a shot. I run as fast as I can from the kitchen toward the marble pillar. Amy ducks down as Stephen fires another shot. I dive onto the floor and slide just as Stephen

329

takes his third shot. In retaliation, Amy fires several shots at Stephen's position, ignoring me entirely.

Stephen signals again. Gunshots erupt at the end of another countdown. My feet grip the cold tile as I take off running. I make it to the hallway and slow down. Stephen is back in the kitchen as Amy opens fire.

The first door leads to a half bath. The next one leads to a guest bedroom. It's decked out in matching everything and has an en-suite bathroom. There is no sign of Stephen's son. I continue down the hallway. There's a linen closet, a washer and dryer, and another bedroom. This bedroom is much like the first, with every piece matching. Stephen's son is in the bathtub, blindfolded and gagged. Zip ties have left his wrists and ankles bloody. An awful smell fills the room.

Stephen's son screams when I remove his blindfold and gag. The way he screams tells me he's deaf.

"Calm down," I sign. He stops screaming. It's difficult to sign in the heat of the moment, but I try my best. "I'm here with your father. I need to get a knife to cut you loose. I'll be right back."

The kid is in terrible shape. He looks like he understands what I'm signing, but he barely acknowledges me.

Stephen watches me emerge from the hallway. To keep Amy in the dark about what's happening, I keep signing. "Your son is alive. I need a knife to cut him loose."

Stephen disappears and returns with a kitchen knife. He throws it across the room. The knife lands just shy of the hallway. A sudden pressure hits near my left shoulder as I reach out to pick up the knife. It all happens so quickly that I didn't even hear Amy's gun go off. Stephen leans out and fires his last shot.

There's a look of confusion and fear on Amy as her head jerks to the side. The bullet forces its way through her skull and into the glass wall behind her. Her eyes remain open as she slumps to the ground. It's painful to watch.

I've never seen a person die before. The only dead body I've seen is that of my grandfather at his funeral. On that day, he wore a peaceful look. But that was all makeup and funeral parlor magic. The look on his face when he died must have matched Amy's. There is a universality in brief confusion followed by a finite stop.

When I try to walk toward her, the pressure near my shoulder turns to pain. It feels like some force is invading my body. There's something wrong with my breathing. Stephen stops at my side and grabs my right hand, applying it to my left shoulder.

"Put pressure on it. You'll be fine," he says.

"Go," I say, taking my hand off of my shoulder to pull my car keys out of my pocket. "He's in bad shape."

Stephen takes the keys from me as I point to the kitchen knife. Stephen picks the knife up off of the tile and disappears down the hallway. My sense of balance fails me as I shamble to the kitchen. The taste of blood mixes with my saliva. The portable phone in the kitchen nearly slips from my bloody hand as I dial 911.

"I've been shot," I say when the operator picks up. "I don't know where I am, but I'm using the home phone. It's a big house on A1A south of Mickler's Landing."

The voice on the other end of the call keeps talking as I set the home phone on the kitchen island and pull out my cell. My father's number has never been so easy to dial. He won't pick up, but it's worth a shot. The call goes to voicemail.

"Dad," I say, my voice raspy from the blood. "I've been shot doing the right thing. I hope I did."

I disconnect and stumble from the kitchen. Stephen opens the front door. He pushes a button near the door before exiting.

The wooziness is unbearable. I'm on my knees before I know it. All I want to do is go to sleep. I fall backward and end up supine near the open front door. The cold tile turns warm as blood pools beneath me. Red tarnishes my hands—sticky red.

My cell phone rings. It's my father's number. My index finger leaves a bloody print on the phone's screen when I accept the call.

"Dad," I say. It's hard to breathe. Each time I try, the ragged breath cuts short with a rattling sound.

"Flynn? What's happened? You said you were shot."

"Still am," I laugh. It hurts.

"You need to call an ambulance."

"I did, but I can't say for certain where I am. Hopefully, they find me."

"Where are you?"

"In a big house... south of Mickler's."

"Where are you shot? How bad is the bleeding?"

"In the shoulder. I think it hit my collarbone," I say. "I think I've lost more blood than I—should've invested more."

"Flynn! You need to get up. Try to walk to the road. Can you do that?"

"I can't. I just—"

"Flynn! Get up! You may have damaged your subclavian artery. If that's the case, you won't be alive long enough for the ambulance to reach you and return to the hospital. You need to find someone to take you to the hospital now!"

"My ride's gone. Maybe it's for the best—I always wanted to…"

"Flynn? Flynn!"

Chapter 58

Stephen

Flynn hands me the keys to his car and points to the kitchen knife on the ground, which I pick up before running to find my son. In my frantic rush to find Jack, I fail to ask Flynn where Amy hid him. Instead of going back, I scream Jack's name while checking behind each door, despite it being impossible for him to hear me.

Jack is in a tub with his hands and feet tied with zip ties. I use the kitchen knife to cut him free and give him the biggest hug I have ever given anyone. It doesn't matter that he's covered in shit. I'm too happy to care about how bad the room smells.

Jack shivers as I wrap him in a towel. I scoop him up and bolt for the front door. Flynn is in the kitchen on the phone, presumably with emergency services. If they are on the way, then there is nothing else I can do to help. Jack and I need to leave before the police show up. The houses are far apart from each other in this part of Ponte Vedra, but someone must have heard all the shooting and called the police. I open the front door and realize the front gate will be difficult to get over with Jack in tow. There is a green button on an intercom system near the doorjamb. The gate opens when I push it.

Halfway to Flynn's car, a man with a gun drawn walks through the open gate and stops me. The 1911 I have tucked in my waistband is empty. This is it. This is the end.

"Stop," the man says. "I'm an officer with the Atlantic Beach Police Department. If you have a gun, drop it on the ground."

"I have one," I reply, putting Jack on the ground. Jack sits there, staring ahead at nothing. I take the gun out slowly and toss it over to the officer. "It's empty."

The officer is in plain clothes. He leans over and picks up my 1911, removing the clip and tossing the two pieces into the grass at a distance.

"Where's Flynn?"

"He's inside," I answer, unsure of how he will react to the next piece of information. "He's been shot."

"And you were leaving him behind?"

"He told me to go. He gave me his keys."

"Is there anyone else inside?"

"A woman. Amy Wright. She's dead. I shot her after she shot Flynn. I only came here to get my son back. I didn't want any of this."

"Inside," the officer says. "Leave the boy out here."

I lean down into Jack's line of sight, signing for him to stay put. He acts like he sees nothing.

The officer maintains a five-foot buffer between us with his gun pointed at my back. We enter the house to find Flynn lying in a pool of blood near the front door.

"Shit," the officer says, running to Flynn's side. The officer puts his gun away and looks directly at me. "If you help me, I'll let you go. I'll say I never saw you."

"What do we need to do?"

A cell phone next to Flynn grabs our attention. Whoever is on the other end is shouting. The officer picks up the phone and makes a strange face.

"Got it," he says into the phone. The officer turns to me. "Go get at least two clean dish towels from the kitchen, and a wooden spoon."

I run to the kitchen and pick up three dish towels hanging from the oven door. The first four drawers I open are full of flatware, mail, detritus, and additional kitchen towels. The fifth drawer is full of kitchen utensils. I take a wooden spoon. By the time I return, the officer has ripped Flynn's shirt open and is waiting with his belt in a loose loop around Flynn's left shoulder. He folds two of the towels length-wise, placing one over and around Flynn's collarbone and the other across the first to make a cross shape. He sets the wooden spoon on top of the buckle and pulls the belt through, tightening it as best he can. He secures the belt by pulling it back through the buckle and then twists the wooden spoon until the belt refuses to budge.

"Hold this," he says, motioning for me to take hold of the wooden spoon. While I hold it, he takes the second towel and ties it around the handle of the wooden spoon to keep it in place.

The officer picks the cell phone back up off of the floor and tells the mystery caller, "It's done." The officer then hangs up and places the cell phone in his pocket.

"Help me get him to my Jeep," the officer politely demands. "Grab his legs."

The officer puts Flynn's right arm over his shoulder and uses his right hand to keep Flynn's hastily bandaged arm close to his chest. I lift Flynn's legs. We rush him outside. Jack sits quietly, ignoring us as we carry Flynn. The officer's Jeep is parked down the road. We cover the distance quicker than I thought we would. It is a little tricky to get Flynn into the seat, but we make it happen. I buckle Flynn's seatbelt as the officer runs to the driver's side. He takes off as soon as the engine turns over.

Sirens roar in the distance. I run back to Jack. He barely acknowledges me when I pick him up.

Chapter 59

William

Durrell fits into four plastic storage bins from the hardware store. He could've fit into two larger containers, but I'm getting old and thought it would be better to reduce the weight in each. That way, I don't hurt my back hauling him around.

The decision was a smart one. The bins are easy to move from the garage to my truck's bed. After loading Durrell, I take off my trusty deerskin gloves and gather tools that could prove useful if something goes wrong with my truck. I'm not a mechanic, but I spent years fixing all kinds of machines. A ratchet and socket set, a torque wrench, vice grips, WD-40, and duct tape all fit into a reusable shopping bag. I wedge the bag between one of Durrell's bins and the side of my truck's bed to keep the tools from getting loose during the trip. Today is the day the clean shovel from my family tree gets dirty. It snuggles on top of the tools before I secure the bed with a tarp and some bungee cords.

The sun has yet to rise. Families are hours away from staking out their claim in the sand. The rhythmic waves, rolling and crashing, drown out the sounds of the morning birds. These are the peaceful hours before the hustle and bustle grabs hold of the beach.

My old truck rattles, pops, and coughs to life. Durrell smiles at me from the passenger seat.

"We're getting an early start to the day. That's for sure," he says.

"That we are," I reply, backing out of my driveway. "We should get there in no time."

Atlantic Boulevard is empty all the way to I-295, which I take north until merging onto I-95. My exit is in the dead zone past the Georgia border. The paved road leads to a smaller road with pockmarked pavement, which leads to another road that's sprayed with tar every summer to keep the dust down and the dirt from washing away, which finally leads to a single-lane dirt road being reclaimed by the surrounding woods.

This property is sacred ground. It's one of the few places I remember from my youth. No one lives here now, but it used to be the center of a bustling commune. The dilapidated farmhouse near where I park my truck used to be crammed with people for breakfast, lunch, and dinner. Now it's only a rotting skeleton feeding the world around it.

"What are we doing out here?" Durrell asks.

"I gave you freedom. Now we have to get rid of what holds you back."

"Out here?"

"My whole family is out here. Well, everyone except for Lily."

"Who's she?" Durrell asks.

The question hurts. Lily said she would leave if I made Durrell a part of my family. I didn't believe her. She disappeared after I set Durrell free. No one has seen her since.

"I don't want to talk about it," I reply.

The bungee cords did their job and kept the tarp in place the entire trip. I unhook one of the bungee cords, pull back the tarp, and pull out shovel number fourteen before putting the tarp back over the bed of my truck and leaving the bungee cord off.

"This way," I say.

The area is all pine trees and wiregrass. It's not densely wooded, which makes the walk easy. The pine tree canopy keeps the sun at bay and holds on to the morning chill. The wiregrass is up to my knees in some places, but the fallen pine needles still crunch beneath me with each step. About a hundred yards in, I reach a part of the forest floor covered in jimsonweed. I find an area near the outer edge of the jimsonweed and start digging. It takes over an hour to dig a hole deep and wide enough to bury Durrell.

The walk back to my truck proves to me that I've misplaced most of the spring I thought still remained in my step. Despite the exhaustion, I have a lot of work to do. I've heard people say it's far easier to build a family when you're young; however, I doubt this is what they had in mind.

My hands are sore and sweaty when I put on my deerskin gloves. Hauling Durrell's first plastic storage bin is almost impossible. I stumble. I take multiple breaks. I expect my back to give out every other step.

337

Eventually, I place the bin into the hole. That feeling of accomplishment gives me a second wind. The newfound energy helps carry the next three plastic containers from the truck without incident. Dirt flies off the shovel until the job is done.

Durrell claps as I top his grave with a clump of jimsonweed. He's been watching me work. This is the first time he's made any noise.

"It's quiet here," Durrell says, leaning against a pine tree. He doesn't look angry anymore. He's at peace. "This is the perfect place to start over."

"Yup," I say, leaning against the shovel. "Not everybody gets a chance to start over. Now that you're a part of my family, we can find you a family together."

"I'd like that. I've always wanted a wife."

"And what about kids?"

"I want four. Two boys and two girls. I want them to be big brothers, the kind I should've been. Brothers that look out for their sisters."

"We'll find 'em. It'll take time."

"I've got all eternity."

Chapter 60

Flynn

Each step forward on the wooden walkway's rough timbers singe and scrape the soles of my bare feet. The sun's intense rays scorch the pier jutting out into a sea of red. It's not a sea of water, but a peculiar scrub brush in vibrant crimson. The red mass moves back and forth in the wind like licks of heatless flame.

A young girl at the end of the pier stands on the bottom railing, holding herself up for an unobstructed view. There's no one nearby. No family. No friends. She's all alone.

The sea of red gives way to a brilliant white as I approach the end of the pier. The white ground extends into the horizon, where it merges with the sky to become one.

"Who would've thought such a thing could exist?" she asks.

"Lily?"

Lily's voice still sounds the same. It's as though time never passed. The shattered crystal on my watch mends as the second hand rolls around the dial.

"You've been waiting since that day for time to start again, haven't you?" Lily asks. "Don't give me that look."

"I can't believe you're here."

"Don't be an idiot. I'm not here. I mean, I am, but this is all in your head. You're not religious, and you do enjoy movies, so I'm guessing this is how your mind wants to see heaven and hell."

"Why am I here?"

"You know why you're here. The real question is, why am I here?"

"I don't know."

A flock of gulls flies from the red grass over the endless sea of white. The birds shrink in size until they disappear from the offing.

"Come on, Flynn. You know why I'm here." Lily turns to me. The ball of energy I once knew cooled down to form this sedate version of my sister. Reassured by her serenity, we turn back to the sea of red. "It's peaceful here, Flynn. But you can't keep it. This is all in your head. You're dying."

"I was shot."

"Yes, you were. And now they're operating on you. This, honestly, unbearable light is from above you in the operating room. You've always blamed yourself, Flynn. What happened to me would've happened. You said it before. If somebody wants something enough, they'll get it. No one can be shielded from the evil in this world. In time, we all have to face the darkness."

"I could've fought. It was an opportunist—"

"I'm stopping you there. You were selfish. That's the only reason you survived."

"I've never given up hope in finding you."

"You need to."

"I can't."

"You have to. What happened to me is a tragedy. What's happened to you is far worse. Loss is singular and absolute. Your pain is continuous. I don't want that."

"You're just a figment of my imagination."

"Yes, I am. But you know Lily as much as anyone ever will. She'd want to cheer you on in the moments you needed it most. She'd want to talk to you after you met the girl of your dreams and dance with you at your wedding. She'd want to convince you that Lily is the best name for your first daughter. She'd want to be there for every big moment of your life. She'd want you to construct your own happy world. She'd want you to stop chasing angels—"

The sun disappears. Everything plunges into darkness. The sky fills with stars in the time it takes for my eyes to adjust. The sight is beautiful. I've only ever seen pictures of the Milky Way. It's as though I stumbled into one of those pictures.

"What happened?" I ask.

"Your brain is desperately low on oxygen. You don't have long."

"That's it? The light goes away, and then I'm done?"

"What is light, Flynn?"

"I don't know. A by-product of the sun turning hydrogen into helium?"

"That's one way to look at it. What does light mean to you?"

"I don't know."

"Stop dodging the question."

"You're me. You know what I think."

"Do I?"

"You're saying that understanding light is something we can't grasp?"

"You can grasp whatever you want. All that matters is what it means to you. It takes eight minutes and change for the light from our sun to reach us."

"It's all the past."

"Light is the past. If we could understand everything light has seen—if you could understand the sadness of being tormented by something so ancient, so beautiful. Chaos and order are one. Toss enough straight lines together, and there's no telling the difference. But light, that all-encompassing warmth, it's something you need to accept. The past is something you need to accept. This false light you've lived with for so long is pointless. We are human, fragile, yet daring to compare ourselves to the divine. All that has ever existed shines down on us every hour of every day, whether we choose to acknowledge it or not. But the truth scares you. The truth that even the stars glowing down from the firmament are dust blown away by the sands of time."

"What the hell are you talking about?"

"That's all you, Flynn. Probably not, though. You've got to be on some real good meds right now. Profligate. Not sure why I said that, but I like the sound."

"This is it?" I say, looking out at the endless stars. They're spinning like time-lapse photography magic. The ground reflects the light into a vibrant swirl of stars.

"Yup. It's all up to you now. The doctors have done what they can. Live or die. It's your choice. And, pardon me for being greedy, I hope you choose to live."

Chapter 61

Flynn

Beeping sounds are a sound sleep's worst enemy. Somewhere in evolution, there must have been an ancestor ape with such a shrill voice that our very DNA shakes us to attention at its mechanized imitation. The beeps keep coming. Beep. Beep. BEEP! The primeval beast in me wakes up to tell them to keep it down.

My father is staring at me. It takes time for my eyes to focus. The compact room has a bed, two chairs, a table, and a TV. The table has several 'get well soon' cards and bouquets along with a balloon that says 'We're even.' Before I can say anything, my father starts gabbing.

"Un homme qui dort tient en cercle autour de lui le fil des heures, l'ordre des années et des mondes."

"Really," I say. My voice is hoarse. My throat is sore. "You can't quit Proust, can you?"

It's been about two years since I've seen my father. He's still thin. It looks like he's maintained the ideal weight of 143 he liked to say he shared with Mr. Rogers. The big difference is 143 meant 'I love you' to Mr. Rogers. My father's interpretation of 143 is slightly cruder, meaning 'A flat ass.' He looks tired. More tired than the sleeplessness from watching over me would have caused. There are extra crow's feet and a distinct darkness underneath his eyes, both of which are undoubtedly a result of his most recent shot at fatherhood. His beard is new to me. I've never seen him sporting a beard before. The sides are jet black with white cascading down his chin like foam on a waterfall.

"Good to see you're back in the ordered world," he says.

"How many times did you quote Proust before I was coherent enough to know what you were talking about?"

"A dozen or so."

"I've been in and out more than I thought. This is the first time I've woken up and felt fully here."

"The lovely nurses have made sure you're receiving your medication."

"I don't remember much that's happened."

"You don't remember getting shot?"

"Trust me. I'm not forgetting that. The last thing I remember is calling for help. Everything else is spotty."

"You were in surgery for a while. The bullet hit your collarbone and ricocheted down into your lung. You lost a lot of blood. Things were dicey, but you made it."

"What the hell is that," I say, pointing to the balloon that says 'We're even.' "Does Hallmark have a bitter divorce section?"

"A gift from an Officer Rittwell. He said you'd understand what it meant. There's also a bouquet of flowers from a nice young man, Kevin, who said he's a friend of yours. He saw a news report about you and wanted to make sure you made it through. He's been showing up and doing his homework in your room."

"Kids these days are so responsible."

"You could learn a thing or two from him."

"What happened with Stephen Collins?"

"Arrested driving south on A1A. A police officer pulled him over for expired tags. They saw the state of his son and arrested him on the spot for suspected child abuse. They only realized who they had later."

"Well, I guess it's all resolved then."

"You have no idea how crazy this all turned out."

"I know Amy was connected to Iain Reid, who was importing something potentially illegal."

"People. The man was trying to import women so he and Amy could start a full-service brothel. A brothel B&B of sorts."

"You're shitting me. How do you know that?"

"This made international news, Flynn. Iain Reid was arrested in Germany. He tried to buy women from a supposed Russian gangster. They were planning to ship the women from Germany to Jacksonville. It ended up being a sting operation. He was in jail before Paul Mahoney died. No one over here knew that. Amy did everything she did to keep their operation from being uncovered."

"So, everything Amy did was pointless?"

343

"Violence is pointless."

All of this was for nothing. Paul. Lou. Amy. Stephen's wife. They all died for nothing. Stephen Collins is going to prison, and his son will be without his parents. All for nothing. Worse than nothing. They wanted to open up a brothel? My father's wrong. Violence isn't pointless. Violence is the unending path of the disillusioned. There is no comfort. There is no warmth. We are all left empty in its wake.

"Helen," my father says.

"What? What are you talking about?"

"You were whispering to yourself," my father replies. "You kept whispering 'Stephen's wife' over and over again. Her name was Helen."

"Sorry. I was thinking about the people that died. I couldn't remember her name."

"Flynn," my father says, moving his chair closer to me. "You don't own the house."

"What?"

"You never owned the house. It will be yours, but I was afraid to make it official after your mother moved out. Your unpredictability concerned me. I was worried you would sell the place, and I wouldn't be able to do anything about it. I printed you out a piece of paper that said you owned it. It's only paper and ink. I lied to you."

"Why are you telling me this now?"

"Curtis called me after the explosion, asking for permission to enter the house. I gave it to him. You called and sounded grateful that I had been looking out for you. I didn't want to admit what I'd done. I was happy with you being happy with me. When you called, all I could think about was how I wanted you to call me more. I left because it was best for everyone. I didn't realize I'd be losing you every day except holidays."

It's for the best. My mistakes cost my father enough of his life. He shouldn't end up in prison to cover up my mess.

"It doesn't matter," I say. "It all worked out."

"I'm sorry for lying to you."

"Don't feel bad. I made a mess. I'm just lucky to be alive at this point."

"I'm not certain luck had anything to do with it. You fought to stay alive, Flynn. You're here because you refused to give up."

"I don't know about that."

"I do. People give up, Flynn. Not everyone can handle moving forward. After your surgery, you were in bed with tubes sticking out from all ends. You weren't even breathing on your own. The first night your face turned a shade of red. I put my hand on your forehead like I did all those times you tried to convince me you were too sick for school. It reminded me of the morning I caught you putting a hot towel on your forehead to increase your temperature to touch. But this time, when I put my hand on your forehead, you opened your eyes. It was slight, but you opened them. In that instant, I knew. Miracles aren't rare and glorious visions; they're opening your eyes."

I can't help but laugh. Using a microwave to heat up a wet towel was a terrible idea. The damned thing ended up hot enough to leave a red mark on my forehead for an entire day. My attempt to avoid a math test I never studied for backfired miserably.

"Do you remember what you told me that morning?"

My father laughs.

"Get your ass on the bus."

Thank you for reading *False Light*. Flynn Dupree's story
continues in *Fires of June*.

If you enjoyed this book, please leave a review on Amazon or
Goodreads. Providing a rating will help me continue to tell stories.

If you would like updates on any future projects, please follow me
on Goodreads, or at www.Facebook.com/SethAlexAuthor, or on Twitter
@SethAlexAuthor.

Made in the USA
Middletown, DE
27 June 2020